BEAUTY AND THE BEAST

"What do you want?" she demanded. "Why have you done this to us? Is it just to shame and humiliate us all?"

A small, amused noise broke in his throat. "You hardly need me to do that. Your father has already made such an admirable job of it."

Purple fire sparked in her eyes. She was stung as much by the truth of the words as by the insult.

"How dare you speak of my father so! Had it not been for you, he would have never have drunk or gambled or. . . ." She halted abruptly and bit her lip as she realized what she was dredging up from the past.

"You would be well advised, Emily, to be nice to me," he threatened gently. "Biting the hand that feeds you is not wise."

She glared at him coldly and furiously. "Then I shall starve and quite willingly," she retorted immediately.

He smiled tolerantly. "And the rest of your family? Are they equally as keen to take up residence in the poor-house?" His silver eyes narrowed. "But I digress. To answer your question, Emily. . . . What do I want? Well, it is quite simple, really. I want you. I have come back for you as I said I would."

The blood drained from her face as his words stirred long and deliberately buried memories. "I have no idea what you mean."

"On the contrary. I think you know exactly what I mean."

Beloved Avenger

BY MARY BRENDAN
Author of A GENTLEMAN'S MISTRESS

ZEBRA BOOKS
KENSINGTON PUBLISHING CORP.

ZEBRA BOOKS

are published by

Kensington Publishing Corp.
475 Park Avenue South
New York, NY 10016

First printing: October, 1987

Printed in the United States of America

Prologue

The small girl fidgeted restlessly before settling back onto her elbows in the soft, luxuriant turf. She narrowed her deep-violet eyes, squinting as her thin fingers carefully picked two long, razored blades of glossy, emerald grass. The prickling green slivers were drawn slowly between the soft flesh of thumb and forefinger before both stalks were abruptly cast aside.

She breathed lightly and contentedly and wriggled further into the grass. She started to hum softly, her legs moving to bend at the knees as her head settled into the grass and her hand came up to shield the sun from her eyes. As it neared her face, she examined it carefully for grass stains, momentarily anticipating her mother's prospective ire. She sighed at their sorry condition and rubbed them thoroughly together in an unsuccessful attempt to clean them. The lightweight material of her dress started to slip above her knees to her thighs, the whiteness of undergarments beneath the lemon-colored muslin openly displayed.

After a few more moments of inspecting her dishearteningly begrimed fingers and roughened palms, she allowed her hands to drop away, the warm afternoon sun gaining full access to her youthful features.

"Are you going to marry Rose Salter then?"

A protracted silence finally made her sit up straight

again and peer determinedly at her companion in the hope of extracting some response.

The young man lay quite close by.

His hands were pillowing his head, and the long, fair hair streamed across his wrists, stirring in the mild breeze. His eyes were closed and his face as relaxed as if he slept.

Emily straightened the muslin of her gown absently, noticing that an unseemly amount of white linen was visible. She glanced quickly sideways at the inert youth and then shrugged to herself and ruffled the gown carelessly, billowing it and letting it fall slowly to cover her outstretched legs. Attempting to be decorous for his sake was unnecessary and the knowledge was comfortable.

Her interest in her dress now gone, she huffed audibly at the young man's continued disregard for her company and her query. When blatant impatience failed too, she crawled craftily across the short space separating them. She grasped handfuls of grass as she inched forward, twisting then silently and stealthily from the earth. Her lips compressed hard as she tried to suppress the childish glee at what she anticipated. Her hand stretched out slowly, her breath catching and her mouth tightening as she neared the open shirt-neck where she intended depositing her handful of grass.

His hand raised as hers descended and she shrieked in surprise and frustration as she was spun onto her back, both hands imprisoned in his, held high above her head.

He was on his knees now beside her, and she glared up at him, her small features sulky and resentful in defeat.

"Clifford Moore . . . you wait. You hurt my hand, you bully. I shall tell my mama and then you will . . . ."

" . . . be in trouble," he finished for her in a mimicking falsetto. He grined at her fury as attempts to free herself proved vain. She quieted after a while, as soon as she realized that her struggles were futile. She turned her head away from him, with a supercilious, bored snort.

He smiled at the side of her face, coated now with strands of sun-lightened mahogany hair; random grass seeds dotted in the glossy tangle.

He released her slowly and she sprung up into sitting position, her expression baleful. He sat down casually, close to her, and looked out across the quiet, silvered stream that lay a few yards from where they relaxed. Emily swallowed any further threats, resorting to sullenness, which she hoped was properly accenutated by a swift shift sideways away from him.

"Stop sulking."

"I am not."

"Yes you are. Why do you always sulk? Typical girl."

Emily stuck out her tongue, and as he turned and caught sight of it, he warned solemnly, "If the wind changes, you shall be like that for ever."

"That is just rubbish." After barely a pause, she asked quite desultorily, and with a smile, "Are you going to marry Rose Salter, then?"

His expression was unaltered; he still scanned the sun-wavering horizon thoughtfully. "Who told you that?" he muttered.

"Cook."

He raised a sceptical brow at her. Emily coloured slightly, mumbling, "Well, she did not actually tell me. I heard her and Sarah Foster talking in the kitchens and they said that. . . ." Her voice trailed into quiet and she turned, following his descent as he relaxed back leisurely into the meadow.

His hand moved to one side of him and he tore a long, slim reed of grass from the earth. He inserted it slowly between his thin lips, the white teeth just visible as they enclosed it gently. His eyes opened to silver-gray slits as he regarded the young girl who surveyed him inquisitively.

"I am not marrying anyone, Emily."

She nodded with a sagacity hardly borne out by her

7

slight stature and the fact of her ten years.

"I thought not, of course. You are much too young. No one gets married at seventeen — not even the servants." She hesitated, then added with provocation, "Which you are, of course, but even so. . . ."

He sat up abruptly, spitting out the blade of grass violently onto the ground at his side. "I am not a servant," he snarled.

"Are," she taunted, glad to have ruffled his composure. She knew he guarded his self-control tightly. She had learned that from watching her mother's constant attempts to rile him with unreasonable demands or accusations regarding the quality or quantity of his toil. But he could rarely be baited. A slight tautening of his mouth, accompanied by a lowering of his eyes — in deference, Emily was sure — was the most emotion she had seen him display toward the adults of her family. Setting him tasks or taking him to task . . . the reaction was always the same.

"Are," Emily chanted doggedly, determined to elicit even greater response from him.

He stared at her steely-eyed but did not react further.

"Are . . . are," she repeated wildly.

He started to rise, away from her, and she suddenly grasped one of his hands in hers, desperately ashamed of her behavior.

"I'm sorry; don't go yet. Stay a while longer. I am sorry. Don't leave me . . . . You know I get bored on my own."

He shook her off roughly. "I have things to do," he muttered ironically, "as you have just given me timely reminder. Saul Milner will have been expecting me this past hour in the stables. I am probably in for a good thrashing." He glanced down at Emily's upturned face. After an intransigent moment, he smiled. "And when your mother finds out that you have been with me, you shall be in for a thrashing too. You know she hates you being with me."

Emily looked about her immediately and warily before dismissing it all with unconvincing nonchalance. "Oh, she thinks I am collecting vegetables for Cook. I said I would. . . ." She added mischievously, "And I will . . . later."

He squatted close by her again, prepared to linger for a few minutes more to please her. He gazed at the crumpled muslin of her dress and noted the green grass stains vivid on the white lawn covering her knees.

"Quite a little lady, are you not?" he remarked drily, indicating with a brief nod the expanse of exposed underwear.

She scowled, wrinkling her small nose, but she drew the lemon material closer to her legs and held it there.

"I wish I had been a boy, like my brother George . . . or you. Then I could have worn trousers. How can you run or climb trees or ride a horse in a dress? I hate being a girl. It is just not fair." She barely paused before demanding, frankly piqued, "Well, will you not even marry me then when I am grown?"

He laughed and brushed the thick hair casually away from her face.

"You just said you wished you were a boy. How can I marry a girl who wants to be a boy?"

Thin, mucky hands moved to cup her face thoughtfully as she gave this salient point her consideration. "Well, when I am older, I might like being a girl," she ventured, but none too firmly.

His silver eyes wandered over her face. "I might like it too," Clifford murmured.

They gazed at each other silent and solemn for a moment before Clifford laughed shortly and stood up. "But as for your parents . . . well, I am not too sure how they would take any such news." He grimaced in mock disappointment and all sense of occasion was lost.

"Rose said you were."

Clifford brushed the clinging, speckling dust and grass from his trousers before glancing at the young girl still seated at his feet. His face displayed his impatience before his words. "Said what?" he snapped irascibly.

Emily deliberately disregarded his testiness and gave a long, exaggerated blink. "Said that you were to be married, that is."

This failed to evoke an outburst or admission either, he merely looked at her steadily before finishing removing the last traces of the meadow from his clothes.

"I heard her telling Jeannie Peters, when they were cleaning the parlor, and . . ."

"I wonder if Miss Emily Shaw does anything other than eavesdrop on others' conversations?" Clifford drawled sarcastically.

She slowly shook her head, smiling infuriatingly, then continued easily, "Yes, and I heard her say that. . . ."

Clifford turned and started to walk away leisurely, his hands thrust deep into his pockets as he strolled, apparently unperturbed.

Emily jumped up and followed him. "Well, why did you go into the stables with her? I saw you myself, and you were a long while. I thought you were going to show her the new black stallion. It is my papa's favorite and it cost such a lot, you know."

She had become sidetracked. Well aware of this, Clifford took the topic up and started extolling the many virtues of the stable's latest addition. The ploy worked for a while. They had strolled a hundred yards or so in amicable conversation before Emily realized she had been outwitted. "You never answered me," she retorted, entirely peeved. "Why did you go in there with her? You never take me in there to show me anything."

Clifford choked on a light laugh as though something

unexpectedly funny had thrust itself upon him. Emily widened violet eyes up at him, smiling expectantly, inviting that the joke be shared. He gave a dismissing shake of his head and turned away, narrowed eyes scanning distant horizons once more.

"You never tell me any of your secrets," she accused roughly, hurt by his reticence. "I tell you all of mine."

Clifford looked down at her and smiled, affection plain in his face as he explained gently, "You are too young, Emily. You do not understand. . ." he faltered, ". . . such things. Wait until you are older."

"You sound just like my mama when you say that," she scoffed in hurt. "It is all she ever says to me." She mimicked in a strange, high-pitched voice, "When you are older, Emily, then you may do this . . . when you are older, Emily, then you may do that."

She made to run ahead, but his hand moved swiftly, arresting her and holding her close. "Look . . . I would take you in there, but you know you are not allowed. It is not my fault you have been banned from your father's stables. You nearly broke the gray's forehock jumping that fence. You frightened both your parents. It is quite understandable. You could have been killed and the mare might have had to be destroyed.

Emily pulled away from him disdainfully. "Well, if they had let me have a decent animal of my own to ride, I would not have needed to creep in there to have secret rides at odd times. The old pony that I had was more like a carthorse. It barely ever got above trotting and then only on three legs, I am sure."

Clifford put up a restraining hand. "Enough," he chided laughingly. "I have heard all this before, Emily." He glanced sideways at her small, bowed head. The long chestnut tresses were shielding most of her face from sight, but as she impatiently shook an irritating lock away from her cheek, she met his eyes quickly. He noticed the thin, slanting set of her mouth and the moist brightness enhancing the violet of her eyes.

One lean, lightly tanned arm moved about her shoulders and then jerked her close as she tried to shrug him away. His grip tightened as he coaxed, "Look . . . the next time your parents go out and you are left with Nannie Greg, I shall let you have a quick ride on the new black stallion. Just around the courtyard, mind you—and only if Saul is out of the way, too."

Emily smiled to herself knowingly before going up at him. He pushed her away from him slightly. "One day, Emily Shaw, you shall get me in deep trouble," he admitted slowly and not wholly in mockery.

Emily peered sideways at him from beneath shaded lids, determined not to let him evade the question of Rose and prospective wedding plans.

"Well, I do believe now . . . because I know Rose has no interest in horses at all . . . I do believe that Clifford Moore must have proposed to her in the stables. I do believe he must have taken her there so that he could drop on bended knee and quote Shakespeare or . . . or . . . ."

A strong hand closed around the back of her neck, exerting just enough pressure to make her hunch her shoulders and shriek. She tried to twist her head free, but the giggling made the effort completely ineffectual.

The imaginary scene became too much for her. She gasped and sank laughing to her knees in the lush grass, flattening the glossy, long stalks and transferring their color to her knees.

"Is that it? Did you propose to her . . . on one knee?" She drew a long breath and wiped her mirth-wettened eyes. "Cousin Cuthbert did that, you know," she gasped. "He is to marry Clarissa soon."

This remembered snippet seemed to dampen her humor somewhat and her breath slowed. One small palm wiped a greyish trail across her cheeks as she smeared the remainder of the wetness from her eyes.

"Cousin Cuthbert and Clarissa are to be married soon and I have got to wear an awful velvet dress." She looked up at Clifford, her top lip curling with the strength of her disgust. She pushed herself to her feet slowly. "It really is the most ghastly thing. It is purple, with a white lace collar and sash and. . . ." She broke off, noting the humor in his eyes.

"I think it sounds just right," he declared in mock solemnity. "I am sure it suits you very well."

She glared at him for a moment. As he noticed the crafty light rebrighten her eyes in retaliation to his quip, he deflected any further reference to his relationship with the vexing parlour maid by stating quickly, "I shall be going away soon, Emily."

This information certainly had the desired effect. Emily stared at him for a few silent moments, then asked "Going where?"

Clifford looked at her steadily and then far away to the southwest, where he could just glimpse the screen of tall poplars that bounded his childhood home, Malvern Hall. He had intended the words as merely a diversionary ploy, to distract her from posing further unanswerable questions. But now, as his eyes found and fixed on the land and residence that were his birthright, he knew that the statement was true.

Emily turned, her eyes following his. She gave a slightly relieved snort. "Oh, that. You know you cannot have it. It is not yours now and you cannot have it back. You have no money. Neither has your mother nor your brother. And the land has been sold off now, practically all of it. My father bought some, and so did Squire Benson, and. . . ."

Clifford cut in quietly with a strange, controlled smile. "But it is mine, Emily, and I shall have it." The words were equable and tinged with wry humour, yet the deter-

13

mination and inevitability in them made her fall silent again. She worried. The threat that he might in fact leave her gnawed at her for a few moments, prompting her at last in her uncertainty to fling at him, "And it serves you right that you cannot have it. If your papa had not been such a terrible man, your family would own Malvern Hall and the estate still."

"And if your dear papa had paid a fair price for the land he bought after my father's death, instead of fleecing my mother of money that would have settled our debts, perhaps we would never have needed to come and scrape for our daily crusts here at Thrushcross Grange at all," he rejoined sarcastically.

Emily glared at him, round-eyed and pinch-mouthed. She had heard as much before, intimated by whispering servants behind half-closed doors. But now, hearing him deride her father's help openly, made her choke out, "How dare you speak of my papa so. Ungrateful wretch. . . ." She let the name hang in the air a moment, glowering at him the while with eyes that sparked purple fire. It was one of her mother's favorite epithets, and Emily had heard her use it on many disrespectful menials.

He seemed unimpressed, so she repeated for good measure, "Ungrateful wretch. You are just jealous because my papa is a good man and your father was a terrible man . . . and a coward. My father would never leave me and Jane and George and Mama alone. He would never shoot himself and leave us alone with nowhere to go and no money. My mama will never have to work at another's house for a living, nor will George or any of us. George is going to be an officer in the Hussars. He will never have to go and work in a poky London office as a lawyer's apprentice as your brother Stephen did." She would have continued with this childish abuse, her fright that he might in fact go away and leave her making her spite ungovernable, but Clifford swung away from her without another word.

He walked on, aware of Emily trailing slowly and silently now at his back, but his eyes fixed and held on the house just visible in the distance. He was glad in a way that he could not see it properly in the hideousness of its decay.

He remembered his childhood spent there, for the most part in carefree wandering and horseback exploration of that large, rambling estate of pasture and woodland. Nearly a thousand acres, and it should all have been his on his father's death. He mused on the bitter irony that he was now working some of that very land, for a pittance, for someone else.

Clifford knew his father had left them destitute and with no living relatives willing or able to help their plight. One distant uncle had felt himself charitable enough to sponsor his younger brother Stephen to study in London as an articled clerk, but the allowance was insulting and would certainly stretch to nothing else. Probably, had he been allowed to do so, it would have been preferable for Stephen to come and work with the rest of them at Thrustcross Grange.

Clifford had been thirteen at the time of his father's demise. He had ferreted and pestered the servants, who were quite willing to oblige him now that their gainful employment had been brought to an abrupt and unexpected end, until he knew every circumstance of this new and untasted poverty and disgrace.

Once aware of the facts, he could hardly credit that the father he had always admired and respected could have been quite so stupid after all; and he had vowed gravely that in adulthood no such negligence would ever blight his own life in family.

Sir Edmund Moore had been very little short of a millionaire in his heyday. Clifford was aware of that. His father had told him this proudly on many occasions while standing by the wide, square-paned window of his oak-paneled study, surveying a domain that stretched as far as the eye could see. He would stare possessively and breathe deeply of the scented land that was his, and Clifford would gaze also, contented to be aware that what gratified his father so would one day be his. His youthful ambition had fired white-hot, and he had promised solemnly that he would keep and expand what his father had managed to amass from nearly nothing. But it was not to be; his father, having started life with nothing, saw fit to quit it the same way; his only legacy the destitution and ignominy that followed his financial ruin and his subsequent suicide.

Jamaican sugar and exploitation of the African trade had been Edmund Moore's making; it had been his downfall, too. Clifford had been aware of the satisfied snickers hissed behind hands, of the fitting end of those with ill-gotten gains, and of upstarts with more money than sense. Superstition had never figured in Clifford's calculations, and he knew that his family's ruin was simply the result of negligence and bad administration.

Edmund Moore had returned from Jamaica with his new wife and his new money and had set about carving himself some respectability. His vast wealth and its derivation made him an ally of those who had come about their fortunes in more or less the same way.

Many well-established families at that time had laid their foundation stones with money from slaving and exploiting West Indian soil and blacks for all they were worth. He had managed to buy himself a seat in parliament with the backing of just such a crony, and then, in his maiden speech, showed that he certainly deserved to be there. His popularity had started to grow.

Ironically, had he stayed at home and attended to his business affairs, especially those concerning the running of his West Indian interest, from which he still derived the

16

great bulk of his income, he might have lived very prosperously. But political life became his all, and so consummate a politician was he, that he was granted a baronetcy for his contribution in the House. His involvement with his new vocation was now absolute, his fate sealed.

Had he only been able to see it, he wold have realized that the machiavellian plotting in the land that spawned his new and immensely comfortable lifestyle far outdid any political intrigue he was likely to encounter in Whitehall. Absentee planters who left their estates in the hands of overseers and checked on them little were sometimes exceedingly less content for having done so — and exceedingly less rich, too. While he felt it his duty to attend wholeheartedly to his political career, the gratified overseers he instructed to act for him felt it their bounden duty to take not only charge but a generous slice of the profits as well. If that meant subjugating the negroes pitilessly to earn those extra pounds that were trickled and then channeled widely aside, they were quite prepared to do it.

But one fine spring morning, the black work force lashed into vengeful fury, rose up, and savaged both their tormentors and then the plantation that had taken their sweat and blood. They burned it to the ground and any survivors of the mayhem were forced to seek refuge with neighboring planters.

The shock of the disaster unhinged Edmund Moore's mind. Unable to cope as various debts were called in by panicking creditors, he tried to close himself off completely from the nightmare, even turning up as usual at the House as though nothing were amiss. But the situation steadily worsened, and a stream of anxious creditors pestered him ceaselessly. One day the bank officials managed to run him to ground outside the House of Parliament, and realizing then that he was about to lose everything, he went home, locked himself in his study, and shot himself in the head.

Clifford's mother had been utterly distraught; not just for the loss of her husband and only kin apart from her children, but for the security and the purpose he had provided.

Edmund Moore had met his wife in Jamaica. Her parents, both of English peasant stock, had traveled to the colonies to make their fortune, much as her husband had.

When Katherine Moore arrived in England she had been young and attractive, good-natured and happy. But her lack of breeding and refinement was undisguisable. She was politely ostracized by polite society, a fact that worried her little but her husband somewhat more, for in his newfound popularity and public life he would have liked his wife to share an equal standing.

Clifford thought of his mother—even now naive and gullible. On learning of their utter bankruptcy, she had wailed; unsure which way to turn or what to do, completely unused to life without a man to guide and shelter her and her family, she was bereft.

But it appeared that there was after all a man to protect her. Squire Shaw, a neighbouring landowner, had stepped in with an offer of "genteel" employment at his home: that she should act as companion to his wife Isabelle and that Clifford should join them and labor in a general capacity about the estate.

Stephen Moore, the younger son, was less robust than Clifford, and their generosity had not extended to him, even though he had wept to be allowed to stay with them. He had subsequently been packed off to London and his wretched apprenticeship.

Clifford sneered to himself; his mother's gratitude for the aid and hostility she was sure she was being offered had been pathetic. Even at thirteen, Clifford had realized that. His mother was guileless, and she supposed everyone else to be the same. Though not quite so innocent now, he acknowledged with a harsh twist to his mouth.

Clifford thought of the Shaws—Squire Shaw and his wife Isabelle. How he hated and despised them, and how well they knew it. He smiled wryly. Yes, they knew it despite his studied politeness and his resolution that they remain unknowing.

He knew they were gratified beyond measure that Sir Clifford Moore, for the title was his on his father's death, got none of the estate or privilege that was his birthright, but now shoveled manure in their stables.

It was not a very large or grand stables, either. At twelve he had had almost as many horses of his own as the squire now had in his entire stock! But then the squire's pursuits were diverse—certainly not wholly taken up with bloodstock. Clifford thought of his mother again, a small, attractive Creole with dark hair and a fine figure. She was too attractive by half. Acting as companion to Isabelle Shaw had seemed a fine solution to an unenviable situation, but the title was soon found to incorporate the more menial duties of an unpaid housekeeper and the general help. Clifford's mouth hardened and his eyes narrowed as he concentrated on Malvern Hall in the distance. She had made the beds on many occasions at the Shaw residence . . . and been coerced to lay on them just as many times. But keeping her mouth shut kept a roof over her own and her son's head; Clifford knew that.

He turned away savagely from Malvern Hall and thought instead of the child walking silently behind him. As though in response to his attention, she trod defiantly on the back of his heel. He ignored her, and soon the soft shoe made contact with the back of his foot again, kicking with more force this time.

He smiled to himself, wondering how she had come of such parents and wondering too why the scruffy little urchin beguiled him so.

He held a hand out behind him and after a few moments she clasped it and then pulled herself round, skipping, to walk at his side again.

"Please don't leave me, Clifford. Don't go away. Who shall I have to play with and talk to if you go? WILL I never see you again? Please don't leave."

He shrugged slightly, disentangling his hand as she tried to imprison it in both of hers, as though she could keep all of him with her as easily.

He stuck his hands in his pockets, out of her reach, and looked down at her intently. "Perhaps I might come back for you: when you are older and your manners have improved."

Emily frowned, her violet eyes narrowing as she sought a suitable rejoinder. After a short moment she sighed and merely started to drag her feet disconsolately through the tall meadow grass.

"Anyway," Clifford muttered. "You should play with your sister. She is more your own age. Ten-year-old girls are not supposed to rush around fields with the servant boys, hitching up their skirts and behaving like little hoydens."

Emily grimaced and sighed more loudly. "I know. Mama tells me so every day. She has washed her hands of me so many times that I think the skin is beginning to disappear. They are so very white, you know." She was thoughtful, slightly anxious, even, and Clifford laughed aloud.

"That is just an expression, Emily. No one actually does so."

Emily flushed uneasily and looked briefly uncertain. "But I saw her. She washed her hands, as she said it. She likes to be clean. She bathes sometimes once a week."

She gazed at Clifford with suitable astonishment before concluding, "And Jane is so boring. All she ever does is talk to her dolls or draw them on scraps of paper or dress them in silly frocks. Sometimes she presses flowers and leaves in her book and. . . ."

Clifford interrupted quickly, "All very proper behavior for young ladies, I am sure." He glanced down at her, asking with assumed gravity, "Have you leaned yet to sing, or play a decent tune on the piano? Last time I passed the drawing room window, I was quite sure some-one within must be attempting to drown a cat—until I looked in and spied you plonking and shrilling."

Emily made a lunge for him, shrieking indignantly. He evaded her easily and started to run; and she followed in half-amused, half-affronted pursuit.

He kept purposely just beyond her reach, turning every so often to taunt her and allow her to practically catch him. She shrieked and batted the air playfully, spinning herself, more than once, completely round with the violence of her swipes.

He slowed abruptly after a few minutes, then stopped, and Emily made to strike him, but he held her at arm's length, his attention quite obviously elsewhere and all his enjoyment gone.

His head was up, like that of an animal scenting danger; his eyes narrowed until they were no more than grey slits, intent now on the whitish bulk of Thrushcross Grange.

Emily's lightheartedness faded. Interpreting his mood exactly, she turned quickly too. She strained to listen, her eyes seeking the stark building, shifting and shimmering in the afternoon heat, nestled in a verdant hollow.

She stared at her home for a moment longer, then gazed enquiringly up at Clifford. But he was oblivious to her now.

A noise reached Emily's ears then, muting and honing on the transitory breeze that kept the damp hair from her forehead and cooled her hot, sticky face. Clifford stood for a second longer and Emily's eyes sought his. But he was moving again, slowly at first, his eyes still with the house. Then his stride lengthened abruptly and he was running faster than Emily had ever seen him run before. She followed automatically, but trailed far behind, her head and heart pounding. She felt icy despite the heat and unable to explain the reason for the dread. But it pervaded her, this feeling caught infectiously from the youth who was pulling further away from her with every second.

Emily entered the white, double-barred gate from the meadow breathlessly, her heart and sides aching badly and her hair and dress flying. She knew Clifford had disappeared into the house long since, but it seemed now uncannily quiet, as though the commotion she was sure they had heard had been no more than a figment of their imaginations. She continued more slowly, dragging weary, stiffened legs towards the kitchen doorway. Then she noticed the servants.

Saul Milner and his brother Tom stood outside the long, low brick-and-beamed stables, their place of work. They too were interested in the house, but when they noticed her, they shuffled around slightly in a wide circle as if to return to their chores.

Emily looked toward them as always, but there was no greeting or smile of welcome on either side this time. The two men looked at each other uneasily before giving up any pretense of work. They became still, leaning against the stable wall once more as they stared towards the house.

As though to reward their unwavering attention, another sobbing cry issued forth from within and then a lower hum of deeper male voices raised in argument.

Emily entered the house through the kitchens, ignoring the abruptly silent and busily scuffling kitchen staff. She stepped out cautiously and unsteady-legged into the narrow corridor that led away from the scullery and toward the main hallway. Her legs and arms were trembling with the strength of her exertion and of unknown yet certain disaster.

The polished wooden floor widened as she reached the vestibule, and Emily gazed at the grouped couples, their agitated faces incongruously gilded by the afternoon sun which streamed through high windows.

Clifford was standing to one side of his mother, slightly in front of her, as though shielding her from the grim-faced couple opposite.

Her own father and mother stood slightly apart facing her, although Emily was sure they did not see her. Their attention was quite obviously with the distraught woman and the tense youth close to them.

The parlor door clicked softly, and Emily's attention was drawn to it immediately. She glimpsed a whitish flash as a host of inquisitive servants protected themselves hurriedly from her view.

The nose in the hallway strengthed again: Emily was aware of Katherine Moore's sobs and of her own mother's raucous remonstrations. But for a few moments then she could distinguish nothing clearly other than the sounds of softly dragging footsteps.

She turned sideways, pacing backwards until she leant gratefully against the wall and she watched her younger sister near her. Jane was trailing a battered rag doll in one hand and clutching tightly at the front of her dress with the other.

She glided closer on small, soft shoes, her face paler than usual and the usually light-blue eyes seeming as dark as sapphires now. She drew level with Emily, then looked away from the figures grouped in front of her in the hall and raised her frightened eyes to meet those of her slightly taller sister.

Emily wanted to reassure her with words but could find none. Instead, she let a clumsy arm drop across the thin shoulders. The stiff lace edging of Jane's large collar scraped the soft skin of her forearm, but she was barely aware of the irritation. Emily patted her gently. She felt the small frame quiver and rock and knew that Jane had started to weep silently.

Emily's troubled violet eyes raised from her sister's bent head just as her mother advanced towards Mrs. Moore. She watched horrified as her mother raised her hand swiftly and slapped the woman quite deliberately, hard across the face.

Emily's eyes darted to her father immediately, sure he would deplore what seemed an unprovoked attack. He appeared to be in some sort of mental anguish, however, and merely stood with his head bowed before it started to move slowly from side to side as though he denied something painful.

Katherine Moore raised shaking fingers to her stained cheek, her head bobbing further forward. Her other hand moved spontaneously, checking the young man at her side who had sprung forward belatedly in her defense.

Clifford shook away the restrictive hand at once and neared Isabelle Shaw purposefully, his face white and set. She backed away, shrilling her husband's name and stumbling on the hem of her gown in her haste.

The squire jerked himself forward, lashing out instinctively with a riding crop he clutched in his hand. Clifford swung away from him, his arms protecting his body, but the crop flailed higher, splitting open his cheek.

Emily gazed in terror at the scene. Her arm tightened absently across the bristling shoulder she still grasped, half-aware that she ought to take Jane away, but she felt unable to move or speak at all.

She watched trancelike as Clifford's hand rose slowly to the wound. He pressed it lightly, then gazed at his stained fingers before he smeared the blood away slowly with a deliberate stroke of his thumb.

24

"You will pay dearly for that." His voice was even and cool, with the same sort of tone he always used when addressing her parents. Emily blinked rapidly as the crop swung again in response to the quiet threat.

Clifford's hand arrested the cane in mid-air. He wrenched it away, hurling it forcefully, and it clattered against the bannister before coming to rest on a stair. As though finally able to force speech, squire Shaw stridently, "Get out. Get out, both of you, and never return! I shall forward whatever money is due to you. Now go at once before more harm is done!"

Katherine Moore raised her eyes slowly to meet those of the gray-faced, gray-haired man opposite. He turned from her at once, one square hand worrying at the large fastenings on his waistcoat. Emily watched his discomposure, wondering distractedly if he might wrench a button off, so frenzied were his plucking fingers.

A strange, clamorous silence ensued, ringing about the high hallway. As though unable to endure it, Jane emitted a gurgling sob, shattering the eerie quiet.

Isabelle Shaw's attention was arrested immediately. Her plump white hands flew to her mouth. "Oh, my baby. Oh, that she should have witnessed this. Where is nannie Greg? Fetch her, someone," she demanded.

But Emily was conscious only of Clifford and his mother as they approached. They walked slowly, Clifford's arm about his mother's shoulder, lean, brown fingers digging deeply into the charcoal material of her dress as he supported her.

Emily stood transfixed, her attention held by Clifford's eyes, which regarded her quite steadily. Her own seemed immovable too, engulfed by his, and yet she was also aware of the bloodied mark streaking the taut, sallow skin from just below one eye the length of his face to his chin.

Emily flattened herself and her sister further against the wall. As he passed, Clifford's mouth tilted, but it was not a smile. "I shall come back for you, Emily," he said clearly, in a quiet, flat tone.

Emily blinked, wanting to run in front of him and make him smile properly and speak to her again. But she merely stood rigid, her sole acknowledgment that he had spoken, a spasmodic jerk of her arm against her sister's thin shoulders.

Her eyes followed them until they turned the corner of the corridor and then her mother was with them, removing Jane from her grasp.

Emily started to walk after the Moores, but her father called her name in a harsh warning tone. She turned and looked at him, sensing a new fear in the pale, moist pools of his eyes. He gestured at her futilely and looked about to speak. But he merely dropped his head forward and shook it slowly from side to side in despair.

Emily looked away from him and gazed the length of the empty, quiet corridor once more, certain that Clifford's words, which would an hour previously have seemed a delightful promise, now seemed intimidating and quite frighteningly sinister.

Chapter One

Jane's needle weaved deftly as she worked a particularly intricate stitch into a cluster of bright red poppy heads. She sat back in her chair and absently patted the perfect example of embroidery that adorned her lap.

She looked up then and across the width of the small, comfortable parlor to where her elder sister sat gazing solemnly at her sewing. Jane smiled to herself and then repeated, more loudly this time, "Emily . . . I was just saying that I have some very interesting news. Mama and I went to the Assembly Rooms last evening and the Lyttleton girls were there. They told us that not only is he back but that the most terrible rumour has started about. . . ."

"Who is back, and from where?" Emily interrupted impatiently. "The Prince Regent from Brighton? Wellington from the war? Georgie from his regiment? Or perhaps it is papa. . . ." she suggested drily, "returned at last from another of his drunken gambling sprees." She ignored Jane's horrified countenance and the way her light eyes swiveled nervously towards the door.

"Hush. . . . Never say so. If mama hears you, you know it will be trouble." Jane caught at her thin lower lip with small, even teeth. She regarded her elder sister steadily, but Emily merely looked dejectedly at the scrap of material covering her own lap. She patted it in imita-

27

tion of her sister's recent gesture, more in this instance to flatten the lumpy stitching she acknowledged wryly than out of any pride in her workmanship. She attempted a new flower head, leaving the one she had scowled over for twenty minutes or more half-finished and disastrously misshapen. The scarlet silk penetrated the smooth linen neatly a few times and then, aware by Jane's silence that the younger girl was watching her artistry, Emily attempted a slightly more adventurous stitch. She yanked at the thread as it refused to pull through the cloth more than a few inches, then raised the material, peering at the underside, noticing at once the necklace of neat knots decorating the silk.

"You keep your thread just a little too long, I fear, Emily," Jane ventured a trifle timidly. "Perhaps if you were to. . . ." Her voice faded as she watched her sister pull impatiently at the thread, trying to untangle the catches.

Emily gave a final, frustrated tug in the vain hope that the looped thread might somehow unravel itself. The red silk gave with a loud ping, and Emily cursed beneath her breath.

Jane's eyes sought the door again and she hissed, "Sshh . . . if Mama hears you talking so, she will stop you seeing Georgie completely when he is home on leave. She insists that he is to blame for your. . . ." She coughed and laughed simultaneously, ". . . your colorful language."

Emily looked distastefully at the blotchy, inept sewing, then threw the colorful sampler forcefully against the cold brick fireplace. Her temper expended, she sighed deeply and closed her weary eyes for a moment. She sighed in defeat and then rose and moved to retrieve the infuriating item from the fender, brushing speckling soot into a smoky-gray trail. She turned it over and inspected the cluster of tight bunches, deciding with a slight, self-mocking smile that they made an infinitely better show than her painstaking efforts on the reverse.

Jane held out a slender white hand and Emily walked to her chair slowly, relinquishing the smutty sampler silently and with a small, grateful smile. She stood close to her sister's chair, watching as her fragile, pale fingers loosened and removed the tangles, then pulled and straightened the scarlet silk into smooth, sleek strands.

The proffered work was reluctantly retrieved, and Emily muttered in a heavy breath, "Thank you, Jane." She paused before adding with a sweet smile, "I am sorry I snapped at you earlier." She began to move away, glancing around the small room casually as she did so. "I do so dislike this house. I wish we could have stayed at the other in Curzon Street. It was so much lighter and airier. This place is quite stifling and oppressive. I simply must go out and get some air." She looked towards Jane with a coaxing smile and suggested, "A walk in the park?"

Jane grimaced a childish refusal and looked towards the long, narrow window at one end of the room. "It is just beginning to rain, and that sky . . . ." She shook her head slowly and regretfully. "I do believe that it might rain all day."

Emily regained her armchair and sank into it slowly. She snuggled back into the soft cushioning, her head falling against one chintz-covered wing. She watched through the window as the first spatterings dribbled and merged, clinging to the glass. Her lids weightened, slightly hooding violet eyes that mesmerically followed the teardrop trailings. She yawned long and wide and a slender hand moved to cover her mouth, and let the other clear soft, mahogany curls from the fair skin of her forehead.

As though only just recalling her sister's words of some time ago, she asked with moderate interest now, "Is our little fat princeling back from Brighton, then? Has he returned to London to give us the rare privilege of watching him squander another hundred thousand pounds or so on some ridiculous pomp and circumstance to mark his Regency?"

Jane glanced at her sister, her expression pained. She was used to the peculiar predilection Emily had for satirizing their Regent, but sometimes she wondered if perhaps she went just a little too far.

Emily's eyes returned to the drizzling window pane as she muttered, "How I hate that man! It is quite obscene to waste so much money while half the populace starves. Princess Caroline has my deepest sympathy. Perhaps she is vulgar and smelly, but his debauchery and extravagance are equally rank."

Jane was scandalized. "Oh, Emily, really! How can you talk of Princess Caroline in such a way—so indelicately? I can see why Mama despairs of you. You most certainly are becoming a bluestocking, and a treasonable one too. I blame it on all those books. If you are not poring over historical or political tomes, you are reading some romantic novel, filling your head the while with fantastic nonsense. . . ." She faltered as she saw the expression on her elder sister's face.

Emily smiled then laughed aloud, quite unperturbed. After a moment her good humour sobered once more. "I do so hate this house, too," she murmured. "I quite liked Curzon Street. The rooms were at least quite spacious and it did have a library, if only a small one."

"You know quite well that we could not afford to live there any longer," Jane chided lightly. "As mama said, running a house of that size costs a small fortune. So many servants, so many rooms to heat and to light. I never liked it much at all. It was damp and cold all the time. I never felt warm the whole winter through." She looked about the small parlor with appreciative eyes, then announced contentedly, "I much prefer it here in

30

Clapham. The house might be small, but it is quite cozy."

Emily pushed herself upright in the armchair again and stated sourly, "Well, if papa did not continually drink and gamble away all our resources, perhaps we might have enough money to keep a decent-sized house and live there without freezing or starving to death every winter."

Emily paused, expecting Jane to spring to their father's defense, but she merely picked up the neglected sewing from her lap and started to stitch a neat outline to a fresh poppy head.

"I heard mama having cross words with that new maid," Jane ventured after a short silence. "I do believe she will not be with us beyond the week. It is a good thing Nannie Greg learned to dress hair. I can see that she will not only be maid to us but mama as well before much longer. I heard Mama say as much."

Dark curls squashed into the chairback as Emily resettled her head, and she remarked drily, "Well, in that case, she will be maid just to Mama. What little time she has left in the twenty-four hours will probably be spent sleeping." She barely paused before asking idly, "What did you say earlier, Jane, about someone returning to town? You never did tell me."

"I would have done, had I the chance," Jane countered slightly abrasively. "You were off on a tangent before I could finish, and berating the Prince Regent and . . . . "Oh," she gasped, "that, in fact, is what I was going to tell you. He was a guest and very highly received, by all accounts, at that august gathering at Carlton House. And not only that — Wellington is said to think very highly of him too and," she lowered her voice and coloured a little as she murmured, "apparently there is some breath of scandal about a mistress they both have. Is that not quite terrible, to share. . . ."

Emily sat upright in the chair and stared at her sister. She demanded slowly, "Who on earth are you going on about? Am I ever to know or may I yet die of old age before this scandalous snippet is dropped within my hearing?"

Jane smiled and prevaricated tantalizingly, "Well, it is your own fault, Emily. You socialize so little that you never get to hear of these things. The Lyttleton girls told me yesterday evening and I must say that mama went quite pale. I thought she might faint. . . ."

Emily's gaze was keen, even ominous now, and Jane added quickly, "Clifford Moore is back in town and apparently he has been back in the country for some while; it is just that nobody knew of it. Of course she made much of the emphasis before continuing, "He is *Sir* Clifford Moore now." Jane hesitated, something about her sister's unexpected fascination with the needlework on her lap, making her fall silent. She watched as Emily picked slowly at some of her stitching with an oval nail, wondering if perhaps she had not clearly heard her news. She had expected her to show somewhat more interest in the information.

Emily raised a hand and pushed tumbling dark curls behind her ear. Her violet eyes contemplated Jane blankly for a few moments before she repeated disbelievingly, "Clifford Moore? Surely he is dead. We heard as much about three years ago . . . that he had died in some ridiculous-sounding drama, privateering or piracy on the high seas or some such escapade." Her eyes searched Jane's calm countenance.

"You must remember, Jane . . . he was killed near the West Indies, I am quite sure of it," she asserted.

Emily stared earnestly at Jane, but her sister was now stitching serenely. She merely avowed clearly without looking away from her work, "Well, I can assure you that it is most certainly true. The Lyttleton girls have seen and spoken to him. They were invited to a rout in Surrey, and he was there, and . . ." she paused for effect, "apparently he is most terribly handsome. What is more, he has an absolute fortune. They said there was more than one hundred thousand a year from sugar plantations and foreign investments, but of course I did not believe them. You know how they exaggerate. Why, I cannot even contemplate the amount . . . and to have that much every year . . . it is quite absurd."

Jane glanced up at Emily, who was staring back widely. To fuel the appetite of this silent, attentive audience, she added quickly, "And Maria was quite swooning, I can tell you; and Margaret seemed very taken with him too." She mimicked in a lilting lisp, "Oh, he's quite charming and so very handsome." Jane wrinkled her nose mockingly. "Apparently he was hard to get close to at all, so beset was he by doting young ladies and their mamas."

"Well, I hope we never see him," Emily cut in quickly and vehemently. "I certainly would never want to meet him . . . not again. Not after that terrible business at Thrushcross Grange." She paused for a moment, then added quietly, "Do you realize, if it had not been for him and his mother, and their foul behavior and lies, we would probably still be living in that lovely old house in the Hertfordshire countryside, instead of removing from one small brick prison to another here in London, as we do now. And every time we move we are incarcerated in smaller quarters."

"I know. I felt so for mama when she heard. She went quite white, and I am sure I saw Mrs. Lyttleton smile slyly."

"Oh, I am quite sure you did also," Emily agreed ironically. "It might be ten years since then, but I have not forgotten, and I am sure there must be others with memories as long as mine." She said with quiet force, "We shall have to avoid him at all costs. He has ruined our lives once with lies and accusations, and should he want to make much of it. . . ."

"I hardly think we need worry," Jane said brightly. "He is rich now and well connected. He is said to be well-liked by both Prince Regent and Wellington. Why would he bother with us at all? We rarely get invited anywhere of note now . . . and you go nowhere in any case. It is exceedingly unlikely that mama and I would ever chance upon him while abroad; I hardly think he will be circulating in the same company we do." Jane gave a small, mischievous laugh. "Perhaps we could capitalize on it after all. I am quite sure we could all dine out for a whole year or more on tales of how Sir Clifford Moore, now so eminent, once mucked out the stables at Thrushcross Grange."

Emily leaned forward in her chair, her hands gripping the arms tightly. "For heaven's sake, Jane, it is hardly a matter for jest. Have you forgotten how Papa was set on the road to ruin? How we have all been set on that same road? I cannot remember Papa touching a drop of alcohol before we left Hertfordshire, yet now he is drunk more days than he is sober. Neither did he ever gamble . . . but soon there will be nothing left at all to pawn or sell to repay his debts and what then?" Emily looked away from Jane abruptly and out through the rain-soaked window. "I hate him," she said finally.

A slight, shocked noise issued forth from Jane, Emily looked briefly at the sewing in her lap before glancing at the driving rain once more. "No, not Papa, although sometimes. . . ." She abandoned the sentence and repeated with quiet resolution, "I hate Clifford Moore. I would hate Mrs. Moore too, were she still alive, although I liked her well enough in Hertfordshire. What I can remember of her, anyway."

"I liked her too," Jane said softly. "She was kind and so quiet. No one would ever have guessed that she was in fact Lady Katherine Moore. She always seemed so modest and unassuming. So unlike Mama." Her cheeks tinged

34

roseate at this indiscretion.

But as though to reinforce her opinion, a woman's voice could be heard quite clearly although the actual words were indistinct.

"I cannot remember hearing her quite so often or audibly at Thrushcross Grange," Jane ventured pensively. "Do you think she has become more raucous in the last ten years or so?"

Emily gave a wry smile and responded drily, "Oh, I doubt it. It is just that at Thrushcross Grange there was more space. We had stables in Hertfordshire that were bigger than this house." She gazed up at the ceiling and around at the room disparagingly.

"Is Papa back then, do you think?" Jane whispered.

"No, if it were Papa back I think we should have heard the front door. He seems to be away from home most of the day as well as most of the evening now." She sighed a little, then mused thoughtfully, "I wonder if she has yet grown to hate him?"

"You must never say or think that. It is not true," Jane said unsteadily.

Emily disagreed. "I think it is true, Jane. And who can blame her? Or us, for that matter? For his profligacy is at the expense of us all, and I feel it increasingly difficult to sympathize anymore, even though I know he is sad." She gave a small, hard laugh. "Besides, his self-pity is so great lately that it makes everyone else's quite superfluous."

She leaned back in the chair, relaxing a little as she realized she was quite hungry. "I should imagine it will be cold mutton again tonight for dinner, and with barely a vegetable to decorate the plate."

Jane sewed quietly for a few moments, then said abruptly, "No one ever mentions Papa when we are out. They never ask how he is or what he is doing."

"They hardly need to; I should imagine his losses at his club are quite common knowledge. No doubt he is the butt of many a joke every time he drags himself away from the tables to crawl home, defeated once more."

Both girls flashed identical warning signals with their eyes before appearing to work diligently at their embroidery. The door opened wider and Isabelle Shaw entered the parlor. She ran the palms of her plump hands across the front of a faded grey satin dress, almost suggesting that she was drying them, but both girls knew that she was attempting ceaselessly and unconsciously to smooth the creases from the worn material.

She approached the vacant wing chair close by the unlit fire, seeking it from habit rather than for any warmth to be had. She settled her small, round frame into the chair and distributed her dress evenly across her lap before eyeing her two conscientious daughters.

Her pale-blue eyes looked from one bowed head to the other. She tidied the fading fair hair into a neater bun at the back of her head, then sighed heavily. This obvious announcement drew attention from her daughters, and both smiled and greeted her politely.

"That dress is not ready yet," Isabelle Shaw remarked. "So tiresome. Jane, you shall have to wear another tonight."

Jane smiled in mute acceptance of this information. Her meek acquiescence did not appease her mother, however, who muttered, "I shall try a different dressmaker next time. The woman was quite insolent, too. I am quite sure she could have finished the gown well within the time, had she put herself to it."

Emily remarked clearly, and without irony, as she sewed, "Perhaps paying the outstanding accounts there might have helped the woman's attitude, Mama."

Jane looked wary; her mother was startled; but Isabelle Shaw managed an even tone. "Your father's fiscal arrangements are no concern of ours, Emily, and I shall thank you to remember it. When he is ready to do so, I am sure he shall settle his dues. Nothing excuses the hussy's unforgiveable rudeness. I shall use Mrs. Baldwin in future; I hear from several acquaintances that she is most obliging."

The temptation to remark that her cooperation was probably also governed by the speed of her remuneration was swallowed as Emily noticed her mother's pale, tightly composed face.

Isabelle watched her two daughters at work for a moment. "I have told Marion Cooper that you will accompany us to Almack's tonight, Emily," she advised levelly, immediately raising a silencing hand as Emily began a spontaneous protestation. "It is no use, I have quite made up my mind. How the dear woman managed to procure us the tickets I shall never fathom. But she has, and at such short notice, and both you girls will be there. Unfortunately, Jane's attire will not be as I had hoped; but you, Emily, as you join in with so little of our social engagements, it is more than likely that no one has seen either of your good dresses before. In a way it is quite fortunate this time that you tend to be such a recluse."

"But Almack's, Mama," Emily demurred hastily, "you know how I hate it there." "Nonsense," her mother expostulated firmly. "Do not talk such rot. How can you hate it there? You have only ever been once before. It was the last time we were presented with tickets, almost two years ago and just after your come-out." She looked reflective for a moment, then eyed Emily thoughtfully as she recalled, "And as I remember, the gentlemen were very keen for you."

Emily made a terse, dismissive gesture.

"What is a poor woman to do?" Isabelle sighed, opening a small, plain fan which she employed sporadically. She inquired of herself again in a weak voice, "What is a woman to do with two daughters, both with their come-outs far behind them and neither any closer to betrothal than they were on their fifteenth birthdays?"

Isabelle glanced sharply from one to the other. "And neither of them willing enough in their mama's opinion to promote their cause, either," she added meaningfully.

She looked towards Jane's lightly flushed face and her blue eyes softened. "Of course, Jane has been unlucky. Due to our . . ." she hesitated, then continued carefully, "our rather strained financial position last year, I could not launch her quite as I would have liked. I could not arrange the outings or engagements or order the gowns that befitted such a lovely young woman." She smiled patronizingly and affectionately at the object of her compassion. She turned to Emily abruptly.

"You, however, young lady, had quite a fine do and three proposals of marriage in six months. What I want to know is why you are still here with your poor mama, who can ill afford to keep you, now you are turned twenty." She ignored Emily's slight scowl, accusing, "You are quite a beauty, Miss, despite the way you twist your face with those grimaces, and well you know how lovely you are. It is high time that you turned the fact to advantage. Your looks will be fading before you have profited from such attributes.

Emily stood up abruptly and moved to the window. Her violet eyes scanned the paler lilac-gray of the heavens. "I do believe it has stopped raining after all. I think I might go for a walk."

"Sit down young lady, you are going nowhere. It will be time to start dressing soon, and I do not want you disappearing and nowhere to be found until it is well past time to leave. I want you to look your finest, Emily and that," she added with grudging admiration and a small smile, "will indeed be fine. I am quite sure Marion is hoping you will not come. She knows that when you two are together, her own two girls suffer from the comparison."

Emily turned from the window and smiled affably. "Well, I am more than willing to oblige Mrs. Cooper in her wishes."

"Sit down." Isabelle extracted a handkerchief from deep within her reticule as Emily resettled herself in the wing chair.

Isabelle dabbed at the tiny beads of perspiration that clung to her hairline and top lip. "I do so hope the room will be well-aired tonight. It is most terribly moist today, and there is bound to be a crush. It could be quite unbearable."

Emily examined her embroidery lengthily and critically. Deciding it was beyond salvation, she dropped the cloth carelessly to the floor.

"Dear Emily," Isabelle clucked. "What on earth am I to do with you? No accomplishments to speak of . . . unless you can call reciting verbatim from history books or Shakespeare or some other such tome an achievement. As for all that silly romantic fantasy you read — Gulliver's travels and the like — no wonder your head is stuffed full of such idealistic nonsense all the time." She shook her head. "You really should have accepted young Mr. Tavistock's offer of marriage. Under the circumstances," her eyes sought the grubby, discarded sampler wonderingly, "I am quite surprised that he ever made it at all."

"Probably because I never showed him my embroidery, Mama. Emily met her mother's eyes squarely, continuing with barely a hint of a smile in her voice, "I thought it wise."

Isabelle's eyes narrowed. "This is no joking matter, Emily. I'm tempted to wash my hands of you completely. He was easily the best of the three that offered for you, and you turned him down out of hand, without even considering the matter. Foolish girl. No proposals have come your way since, and really, with your attitude, I cannot be surprised.

Jane tells me Clifford Moore is back in town, Mama."

The ensuing silence stretched a trifle uncomfortably.

Isabelle's color heightened. "Yes, I know. Various acquaintances have made it their business to inform me of his presence . . . several times." She smiled bitterly as she added, "And of his new status too, of course. Memories can be very long but very selective in what they recall. He is most definitely sought after by all the top hostesses, and accordingly I could almost hear our names being dropped from many a guest list. Of course, you cannot blame them. I suppose it is a very delicate situation, and he is so well connected now, patronized by the Prince Regent and Wellington. I have heard no end of tales to account for it . . . that he has loaned the Regent money and that there is some talk of help with the war effort."

"But what does it matter, Mama?" Emily interrupted gently. "We move in a different circle from people like that now. He is nothing to us anymore, and neither are we to him. He is hardly likely to bother seeking us out for reasons either fair or foul. There should never be any reason for any of us to meet him. It would be madness for him to try to even old scores, would it not?"

Isabelle stared ahead at nothing in particular. "They say he has had Malvern Hall repaired. It has been carried out over a number of years and is all but completed. A select few have viewed the results, and it is rumored that the Prince Regent was so impressed, he rushed back to London and started planning with architects for alterations to Carlton House the very same day."

Emily sneered, "Perhaps he might also see fit to ask his newfound friend to pay for the works, instead of dipping into the country's coffers to satisfy his latest whim for a gothic tower or a Chinese room." After a moment she asked her mother sharply, "Where is Clifford Moore? Is he in London still?"

Isabelle shook her head reassuringly, reading her

daughter's mind at once. "No, we will be quite safe tonight. It is nearly the end of the season, anyway. Many have already left for their country estates, and he is one that has done so. I daresay he will not return until next year." She gazed steadily at Emily. "So, I really do expect you to go to Almack's tonight and act as companion to your sister. No doubt Marion will want me to sit with her for the best part of the evening. I daresay that is the reason she got the tickets. And because the end of the season always brings with it more availability, once the haute monde start leaving town. She will probably bore me rigid with accounts of her family's successes. But what matter? It will be worth the agony so long as you two girls benefit from it."

She looked at Jane and smiled. "I do believe Mr. Rochford will be there this evening."

Jane blushed and hung her head slightly, although a smile hovered at the corners of her mouth.

"I think it possible we may hear some good news from that quarter soon. He really was most taken with you last time you met. I must say, I quite expected him to call the next morning out of reason more than mere courtesy. I assume the delay is because he is shy. He has always struck me as being rather a timid man. Even so I am sure he could be prompted to approach your father were the encouragement . . . ."

Emily cut in with a disgusted snort, "Mr. Rochford?" She looked from her mother to her sister, appalled. "Why, he must be forty-five if he is a day! A widower, too, with three children." She fumed with such vehemence that the insult could have been her own rather than Jane's.

"Jane could do much better than that. Why should she settle for being nursemaid to another woman's brood? It would be hard enough work should she have children of her own. Why can she not wait until she finds someone she can love and respect?

Isabelle bit out crisply, "Mr. Rochford has quite a reasonable income and a large estate, plus a very nice country residence in Kent." She added through lips that twisted strangely, "And remember well enough, both of you, when gazing dreamily around for romantic illusions to take into womanhood, that love and respect do not last . . . neither do they pay the bills."

Emily shifted further along the small bench seat, making room for Jane, who was smiling sweetly at a tall, dark-haired Hussar who had returned her to her seat.

As he turned to leave, Emily stared wistfully at the back of his tunic and sighed, "I wonder how Georgie is. I hope he will be home soon. I would dearly love to see him."

There was no response to this plaintive wish, so Emily turned and looked at her sister. But the younger girl's attention was still held by the cavalry officer who had turned and flashed a brief white smile across his shoulder.

Jane flirted deftly, her fan opening and fluttering prettily as she subtly displayed gratitude and pleasure at his interest.

Emily gazed after the uniformed figure again, this time with more interest. "Now he looks quite charming. What was his name?"

The discarded fan dropped into Jane's lap now that the handsome hussar had disappeared from view, and she sighed, "I am not too sure. I believe he said his name was Philip something, but he trod on my foot at the crucial moment and I missed the rest." She was still gazing pensively after him. "He is most terribly distinguished-looking, though—don't you think?"

"Most awfully clumsy too, by the sound of things," Emily noted dampeningly, as her eyes scoured the crowded ballroom for likelier male prospects for her sister. She looked back at Jane, and noting the wistfulness in her blue eyes, she encouraged spiritedly, "Forget him.

A permanent liaison with him could ruin your dancing days for all time, and you know how you like to take a turn around the floor."

Jane's eyes focused on her sister and she smiled. She glanced down at the sapphire-blue of her dress, smoothing the silk with thin white fingers. "Do you think this dress looks presentable? I am sure I heard Mary Cooper murmuring about it behind her hand. It is such a striking color — a blue that is not easily forgotten — and I did wear it the last time I saw them at that midsummer ball."

"You look quite magnificent, Jane; you know that. You have been asked to dance more times than any other girl in the room, I am sure of it," Emily reassured her firmly.

"Only because you refuse every man who approaches you and then they feel obliged to ask me instead," Jane countered, a tinge of resentment sharpening her tone.

"An abrupt, light snort indicated Emily's opinion of that statement, but Jane locked her fingers together and examined the white knuckles carefully. She said slowly, "You know very well it is true. I am amazed that I am paid any attention at all when you are near, and if Mama finds out you have been turning away every suitable man who presents himself, she will be quite furious." Jane looked sideways at the slim, fair column of her sister's throat and the way long, loose ringlets clung with glossy brilliance to the nape of her neck. Her dress was of amethyst silk and austerely plain in style, but as Emily turned her head and Jane received the full effect of the wide, jewel-bright eyes, she realized dispiritedly that any adornment would have been merely superfluous.

"Well, I have made a quick search," Emily informed brightly, ignoring her sister's doleful homily completely, "and I must say that I do believe the doddering Mr. Rochford has not yet put in an appearance. You could yet be luckier tonight than you imagined."

"He is hardly doddering, Emily," demurred Jane, but with a small smile. "He uses a stick only rarely, you know. His knees suffer only when the weather is excessively damp."

Emily grimaced in mock horror and muttered, "Heavens . . . let us pray then that this evening's humidity keeps him indoors, else your shins may end up as bruised as your already battered toes."

Jane made a laughing speech in her elderly beau's defense, but Emily's pained expression made further words on her own estimation of that gentleman's sprightliness totally unnecessary.

Emily endeavoured to find some comfort in the hard wooden chair she fidgeted upon. She glanced at Jane, about to speak, but her sister's attention was now quite definitely engaged elsewhere. She was once more flirting in a silent yet unmistakable way with the dark-haired man who had recently danced on her foot. He now lounged against the wall, near to where they sat, and gazed Jane's way with large, brooding eyes.

Pleased by her younger sister's obvious success with the hussar, Emily nevertheless leaned her head back against the wall and sighed. Her boredom was mounting steadily, and she knew the restlessness would soon be hard to control. She glanced yearningly toward the far end of the room, where there were large, open windows leading onto a terrace. She would love to escape for a while, but dismissed the notion almost at once, aware that such behavior was unacceptable and would vex her mother should she find out. She decided on impulse to count the people lining the opposite wall, determined to amuse herself at least for a minute or two with the childish game. She started immediately, her lips barely moving as she chanted to herself, and it was some while before her mind caught up with the rapidity of her eye movement.

Her sight flicked back along the groups of people to a

point almost exactly opposite where she sat, and she breathed out softly—one hundred and two—automatically, although all interest in her little pastime had now vanished.

She stared rigidly and without breath for a moment as the heart-thudding force of recognition mingled with a strange uncertainty.

She was aware of a slight curve to his mouth as he acknowledged her arrested attention, but there was nothing in his manner at all that suggested hostility, or warmth, or even greeting. She was oddly sure that he had been watching her awhile, and she tried to reason why she, in her countless idle explorations of the room and its occupants, had missed him.

Violet eyes detached abruptly from silver-gray, and she searched anxiously and immediately about her for her mother. She was unable to distinguish Isabelle Shaw's crimson-clad figure anywhere in the bright, crowded room. Remembering then her closer relative, she turned toward Jane at her side. But at that precise moment, Jane's wiles paid off. The dark and moody cavalry officer presented himself once more, and holding out his hand and bringing together the heels of his highly polished boots, he requested Jane join him in forming a quadrille.

Emily watched her sister for a moment as she disappeared amongst the throng. She looked ahead again then, slowly and more calmly now, for she was instinctively aware that he was still watching. Their eyes met and held for an infinite moment while her mind registered remote surprise that she had recognized him so easily.

She was sure he did not look the same; or rather, he no longer fitted the ephemeral vision she had kept of a tall, fair youth whose memory urged her to recall hazy summer days both warm and sunlit.

That the name of Moore was a bitter reminder of her family's grief and ignominy and their withdrawal from the

45

home and countryside she had loved, had always confused and disturbed her. She had found it difficult to reconcile the paradox, but now as she stared at the familiar stranger with short, silvered hair and sun-darkened skin, she could sense every association with halycon days receding irrevocably from her mind and only the fear and resentment remaining.

He pushed himself away from the wall abruptly, breaking her trancelike stare. She realised intuitively that he was about to come over to her. She stood up immediately and proceeded to mingle, jostled by those grouped close by. She managed to smile and adequately to return the occasional greeting and was aware of vaguely surprised eyes following her lone progress through the room.

A young man interposed himself and bowed neatly. After a confused instant, she realized that he was suggesting they join the last quadrille, which was forming slowly and still required another couple. Emily started to demur, but as she turned, constantly seeking her mother's bright and colourful form, she noticed Clifford Moore again. He was matching her progress along the room but on the opposite side, and his attention was still very much with her.

The young man still hovered at Emily's side. She smiled instantly and, slipping a hand through his arm, almost propelled him toward the couples grouped on the dance floor.

As they danced, Emily scanned the crowded room with minute purpose for her mother. She espied her at last, sitting barely fifteen yards from the dance floor. She was conversing animatedly, half-hidden by an amply proportioned matron wearing a puce silk gown. The woman laughed heartily and her bosom undulated in heavy ripples, silver brooches bobbing and dipping on the storm-colored swell; ostrich feathers adorning a turban headdress were set ashiver. The woman turned Emily's way then, eyes bright and razor sharp as she scoured the dancing couples. She raised a gloved hand and made a small wave at Emily, and it was a moment before Emily realized that beneath the tasteless disguise was, in fact, Mrs. Cooper.

The dance pattern was now taking Emily and her partner close to the side of the room she most wanted to avoid. She sought the dark face, noticing thankfully that his attention was now elsewhere.

He was beset by a crowd of people; mainly female, Emily noticed with an odd sourness, although she recognized the Earl of Craven and another gentleman there also. She watched him avidly, now that she could do so unobserved, noting at closer quarters that his clothes were immaculate: dark and of fine material and, even to her inexperienced eye, quite obviously expensive. A small girl dressed in pink, encouraged by her mother, imposed herself urgently on his attention at that point. He gave it to her, but as his eyes moved from his male companions to the determined lady, his eyes skimmed the dancing couples once more and found Emily's watching him.

The music ceased at that precise moment. Emily's partner bowed and tried to draw her arm through his in order to return her to a chair.

Emily refused prettily, disentangling herself quickly. She gave the disappointed man a winsome smile before hurrying lightly toward Jane and the hussar. She adroitly excused them both, murmuring about the necessity of locating their dear mother, and was, in an instant, dragging Jane toward their seated parent.

"Thank you, Emily. I am glad you did that," sighed Jane gratefully. "Did you notice that oaf crushing my toes mercilessly? Handsome he may be, but . . . ooh, my feet. I can barely walk. I do believe I am quite crippled." She attempted to slow their speeding pace with a slight limping step, but Emily's next words cured her lameness considerably.

"And did you notice Clifford Moore? He is here, and after all Mama's assurances that he was most definitely in Hertfordshire! I have just seen him, and he most certainly recognizes me . . . or rather, us. I am not sure how or why, but then I recognized him easily too, and he is quite different, nothing like I would have imagined. . . . He is. . . ." She paused and then stuttered a few times before giving up attempting to formulate any description of him. "But he is most definitely interested in me . . . or us. He barely took his eyes away, and his attitude. . . ." Emily gave a small, unsure laugh, finding nothing to actually accuse him of. "Well, let us just say that it hardly seems benevolent," she finished lamely.

Jane paled, searching about her swiftly and warily. "How do you know? Did he speak to you? What did he say then to make you think so?"

"Oh, we did not speak. We did not need to. One look was enough to discern what his feelings are towards me . . . us."

They gained the small sofa on which Isabelle Shaw was comfortably ensconced with her bepurpled interlocutor.

Emily bent toward her mother immediately with a bright smile and speech so forceful it did little to justify the words she was uttering.

"I have such a terrible headache, Mama, that I feel quite faint. Do you think we could leave now?" She raised a limp hand, pressing the back of it against a white temple, and shielded her eyes with fine dark lashes.

"Oh, my dear," Isabelle breathed out on a vexed sigh. "What a dreadful pity! The one evening I manage to drag you away from home and books! You *did* look as though you were enjoying yourself with that nice Mr. Sullivan." Noting the bewilderment in her eldest daughter's eyes, she explained, "He that you were just dancing with, Emily. Mrs. Cooper was telling me that he is quite an up-and-coming young gentleman these days."

"Mama, my head is about to split," Emily informed through closing teeth.

"Perhaps some refreshment, dear," suggested her mother helpfully. "It can be barely past nine o'clock, and it would be such a shame to leave early. I am sure supper will be announced soon."

Mrs. Cooper had been following the conversation between parent and offspring, her turbanned head lolling from side to side sympathetically as she identified first with the mother's sentiments and then the daughter's. She settled her head on a stout neck, ostrich feathers nodding as she drew her conclusions. "Young girls overtire so easily, I find. Not like in our heyday, eh Isabelle? Could dance till dawn and then some more! But I have noticed it with my own dear Caroline . . . simply no stamina, you know."

"I really believe I shall soon swoon," Emily threatened. "I should like some air at once, before I faint dead away."

Mrs. Cooper's attention was now riveted on something past the two girls who were standing by her sofa. "Why," she murmured in an awed tone, "I am certain I just espied Lady Jersey, and with her is. . . ." She hesitated and looked toward Isabelle. She muttered in a sly undertone, "Of course, the whole town is talking of him, and I must say that all I have heard has hardly been reputable or fit for the ears of young ladies." She slanted meaningful eyes towards Jane and Emily and inclined her head, pointing feathers at them. A plump hand covered her rapidly working mouth. "Of course, he is so rich now, and so well connected. But people have short memories, Isabelle. You must not fret or let it worry you." Her heartening reassurance had been losing volume steadily. She smiled widely and gasped out through stretched lips, "Why, I do believe they are heading our way."

Unfortunately Isabelle had not been following her

friend's rambling speech. She was in fact at that moment searching the floor and the sides of the sofa for her reticule.

"Ah, Mrs. Shaw, please, do not get up . . . not on my account." The light, humorous words drew a ripple of appreciative amusement from the surrounding guests.

Emily straightened slowly and stiffly away from her mother, not needing to look in the direction of the smooth, well-modulated voice to know whence it had come.

Isabelle smiled automatically, as she invariably did when an attractive and well-dressed man spoke to her. But her eyes were drawn quickly to the august personage of Lady Jersey. She dropped her head a little in deference and made a clumsy and unnecessary bob.

Emily cringed inwardly and closed her eyes momentarily with the strength of her embarrassment. She watched her mother, noticing that she smiled charmingly at the man for a brief moment before the smile fixed. Suspicion and then recognition glimmered, and Isabelle glanced quickly and uncertainly at her eldest daughter.

Something in Emily's tense countenance made words or gestures superfluous. Emily's hand moved to support her mother almost before the woman had taken the first stumbling step backwards into the sofa. She helped her mother to reseat herself with a semblance of dignity. Then her eyes rose to coldly meet the watchful gray ones of the man opposite. They stared at each other for so long that a vague murmur stirred amongst those grouped behind him. He smiled to himself and looked away from Emily and at Isabelle, sitting quiet and still with head bowed. His eyes lingered dispassionately.

"How are you, Mrs. Shaw?" He murmured coolly. "Well, I trust?"

Isabelle merely nodded and smiled weakly as her eyes raised to his.

"Jane?" he enquired softly.

Jane's already hot face reddened further as she whispered, "Well, sir. Thank you."

Gray eyes turned to Emily once more, but before he could utter her name, she stated with wintry formality, "Very well, thank you."

She bent swiftly to her mother, urging her to rise so that they could leave. Marion Cooper, noting her chance to make known her presence in such company as might never assemble before her again, informed them obligingly, "Emily dearest wants to go home. She feels faint, you see. I expect she needs some air."

Clifford gazed unwaveringly at Emily, and as their eyes met, he smiled. She felt certain he knew her real reason for wanting to leave so abruptly. "Perhaps you would allow me to take Emily for a short stroll on the terrace," Clifford said to Isabelle. "I am sure the night air would benefit her."

Isabelle stammered, "I think . . . I think it must be up to Emily . . . should she want to go . . ."

Emily felt her face burn. As she looked at Clifford, she noticed the thin scar that marked his left cheek. She stared openly for a heart-stopping moment as horrifying memories were stirred by the pale slash that ran against the tan of his skin from cheekbone to chin. She looked away swiftly without meeting the silver eyes that watched her so steadily.

"I think my health will be best served by quitting this place at once," she stated quietly. It sounded churlish and she wished, as she helped her mother to her feet, that she had declined more politely.

Isabelle's composure had now recovered to such a degree that censure was quite clear in her face. She widened her eyes meaningfully at Emily before looking warily at Clifford Moore.

He nodded briefly, his gaze tarrying on Emily's

flushed, averted face, before he allowed Lady Jersey to lead him away.

"Such ill-bred girls, I fancy," she opined quite audibly as they strolled away.

Isabelle Shaw scuffled her shoes on the pavement and picked restlessly at her pelisse as she paced the cobbles.

Her daughters both stood silently, lost in thoughts of their own.

"I do believe we shall never be invited out again," Isabelle bewailed for the fifth time. "You could have been more gracious, Emily, more discreet in your dislike. Would it have hurt to have promenaded with him? Marion Cooper was quite green. So was every other female in the room. Every mother at Almack's tonight would dearly have liked her daughter to have had the opportunity you chose to discard . . . and so rudely, too."

"I wonder whose memory is lapsing now, Mama," Emily muttered drily.

"The incident was years ago, Emily. We have no need to dwell on it so. What is the matter with you? Do you really think he is likely to want to reattach himself to some sordid scandal after all this time? He is a man grown now and with very favorable prospects to recommend him. He seemed most civil; there was nothing improper in his manner at all . . . a little abrupt in his speech, perhaps—but nothing more. He sought us out especially and was most courteous. I am sure he has forgotten the past."

"Do you think he has forgotten that mark on his face?" Emily demanded in a hard tone. "He must be reminded of the incident every time he looks in a glass. Quite often, in other words, judging by his conceit."

Emily scanned the road yet again for a hackney cab, her hands gripping her shawl tightly about her.

"How can you say that?" her mother huffed. "You go too far with your dislike. Especially when I recall how you used to follow him about as a child and catch at his hand at every opportunity. You were sent to your room without supper more times than I can remember for doing just such, and still you would not be separated from him. It used to vex your father and me, no end."

Emily turned swiftly away and started toward the cab that had just been halted for them by a footman. She clambered aboard and stared sightlessly through the window, oblivious to her mother and sister.

By the time they reached the small Clapham house, Emily felt completely drained. An uneasiness fluttered within her stomach and knotted in her head until her previous shammed migraine was a fact that lasted long after she had retired to her small bedroom. It kept her restless and wakeful until the first streaks of dawn colored deeper rose into the pink bedroom curtains and she at last slept for a short while.

Chapter Two

Emily snapped the book shut with an irritated sigh. "Must we discuss this interminably, Mama? The incident was three days ago. I really cannot think of anything more to say on the subject. I'm sorry you think I have ruined your social standing. But after all, you and Jane . . . none of us has been sought socially for some while now, except perhaps to make up numbers now and again."

Isabelle inhaled deeply, eyes glaring." Oh, what is to be done with you? That a poor woman should have her own dear child speak to her in such a way." She twisted her hands together. "I leave you to your own devices. If you will not attempt to be more amenable and dutiful, then you must resolve to live your life as best you can. And that, my dear child, means one thing. . . ." She said the next words as if they caused her physical pain: "You'll be an old maid, Emily."

Emily idly turned the pages of the book in her lap. "Why, I quite embrace the idea. It suits me better than would a life of mindless socializing or drudgery depending on a future husband's financial resources. Neither recommends itself to me overmuch."

"Do you think it recommends itself to me or your papa that you should burden us with the cost of your keep?" Isabelle demanded brusquely.

"No," Emily replied. "I have already thought about the necessity of earning a living. It seems sensible, especially as papa seems intent on frittering the small resources we do have so self-indulgently."

Isabelle Shaw stood before Emily's chair with her hands

clenched and her small body held tautly. "How dare you! How dare you speak of your own father so . . . and to me. Remove to your room at once! I will never accept that sort of attitude from a child of mine . . . I will not. Don't walk away when I am talking to you," she commanded on a slight screech.

Emily halted wearily by the door. "I am very sorry, Mama. Please forgive me," she began softly, "I speak sometimes without thought. I would never intentionally hurt you. You know that."

Mother and daughter faced each other for a moment across the width of the small room. Emily smiled, her eyes soft, filled with mingling affection and remorse.

Isabelle searched quickly in her reticule and, retrieving a scrap of lace, she held it to her moist eyes. She sniffed and raised her chin away from the lace collar of her morning dress before settling her head satisfactorily. She sniffed once more, then asked, "What sort of employment did you have in mind for yourself?"

Emily was well aware that the choices open to her were limited. She ventured with a wry smile, "Well, I thought of acting as a companion . . . or governessing would be another possibility."

Her mother snorted a satiric laugh." And I was under the impression that you backed the abolition of slaving. Now you inform me that you personally intend helping to perpetuate that vile trade." She cautioned her daughter quietly yet passionately, "For that is what it is, Emily — you realize that, don't you?"

"Oh, yes, Mama. I have no illusions about what sort of life it would be, living with a strange family and holding position somewhere between servant and unwanted guest, disliked and distrusted by domestics and held as inferior and contemptible by employers. Eating, sleeping, and reading is the most enjoyment I would expect from such a life."

"Reading?" her mother repeated scornfully. "Do you think you would have time to read? After you had finished for the day trying to instill some of that basic training into the heads of recalcitrant brats, there would be no time left for pleasurable literary pursuits. And as for eating and sleeping — you would eat little and be allowed to sleep a bare minimum of hours." Isabelle gazed at her daughter intently. "You forget, Emily, I know what the occupation entails. My own dear sister was a governess most of her short life, and I vow that it was the ghastly rigors of that horrid profession that brought about her own mental exhaustion and finally killed her. She was up and working from dawn till dusk and it was expected that every minute that was not filled trying to discipline and tutor defiant offspring should be spent in general housewifery. She was expected to hem dusters and sort linen with the menials. And as you so rightly perceive, the servants still despised her for her slightly superior status just as much as the master and his wife despised her for her dependency on their meager charity." Isabelle looked at Emily, taking in the beauty of her countenance and the slender yet enticing figure. She shook her head slowly. "And should you be unlucky enough to be accepted into a house where there is a young blood with unruly passions, you would be persecuted mercilessly. That happened to my dear sister, Angela, too. Her reputation was ruined by the vile lies of one such young buck who had tried unsuccessfully to seduce her. But young men of quality are believed; or they are excused, again and again, no matter how many times the same accusations are leveled at them. Yet it takes only one hint of salacious slander to destroy a young woman's life. Angela was henceforth ostracized by polite society and lived the remainder of her short life teaching brattish upstart peasants, with money from industry, out in the countryside."

Isabelle sighed with warning and compassion. "It is no life for anyone, Emily, but especially not for such as you. You are too spirited and intelligent . . . too beautiful." She gave a small, wry laugh. "Altogether too fine . . . and someone somewhere would take perverse delight in sullying and devastating that perfection, either with punishing toil or lust. It would break you completely, I know it."

Emily nodded. "I know that, Mama, and yet so could marrying unwisely. That is why I wish you would not keep pressing me to find myself a husband. I have met no one I want to spend the rest of my life with, and I would rather be alone and take my chances providing myself with a living. Should I join a family in some capacity and find that we do not suit, then at least I could leave and try again. But with a husband, I would be tied interminably, and that would be the surer hell, however eligible the man may appear to be outwardly."

Isabelle stared at her daughter, disturbed, yet conscious of the logic in her argument. "But it is a woman's calling, Emily," she persisted, "to marry as well as possible and provide her husband with children and a comfortable home. It is what all young ladies aspire to. . . ."

Emily shook her head, her lower lip caught between small teeth as she regarded her mother gravely. Isabelle opened her mouth to reply, but was cut short abruptly by the sound of the front door slamming.

"That will be your father home now. I have things to discuss with him." Isabelle moved quickly to the parlor door. She passed Emily without another word, closing the door firmly behind her, practically in her daughter's face.

Emily stared at the faded white paint on the door, noting that it was starting to crack and lift in various places. She turned back into the room and looked toward the small clock on the mantel. It was seven-thirty, and she knew her father had been absent from the house since approximately the same time yesterday evening. She thought of him, wondering if he was drunk, wondering if the sight of him would make her feel as disgusted as it had the last time she had been unfortunate enough to encounter him stumbling in, maudlin and pathetic, after a crushing loss at the tables the night before.

Stepping into the hallway, Emily made for the narrow, thinly carpeted stairs, intent on seeking sanctuary in her room with her books for what remained of the day. She gained the bottom step just as the voices rose in the small study opposite. She hesitated, but briefly, knowing too well that the altercation would take its customary form: accusations and recrimination on her mother's part, followed by her father's abject excuses and apologies and vain promises of future self-control and moderation. She mounted the stairs slowly, leaning heavily on the bannister rail.

If Isabelle noticed anything other than a customary dreary dejection in her husband after one of his failed nights out on the town, she gave no indication. She launched directly into her diatribe. "This really is too much, Charles. It is past seven-thirty, and I have not seen or heard from you since yesterday evening at eight. It really is beyond the bounds of decent behavior. You promised me quite faithfully you would return at nine-thirty last evening for cards with the Morgans." She paused, eyeing her husband sharply for some sign of remorse or a glimpse of some feasible excuse in the hatching, but there was nothing. His heavy head still hung slightly, and the palm of one hand worried incessantly at the rough stubble spiking his face.

Isabelle reiterated her position with slightly more affront, annoyed that his worsening behavior seemed to worry him not at all. "I was utterly mortified; by ten-thirty I was quite out of excuses and in the end had to plead a migraine just to get rid of them. I expect we shall be the butt of every joke. . . ."

Charles raised his head to gaze at his wife, then cut in with a rasping, humorless laugh, "Yes, I do believe you are right . . . and there will be plenty more for them to snigger over than my nonappearance at some piffling bridge session. Damn the Morgans and damn the cards. . . ."

Isabelle gasped out, "Well . . . a fine way for a gentleman to speak to his wife." She seemed suddenly to take account of the despair in his features and the pronounced hunch of his shoulders as he slumped into the worn leather chair by his desk.

She stared at him unwaveringly and his uneasiness increased, his slack head swaying first one way then the other. His elbows moved to prop themselves against the battered yew top of his writing table, and his head sank forward slowly and gratefully to rest heavily in broad palms. Thick fingers started a slow massage of his scalp, lost from sight within his wiry gray hair.

Isabelle fumbled, unsteady-fingered, with the plain gray cotton of her skirt. "I take it this dismay has more to do with another pecuniary calamity than lovelorn hankering after some outpriced mistress."

Charles snuffled a gruff laugh. "I have had no mistress for some good while now. Expensive luxuries are something I certainly cannot afford."

"And basic necessities are something I cannot afford," she snapped back bitterly. "I have been informed by that upstart Claudine that she will not take another order from us for materials or buttons or ribbons or. . . ." She faltered and one hand went to press at her forehead for a moment. "Such disgrace . . . that we cannot even afford to pay the haberdasher's bill."

Charles slouched back abruptly in the chair and his hands flopped limply to his sides. "I am afraid, Isabelle, that I have some bad news." He sensed a hysterical urge to giggle at the understatement but emitted no more than a sigh.

"I thought as much," Isabelle uttered crisply. "I could tell it straightaway. You have lost again. How much this time?" Another hundred pounds? More?" She gazed at him with unconcealed contempt. He began to speak, but she cut him short. "Well, no matter. I anticipated as much last week." She smiled acidly. "I do every week and have taken steps to economize accordingly. My new maid; I have dismissed her already. 'No doubt I shall have to cut back further in the kitchens if we are to survive this winter . . . but where, heaven only knows."

"We have not survived, Isabelle. We are totally bankrupt." The information was quiet and even and he looked up from the mellow wooden desk top to his wife. "You are quite right. I did lose again last night, but not hundreds." He gave a small, hysterical laugh. "No, indeed; not hundreds. It was thousands, and so many that I will not bother telling you just how many. I have not the credit or any expectation at all of ever being able to find enough for what I owe this time. This house and your jewelry and what little the girls have is all the security I have left. And if every other creditor now called in their outstanding duns, I would not even have that small amount to lay against what I lost last night."

Isabelle stared blankly, the enormity of the situation uncomprehended. "Well, you will have to visit your cousin. Plead your case there again. Heaven knows I hate that you have to; he makes such a parade of his condescension. But when there is no alternative. . . ." The words tailed off as she watched her husband shake his head wearily.

"Where do you think I have been all this time, Bella?" he inquired gently. "I arrived at his house before nine this morning. I pleaded with him until eleven, and he eventually had me forcibly removed by his footmen. He is without pity. Everyone is without pity." A weary hand moved swiftly across his face. "I lost badly . . . in every sense of the word and all those present at Watier's were well aware of it. So will the whole town be soon. But it is of little import to them. Just another risible blunder by that drunken oaf Shaw. It will humor them but for a short while. None of them cares that much anymore; I am indeed beneath contempt." He picked up a quill from his desk and then let it fall from his fingers. "I have since visited every likely usurer . . . every Jew, but without success. Those that will lend want to do so on such terms as it would be ludicrous to accept. I cannot get another ha'penny, Bella. We shall have to visit the pawnbrokers if we are to eat this week."

Isabelle back-stepped gingerly until her calves touched the small sofa and then she sank slowly into it. "What do you mean this house and my jewelry are all the security you have? You cannot touch those things . . . my home . . . my jewelry. You cannot use such precious things as collateral."

"You do not understand, Bella. The house is no longer mine. I have as good as signed it away. It was lost when I played him last night. He intended that . . . I know it now. He intended that I should be left humiliated and bankrupt. And yet when he walked in to Watier's last evening, he was cordial and talkative and his company brought me more companions than I usually have in a fortnight. He was so pleasant; and I believed that he was as keen as I to forget past differences and to show those hoping for some sign of animosity that there was none to be had. And then he suggested cards. I was more than willing to oblige . . . and lose a few pounds, too, to keep his influence and friendship, for he is so well-connected now. But I was drawn in too deep, Bella. I know now that it was always his intention. Once I had lost five thousand I knew I had to continue to try and recoup some of the money." He shook his head despairingly. "But I just could not. He plays well, too well for me." He turned in the old leather chair to look directly at his wife.

"Clifford Moore has ruined us, Bella. He has come back to torment and shame us. He is coming here tomorrow afternoon at two-thirty to do just that: apprise us of his terms to settle the debt."

He gazed at his wife for a long while, but she could manage no more response than a weak, uncertain gesturing. He added quietly, "There will be no mercy. He means to finish me off, have me committed to a debtor's prison, no doubt, and you and the girls to the poorhouse."

Isabelle shrieked out, "No! You must be lying! We saw him but the other day, the girls and I, and he was most courteous. He would not . . . he would not. It is you he hates, not us. We gave him no reason. It was all your fault: You and your filthy lechery and your lies. Oh yes, I know now that you lied; probably I knew then, too. You and *Katherine Moore!* That ill-bred slut from some Jamaican hovel with her coarse ways and vulgar dress and dialect. And what could you expect? Born as she was of English peasants hoping to seek their fortune in the colonies. A full-blooded Creole," she sneered.

Charles Shaw stood up abruptly. "She was never coarse! She simply wasn't a preening, simpering, empty headed female. Her simplicity was quite refreshing, let me tell you."

There followed a soaring silence.

Isabelle turned her head stiffly and glanced at the door as though to judge who without might have heard the raucous exchange. "The girls will have to know of this," she said at last. "They will have to be warned of the future that awaits them, the shame and disgrace. I will fetch them now and you can relate to them, as you have to me, how your disgusting profligacy has brought ignominy to all of us."

Emily shifted position on the bed, then moved her hands back to cup her face once more. She read steadily, but as the muted noise in the room below her crescendoed again, she pressed her slender hands against her ears. She attempted to read on but was distracted by the voices still, uncertain now whether they were in fact audible or merely within her head. She rolled onto her back in frustration. The house was quiet once more. She sat up, swung her legs over the edge of the bed, and went to her dressing table. Sitting on the low satin-covered stool, she stared at her reflection in the glass for a moment at the large, troubled eyes and the excessive pallor of her complexion.

She glanced out the window, wondering what time it was. It seemed that her parents had been arguing in the room below for hours. Absently she began to remove the pins from her hair until her loose curls bounced softly against her shoulders.

There was a light rapping at the door. A slightly stooped woman, who looked to be nearing seventy, entered briskly. She smiled in greeting and straightaway helped with unbuttoning the back of Emily's dress with fast, deft fingers.

Nanny Greg had been with the Shaws ever since Emily could remember. She knew the old woman was some sort of distant poor relative who had been taken into the Shaw household as nursemaid when George was born. She had been nanny to all three children. Although her parents were in an embarrassing situation with the servants, Emily knew that Nanny Greg would never leave them.

Emily smiled at Nanny's paper-thin lined cheeks and bright dark eyes. "You know I am quite able to undress myself now that I am grown up," she said.

The old lady waved a dismissing hand and finished unbuttoning, then slid the shoulders of the dress away from Emily's creamy skin.

63

Emily undressed quickly and Nanny Greg held out her night things for her to slip into.

"Sit down and I shall brush your hair for you," the old woman suggested, gazing shrewdly at Emily's pale, tense face.

Emily reseated herself feeling quite weary. She gathered the thick, heavy hair away from her face, lowering it across her shoulders.

A veiny, brown-speckled hand moved to the dressing table top and Nanny Greg selected a large, silver-backed hairbrush. She collected several long, dark tresses and began to draw the brush firmly yet gently through the silken hair.

Emily relaxed, allowing the woman's skill to soothe her. As her gnarled, arthritic hand skimmed the satin length of hair slowly, her small black eyes met Emily's violet ones in the mirror. "How is it you can look like this and yet talk and act more often than not like a veritable harridan?"

Nanny Greg gathered the hair, twisting it into a soft chignon at the back of Emily's head. She held the dark mass there for a moment as she approvingly examined the slender throat and shoulders and fair, flawless skin of her young charge. She smiled and asked wryly, "And what I want to know too, is why you are still here with your old nanny at twenty years old, when you should be a lady at some fine house, with a fine accomplished maid to tend you to perfection, and a doting husband to pamper you."

She allowed the hair to fall, swinging and rippling thickly against Emily's plain white nightgown in a chestnut cloud.

Emily ignored the query and the old woman's eyes, which she knew still watched her in the glass. She raised slender arms and gathered her hair once again into a high bun as Nannie Greg had done. She turned her head slowly and inspected her profile with a slightly critical grimace.

"So you saw Clifford Moore the other evening, then," the woman stated baldly.

Emily abruptly released her hair and stood up. She moved to the window, and drawing back the curtain a little, peeked out at the sky, scanning the gray-black for a sign of the moon.

"What did he say to you?"

The curtain fell back into position and Emily turned toward Nanny Greg with an abrupt, mirthless laugh. "You obviously know that already. If Jane has told you of our brief encounter with him, I am sure she recounted the incident verbatim."

Nanny Greg smiled wryly. "It is hard to believe that this is my Emily of a decade ago, who would follow him about like a loyal puppy at every opportunity. Of course, he was just as smitten with you." She laughed as Emily colored and turned away. "That lad was in more trouble on your account at Thrushcross Grange than for any other reason. I am sure if he was beaten once it must have been a dozen times for shirking work during the day to be with you."

Emily reseated herself on the bed and picked up her discarded book.

"If he avoided work, it was no doubt laziness," she remarked woodenly. "He was probably an idler." Nannie Greg shook her head. "Idlers rarely make themselves into millionaires within ten years. It is no mean feat to achieve such, but he has, so it is rumored."

"Frankly, I care little what he has or has not done or achieved," she said coolly. "My only concern is to stay well clear of him."

"Perhaps you'll get over your aversion to him. After all, Jane says he was quite charmingly polite."

Emily stood up impatiently and turned down the bed cover, averting her face from Nanny's.

"You must not judge every marriage by the relationship your parents have," Nanny Greg went on implacably. "Not every wife is soured by the man she marries. Many couples that marry for love remain in that blissful state of union until one of them dies. I did with your great-uncle George. Your parents—."

"My parents' marriage is none of your concern!" Emily said harshly. As soon as the words were out she was appalled by her rudeness. "I am sorry. It is just . . . I would rather not be reminded of the past . . . of Thrushcross Grange. I did not mean what I said. I know you are related to Papa and therefore have a right to be interested in his . . . our welfare." The violet of Emily's eyes gazed brightly and Nanny Greg shuffled on slippered feet to hold her in a thin-armed embrace. Emily clung to the woman tightly as she murmured on a choking sob, "Oh, Nanny. . . . I have such terrible dreams lately. I run and run from something evil that I cannot see, but never escape it. I am sure some disaster is about to befall us all, I am sure of it. . . ."

"Hush. . . ." the old woman said soothingly as she stroked Emily's dark hair. "No, Emily, there is no disaster—not for you—you were not born for it. You will be happy, if you allow yourself to be so. At the moment you avoid every opportunity that could bring it to you."

A peremptory rap sounded at the door. It was Emily's mother, come to bid her good night. Nannie quietly left the room as Isabelle entered.

"Good night, Mama," Emily said.

"Hardly, Emily," her mother stated quietly.

As they gazed at each other in silence, Emily felt a chill crawl up her spine and she reflected instinctively on her recurring nightmare. Her eyes lowered to her hands in her lap. "No, I suppose not."

A sonorous half-hour chimed and Emily's eyes were

redrawn to the clock as were all others in the parlor.

Jane and her mother looked away from the timepiece simultaneously, returning to the embroidery in their respective laps.

Emily gazed out through the window at the grayish afternoon light. She listlessly retrieved her Jane Austen novel, reading diligently for a few minutes. But after a few paragraphs she gave up and closed the book sharply.

"Where is papa?" she inquired.

"In his study, I imagine," her mother replied curtly.

Jane's anxious eyes sought Emily's, who tried again. "Is Nanny Greg not coming down?"

"I doubt it. She is probably in her room, mixing potions for headaches", Isabelle said. At times I believe we have a witch in the house, she spends so much time in that cupboard brewing and stirring." She pressed a plump, white hand languidly to her brow. "Probably later, though, I will be quite grateful for her sorcery. I can already feel the start of a migraine," she muttered.

Silence ensued for a while, and then Emily posed tentatively, "Have you informed . . . have you or Papa written to George? Told him of our . . . troubles?" she finished feebly.

"I have written to him this morning," she answered without looking away from the sewing in her lap. "The letter is ready for posting; I shall do so after Moore has visited." Her pale eyes shifted to the small gilt clock on the mantelpiece once more, the hands showing two-forty. "If he intends coming, that is," she added acridly. "No doubt he means us to sweat and fret in his absence, torturing ourselves over what our fate shall be. Not that it takes a great deal of imagination. Those who are penniless have very little choice in their existence."

"Mama, do not upset yourself . . . not yet," Emily comforted softly. "Perhaps he has not come because he intends giving Papa time after all to try and settle the debt. Perhaps he will allow us to pay it off as and when we can." She hesitated, aware of her mother's wretchedness and the dark hollows beneath her sleep-deprived eyes.

Emily ignored her younger sister, who was now weeping silently into a scrap of white lawn, her head bent low to conceal her misery. "After all, what would he want with this house?" She said with false brightness. "He hardly needs it himself. He has Malvern Hall and a London mansion, so I hear, and besides, it will bring in but a small amount when sold."

As both Isabelle and Jane had cherished the hope that the reverse might be true, two handkerchiefs now pressed noses and sporadically shielded eyes. Emily sank despairingly against the cushioned chairback. She regarded the clock again: it was nearly ten to three. She stared at it mesmerized, thinking that the slow ponderous ticking seemed to strengthen with every measured oscillation of the shiny, gilt bob. She was quite certain then that it was no longer their own dainty clock at all she was hearing but some neighboring steeple. Unable to close her mind to the resounding throb, she rose abruptly. "I am going to my room to write a letter."

Emily shut the parlor door quietly. She moved into the hallway, noting anxiously that the front door was ajar. Her heart thudded with icy slowness and she leaned to one side to peer cautiously outside. She glimpsed the fair, curling hair of Betty, the young kitchen maid, on her knees on the step. She was scrubbing at the stone between periodic bouts of raising herself onto her knees and peering over the privet hedge and along the street. Emily wondered absently if there were not some interesting spectacle taking place in the road, but she was unable to raise enough enthusiasm to go and look for herself.

Her thoughts turned abruptly to her father and the ambivalence she had felt for him when he had told Jane and her of his ruin and their complete poverty. The pathos and disgust had warred within her as she had stood silently and dutifully, listening to the long-expected words.

She felt pity niggling below the blame once more at the thought of him incarcerated in lonely ostracism within his own home. She turned and paced quietly toward the study door.

Her soft shoes made no sound on the threadbare brown-and-green patterned carpet. She halted and stood uncertainly by the door, her hand half-raised as though to knock. Then, as she heard the clinking contact of glass and decanter and the liquid pouring, she let her hand fall to her side once more. She waited, listening for a moment. The glass found the table again and was noisily and immediately refilled. She turned slowly away, half aware of another noise to be heard in the hallway now.

Betty was indoors again, but without her bucket and brush. Emily watched as she smoothed her pinafore hastily. She widened the door further, smiling up into the face of the fair man who entered with a slight nod.

Betsy curtsied quickly but with deep reverence, eyes lowered demurely, then raised and widened with flagrant flirtation. She was standing quite ridiculously close to him, barely allowing him room inside the doorway at all. As Emily regarded them unseen, the girl arched her back, her shoulders spreading. She straightened the white, starched apron top with slow, sensuous fingers that skimmed and flaunted her breasts quite openly.

Momentarily lost in disgust for the kitchen maid's shamelessness, Emily took a few seconds to realize that the fair visitor was more interested in watching her. Emily flushed beneath the steadfast gaze. Conscious now that she had been observed, she moved towards them a few steps. "That will be all, thank you, Betty," she dismissed coldly.

The blond girl spun around then to look at her with a sullen pout. She curtsied again, exclusively for Moore, the blatant offer still apparent in her sly, upward-slanting eyes.

He reacted with a slight, acknowledging movement of his head and a small, cynical smile.

As Betty passed Emily on her way to the kitchens, she tilted her chin in a small sign of victory.

Emily felt the blood slowly suffuse her face once more; she was naturally enraged and mortified by the disrespectful exhibition. The servants were of course aware of their straitened circumstances, but to parade their contempt so overtly and in front of such as he, the instigator in all their disaster, was insufferable.

They were now quite alone in the dark corridor. Emily glanced irrationally at the various closed doorways as if longing to escape.

He commanded softly, "Come here." Emily looked at him swiftly, startled by the words and his presumption at using them. "I . . . I shall tell my father you have arrived," she stammered.

"Emily." The name was spoken quietly and yet compellingly. Emily, wary, moved closer, halting as soon as she could distinguish the silverish scar on his cheek. Her eyes lowered to the top button of his jacket. The tense silence protracted. Emily raised her eyes for a moment. He was still watching her with remorseless intent.

"I . . . we thought you might not come today after all", she said uncomfortably. "I shall tell the others you are here now."

"Not yet," he said curtly.

Emily looked away from him quickly and regarded the faded, chocolate-brown wallpaper lining the hall. She stared at it unblinkingly, feeling more ashamed and furious at its miserable presence at that moment than she ever had before.

"What do you want?" she demanded coolly. "Why have you done this to us?" Is it just to shame and humiliate us all?"

A small, amused noise broke in his throat. "You hardly need me to do that. Your father has made such an admirable job of it alone."

Violet fire sparked in her eyes. She was stung as much by the truth of the words as by the insult.

"How dare you speak of my father so! Had it not been for you . . . you and your mother, he would never have drunk or gambled or —" She halted abruptly and bit her lip painfully as she realized, quite horrified what she was dredging up from the past. It was not what she had intended at all, for surely memories of the past would only incite his quest for vengeance.

She stepped back from him a few paces. "I shall fetch my father now," she said.

Long, bronzed fingers closed upon her wrist, halting her. At the first light touch, she attempted to throw him off with a quick jerk, but he drew her resolutely closer. "You would be well advised, Emily, to be nice to me," he threatened gently. "Fighting against the hand that provides for you is not wise."

She glared at him coldly and furiously, attempting to twist her wrist free. "Then I shall starve, and quite willingly," she retorted.

He smiled tolerantly. "I think you probably would, but. . . ." He hesitated, then queried with mock concern, "But what of the rest of your family? Are they equally as keen to take up residence in the poorhouse? I would not recommend it," he advised, releasing her hand.

She backed away from him, her trembling fingers massaging the slight mark where he had held her.

"You have changed little in ten years, Emily . . . in looks or nature, judging by this absurd defiance."

His eyes moved slowly across her features and Emily

felt the heat in her face increasing. He raised a hand to touch her cheek and she flinched as though he had stung her. His hand moved away leisurely, just touching her dark, soft hair before returning to his side.

"Are you not now supposed to make some polite observation on my appearance also?" He suggested with wry mockery.

A mellifluous smile was delivered this time as she looked at him.

"Were it within the bounds of honesty to do so, I would indeed try to think of something," she returned with honeyed irony.

Her eyes slid compulsively to the scar etched lightly into his skin and away hastily. Her eyes closed as she regretted the sarcasm and what he might think she was implying about his disfigurement.

"I cannot pass comment . . I hardly remember you."

He laughed sceptically. "You recognized me well enough the other evening at that awful gathering place . . . what was it called? Ah, yes, Almack's. Do you go there often?"

"Rarely. I have been there only twice. I never like going out."

"Good," he rejoined. As she looked at him sharply, he explained with a smile, "Neither do I." Emily raised her eyebrows in a studied show of disbelief.

His smiled deepened. "Oh, I went because I found out you would be there. I wanted to see you, I can socialize well enough when I need to. Otherwise, I prefer my own company."

"You surprise me . . . nay, astound," Emily mocked.

His silver-gray eyes narrowed. "But I digress. To answer your question, Emily . . . what do I want? Well, it is quite simple really. I want you."

She stared at him, all hint of sarcasm gone.

"I have come back for you as I said I would," he reminded her gently.

The blood drained from her face as the words stirred long- and deliberately buried memories. "I have no idea what you mean. I—"

His mouth curved slightly. "Oh, I think you do. You were not so young . . . ten years old and remarkably bright. I quite believe you remember me as well as I do you." His eyes flicked over her figure unobtrusively as he remarked, "You were always beguiling and passionate as a child. As a woman. . . ." He paused, his eyes returning to her face. "Go and get your father now, Emily," he commanded.

She obeyed as though hypnotized, approaching the study door slowly. She knocked once and her father opened it, a glass still in his hand.

"Ah, Emily, my dear. Come to see your old Papa?" His breath reeked of alcohol. His pale, moist eyes blinked, then focused on the tall, fair man standing near the front door. He drew a shuddering gulp of air before he said with acerbic cordiality, "Ah, do come in. I was just wondering where you had got to. I have some very good port in here—my last bottle. I am quite sure you must want to help me finish it off."

Clifford Moore walked forward leisurely. Emily watched him, noting that he looked quite magnificent in his immaculate, expensive clothes against the backdrop of fading brown wallpaper.

"What I have to say concerns Emily," Clifford said. "I want her to be present."

Emily's stomach contracted sickeningly. Her frightened eyes sought those of her father.

"I think I know what is best for my own family," he gritted, outraged. "I deal with the business in this house. I do not worry my wife or daughters with such matters.

Clifford raised his eyebrows in sarcasm. "Do you not?" he inquired. "I would have imagined otherwise."

Mortification reddened Charles's florid face even further and moved closer to him at once in a quiet gesture of sympathy and unity.

"Well, we could talk here, if you like. I am sure the servants would be most gratified," Clifford said smoothly.

"Show our . . ." Charles hesitated before spitting with quiet acrimony, ". . . our guest into the parlor, would you please, Emily. I am quite sure he will never be satisfied or take his leave until he has gloated over the sight of an impoverished woman and her two daughters."

Clifford entered the parlor, moving unhurriedly towards the long, narrow window that looked out over the street. He gazed through it for a moment before turning slowly and standing with his back to it.

Emily watched him, noting that he seemed to block what little light was to be had that day, making the room appear more than usually drear. She glanced at him with more purpose: an icy halo of light hovered above the silver-fair head, his face in shadow. He murmured the names of the two women seated on the sofa in formal greeting, then spoke to Charles.

"I am prepared to write off the debt if certain conditions are met." He paused, watching closely as Charles's attention was immediately arrested.

Emily sat unmoving, her face pale and marblelike in its stillness as she gazed at her hands clasped in her lap.

Clifford looked at the top of Emily's dark, slightly bowed head and what could be seen of her features. He stated relentlessly, "I want Emily in return for the fifteen thousand pounds, ten shillings and sixpence that you owe me."

Charles stared at him stupidly, repeating idiotically,

"Ten shillings and sixpence?"

Gray eyes moved reluctantly from the emotionless girl and returned to her father. "Oh, that was money due to me from some years back. You said you would send it on but it never actually arrived." He added in an amused, patronizing tone, "I expect you did not have the workhouse address. But no mater. I shall waive any interest accrued over the ten years or so I have waited."

Isabelle blinked rapidly, knowing exactly to what he referred. She looked anxiously towards her husband before her eyes fell on the inclined head of her eldest daughter.

Conscious of Isabelle gazing at her daughter and then at him with alarm and suspicion, Clifford said with deliberate condescension, "I am prepared to marry her."

Emily looked up briefly in surprise.

After a couple of false starts, Isabelle managed to stammer out, "Well, I do not know what to say . . . such a surprise . . . I must say. I had no idea. I just do not know what to think or say."

Her awed, deferential tone suggested that she knew exactly what she would like to say.

"Well, I do," her husband rasped.

He gazed at his tormenter with pain-ravaged eyes and choked out savagely, "Do you think . . . do you really believe I would allow you to take a daughter of mine on whom to vent your spite and deviance? Do you imagine I would offer her up as some human sacrifice to sate your warped sickness? Or let you take her away from her home and family and into your custody to abuse and humiliate her as you wish? I would not allow a horse of mine to enter your stables for fear you might torture it to death from sheer malevolence. Yet you expect me to grant you Emily to appease your foul vindictiveness! I would rather sell this house and every stick of furniture in it to repay you, than imagine you to as much as touch the hem of her skirt."

Emily raised a hand to touch the clammy skin of her face; it pricked icily as though something crawled upon it. She blinked rapidly, knowing that her father had just put into words and forced upon her, the horror she had not yet allowed her own mind to acknowledge or dwell on.

"This house is not worth more than. . . ." Clifford hesitated and made a slight assessing grimace, "Two or three thousand pounds at most. As for the furniture—" his eyes flicked with disparaging quickness across the few unpretentious items that they had left in the room, "you would be lucky to raise five hundred pounds in total for what you have within the whole house, if it matches what is in here."

Isabelle looked at her increasingly rubicund husband with round, frightened eyes, the denigration of her home and furnishings passing unchallenged in her agitation. She whispered weakly, "I think we should perhaps . . . I think, Charles, we should talk about this. You might have been a little hasty and unfair in your judgment. I really feel we ought to discuss things. . . ."

Her husband turned, stonefaced, to stare at her with bald disgust. Isabelle put a hand to her throat as though to ease a sudden constriction. She murmured timidly, "I just thought we ought to be realistic. We have to consider everybody's future . . . mine," she continued quickly, "yours too, and Jane's and. . . ." She looked at her husband fiercely. "What of Georgie? What will become of George if he has to leave the hussars in disgrace? What will become of his career?"

Emily listened numbly to her parents wrangling over lives and futures. And even to Jane, now venturing a few hushed, timid words as she endorsed her mother's case.

Emily raised her eyes slowly, seeking Clifford's face, and she gazed at him with a silent yet vivid entreaty. He returned the stare impersonally at first, then as though swayed involuntarily, a slight, self-mocking smile enhanced the thin curve of his mouth. Emily knew then that he was completely without pity. She stood up slowly. The low, sibilant altercations among the other members of her family ebbed, then ceased; all eyes were set intently on the slight figure standing quite still.

"There is no need for any debate . . . no need for anything at all." She gazed at a spot on the carpet

76

somewhere midway between herself and her detested suitor. "I would not . . ." she faltered as though unsure which words were most appropriate she resorted to, ". . . marry him were my life to depend on it." Her head turned toward her family and she accused in a trembling voice that hinted at pleading, "And I would that none of you ask or expect it of me." She walked calmly toward her father and the door.

"Emily."

Her name came from behind her and she slowly turned to face him again, hatred and fear glossing the violet of her eyes.

One side of his mouth lifted slightly. "Far be it from me to insist upon something to obviously unwelcome. I withdrew the offer."

"No!" Isabelle rose swiftly away from the sofa, shrilling agitatedly, "She did not mean that she would not—"

Charles glared at his wife. The woman sank slowly back to perch uncomfortably on the very edge of her seat, her hands raised to grip tightly at her face.

"I have another suggestion. Perhaps Emily, in her innocence, might prefer it." Clifford moved away from the window as he spoke to a small escritoire in a corner. He picked up a delicate porcelain figurine and looked at it thoughtfully for a moment before upending it casually to examine the maker's print on the bottom. "My late brother's wife lives at Malvern Hall with her young son. Amanda has had a series of companions and nursemaids to help with the child since she has been resident, none of whom has made any favorable impression on me. She has one now with neither wit nor beauty to recommend her." He replaced the statuette with an abruptness that confirmed his interest in it to have been minimal. He gazed fully at Emily. "You, however, have both, and I am willing to waive the debt on those terms too: that you join my household at Malvern Hall as companion to my sister-in-law."

Emily wiped her damp palms against the dark material of her plain skirt. she retorted impetuously, "I would never join your household under any guise," "Much as you might think me some credulous fool, I am not. My innocence was lost years ago."

She blushed abruptly at her ingenous turn of phrase. Her long dark lashes swept down to shield her violet eyes, but not before she had read the amusement in his face.

"Your qualifications for the position appear to be improving by the minute, Emily," he remarked.

Isabelle's face crimsoned. Her hands worried each other incessantly as she countered in her daughter's defense, "She did not mean . . . she intended to say that she is no longer. . . ." She floundered, looking about eagerly at her family for aid in finding some way out of the mess.

Emily kept her eyes lowered, sensing hysteria threatening. She fought to dismiss the whole farcical episode as just part of one of the lurid nightmares that came so often.

"Naive," her mother burst in upon her delirium, her relief and satisfaction at having solved the verbal maze quite evident.

Unable to endure any more, Emily turned abruptly to her father, her eyes begging that she be allowed to leave.

Charles was staring at his persecutor through the film misting his weak, pinkish eyes. "Companion? What made you think of such?" he asked dully. "Was it because one of your own family . . . your mother . . . served in that capacity in my household?"

"So she did," Clifford agreed with mock recall. "She was companion to your wife as I remember . . . or so she was termed." He paused before insinuating quietly, "I believe she served you also."

The two men gazed at each other, eyes locked for an infinite moment.

"Of course, I would expect no more and no less of

Emily," Clifford informed in a quiet, reasonable tone. "It seems condign, does it not?"

Charles's watering eyes sought the ground. He shuffled his feet against the worn carpet, the muscles in his cheeks contracting jerkily. "I will not give this madness further credence by listening to it or by allowing my family to be further distressed by it. Leave and do your worst." He made to turn and open the door, but Isabelle was on her feet in a flash.

"No! We have to resolve this . . . and today. I have no intention of embracing destitution and disgrace if it can be avoided and at such a reasonable cost. It seems to me that Sir Clifford has been most generous in his offer of marriage to Emily, and I feel that neither you nor she . . ." Isabelle glanced hard-eyed at Emily then ". . . have given the matter the consideration such honor merits." Her hands smoothed creases from her dress as she offered coldly, "Should you wish that your daughters and I not witness any further dealings you have with Sir Clifford, then we will remove from the room and leave you alone to conclude the matter."

She turned then to look at Jane. The girl rose immediately and gratefully at the silent signal.

Emily started to leave with them but was halted by the next quiet command.

"Emily stays."

Emily swung round. "No," she cried.

Clifford smiled, the caress in his eyes as he looked at her belying the remorselessness in his tone. "Oh, yes," he murmured.

Their eyes held exclusively, as they were as alone as they had been earlier in the hall. Emily felt the gray eyes engulf and subdue her and she turned her head away savagely and gazed at the wall. "You can talk for as long as like with my father," she murmured, shaking but firm. "You can intimidate and tyrannize until he succumbs, but it will make no difference. My answer will still be the same. I will not go with you under any pretext. I would rather take my chances with my family in the poorhouse or on the streets than sample what you have planned for my future."

Her hand touched the door handle as Clifford remarked levelly, "I am surprised at you, Emily. I never would have believed you capable of talking such immature rubbish."

He smiled as she glared at him. "Innocent you may be, but I had not thought you simple-minded too. "You know the difference between life at Malvern Hall with me and trying to survive in the workhouse . . . or some worse establishment," he added softly.

"Do I? I imagine it would be much the same thing," she replied coldly.

Charles cut in abruptly. "How long would you require her presence? Four years? The same amount of time your mother was resident at Thrushcross Grange?"

Emily looked in amazement at her father.

"Perhaps," Clifford shrugged casually, "Perhaps less . . ." He noted the skepticism in the grunt, ashen face and smiled sardonically. "You need not fear that you will be bothered by me again at some future date for the money. I will, of course, lodge legal documents to that effect with your solicitor . . . and mine."

Charles's eyes were full of torment. "Your mother was a widow in her thirties when she came to me. Emily is but twenty and she is, innocent, despite what she has in her artlessness implied. But then you know that very well and, of course, it hinders her case; for if there was nothing to sully she would be of no use, would she?" He halted and swallowed jerkily. "She is pure . . . in every sense, and knows nothing of life or how to live in the world. For the most part she inhabits a world of her own . . . a fancy where all is fair and just. And I don't know why I am telling you this, for I fear with every word I utter I damage her further. Please, I beg of you, let her be. Take whatever else you want, the house . . . the furniture, but let her be. She would be of little use to you, for she cannot compromise her dreams. You would destroy her so easily . . . in such a short time as to never appease lust or vengeance. Give me more time and I will get the money, I swear it."

After a moment, he lied desperately. "I have other sources to try, and I am sure I could let you have half what is owed within the month if you will but wait. Seeing me crawl must be worth half the amount surely. I will crawl on my knees if need be."

He sagged as though he might indeed fall to the ground. Emily, her emotions chilled but her eyes hot, caught at his arm and clung to him tightly, as though to prevent him from lowering himself further.

"Well, this is most gratifying, I agree," Clifford allowed with mild amusement. He waited for the glimmer of hope to quicken in the distressed, watering eyes before he crushed it ruthlessly with a callous smile and quiet words. "But it is not nearly enough. And as for the money . . . I have no immediate need of another fifteen thousand pounds." His eyes lingered deliberately and contemplatively on Emily as he tormented further, "I have other . . . more pressing needs and they will not be put off longer. Money is not the essence of this and well you know it."

Charles Shaw quoted stridently, " 'Vengeance is mine, saith the Lord. . . .'" 'For God's sake man, have a little pity. I implore you as a Christian, show some compassion.' "

"Why should I?" Clifford asked with a surprised laugh. "You showed my mother none . . . or me, for that matter."

He halted by the door, so near to Emily now that their hands were practically touching. But he kept his eyes on Charles. "I have already instructed my lawyers to draft documents enabling me to have you removed from this house and onto the streets, and suing for the remainder of the money due. It would be implemented and achieved speedily. I will do everything within my power to make it so."

Charles merely nodded, utterly and hopelessly defeated. "I need time to make a decision."

"You have until this time tomorrow. You can send word to me at my Grosvenor Place address. If I have not heard by that time, I will assume you refuse my terms, and proceedings will start to recoup every last penny that is owed."

He smiled at Charles's bent head. "I'll wager that I can have you imprisoned by the end of the month."

Emily allowed herself to look at the tanned face of the tall, fair man who stood so close. She could smell the warm, fresh scent of him, see individual threads in the fine, dark clothes that he wore. She wondered numbly why it was he did not smell or look as foul as his character.

Charles Shaw drew a final shuddering breath. "I would kill you if I could and enjoy it."

"In your position I would feel the same way," Clifford replied mildly. "I once did feel exactly the same way."

Chapter Three

"Go away."

After a short pause Isabelle said quietly but firmly, "Emily, I insist you open this door at once before my patience expires."

There followed another silent interval. Isabelle sighed in exasperation. "Emily . . . open this door! I have something important to tell you that concerns us all, and I cannot shout it to you through the door."

Emily sat on the side of the bed, silent and still with her hands folded in her lap.

The preemptory rapping came again. "Emily, this is quite ridiculous. Let me in at once so that I can tell you what I have decided."

At last Emily rose stiffly and unlocked the door. Her mother bustled in immediately and with such force that Emily backed away. The two women stood eyeing each other for a moment, then Emily turned away abruptly, her loose, dark hair swaying starkly against the snowy shoulders of her cotton nightdress. She perched on the edge of the fading rose satin coverlet.

Isabelle sighed as she took in the tears that tracked the pale, fine skin of her daughter's complexion.

"Emily. . . ." she whispered.

Emily looked up at her mother then, tears starting to well in her eyes again.

"What is to be done with you?" her mother asked with exasperated concern. "You receive an offer of marriage from the most eligible man in town and it throws you into utter despair! But apart from that, and more importantly, you know you have it within your power now to save us all from poverty."

Emily turned her head away. "Dear Mama . . . what is to be done with you?" she despaired. She hesitated for barely a moment before stating adamantly, "I do not wish to talk of it further. I have made up my mind and you will not persuade me otherwise."

"I know that well enough, Emily; it is one of the reasons I have come up to speak to you again.

Isabelle moved to seat herself at the small dressing table, smoothing her dress carefully. "I have been with Jane," she said. "She is distraught, fretting about the life that awaits her in the poorhouse. Why it should frighten you less than the prospect of marriage to Sir Clifford Moore I cannot fathom, unless perhaps your imagination is lacking."

"I think the opposite is true," Emily laughed bitterly. "Perhaps if my imagination were less well-developed, I could bear the thought of it. "I would rather take my chances alone or with the rest of you than go to him."

Her mother snorted her frustration. "Can you not understand, you stupid girl? We none of us need to take chances. We can all survive this; you, I, Jane, Georgie, and even Nanny Greg would be salvaged if only you would be less selfish and more sensible and realistic. You are twenty now, and despite what you say, you must marry soon. It seems sensible, as you appear to have no particular preference for any man, that you should do so as advantageously as possible." Her argument afforded her nothing, and Isabelle muttered exasperatedly, "Good grief, my girl, you were only two days ago talking rubbish of how you would seek employment because of our financial hardship. Now exactly such an opportunity has presented itself and you turn it down. The chance to marry this prospective employer has also been offered and you shun that too. What on earth do you want?"

"If it were any but he, Mama . . . ." Emily explained sadly. "Well, it is not and never likely to be," Isabelle snapped. "He now holds the outcome of our very existence within his hand and has no intention of letting that slip until he has you."

"And how he loves it," Emily remarked in a harsh whisper. "How he savors every torment — being able to manipulate us so. He can tear us asunder or allow us crumbs of comfort as he will. He can beset us with disaster and make us bicker and squabble amongst ourselves as he pleases. He sets us one against the other until our disgust for him is no less than we feel for each other. Can you not see what he is doing, Mama? And watching every sordid, amusing moment with intense satisfaction."

"I know that very well, Emily, but we are not without a trump card ourselves. You are worth fifteen thousand pounds to him, which means he wants you very much." She shook her head impatiently at the shamed expression on Emily's face. "Don't be ridiculous, Emily. If it were simply for that . . . how many whores do you think he could purchase with that amount? Enough to see him through a lifetime!"

She looked away from Emily then and smoothed her gown once more with long, soothing strokes. "But . . . this is not what I have come to tell you, Emily. As I mentioned, I have been with Jane. She has suggested that if you continue to refuse to marry him, then she will offer herself as substitute bride."

Emily gasped. "You would allow Jane to go with him, knowing what you do about our families' histories — that he is ridden with vindictiveness?" she demanded, incredulous.

"I would encourage her, Emily. *She* is a good and dutiful daughter and thinks of her parents and the rest of her family as well as herself. It was her own idea when she learned of your continued refusal and do not talk of this supposed vendetta he is waging against you. I concede that he likes your father and me little. But do you really think he would take a wife and then abuse her and risk ruining this new and shiny reputation he has now?"

Emily laughed acridly. "What a man does in his own home—especially away in the countryside where none may ever hear of it anyway—is, I am sure, ignored as his own business. Papa believes, as I do, that I would suffer. We both know that none of his hatred and vengefulness has evaporated; it has merely been ten years in the festering."

She was silent for a moment. "What exactly did happen between you and Papa and the Moores that day, Mama?" she asked.

Isabelle stood up suddenly, plump hands waving dismissively. "Nothing that can alter anything now."

"I think I have a right to know now that it affects me to this degree," Emily insisted.

"I am sure you must already know," Isabelle muttered stiffly. "Gossip was rife in the early years. I heard many times of it myself. It was an unfortunate business, but one which merits neither the attention nor the time it has lasted. It was mainly to do with an old brooch of mine, and not a very valuable one, either. Mrs. Moore. . . ." She paused and gave a short laugh, "Lady Moore, I suppose I should say—but it always sounded so ridiculous to call her by her title once she was resident in our home as a housekeeper. Katherine Moore had always admired the brooch, and when it went missing that summer's day, it was discovered by your papa in a drawer in one of her rooms. She denied the theft and accused your papa of planting it there and . . . ." She hesitated, then finished in a strained voice, "She accused your papa of having carried on a secret liaison with her over the years. It was utter rubbish, of course. Charles said as much, and of course I knew the truth. We were furious, not so much at the theft as at the abuse of our trust and loyalty. We had always believed her and Clifford to be duly grateful and appreciative of the sanctuary we provided for them after Sir Edmund Moore's death.

"But it seems it was not so. Naturally, after such filthy aspersions being bandied about, they were forced to leave immediately. Some six months later I heard from your papa that Katherine Moore had died of a brain fever in the workhouse and that Clifford had gone abroad."

Isabelle glanced at her daughter's pale, set face. "Naturally, I was shocked to find out that they had ended up in such an institution, but under the circumstances there was no way they could have stayed under the same roof with us. I believe now that the poor woman was probably addled in the wits at the time of the theft. When she leveled those awful accusations at your father, I expect her health was already in decline. I am sure we are not at all to blame. If we are, it can only be for not guessing of her affliction and being more compassionate." She sighed her regret.

"Of course, your father feels guilty. It is why he can see treachery where perhaps there is none. He feels he is to blame that the poor creature should have died in such distress and in such a place. But of course you must have heard all of this."

Emily nodded slowly. "Yes . . . it is exactly what I had heard." "If you want to know anything further, you should speak to your father, for that is all I have to tell of the incident."

"And you are prepared to let Jane go with him?" Emily said. "He has withdrawn his proposal of marriage. If he will not reoffer it, will she go under the other terms he suggested? As companion to his sister-in-law?"

"Oh, there is no need to go into that." Isabelle grunted a wry laugh. "I have already written to him informing him that Jane is willing to accept his terms, whatever they may be, but I hold no hope at all of him agreeing to the revision. I expect a note shortly to that very effect."

Emily looked at her mother searchingly.

"I merely undertook the task to display that Jane and I are amenable to his proposals and more than willing to try and comply with his wishes. But he will not allow us to dictate any part of the conditions of our humbling, and of course, and more importantly, it is only you he wants." She breathed out on a vehement sigh, "I wish to God Jane would satisfy him. Her attitude is selfless." She smiled wryly. "Well, perhaps not entirely. Jane is not so ingenuous as to pass up the opportunity that presents itself here. I have to tell you, Emily, she did not appear that much of a martyr at all when she suggested it."

Emily remained unresponsive. Isabelle glanced at her from beneath her lashes and remarked evenly, "Of course, had he come and openly declared he would take you as a mistress and set you up in some dreadful haberdasher's or the like, we could not have refused, our circumstances are now so dire."

"Well, I assure you I would have," Emily breathed out, taut-lipped.

Isabelle shook her head wearily. "Why will you not be sensible, Emily, and thank God that this infatuation he has with you has lasted a decade. As a child you could twine him about your little finger and took the greatest pleasure in doing so, and frequently. I saw it many a time. You were extremely fond of him then, even idolised him; and for some reason, even though he was a young man and you but ten, you held the same fascination for him. You must use that now; nurture and exploit it and we will all survive and very well."

Emily turned her head away to stare out the window.

"You have a unique power over him, Emily," Isabelle said softly. "Which means . . . if you wish to . . . you can hurt him deeply, more deeply than he will allow himself to harm you. For there is something in the way he looks at you—"

"No!" Emily cut in harshly. Her hand brushed across her moist cheeks.

"Do you want Nanny Greg to die this winter in some filthy institution such as the one where Katherine Moore perished?" Isabelle hissed fiercely. "You know she is frail, and yet I quite believe she would outlive Jane by some while. Jane was never reared for that sort of deprivation; you know she is delicate. She would not survive the first months and I give myself but a short while longer." She looked at Emily and declared quietly, "Strangely, for all your idealism and need for perfection, I believe, of all of us, you would have been the one to come through the ordeal. And yet he will never allow you to stay there. You can go to him unwillingly now but with some honor, or perhaps in a month or so, most gladly and greatly humbled." She cautioned gently, "Should he take advantage of scooping you from the gutter at some future date, Emily, the most you could then hope for would be the haberdasher's you have just scorned. And you would show unstinted gratitude for it."

Emily sat with her head bowed and her eyes closed. The faces of those dear to her paraded across her mind in painfully slow succession. She thought of Nanny Greg and of her mother's words on her ability to survive the winter and knew that she did not exaggerate. She dwelt on her mother and her fragile, soft-spoken sister, aware that there had been no overstatement in their inability to withstand hardship either. She could see George, handsome and proud in his hussar's uniform. But she mused most lengthily on her pathetic papa. The anguish increased, despite the antipathy and blame she felt and knew he deserved. She wondered how long he would survive the rigors of a debtor's prison without the comfort of a bottle in which to drown his misery and memories.

She raised her head slowly. "I cannot write to him myself. You will have to do it. Say that I am willing to accept the terms he has offered. Papa will have to sort out the legalities; ensure that he has signed documents so that Clifford can never go back on his word should he tire of the game early and want his money instead."

Isabelle closed her eyes in heartfelt gratitude at this capitulation. "I will intimate that you are keen for him to reoffer his first proposal of marriage."

"No," Emily said fiercely. "This way, at least, I am not tied to him forever. It will probably only be a short while, and then I may have some life to myself again."

"But . . . you cannot go as a companion," Isabelle objected. "Gossip will start. Your reputation will be shredded. It must have been noticed the other night at Almack's that he was interested in you. What do you suppose people will conclude if you now join his household under such a ridiculous guise as companion to his sister-in-law, who I hear tell is quite young and no better than she ought to be."

Emily laughed, her feelings verging on hysteria. "Perhaps he means to make a collection of young women, thereby ensuring that they are all no better than they ought to be. Perhaps he has propositioned another ten young ladies like myself to join him at Malvern Hall for the winter months. After all—he cannot hunt and shoot all the time." Brilliant tears enhanced the violet of her eyes again.

"Emily . . . ." Isabelle soothed. But Emily shook her head and stood up abruptly. Her hand savagely brushed away streaking, hot tears. "Write and tell him, Mama, that we are venal enough to accept; but make no mention of his proposal of marriage or I will not go with him at all."

Isabelle stared at her anguished yet still proud daughter for a moment longer. Then, as though suddenly startled into motion by the notion that she might in fact retract this submission if it was not acted upon at once, she quickly left the room.

A silver salver hovered at the edge of the open newspaper, and Clifford's eyes moved from the print on the page to the white folded sheet lying on the light-reflecting platter. His eyes lingered, then moved to the white-gloved hand holding the tray. A thin strip of satin-ebony skin showed starkly between the white lawn of cuff and glove. Clifford's eyes raised to meet those of the black servant who was standing impassively at the side of his leather wing chair. The man returned his master's gaze steadily.

"Another note, Heath?"

The black man allowed an almost imperceptible smile to curve the full, finely carved mouth. "It would seem so, sir," he answered.

"Did you deliver my own reply earlier?"

"Some while ago now, sir."

Clifford broke the seal and unfolded the paper, scanning the few elegantly scripted lines. He read it twice, then allowed his hand to drop a little; the half-closed sheet tapped gently against the thumbnail of his free hand. A small smile touched the scar, raising it at one side of his mouth.

"Good news, sir?" Heath inquired politely.

"Improving, Heath . . . but it could have been better." He glanced sideways at the passive servant as he emphasised wryly, "It most certainly could have been better."

Clifford descended the elegant sweep of stairs quickly and silently, his shoes clattering only as they hit the grained marble flooring of the opulent entrance hall. An extravagant crystal chandelier starred the hall, diamond light sparkling iridescently along the soaring marble pillars. He made for the great oaken double doors that led out onto Grosvenor Place, giving his appearance a cursory inspection in the ornate mirror dominating one wall. He adjusted his cravat slightly and then stared thoughtfully at his reflection for a moment. He made to turn and leave just as he heard his name echo hollowly around the quiet white space.

His hand moved to make a final adjustment as his head turned slowly. He raised his eyes to the stairs with bored leisure, watching the whispering approach of his sister-in-law.

Amanda descended the wide curve of stairs with stately, measured steps. The ice-blue satin gown she wore matched exactly the shade of her eyes, and it swayed, curving against her legs with deliberate allure.

Clifford turned to watch her narrow-eyed as she neared him with sensuous grace. On noting his full attention, a gratified smile hovered about her rouged, pouting lips. She raised her white hands to his lapels. They gained his cravat, fidgeting with the frost-white silk.

Clifford lifted his hands to cover hers. He returned them to her sides, turned back toward the mirror, re-examining and readjusting his cravat, and rectified her disturbance.

She watched him carefully and his eyes shifted to meet hers in the mirror. "Where are you going?" she asked. Her hand caught at the dark suiting of his sleeve and she ran a long, oval nail along the soft, fine, luxurious cloth.

"Out, Amanda . . . I am going out." He flashed her a white, casual smile.

"You have not taken me out for a while now. You know I wanted to see Kemble on stage. You promised to take me . . . ." she complained.

"I promised nothing."

The possessive grip on his arm tightened. "May I come with you?" she pleaded, she pouted and pressed against him.

"No . . . I have business to attend to."

Suspicion was plain in her eyes. "Before we leave for Hertfordshire I intend holding a soirée here," he said. He watched her eyes brighten at the information.

"And I shall be hostess!"

He nodded slowly, then added in the same cool, even tone, "I want the evening to serve as an introduction for you and your new companion, Emily Shaw. But more importantly, I want it to introduce society as a whole to the arrangement."

Her face hardened, her mouth firstly pursing then setting in a thin line. Clifford, aware of her pique, continued quietly, "Should any hint of impropriety attach itself to her employment at Malvern Hall. . . ." He smiled and went on with intentional understatement that he knew would nevertheless be well heeded, "I would be most put out, Amanda. I expect you to do your best to ensure that no such thing occurs."

"I have no wish for a new companion," she protested abrasively. "I have an adequate one at present. She suits me; she is middle-aged and dependable. I have no wish for a strange young woman at Malvern Hall with my son and me." She paused, then stated more vehemently, "Or with you."

Clifford smiled ruefully. "Believe me, Amanda, I also have no wish to see Emily Shaw as a companion. But it seems that, for a while at least, we shall both have to tolerate the situation."

He acknowledged her augmenting hurt and resentment

with an increased sardonic twist to his mouth. "You will enjoy yourself, Amanda. Think of all the young gallants sighing and dying for a glance from those blue eyes. You will no doubt be propositioned the evening long."

She glowered at him, whispering throatily, "You know very well there is only one I seek to impress and only one proposal I wish to hear."

His amusement increased. "Ah, yes, Wellington, is it not?" he taunted. "If he is in town, I shall see if I can persuade him to attend."

Her blue eyes blazed. "You have shared one mistress with him already. Is that not enough? And I will not have that . . . that girl . . . as a companion. Just because you have old scores to settle. I want nothing to do with her."

"I think you forget yourself, Amanda, and to whom you speak. Perhaps you would benefit, like your son, from an early night."

The dismissal was explicit but she allowed a small, hesitant smile to just relax her mouth. "Surely that might benefit you too," she replied softly.

He turned away and walked to the door. "Don't lose any sleep waiting up for me."

Emily looked about her; they were practically alone in the magnificent drawing room now. Only a dozen or so people remained, most of the other guests having drifted away to the music room to partake of that entertainment.

She rose slowly and made her way across the splendid, spacious room. She seated herself in a vacant chair close to her father with a concise smile for a pair of middle-aged ladies who had just risen to quit the room. They each gave her a piercing look and smiled knowingly, barely waiting to move out of earshot before their speculation resumed in earnest.

Emily felt her fact heating for the thousandth time that

evening. She attempted to ignore the uneasiness yet again and looked at her father. His fingers drummed a rhythmless tattoo on the table top.

"Hungry, Papa? Jane said that at dinner there was all manner of delicious. . . ."

"No, I could not stomach a morsel," her father interrupted curtly. "I would choke on a glass of water in this place."

"But downing our host's brandy or port seems to be quite another matter," Emily retorted.

Her father chuckled appreciatively. "And why not?" he rejoined. "He has seen to it that I cannot afford to buy my own solace, so let him provide it for me."

"Please, Papa—" she pleaded, but he interrupted.

"What about you, my dear? You have eaten nothing." He made as though to rise and the mahogany table close by shuddered as he bumped it, thinking to retrieve for her some dessert.

"No . . . sit down, Papa, please. I am not hungry at all. I think his hospitality affects me in the same way it does you. I have felt quite sick the evening long."

"Are you not having a good time on this grand occasion, my Emily?" Charles inquired with sour mockery. He looked around the nearly empty room, its beauty and elegance much enhanced now that the full majesty of architecture, furniture, and furnishings could be fully seen and appreciated. He threw his head back, examining the intricately carved ceiling that had already attracted Emily's attention several times. "Who would have believed that our persecutor could be so ingenious as to make public our shame? Not only does he plot our disaster and then bring it about—he takes credit for rescuing us from it by his munificence, and with such apparent frankness and sincerity that no one dares hint aloud at what they privately suspect—that he is merely furthering his own base cause. He certainly lives and entertains well. Wellington and a clutch of lords and ladies in one soirée.

"Did you see Wellington? I hear he is quite a ladies' man . . . ." He laughed and remarked coarsely, "Apparently he shares his taste in women with that silver-haired Janus in whose home we sit."

Emily looked at the table in front of them. She traced a finger along the reddish grain, knowing that her father had already drunk too much to speak properly in front of her. But she felt unaffronted—even slightly drunk herself—although she had tasted no more than two glasses of lemonade the whole evening. "I cannot see what a great man such as Wellington would like about him at all," she remarked tonelessly.

Charles laughed. "Oh, they have a common interest . . . a very common interest." As though realizing then who in fact he spoke to, he coughed and reddened, mumbling some incoherent apology for his oafishness. A hand rose to rub roughly at his eyes.

"Tell me, Papa," she urged quietly. "I would like to know something of this man who has bought me."

Charles harrumphed in his throat and looked at the daughter who sat watching him so gravely. He realized that during the past few days practically all formal barriers between himself and his family, but especially between himself and this daughter, had been battered mercilessly and all but destroyed.

"Wellington and Clifford Moore share, or shared, I know not and care not which, a mistress. It was at one time supposed to have caused them quite some amusement that Hannah Watson, a lady of ill repute, found it difficult to choose between them. One such incident was rumored to have taken place some months back. Wellington had returned hotfoot to this . . . er, lady's abode from the Peninsula, only to be locked out in the street in the rain while she entertained Clifford Moore in her rooms above. Wellington apparently knew none of this at the time. He stood for an hour or more like a drowned rat pleading to be let in, thinking she was merely dallying with him."

Charles stared at his daughter's sweet, melancholy countenance and clumsily covered her hand with his. "Ah, my Emily," he murmured affectionately. He clasped the small, pale hand within his own and squeezed it tightly. "Did you see our porky Regent too?" he inquired on a lighter note. "I just glimpsed him through the throng. Quite something, is it not, to persuade the Prince Regent to put in a fifteen-minute appearance at a soirée?"

Emily let out a wry laugh and her fingers, held within the podgy, thick hand, tickled playfully. She gave a slow nod. "Yes, I own I did notice him," she mocked. "It is hard not to; he is such a gross size. Needless to say, as I espied him in the music room, it was enough to make me seek this peaceful haven once more."

"No doubt he has come in the hope of availing himself of another loan from our wealthy benefactor," Charles sneered. "I hear that Moore has provided him with funds in excess of twenty thousand pounds . . . and there was I, owing him a piffling fifteen thousand."

He looked around the room again in lingering assessment. "And to think you declined to be mistress of all of this," he muttered conspiratorially. "They do not know that, do they? He has not, I'll wager, let it be known that Emily Shaw, daughter of that buffoon Charles, spurned his hand in marriage."

Across the room Clifford and another gentleman entered and walked leisurely to the brightly roaring fireplace. Emily watched him place his glass on the mantel and then greet someone who came immediately to stand by them. As he talked, one foot moved unconsciously, resting proprietarily against the highly polished fender.

For a moment she watched him quite openly. Apart from a brief, courteous, and quite impersonal welcome on arrival, she had barely seen him; or rather, she had seen him, but he appeared barely to notice her. The few times their eyes had met had been fleeting moments before his attention had been drawn immediately to something or someone else.

There had been a formal introduction to his sister-in-law, Amanda, thankfully before the majority of the other guests had arrived and in a small private salon. The older woman had been amiable, but Emily disliked her at once. She sensed deceit in every pleasant smile and compliment. And those assessing, limpid blue eyes made the frosted blue silk she wore appear quite warm in comparison.

The introduction over, Clifford had removed himself at once, leaving Amanda and Emily to sit and attempt to converse with something like cordiality. But Emily knew that her own relief was matched by that of her new mistress when Amanda rose after some ten minutes of trivial discourse with the excuse that she had to visit her son in the nursery.

Clifford had shifted position now and stood with his back to the fire, his companions facing him. He was watching her and her father quite steadily as he drank from his glass. Then he made his excuses to the two men.

Emily averted her eyes as he approached, feeling absurdly piqued that he had so ignored her until now.

Clifford seated himself unceremoniously in a chair he had drawn close to their table. "I hope you are enjoying this evening."

Charles stood abruptly. He drained the last drop of alcohol from his glass before replacing it on the table. "I think I require something to eat after all," he said.

Emily's eyes yearningly followed her father's stout figure as he walked away, dismayed that she had been abandoned.

She looked up into the steel eyes that watched her so relentlessly.

"You have . . . a very fine house. . . . It is quite magnificent," she said uncomfortably.

"I am glad it pleases you," he said, and then: "Have you reconsidered my proposal, Emily?"

The color drained from her cheeks. "You have already been notified that I accept your offer of employment," she said coolly. "I was sure you understood my mother's obsequious little note. Otherwise, why arrange this farcical gathering of society to publicly applaud your boundless generosity? And I am sure your benevolence will be spoken of for years to come — how you treated an impoverished man and his wife and two daughters to a taste of Moore charity."

He smiled. "Farcical, yes. But if you will persist in cleaving to my offer of employment at Malvern Hall, then it is as well to have some concoction of half-truths surrounding your removal into my custody. Your reputation would suffer otherwise. Mine too, of course, but not irreparably." He sat back in his chair and sipped from his glass. "Of course, it is my own fault, for allowing you any choice in the matter."

"You know as well as I that my reputation is ruined the moment I leave London. Your sister-in-law has no need of another companion. She tells me she has one already and a nursemaid for the child. I am sure if I know that then others must too."

He leaned forward. "Shall we start again then, Emily? I think I was rather hasty in withdrawing my first proposal and most definitely unthinking in offering an option." Emily averted her face.

"Your mother and sister appear to be enjoying themselves, at least," came the soft, mocking comment after a moment.

Emily watched as Isabelle and Jane Shaw entered the room with some gay friends. She reflected bitterly that their host's patronage of her family had elevated their social standing once more.

Out of the corner of her eye she saw a length of aquamarine-blue silk detach itself from the throng. Amanda paused and stared across at Emily and Clifford, her smile fixed. Then the blonde woman was swishing lightly and purposefully their way.

Unable to countenance the company of both Clifford and his superficial sister-in-law, Emily rose immediately. She was aware of Clifford moving his chair back to stand also.

"Please . . . do not bother to get up," Emily deterred swiftly. "I must speak with my mother." She turned and walked away. Passing Amanda in the center of the room, she matched the small, crisp smile with one of her own. Emily hoped to slip by her mother unseen, although she knew it would give the lie at once to her excuse for leaving Clifford.

She gained the cooler air of the hallway and breathed deeply of the refreshing atmosphere. Strains of light melody drifted in along with muted laughter and chatter, then light, gloved applause.

She stepped backward into a slight recess, yielding gratefully to the cold wall at her back. Her hands pressed against the chill, watered silk lining the walls, then she held her palms against her hot cheeks.

She looked longingly at the stairwell; the clean white marble columns below were just visible from where she stood. She walked over and gazed down at the brightly lit vestibule; crystal droplets of the chandelier threw glints of refracted light against the towering, pearly pillars.

She descended enchanted, and moved instinctively toward the massive doorway. A pair of footmen stood rigidly against the creamy walls and she hesitated, wondering whether to inquire of them whether they had seen her father leave. She gazed at them and noticed curious eyes swivel her way, although their heads never moved.

They looked friendless and intimidating in their immaculate gold and blue frogged livery. Aware that they were still watching her slit-eyed, she made a small, hasty smile, then walked away to a corridor that lead at a tangent away from the stairs. She halted after only a few yards as she realized what she was doing: making an impromptu tour of the house was not what she had planned at all. She half-turned, knowing that she should return to the rooms above.

Her muddled indecision was interrupted by a sound from the far end of the corridor.

Emily silently gazed in awe as a man approached on quiet, fast feet. He was also dressed in the blue and gold livery, and one hand balanced a silver tray laden with a crystal goblet.

He drew level with Emily and nodded deferentially. She stared openly at the handsome hauteur of his countenance, her attention held by the impossibly light agility that belied his size and stature.

Emily stood immobile, awestruck, as the black man disappeared from sight. She had heard and read tales and seen pictures of those who were captured and traded as slaves, but she had never before actually seen one in the flesh.

A weird moaning sigh reached her ears at that moment. She glanced at the door nearest her and moved hesitantly and warily closer. A coughing groan sounded again. It was her father. She turned the door handle and it yielded at once, swinging inward on silent hinges.

Emily closed the door with equal stealth, then turned into the room. It was unlit, the only brightness coming from a fire that was slowly disintegrating in the hearth. She scanned the room by the dying glow, noticing that it was some sort of small study or library, book-lined and austerely furnished, yet still displaying the same fine elegance of the rooms above. She glanced down at the floor; the wooden boards at the perimeter were highly polished, but the majority of the room was covered by a pale, creamy rug that spread from just in front of where she stood to the clawed feet of a solid, dark wood desk. Her eyes fastened on the desk top as something stirred and grunted out a sigh.

Emily felt her stomach contract into a tight, painful ball. She stepped onto the whitish rug and walked towards the slumped figure of her father. He was fidgeting in a dark leather chair that groaned as he moved. His arms were folded across the mellow gold leather-topped desk; wiry pewter hair was all that was visible of his head. A half-empty glass of port was close by one slack hand. Emily's eyes slid at once to the equally depleted crystal decanter on the other side of his sagging frame.

"Papa. . . ." she whispered urgently. He stirred a little, attempting to raise his head. As though he found the effort too great he sank back.

Emily closed frightened eyes as she realized that he was quite stupefied with drink. The necessity of getting him out and home with a minimum of fuss and witness was vital. She felt sure she could not endure any further embarrassment that evening and knew well enough that her mother would probably expire on the spot were she shamed in front of such company as was here tonight. She realized she would never be able to move him alone and she dithered for a moment, unsure whether to beg assistance from a footman. If she did, obviously the incident would later be recounted, and with much scornful amusement she was sure, but at least it would be only secondhand news.

First she would try to wake him. She moved swiftly around the desk and shook his shoulder forcefully. His head lolled and he made a thrashing protestation with one hand. The half-empty goblet crashed over, spewing its contents onto the old-gold leather top of the polished mahogany desk. Emily scrabbled quickly at the blotter, trying to remove it hastily from beneath her father's bulk to contain the spread of the liquid. But his weight impeded her and she watched horrified as the claret pulled itself slowly towards the edge of the desk and then dripped in long, slow globules onto the carpet.

Managing to remove the blotter at last, Emily covered the dark spreading stain on the desk with the absorbent sheet, the entire surface area darkening immediately.

She righted the glass and gave her father's shoulder another sharp, despairing shake. "Papa . . . please, Papa . . . wake up . . . we have to go quickly. Please, we have to go before the others start to leave."

Emily grasped at the fresh sheet of blotting paper and pulled herself around the desk quickly to gaze with increased desperation at the blood-red blemish on the cream carpet. Dark curls tumbled softly against her cheeks as she crouched down.

"Leave it." The command was quiet and yet compelling. Her head jerked up at once, her heart pounding painfully in her throat at the startling, unexpected noise.

As the fire threw a grotesque, ceiling high shadow of the approaching man, she sank forward petrified onto her knees in the soft wool pile.

Clifford approached the desk, ignoring her as he stared down impassively at the inebriated, slack-mouthed man.

Hot, hopelessly ashamed tears stung Emily's eyes. The blotting paper fell from her insensate fingers to the carpet. She murmured with what dignity she could manage, "I am very sorry . . . he did not mean it. It was an accident. I think it was my fault. I startled him and he knocked the glass over." The apology trailed into lengthy silence. Thinking perhaps that he expected her to furnish further regrets or explanations, she added unsteadily, "I am afraid he is drunk."

"Obviously," he said curtly.

Emily drew herself up onto her knees. His hand stretched out leisurely, offering assistance. She placed her fingers in his and a cool, firm grasp pulled her upright.

She stood passively for a moment with her hand resting unrelinquished in his. She murmured quick thanks, then tried to slip her hand free. His grip increased a little and he drew her slightly closer, his eyes dark and intent. She apologized again in a hushed, tremulous voice, "I . . . I am very sorry your carpet is ruined. If you were to summon one of the servants straightaway, perhaps the worst might still be avoided." She attempted once more to disengage her hand, as though quite prepared to undertake the task herself.

Instead of releasing her, he caught hold of her free hand as it spontaneously tried to lose itself among the folds of the amethyst silk dress she wore. He shifted position so that he was resting against the desk, his back to her softly rumbling father, and pulled her closer.

Emily turned her head instinctively as his face neared hers and she felt his mouth brush against her hair. She stood rigid and mute, utterly mortified by her conviction that he felt he had the right to make free with her already in reparation for the damage sustained to his furnishings. His hands still held hers and he moved them behind her, crossing them over her back. He eased her gently closer, his mouth touching her neck softly beneath the loose curls.

She jerked her head away from him, turning as far from him as possible. "I would rather you deducted the price of the carpet from my future remuneration," she murmured coldly. "I trust I will receive some whilst in your employ."

Clifford straightened slowly, his hands releasing her slender, straining fingers.

"If you knew how much that rug cost, you would not even suggest it," he countered mildly.

Emily stepped back at once, freezing him with violet eyes.

"Besides," he added evenly, "I believe you were paid in advance. At an average companion's salary, fifteen thousand pounds should keep you with me for the next thirty-five years or so."

Emily looked away from him to her father, who started to snuffle. She stared at the motionless gray head, at that moment hating him fervently, yet envious too of his momentary comfort and oblivion. She watched the straining dark material across his shoulders, rising and falling as he slept peacefully, and wondered how long he would be allowed to rest in that blissful insensibility. She knew well enough that their shame-free passage home that night now depended solely on the mood and benevolence of the tall, silent man opposite.

As though guessing her thoughts, he said evenly, "He will have to remain the night. I cannot get him out of here unobserved in that condition."

"No, I don't want him to stay here," she quickly blurted.

"What do you think I am going to do, Emily? Murder him in his sleep?"

"You have done everything but that already. I would not put anything beyond you."

Clifford smiled tolerantly and said softly, "Well, if his welfare at my hands scares you that much, Emily, you are very welcome to stay also . . . simply to guard him, of course."

She stood silently and the thought that snaked its way into her mind appalled her. In a voice that shook with disgust, she said, "If . . . if I did stay here tonight . . . would you forgo the conditions for waiving my father's debt?"

Tears of humiliation dampened her lashes just as his hand moved out abruptly, spanning her face. He tilted it upwards so that she was forced to look at him. The wetness slid against her skin, and she tried hastily to shake off the restrictive grip, but his fingers tightened.

"Fifteen thousand pounds for one night is rather a lot, even for you, Emily," he mocked in a hard, quiet tone. "I think it would serve me better to wait, and take you to Hertfordshire, and get my money's worth."

He released her abruptly and strode away to a bell pull close to the hearth. He stood by the fire, silent and unmoving for a moment, before he suddenly kicked the fender, savagely prompting the glowing coals to give a last shower of life before being dislodged into final flame.

For some reason it was at that moment that Emily noticed just how well groomed he was. His hessian boots were highly polished and the dark-blue velvet jacket stylish and immaculate. His hair was silver-clean and fire-reflecting, tinted now with copper lights, as was his smooth-shaven, tanned skin.

His hands thrust into his pockets and he turned abruptly to gaze at her. "Your father stays here — you go home," he stated tersely. "I shall make arrangements for you and your mother and sister to leave immediately. You can take one of my carriages."

"We will get a hackney cab, as we do usually," she rebuffed.

The servant she had seen earlier that evening entered then.

Under Clifford's direction, he approached her father and cleared the desk of its scattered contents, removing the decanter away safely to another table.

Emily's eyes were hard as she looked at Clifford. "You are acquiring quite a collection of slaves, it seems," she bit out contemptuously. "I find it hard to believe that even someone as arrogant and despicable as you would flaunt your inhumanity quite so openly by bringing the wretched creature to London to be gawped and tattled over."

She tried to sweep away from him disdainfully at that point, but he caught her forearm in a steel grip, his fingers cutting deeply into her soft flesh. "He is as free to leave this house as you are," he laughed softly. "Freer . . . for it is quite likely if you do not remove yourself immediately I shall change my mind about the terms for keeping your father from debtor's prison. They might easily also include your presence here tonight."

Emily swung from him. She jerked open the door and then slammed it behind her. She hastened along the corridor toward the stairs then slowed her pace considerably and tried to regain some semblance of calmness and poise.

Amanda was standing at the foot of the stairs bidding gracious farewell to several guests. Her hard, concentrated gaze searched Emily's face; then the frosted eyes were staring past her into the silent, empty corridor. Emily passed Amanda, then mounted the stairs quickly and went in immediate search of her mother.

She found her easily, with Jane and Mrs. Cooper and her daughters, making preparations for departure. Emily managed to prise her happy mother away from Mrs. Cooper and explain her father's predicament in a few concise sentences.

"Well, I shall have to write and thank Sir Clifford in the morning," her mother said. "I cannot imagine the extent of my shame had your father made his departure on all fours."

"Come, Mama," said Emily, "let us leave now. We can hail a hackney cab or perhaps beg a ride with the Coopers. We can simply say that Papa left early as he felt unwell."

But even in this Emily was to be thwarted, for they were met at the bottom of the staircase by Clifford's black servant, who bowed stiffly and said, "I will show you to your carriage."

Isabelle was so effusive in her gratitude toward her host, who was now standing beside Amanda, that Emily could not decline the carriage without drawing a good deal of attention to herself. Without looking at Clifford, she stiffly followed her mother toward the door.

Clifford's eyes took in the length of Emily's stubbornly presented back view and his lips twisted wryly.

Chapter Four

The coach lurched and Emily's gloved hand rose instinctively trying to prevent her head from making contact with the padded coach again. It tapped more lightly this time, her thick, chestnut hair cushioning the worst of the blow. She opened sleep-heavy eyes and blinked, trying to clear the moisture filming them as she shifted further into the middle of the coach seat.

"You banged your head on the side of the coach," Amanda informed, a humorous glitter firing her eyes. "Lucky, is it not, that the interior is so well padded, else you could have done yourself some real harm with your thrashings."

Emily glanced at the woman uncertainly and Amanda explained, "Oh, you have been dreaming for practically the whole while you have been asleep. You have been twisting and turning and muttering all manner of nonsense. Obviously it was more of a nightmare. You seemed most terrified of something . . . or someone?" she hinted slyly.

Amanda moved a fur-trimmed gloved hand to absently stroke the fine fair hair of the boy resting against her. He stared unsmilingly at Emily too for a moment, then he turned from his mother and her caresses and stared indifferently through the coach window.

Emily probed gently at the tender place on her brow once more before following little Richard Moore's example and gazing through the window of the undulating coach at the hazy gray horizon.

The wet green countryside passed practically unobserved, Emily's eyes wide but sightless as she stared out into the light drizzle. She heard Amanda advise, "We should be there quite soon. I believe this is St. Albans already. But then you must know the landmarks quite well. You used to live quite close by, I believe." "Yes, that's right."

"How long is it since you last saw Malvern Hall?"

"So long I can barely remember seeing inside it at all. I think we were all invited to dinner there a few times, when I was about seven or so, I suppose. Just before Sir Edmund . . . ." She hesitated, then continued, "Just before Sir Edmund's death. But I remember little of any of the Moores, or of their house."

"Stupid, cowardly man, "Amanda spat.

This vehement denunciation made Emily glance across at Amanda.

"Oh, he was," Amanda informed glibly, with a smile. "Stephen thought so too. If it had not been for his father's idiocy when he lost everything then disgraced them all, and his own memory into the bargain, Stephen and I would never have had to endure such hardship in our early marriage. There was never any money for luxuries or fine things."

"But then, I suppose if it had not been for Sir Edmund's death, you would probably never have met Stephen at all, let alone married him," Emily remarked woodenly.

Amanda's eyes narrowed and her mouth thinned. "Whatever do you mean?"

"Just that is is unlikely Stephen would have gone to London had the . . . accident not occurred," Emily reasoned. "No doubt he would have stayed in Hertfordshire and finished his education, then gone to university or traveled abroad." To change the subject, Emily asked quickly, "When did Stephen die? Was he ill?"

"Oh, he has been dead these past three years now," she replied easily. "He was killed fighting on the Peninsula.

He was only twenty-four and there only about nine months. He was a fool to go. He used to tell me that when they were boys, Clifford used to thrash him at every competitive sport. He should have stayed and completed his studies n law. Of course it is hard to blame him," she added more charitably. "It was a deadly boring life — poring over ancient volumes into the night. He was hoping that once he was qualified we would go to the West Indies and join Clifford. There is money to be made there, and not only by planters. Solicitors and businessmen of all sorts can find quite excellent prospects in the colonies. I am not too sure I would have liked to go: such a climate! And full to the brim with black savages."

"No doubt those black savages would also prefer to be elsewhere," Emily remarked drily, "back in their homeland and free."

Amanda raised a hand to smooth pale strands of hair beneath her fur-trimmed bonnet. "When Cliff came home he looked for Stephen and found us instead. I believe I compensated somewhat for the loss of his brother. He knew Stephen had married. He used to send us money sometimes but was never very forthcoming about where he was or what he was doing.

"Clifford wrote and asked Stephen more than once to join him in Jamaica. But Stephen was stubborn. He wanted to merit a share of the business by qualifying first. Quite honestly too, I think the idea of living there amongst the blacks frightened him more than fighting the French did. Every time he read of a slave riot in Jamaica he would fret and bewail Clifford's fate, fearing him dead or tortured."

She laughed and raised quite astonished eyebrows as though the very idea that her brother-in-law would submit to such a thing was beyond belief.

"Unfortunately, it transpires your late husband's fears were totally unfounded," Emily said quietly and with a bitter smile.

Amanda stared at her, astounded at this impertinence.

Regretting having allowed any insight into her attitude toward her new employer, Emily scanned the countryside briskly, asking hastily, "Is Malvern Hall close by now?"

Amanda was silent for a moment longer. Then she smiled, knowingly, and replied, "Oh, you will know when it is. It is quite magnificent now and dominates the countryside for miles. A whole new wing has been added over the past years. I occupy all of that with my staff," she added arrogantly.

Emily ignored the information and Amanda's smug smile.

"I know of Clifford's hatred of you and your family and what caused it. I know everything. Stephen hated your parents, too. He never forgave them for not allowing him shelter as they did his mother and Clifford." She laughed shrilly, "Of course, all things considered, it was hardly any refuge at all."

Emily ignored the jibes completely, knowing she had already been provoked into revealing more of her feelings than she wished.

Amanda smoothed her gloves against each other and continued, Before Clifford went abroad, "Stephen learned of his mother's death and that they had both been turned out to the poorhouse by their father." She watched Emily carefully for her reaction. "I suppose now that I am a Moore, I should hate you too."

Emily turned then and looked directly into the cold, water-blue eyes. Amanda said patronizingly, "But I think if you are sensible and do exactly as you are bid and never vex me, we might get along tolerably well for the short time you stay at Malvern Hall. And it will be a short time. He will tire of his punishment and your presence very quickly. He bores easily and you will soon irritate him. He has only brought you here to wound and degrade your father . . . to bring him to his knees. Personally, I would have deemed that already achieved and left the poor wretch now to wither in his own pathetic way. But Clifford can be quite exceedingly cruel."

Emily looked through the window of the coach again abruptly, biting her tongue to prevent herself from retaliating against this spite. Yet even though she disliked of Amanda, she realized that the woman was going to prove a most welcome, if unwitting, ally. As the coach neared its destination, she thanked Providence for Amanda's quite obvious jealousy and possessiveness where her brother-in-law was concerned.

"I've been a good boy, Uncle Sir Clifford, honestly I have. Is that not so, Mama?" The thin, slightly built boy jerked back his head on a stalklike neck, raising his eyes to his mother.

Amanda patted her son's smooth, pale cheek as he knelt by her chair and then nodded confirmation.

Clifford was dressed in riding clothes and held a small riding crop behind his back. "I think perhaps we ought to ask a rather more unbiased witness as to the truth of this highly unusual occurrence, Richard," he said solemnly.

The small boy's gray eyes moved to Emily. She was sitting quietly in a soft velvet chair by open french windows in the elegant small salon at Malvern Hall.

Emily raised her teacup to her lips, sipping slowly from it.

Clifford watched her silently as she replaced the cup on the saucer in her hand.

"What is your estimation of Richard's behavior today, Emily?" he inquired evenly.

"I believe he behaved very well the whole journey. He was so quiet I hardly noticed him in the coach," she replied.

The boy's face split in a sunburst smile as he gazed

proudly up at his uncle. He jumped up then and followed Clifford to the mantel shelf, where there was a dish of sweetmeats. Richard received them gladly.

"Thank you, Uncle Sir Clifford," he muttered solemnly.

He turned with a happy smile and crammed a mouthful of his sweets as he ran toward the open glass doors. He dazzled Emily with a split-second smile as he went, allowing her a glimpse of the tasty treat within his mouth.

He skipped out onto a stone-flagged terrace. This in turn led to narrow stone steps that descended gracefully and lengthily to magnificently proportioned gardens.

Emily watched the boy as he scampered down to the rain-wet lawns. He began to spin himself around in aimless circles, arms outstretched, and then sank giddily to the turf. He examined his dish of sweetmeats, relishing his next choice.

"If anyone was restless and unsettled on the journey," Amanda said, "I am afraid I have to accuse Emily of it. She quite frightened both Richard and me with her violent thrashings and mutterings."

Emily dropped her eyes, feeling color sting into her face.

Clifford pulled a chair round to face Emily. The tip of the riding crop touched the richly patterned, oriental carpet between his feet. He began to sketch some design on the carpet with it as he asked evenly, "Oh? Why was that?"

"She slept for the best part of the journey here, but hardly peacefully," Amanda said smugly. "She was having the most frightful dream . . . a nightmare, twisting and turning in her seat and crying out for most of the time. It was difficult for Richard and me to rest at all. I was going to awaken her but then she jolted herself against the carriage and banged her head quite hard, waking herself."

"I am sorry that you and Richard were distressed by my

presence," Emily said. "I assure you it would have suited me better too had you been allowed to return here alone."

Amanda looked toward her brother-in-law, slightly raised eyebrows mocking this quiet, haughty speech. But his attention was all on the mahogany-haired girl across from him.

He stood up and approached Emily's chair. Tanned fingers extended to caress the dark, soft hair close to her forehead, as he began to examine the bluish discoloration by her temple.

Emily suffered in silence.

"What were you dreaming of, Emily?" he asked.

"I have no idea . . . I can never remember," she lied. She rose abruptly, moving away from him. "May I be shown to my room now, please?" she asked with cool civility. Immediately she wished she hadn't spoken. It was quite probable she would not be given her own room. Perhaps she would be expected to share a room with other servants. It was usually the case that staff boarded together. Perhaps she would not even have a bed, but rather some meager pallet on a floor in an attic room with other menials. Humbling and humiliating her was, after all, Clifford's motive for bringing her to Malvern Hall. She sensed loneliness and despair threatening her composure yet again as she realized he might even show her to his own room straightaway.

She knew from the intensity of his gaze that her distress was apparent.

"Sit down for a moment, Emily, and I will show you your room in a short while," he said softly.

Amanda let out a sharp laugh. "I do believe that is one of my duties . . . showing her where she is to sleep. She is my companion after all, and will therefore occupy one of the rooms in my suite in the west wing."

Clifford turned leisurely to his sister-in-law. "Emily is here at my bidding and my convenience. Her removal here to act as your companion was merely a ruse to ensure our reputations."

"Where does she sleep, then?" Amanda demanded, her blue eyes blazing.

"On the first floor."

"But your rooms are on the first floor!"

"Thank you for reminding me, Amanda, but I had not forgotten."

Amanda pouted at this freezing sarcasm.

Emily turned away, feeling more wretched than ever. She watched Richard as he mounted the stone steps with the empty sweet tray in his hand. He entered the small salon again, his breeches and light jacket grass-stained and damp from the lawn.

Clifford interrupted what was a tense silence. "You will want to rest before your outing this evening, Amanda. I suggest you remove to your rooms and freshen yourself." He looked toward the newly arrived boy with his soaked and grubby clothes and smiled shortly and indulgently as he took in his nephew's disarray. "And take Richard and dry him off before he catches cold."

Amanda's gaze alighted first on her soiled son and then passed on carelessly to Clifford. "Outing this evening?" she repeated in a puzzled tone. "To where?"

"I have accepted an invitation from the Dobsons for you. They are holding some sort of evening at home . . . seven-thirty . . . cards, I believe. It will give you just enough time to rest and refresh yourself before you leave." One hand moved to his waistcoat as he spoke, extracting a heavy gold watch, which he glanced at laconically. "It is only a quarter to four now."

Amanda spoke over his words sarcastically. "Thank you so much for your concern over my social invitations; unfortunately, this time it is wasted. I do not wish to go. I am quite exhausted by the journey from London and have no desire to travel anywhere else today at all."

116

"I have arranged for you to go, Amanda," Clifford insisted. "Please do not vex me with your dissension."

Amanda's weak blue eyes stared into his silver ones for a long moment; then they dropped. "I am so sorry, Cliff . . . you know I never mean to be disagreeable, it is just that I am quite weary. But I am sure that if Emily and I rest for a few hours or so we will be quite fit to enjoy ourselves this evening." Aware of the quickening interest in Emily's face, she added with sly sugar, "It really is rather thoughtful of you, Clifford, to arrange for her to meet some of my little circle of friends so early on."

Clifford smiled too. "Emily stays here. I have things I want to discuss with her this evening." The silence that followed was palpable.

"Surely they could wait; after all, she will be here some weeks," Amanda reasoned shrilly. "I am sure one evening — and her first at that — will not make any difference."

"If you are that desperate for female companionship tonight, I am sure Mrs. Tadworth will be more than pleased to travel there with you. She has already intimated as much."

"Mrs. Tadworth?" Amanda gazed about astonished, as though she might espy the unwelcome woman in the room somewhere. "What is she doing here still? I believed you to have dismissed her. I have no need of her now." She smiled insincerely in Emily's direction. "I realize now that it was a good idea of yours . . . arranging for me to have a younger companion. Mrs. Tadworth was unbearably stifling with her middle-aged ideas and those endless tales of her late husband."

Clifford cut in impatiently, "Quite so . . . I should have words with her. Now take young Richard away to some clean clothes before he is chilled."

Emily looked toward the young boy. He gazed back at her, then up at his uncle; and for a moment she glimpsed some unbearable sadness in the child's large-pupiled eyes. They reddened and shone but his mouth pinched, stilling the trembling of his lips.

Emily sensed an overwhelming desire to reach out and pull him close and put her arms about him.

Richard looked at her again with bright, fierce eyes, then turned away from them all, walked to the window, and stared quite casually over the gardens.

Clifford was watching the boy too. "Take Richard away now, Amanda," he said firmly. "He seems quite over-wrought . . . as do you."

Amanda rose swiftly, choking out, "I *do* want Mrs. Tadworth removed, and I have already accepted the replacement you chose for me as being adequate. I am pleased with Emily and accordingly wish her to take up her duties immediately. I wish her to join me in going to the Dobsons' tonight."

Emily stood up also then, realizing that this was probably her only chance of escaping whatever it was he had obviously planned for her first night at Malvern Hall. "I would very much like to accompany Amanda tonight," she managed with surprising calm and a reasonably steady voice. She continued with strengthening composure, "I am not tired and I would rather go out than stay in this place alone."

A barely perceptible smile just creased the thin white line near Clifford's mouth. "You will not be going out, Emily," he denied her softly. "Neither will you be alone. I have no intention of going out tonight myself . . . have no fear on that score."

Emily tried to emphasize her desire to socialize, but the words were lost as Richard started to chant some childish rhyme in a high-pitched, tuneless voice. Clifford reiterated with slightly more strength, "Retire to your rooms, Amanda, time is passing and I have things to do."

She rose suddenly and walked toward him, holding

herself tautly. She halted close to him and glared up into the impersonal face.

"Do not forget your son, Amanda," he reminded with a cool smile. "Remove him before he shatters every window in the place."

"Richard . . . come," Amanda commanded. "Your uncle wants you removed from his presence." The child approached his mother with reluctant, dragging feet, his eyes downcast and his song finished.

Clifford shut the door immediately after they had quit the room.

He turned and looked at Emily for a moment before approaching. She felt the knot within her stomach tighten, then writhe to free itself. He halted quite close in front of her chair, and she was acutely conscious of close-fitting beige material encasing hard-muscled legs. The riding crop was still clasped loosely in one hand. He moved it behind his back once more, gripping it with both hands before tapping it against one open palm slowly. He walked past her and to the french windows. She did not turn to watch but was instinctively aware of him gazing out over his magnificent lawns and immaculately tended gardens. Shrubs and flower beds stretched as far as the eye could see.

"How did your parents react to your departure this morning?" he inquired casually.

"My mother conveys her kind regards and hopes she finds you well. My father. . . ." She hesitated and looked up at the expressionless face as Clifford turned to stand in front of her again. "My father was suitably, and I am sure for you, most gratifyingly wretched. He sends every possible ill wish that he can think of and hopes, as do I, that each one of them fatally befalls you."

Clifford smiled to himself and then to her. "Surely one would be enough to fatally befall me, Emily." She ignored him and he continued with deceptive softness, "You really must learn prudence, Emily. My tolerance of this continued impertinence is rapidly diminishing. As I told you once before, it would pay you to be nice . . . very nice . . . to me."

There was no response to this caution, apart from an increased unsteadiness in the fingers in her lap.

"Come, I will show you to your rooms now."

Emily stood up and walked away from him. "You just mentioned how very busy you are," she reminded quickly. "There is really no need for you to waste time with me. I will not be at all offended if a servant shows me where I board. I am sure if you were to give me directions, I could find the room myself."

He smiled, his head inclining in mocking acceptance of her concern. "It is true, I am very busy today, but I think I can spare ten minutes to welcome you." He had neared the door as he was speaking and he opened it and held it for her. She passed him silently.

He lead the way to the stairs and Emily looked around her surreptitiously.

A large, round woman of about forty, dressed in a grey serge uniform, turned the corner of the landing above them and started to descend. A wire ring of keys clanked as she moved closer, and as she dropped a low curtsy to her master, the jangling increased. Round brown eyes moved to Emily's face, and the woman smiled at the new arrival once more in welcome.

Clifford halted and made to introduce them, but the woman ventured quickly and politely, "We have already met, sir. Mrs. Moore introduced Miss Emily when they arrived earlier today." She gazed squarely and amiably at Emily.

"May I assist with your unpacking now, miss? Or perhaps get one of the chambermaids to help?"

"No, I can manage, thank you." Realizing belatedly that much could have been gained from this chance meeting, Emily corrected herself stumblingly and hurriedly, "Yes . . . yes, perhaps you would help me now with it. If it is not too much trouble. It would prevent. . . ." She glanced at Clifford, reading the amusement in his face as she strove desperately to rid herself of his presence. She knew he was also waiting to hear how she would address him. She swallowed the urge to say merely "him" and uttered tonelessly, "It would prevent Sir Clifford wasting his valuable time too if you would show me where my room is."

The housekeeper bobbed obligingly.

Clifford turned on the stairs and said to Emily alone, "I shall see you later at dinner, then. Mrs. Phillips here will advice you when and where we eat."

The woman dipped again, setting the keys aclink as she assented dutifully, "Of course, sir."

After Clifford left them, an unconscious, long, slow sigh of relief escaped Emily. She turned back to the housekeeper.

"It really is very kind of you to offer to help me with my things, but I could manage alone if you are busy," she said. She mounted a few stairs, adding, "I have so very few clothes, I could manage alone quite easily."

"Nonesense. It will only take a short while, and you are a guest."

Emily glanced back tentatively but could detect no irony, and she wondered if Mrs. Phillips was unaware of her own ostensible role as Amanda's companion.

Emily's eyes darted along the hallway, from one door to another interspersed along the paneled walls. She wondered which rooms were his and which were hers, wondered too if this genial woman who was making pleasant remarks on the inclemency of the weather thought it unusual that her master should have chosen to situate a young lady's bedroom so close to his.

Mrs. Phillips' eyes met hers and the woman smiled.

Emily returned the friendliness, but reticently tempered it with the cynicism she was probably being paid enough not to think about Clifford's morals at all.

They had nearly reached the end of the corridor when Mrs. Phillips halted. Raising her key ring, she selected one and inserted it into the lock. It turned smoothly and she swung the door open. Emily walked in slowly, her eyes circling in leisured assessment of her accommodation.

She realized all fears of being hounded into a small attic chamber had been completely unfounded and now also knew why Mrs. Phillips had deemed her a guest.

The woman stood and watched as Emily perused the room slowly, then she remarked, "I wondered why he chose this room; but I see now. Violet . . . it matches the color of your eyes quite exactly. He had a room decorated in every color of the rainbow. I'm not too sure what he selected for the rest though. There are so many bedchambers in this house that I scarce can keep count of them myself. The whole of the eastern wing is closed, unused, apart from his rooms, of course."

Emily looked at the woman swiftly and ventured, "I thought his rooms were on this floor."

"Oh, so they are; but as you mount the stairs you turn left. That takes you directly into the east wing of the house." She smiled at the fair, thoughtful face, commenting, "I still get lost myself at times. I have only been in residence for six months." She bent swiftly and unfastened the catches on Emily's battered trunks. She raised the lids and started to lift out clothes, shaking them loose of wrinkles and placing them carefully on the bed.

Emily turned and examined the chamber from ceiling to floor once more, noting that the drapes and bedcover were of the same violet material. "It looks as though everything is brand new," she murmured.

"Yes, it is." The woman still shook and spread clothes

as she informed, "It has been redecorated since I have been here—only finished just recently. It has never been used, not to my knowledge anyway."

The woman laid the remainder of the clothing on the large high bed. She bent towards the amethyst silk gown and smoothed the cold, sleek material with a work-roughened hand. "You will look quite beautiful in this," she sighed.

Emily smiled as Mrs. Phillips straightened and rustled to a doorway off the main bedroom. "Now there is a dressing room and a small sitting room through here." She entered and after a moment returned, poking her head around the door. "Do you not want to see?" she queried, surprised.

Emily shook her head quickly but managed to smile gratefully. "No—I shall look later, thank you."

The woman nodded, moving back into the main bedroom. She opened a wide, high rosewood wardrobe which was beautifully and intricately inlaid with brass as was a matching chair nearby. Mrs. Phillips started shaking out dresses and hanging the clothes neatly.

Feeling superfluous, Emily walked to the large, square-paned window and looked out over the spreading lawns before lifting limpid violet eyes to gaze into the distance. Her heart paused heavily for a long moment before recommencing with hammering speed. She gazed at the white angular bulk of the home she had not seen for ten years, recognizing it immediately. His reason for choosing the room became achingly apparent. It had a quite marvelously tormenting view of Thrushcross Grange, nestled in a lush green valley yet on slightly raised ground so that it was quite visible still.

Emily tore her eyes away from the building and scanned the land close by. Then more slowly, she looked for signs of life, as she wondered who was resident there now. She gazed back at the two large squat chimneys rising from the gray slate roof but could distinguish no smoke against the watery-pale sky. She looked again at the fields and meadows but it all seemed quite desolate.

Emily turned quickly and looked at the woman who was busy closing her empty trunks and locking the wardrobe doors. "Mrs. Phillips . . . ?"

The woman waved a hand once more. "Call me Margaret . . . everyone does."

"That white house in the distance over there . . . do you know anything of it? Does anyone live there now?"

The tall, plump woman joined her at the square-paned window and squinted myopically in the direction of Emily's pointing finger.

Oh, that . . . you mean Thrushcross Grange. No one lives there. Not as far as I know, anyway. He doesn't rent it as far as I am aware and he certainly wouldn't live there instead of here, would he? I believe it is almost derelict, so Tom Mansfield said. He's one of the gardeners and. . . ."

She would have continued, but Emily, shocked, whispered the words, "Who owns it, Margaret?"

The woman's gaze moved from the white house afar to the large, violet eyes that were watching her intently. "Oh, it belongs to Sir Clifford, same as most things round here do. There's hardly a building or piece of land you can set your eyes on roundabouts these parts that doesn't have the Moore crest on the deeds. 'Course, there is that bit. . . ." She pointed out and Emily glanced, but barely interested, in the direction of the housekeeper's aim. "That strip of land between Thrushcross Grange and the Bentons' farm aways to the north. Now that belongs to Jonathon Cross, and as far as I know he is not letting anyone lay hands on it." Margaret glanced uneasily at Emily, her ruddy cheeks blooming further as though aware she had presumed too much. But Emily was not even looking in the direction of the acreage in question but away to the northwest, once more captivated by the childhood home she still loved.

The woman bustled away from the window and made a brisk, workmanlike show of tidying the trunks away. "Well, now, Miss Emily," she said crisply, "dinner is at eight, but you will hear the gong, and if you'd like to wait at the bottom of the stairs, I shall show you where the dining room is."

Emily cut in sharply, "I am afraid I will not be down for dinner tonight. I am completely exhausted. Would it be possible to have a tray in my room? Something cold would be fine."

"Of course . . . I don't see why not, miss. Naturally you're tired. I'll bring it up myself at eight." She retreated and was gone.

After Margaret had left, Emily closed her eyes, the relief of being once more in solitude and relative safety rendering her paradoxically weak and nauseated. She walked the few steps to the bed and sank gratefully into the soft, airy cover. She examined the room slowly once again. She had never been in a bedroom like it. Expense was apparent in every drape and fold of heavy material and each item of pink-veined rosewood furniture.

She looked toward the dressing-room door, knowing that there was no need to investigate to realize that it would be just as lavish. She felt wistful tears blur her vision, wondering if she would not, after all, have preferred a tiny box room with meager furnishings. It would certainly have reminded her more of her home and the life she had grown used to.

She leaned forward, removing her shoes. Then she rose, walking in stockinged feet and with little enthusiasm, to inspect the other rooms that were hers.

Emily woke with a start to find Margaret Phillips above

her, recoiling also. "I'm so sorry, miss. I didn't mean to frighten you. It's almost eight o'clock and time for dinner soon. I thought you might like me to help you to get ready." She smiled apologetically.

Emily put up a slightly trembling hand to her forehead, holding the loose dark hair away from her face for a moment. "It is quite all right; you just startled me, that is all." She pushed herself further upright in the chintz-covered chair she had slept in.

The small sitting room was lit now; oil lamps burning here and there lent an even warmer glow to the rosewood furniture. Emily glanced at the book she had been reading prior to her slumber. She closed it and, rising, moved to replace it in the bookcase whence she had removed it some hours earlier.

Her movement reawakened the gnawing feeling in her stomach. She turned to Margaret with a shy smile. "I am quite famished, Margaret; I do hope you remembered my dinner tray."

The woman looked uneasy. "Actually, miss, I'm glad you are starving, because Sir Clifford is prepared to wait dinner until nine to allow you ample time to refresh yourself before joining him." She noted the immediate shock and dismay in the young woman's face and added quickly, "Naturally I did tell him that you had requested a tray and felt happier eating alone tonight but he said . . . well, he wouldn't hear of it."

"Please inform Sir Clifford that delaying on my behalf is quite unnecessary. I shall still eat in my room. Convey my apologies please, but — "

"But he insists, miss, and if I do say so, in the tone of voice that means he doesn't intend hearing more on the subject," Margaret returned coaxingly.

Emily sighed and seated herself at the small escritoire and sorted through the quills. She selected one and a sheet of paper and wrote a short note informing him that she had started to prepare for bed and would, accordingly, make do with a tray in her room. She thanked him for his concern in a way that conveyed she had no use for it, signed the note, then folded it and handed it to Margaret. She knew quite well that the slip of paper would become unfolded on the way to its recipient, but its confidentiality was of minimal import. The woman looked at the paper before taking it reluctantly and with a wry grimace that conveyed exactly her feelings on its use. She hesitated for a moment as though indisposed to deliver the message at all.

"I could help you dress, miss and style your hair," she coaxed.

Emily made no reply, but merely shook her head with a small, unyielding smile. When Margaret had reluctantly left, Emily searched for the escutcheon and the key. She walked to the latter quickly, turned it before going into the bedroom, and locked that door also. Her stomach rumbled hungrily again and she realized she was quite ravenous and that a sandwich would go little way toward slaking her appetite.

She sat down at the dressing table and unpinned her loosened and falling curls, then brushed her glossy, dark hair thoroughly, taking comfort and satisfaction from the simple task. She examined her face in the mirror, one finger raising to touch the light bruising near her temple. Her eyes were drawn to the door's reflection in the mirror as she heard the light tap. Her stomach lurched, then she smiled at her needless alarm, realizing that no such gentle announcement would have come from the master of the house.

She rose swiftly and unlocked the door, allowing Margaret to reenter the room.

The plump woman proffered a letter, and Emily looked at it without making any move to take it. "What did he say?" she asked stupidly, realizing even as she uttered the words that if he had meant to communicate any verbal message, he certainly would not have bothered to write one also.

Margaret merely offered the letter in answer. Emily took it and slit it open immediately.

The writing was black, glaring, and obviously impatiently scripted and folded before the ink was dry. There were only a few lines which she had gained the sense of even before she had read the exact words. She reread it slowly:

This is the only note I intend writing. Come down immediately — your state of undress will not trouble me.

He had not bothered to sign it, and Emily allowed the paper to fold back upon itself.

She glanced at the attentive, curious housekeeper and tried to fathom what to do next. Antagonizing him further for whatever reason seemed pointless, however genuine her fatigued. After a few further indecisive moments, Emily simply murmured, "Would you mind helping me to dress, Margaret? It seems I would like to eat downstairs after all."

Emily's eyes roamed slowly across the laden table. What was on it now would have lasted her whole family for a week. She looked at the meats: capon, joints of beef and lamb, and hams and tongue too.

There were plentiful dishes of vegetables; almost a dozen, she guessed; and when this course was finished there would be yet more. They had already eaten soup and fish and the hunger that had soured her stomach was already sated.

Her violet eyes flitted from one delicate, gold-rimmed tureen to another, the fine elegance of the vessels' shape and design passing almost unnoticed as she marveled at their contents.

The servant carved meat for her and laid it neatly onto her plate. Her eyes lifted from her plate and followed him as he moved with smooth grace to the opposite end of the highly-glossed yew table. It was a small table, barely fifteen feet long, and Emily knew this could not be the largest dining room in a house of such grandeur. It was obviously merely a family eating room. The vegetables now served also, the servants began quietly to withdraw.

The black man neared Emily once more, this time with gravy, and she looked up into the unemotional dark face and murmured, "Thank you."

The man's liquid gaze met hers. He inclined his head, responding politely, "Miss Shaw."

She smiled again, but felt slightly unsettled, surprised that he knew her name. She looked then at the fair man seated at the other end of the table. He was watching her unwaveringly, and as their eyes met, he smiled.

"There is no need to be quite so humble in his presence, Emily," he commented easily. "I am sure he is well aware of your sympathy."

Emily watched the door close as the man quit the room. "It is more of a shame, then, that he is not made aware of yours," she countered scathingly.

He pointed at her plate with his silver knife. "Eat your dinner," he ordered. "It will get cold."

"I don't want it. I have already had more than enough. What has he eaten today? Kitchen slops?"

Clifford's eyes rose slowly and steadily from his plate. Emily's met them briefly before she stared again at the door, feeling the injustice of the black man's plight. She rose suddenly, unable to bear it any longer. "Well, I shall let him eat this," she uttered clearly and defiantly. "I have no need of it." She picked up the plate and made for the door that the servant had left by minutes before.

She heard the scrape of Clifford's chair against the polished wood floor and then his cursing below his breath, as he threw the napkin violently after the dinner plate he had just pushed away.

He was in front of her in two paces. "Sit down, Emily, and do not be ridiculous," he gritted through tight lips. There was a short silence before he added, "He has eaten already. So would we have by now, had you not indulged in childish sulking in your room."

She made to sidestep past him, still clutching the dinner plate in both hands, but she merely brought herself closer to him. A sudden absurd urge to tip the meal down him bedevilled her and the more she tried to quell the dangerous notion, the more compelling it became. She glanced up at his face, unable to prevent a small, betraying smile, as some vague memory of similar youthful escapades forced upon her.

He smiled also, but warningly, and his voice was cool and gently menacing as he threatened, "Please don't, Emily. I am well past such puerile pranks."

The door opened at that moment and the black man reentered. If he was surprised at seeing his master and Miss Shaw standing, and with a full dinner plate between them, he gave no sign of it.

Clifford moved away and, reseating himself, picked up his knife and fork once more. "Ah, Heath, I am glad you are back," he remarked easily. "Come, tell me what have you eaten this evening? Was it swill from the pigs' bin?"

The handsome dark features remained impassive. "No, sir," Heath responded.

"Probably some sort of putrid offal then."

"No, sir."

"Bread . . . cheese . . . water?"

"No, sir."

Emily stood mortified, the plate still clasped in her hands. She turned back slowly toward the table. She

130

watched the unperturbed servant refill her wine glass, then walk sedately to the other end of the table to replenish Clifford's.

"Come, tell us then, Heath, what you have eaten today. Miss Shaw is quite certain you must be unfed and is accordingly desperate to offer you her own meal."

The black man returned the wine to the sideboard. "All the meals, sir, or just dinner tonight?" he inquired phlegmatically.

"Just tonight will do, thank you, Heath. Perhaps tomorrow you could supply Miss Shaw with a sample menu . . . things you are most likely to partake of during a day, so she will not have to fret for your welfare further."

"Certainly, sir. For dinner, Miss Shaw, I had a roasted chicken with potatoes and cabbage; a baked onion and. . . ."

Emily missed the rest of the details, conscious only of the soft droning hum of his well-modulated voice as he itemized his repast for her benefit. She returned to the table and placed the plate back on it but did not sit down. The incongruity of the situation and her behavior engulfed her suddenly, and she was acutely conscious of Clifford's eyes on her as he ate, watching her remorselessly.

Heath had finished his account and was now addressing his master: "Will that be all, sir?"

"For the moment, Heath, thank you."

The man quit the room with a small bow in Emily's direction, but she found it impossible to look at him this time. The heat in her face increased as she became aware of Clifford sitting back in his chair, as though finished with his own meal, regarding her intently and silently.

"Are you going to sit down and eat that, Emily?" he asked mildly.

"No." She rounded on him then, taunting sweetly, "Why . . . would you like it?" She half-raised the plate again and held it out for a moment, the desire to throw it at him returning with almost inexorable force.

He watched her, this time smiling with amusement, and she knew that now he was further removed, well into ducking distance, he was daring her to it. Any opportunity for a confrontation leading to physical contact between them was exactly what he wanted.

Their eyes held, then Emily looked down at the plate and replaced it carefully. She turned her back on him, the trembling beginning anew as she wondered nervously why she was provoking this friction quite blatantly and unnecessarily, even though she understood what the outcome was likely to be.

She heard his chair grate away from the table once more, and he walked to the fire, carrying his wine glass.

"I always thought getting through a meal with Richard at table was bad enough," he muttered drily before he tipped his glass, draining it.

Remembering that they were not completely alone, Emily asked quickly, "Where is Richard? Perhaps he would like to—"

Clifford cut in on a wry smile, "It is ten o'clock, Emily. Richard is no doubt safely in bed." He paused and half-smiled, as though something else could have been added but he was exercising admirable restraint.

Emily's hand went to the silver knife on the table in front of her and she rearranged the cutlery into neat lines before looking again at the wasted meal. She realized that none of her family had enjoyed such a meal since last Christmas, yet she had just turned it down.

Her fingers retidied the gleaming spoons and forks, forming a different pattern. She sought in her mind for an excuse now to take her leave of him and escape to her room. She had done his bidding and dined with him; now she wished to sleep, yet she was wary of mentioning retiring for the night at all.

"Will Amanda be home soon?" she posed pensively, raising violet eyes to his.

He turned sideways and placed his empty glass on the mantel shelf before staring into the roaring fire. "I doubt it. She will probably stay the night in this storm." As though confirming the sense of this prediction, a renewed howling of wind could be heard outside above the rain spattering fast against the window glass.

Emily's head spun first in the direction of the noise and then to the fire as it smoked and hissed.

Her eyes found his again, reproachfully. He laughed, muttering drily, "Is it my fault, Emily? I can hardly control the weather."

She regarded him with mounting circumspection, unconvinced he had no powers, and quite certain that they were of the very darkest variety now that even the elements seemed to be conspiring against her.

He moved away from the fire then and toward her. Taking her hand casually as he passed, he pulled her toward the door with him. He walked into the corridor and toward the stairs, and Emily, no longer merely cautious and reluctant, tried feverishly to free herself.

They passed the stairs and approached a doorway she had previously seen but never entered.

He opened the door, pushing it wide before releasing her. "The library," he announced. "Now there must be something in here to please you."

The room was already lit, and she walked in slowly, dumbstruck by the magnificence of the appointments, but more by the thousands upon thousands of books racked and ranged from floor nearly to ceiling. She moved forward slowly and allowed her eyes leisurely to climb and rove the tiers of volumes. Her eyes settled for a brief moment on the oaken ladder at the far end of the room. She turned slowly in a complete circle and studied the marble fireplace, where yet another high fire was lit and now crumbling slowly in the hearth.

Clifford walked past her and sat down in a large, comfortable-looking armchair that had small tables close by either side. A decanter and glass were set out on one as though patiently awaiting his need.

Emily walked further into the room too, her eyes once more with the books. Part of her wanted to pretend disinterest, but the lure was too great. She approached the nearest book shelf, and with her head tilted a little to one side, she started to scan the titles as she wandered the row. After a few minutes of superficial perusal, she was totally absorbed, her eyes scrutinizing thoughtfully and once in a while her fingers rising to remove an interesting title.

She discovered a volume of gothic tales and opening the wine-red leather cover, studying a frontispiece drawing of goblins and elves in a high wooden glade. She gazed entranced at the scene, then read the wording below the sketch, her lips moving soundlessly before she began to turn the pages slowly with rapt attention.

The decanter and glass chimed together and Emily raised her eyes speedily. He was watching her and she turned at once, about to replace the book. But the sacrifice was too great and much too soon. She closed it and walked to a nearby small sofa-chair and sat down with it instead.

"You should move nearer the fire; it is quite cold over there."

"I am warm," she lied glibly, one hand contradicting absently as she rubbed it against a bare, chilled arm.

As though to endorse his advice, the slightly open library door crashed loudly against the wall, swinging on its hinges in a blasting draught.

Clifford rose at once with a muttered oath and moved to close it. While he was away, Emily moved swiftly from the small sofa, which she had lately realized was more than big enough for two, and did, indeed, seek the fire, opting for a small, single armchair.

He returned to his chair and sat down, watching her. She turned the pages of the novel slowly, eyes downcast, a slender hand moving every so often to clear the tumbling mahogany curls from her eyes as she read.

"This occupation you have found, Emily, is rather exclusive, is it not? Watching you read amuses me little."

Large, violet eyes sought his face briefly before returning to the open volume. "There are plenty of books; why do you not choose one yourself," she countered sourly. She gazed at him more purposefully and mocked, "You did learn to read, I suppose? I realize your schooling was abruptly curtailed."

He smiled at the insolence. "I would rather you provide me with diversion," he murmured.

Emily looked at him swiftly and guardedly, her eyes alert. "Watching you sew might be quite entertaining, I think," he suggested softly. "I am sure I could find you something to embroider."

Emily returned caustically, but with a vestige of humor, too. "Had I known you were to be quite so cruel, I would indeed never have come. Starving would have been infinitely more preferable to a life of enforced needlework."

"You would never have starved, Emily. Young women who look as you do rarely starve. They quickly find a quite lucrative means to support themselves."

"I assure you that I would rather starve," she replied haughtily. She realized then that the antithesis to this high principle was that she sat with him now and had just eaten very well. Had it not been for my parents and Jane and Nanny Greg and George—" "And I assure you, you would not have chosen the poorhouse above mine for more than a week," he countered obdurately.

She looked up then and met his eyes squarely. "Had it been just me, I would have chosen any amount of poverty

135

above you forever," she said. "Perhaps if you had been someone else, I might have succumbed."

Emily looked away uneasily from the steel eyes and back to her book.

"Well, as your accomplishments with the needle have hardly improved over the years, perhaps you would rather please me in some other way." He remained silent until she looked up at him. His head inclined in the direction of the mirror-bright piano that stood regally in one corner. "Perhaps you would prefer to play . . . or sing for me. Or is that gift still undiscovered too?"

"It would certainly mean that torment is more evenly distributed between us, had you to sit and listen to my dubious musical talents."

"In that case, perhaps I'll settle for having you read to me."

"I much prefer to read to myself," she said obstinately. "I stumble when reading aloud, and my tone is not good."

He spun the stem of his goblet between finger and thumb. "Well, what does that leave us with, Emily, to while away the long, dark autumn evenings?" he queried softly.

Emily stared down at her book as the silence throbbed interminably.

The glass found the table again, shattering the tension. "How about cards . . . Can you play?"

"Not very well," Emily admitted tentatively, as an unsteady finger traced a line of print.

"What can you play a little of?"

"Games that take more people . . . whist and loo and five card brag."

"Who taught you brag?" he asked with amused surprise.

"George . . . when he was on leave. He taught Jane and me one afternoon. I won a florin from him."

"Well, I am not sure I want to play if you might beat me," he murmured with mock reluctance. "I never like to lose." He got up and walked to an imposing looking desk and opened it. He withdrew a pack of cards and Emily looked agitatedly at them as he returned to his seat.

"I never said I wanted to play," she flustered. "I can barely remember what to do, and besides, we played with three of us and. . . ."

"You can play with two," he said on an unrelenting smile. He reseated himself and started to shuffle the cards. Pulling one of the tables at his side round in front of him, he placed the deck on it.

Emily stared at it nervously then shook her head. "I have forgotten already how to play, it is no use."

"I shall help you . . . first time round."

"I have nothing to stake . . . I cannot play." A daring thought suddenly occurred to her. "But if I won. . . ." She gazed at him uncertainly. "Would you wager my father's debt on just one hand of brag?"

He retrieved the cards from the table and leant back in his chair, shuffling them automatically. "And if I win?" he asked quietly, his eyes lightly challenging, "what will be my prize?"

She was silent, staring at the cards in his hands. His attention returned to them too.

"A thirty thousand pound debt, it seems," he mocked himself drily.

"There is no thirty thousand pounds," she contradicted fiercely. "Fifteen thousand is paid. I came; the debt is finished now."

He nodded slowly and acceptingly. "Why are you trying to resurrect it then, Emily? It was your idea; I had no intention of playing for anything other than pleasure." He smiled ruefully.

Emily sat quietly for a moment, then her fingers moved to the small pearl ring on her right middle finger. It had been her grandmother's and her parents had given it to her on her eighteenth birthday. She realized its value was little, perhaps fifty pounds at most, but she withdrew it from her finger and looked at it on her palm for a moment.

She rose and walked to the card table and, as there was no other chair close by, she sank slowly to her knees, then placed the pearl ring on the table.

"It is not worth that much . . ." she admitted, "but it is not valueless either. We could pretend it is worth more, for if you lose it will not matter how little it is worth." She raised large, appealing eyes to his, silver and violet merging for a moment before he looked at her offering with a smile.

"But if I win, presumably you then owe me twenty nine thousand and nine hundred and fifty pounds, is that it?"

She said nothing but snatched up the five cards he had dealt her while he had been speaking, afraid he might withdraw from the bet completely. He picked up his cards and glanced at them in a cursory way before looking back at her and smiling.

She returned a small, apprehensive smile, then pleaded, "Might we forget about the wild cards, for I cannot remember what to do with them?" Before he could reply she added hastily, "Will you write it down . . . the bet?" She glanced about anxiously, murmuring to herself, "There is no one here to witness it."

His smile deepened. "I see you trust me to my honor, Emily," he remarked. He looked at his cards, saying, "Of course, you realize you are on your own now . . . no help."

She glanced at him quickly and quite startled, as though still expecting clemency, but he was looking thoughtfully at his cards. He discarded two almost immediately, laying them face down on the table.

Emily perused the cards in her hand, forcing concentration. She sensed her heart hard against her ribs as she strove to decide what was best to do with them, doubly flustered by the fact that he had finished his own hand so quickly and with barely a glance at them.

"You have not commented on Malvern Hall, Emily. Is it as you remembered?" he asked conversationally.

She shook her head, her eyes fixed on her cards. "I remember little of it, but I know it is nothing like it once was."

She rearranged the cards in her hands, and then a betraying smile softened the pursed set of her mouth, as she realized she might be able to do something with them after all. She decided at last which cards to group and did so, before looking up at him with a rare, natural smile, her optimism disclosed guilelessly and at once.

He felt tenderness pervade him, desire and affection knotting his stomach at the unaffected display of innate sweetness. His teeth caught at his bottom lip as he waited for her to discard her unwanted cards.

"I get the impression you do not like my house, Emily," he commented softly. "Is it just that it is mine, or the way I have renovated it?"

Emily bit at her lower lip, unconsciously copying him, and arranged her skirt more comfortably about her. "Both," she returned absently.

"Why do you not like it?"

"Oh, it is most opulent," she conceded sincerely. She gazed about the room they were in, assessingly and honestly, noting and marveling once more at the fine, high ceiling and gold-leaf work on the friezes and around door arches. "It is very sumptuous . . . but you know that and intended it. It is obviously costly, contrived and calculated to very best effect. But it will always be just an ostentatious palace, never a comfortable home. The whole building is as cold and soulless as you are," she stated quietly, "a monument to your avarice and arrogance. It has no heart and it mirrors you exactly."

She glanced back anxiously at the cards in her hand, feeling perhaps that her rash candor might have somehow affected her chances of success. She hastily discarded two and stared at the pair of queens and a six she retained, knowing that they still looked quite favorable.

She looked up into gray eyes again and the scar at the side of his mouth just tilted. "Show me your cards, Emily," he said coolly as he spread his own face up on the table.

She stared at the three tens that had won him the game and then at the cards in her own hand before letting them drop to the table next to her pearl ring. "Congratulations," she whispered huskily as she made to rise. But his hand moved swiftly, fastening about her wrist and holding her still and close.

His free hand moved the light table to one side of his chair again so that there was no obstruction between them now. She fought to pull back and rise, but it was impossible, and she rested silently and rigidly against his chair once more.

"The Prince Regent was most impressed when he visited Malvern Hall," he informed casually. "I hear he has copied some of my drawing room almost exactly at Brighton Pavilion . . . yet you do not like it."

Emily remained quiet and tense, her head bowed a little.

"Wellington also expressed his pleasure at seeing it . . . so did many others and yet it pleases you not at all," he softly derided.

She glowered up at him at that point, her hand twisting ceaselessly in a vain attempt to free itself. "I am not surprised Wellington liked it. . . . I hear you have similar taste when it comes to gaudy, showy pieces," she scorned pointedly. "I should imagine this . . ." she spat the word and moved her head abruptly to indicate the house in

140

general, "would suit him as it does you, quite admirably."

She noticed the hard smile curving his mouth as he understood the comment, and was furious with herself then for deigning to mention their 'common interest,' as her father had termed it.

"Well, Emily, I am most gratified that you are showing such concern in all my affairs." His smile softened a little. "I hope you are not going to believe everything you hear . . . the truth distorts very easily."

She turned her head from him disdainfully as though completely disinterested in anything he might have to say.

After a moment of inner turmoil she was unable to prevent herself blurting out, "And of course his Royal Highness would admire it too, with all its effective sham and facade created to screen the gluttonous degenerates it nests. But more, I suspect, because it has given him yet again reason to stampede down to the coast and press hundreds of laborers to toil erecting him some tactile fancy. And why should they care to rest? And why should they mind if their hard-earned bread money then gets clawed back in taxes that pay architects' fees? And all for some gilt and glass Chinese monstrosity or the like. After all, they can gawp at it when it is finished . . . if they manage to survive that long. A colossal debt must surely deserve colossal profligacy . . ."

He shook her roughly to halt her. Her head jerked back and she glared at him, breathing rapidly.

He gave a small, disbelieving laugh. "You talk treason like no one I have ever heard before. Leigh Hunt is serving two years in jail for a lesser sedition of the Regent."

"Well, I am incarcerated, too, and care little for my prison," Emily cried harshly. "You asked me what I thought of this grand house and I will tell you. For all its fine veneer, no one had a more odious or decadent jail . . . or jailer . . . than I. It is the ugliest place I have ever seen."

She tried once again to free herself, but his grip was viselike. Her breath caught on a defeated sob as she subsided once more close to his chair.

He turned her head toward him with treacherous gentleness. "I shall take you to see Thrushcross Grange tomorrow; then we shall see what is hideous and decaying," he said softly.

She looked up at him then for a moment before staring soulfully into the burning coals of the fire. "It does not matter what you have done to it . . . how you have abused it. You can destroy it completely. Perhaps you already have. It is too far away for me to know if it is now any more than a shell. But you cannot take my memories of how it was, and you will not make me love it less."

The backs of his fingers just skimmed the side of her face and she shrank away instinctively, her eyes closing.

He gave a small, hard laugh and mocked softly, "Now who would believe this is the same child who dogged my every move when once I lived there with her! Once she clung to me . . . begged me not to leave her. Now she cringes every time I touch her." His fingers became more purposeful, caressing the satin skin along her jaw with sensuous, leisured strokes.

Emily remained quiet, her heart beating too deeply and slowly, her skin icy but alert to every movement. She ached to turn away but felt lulled into inertia by the artful, soothing fingers. She realized at that wounding moment that her vulnerability was perilous, certainly no match for this smooth, practised craft he would use when it suited him. The knowledge that she had not even been able to withstand him or the pain of loneliness and fright beyond the first day made her eyes burn and sting.

She felt the tears welling up and so shut her eyes tight, determined to stem the traitorous flow, her throat throbbing with the effort. But the water squeezed through her lashes defiantly and trailed slowly down her cheeks. She sensed the sliding wetness near the insidious fingers, and before it made contact, she turned her head quickly, her free hand moving up to her face to try and shield her despair.

His hand moved further away from her and his grip on her imprisoned wrist relaxed and then removed.

She swallowed noisily with constriction in her throat and moved her free hand up to her face to try and contain the depths of her grief, the height of his gratification. For even in her misery she knew, with futile fury, that she must have contented him, displaying so obviously how low he could bring her, and how easily — with a single, deceitful touch.

He got up and walked away. After a moment, Emily gained control of her breathing and wiped her face with the backs of her hands. She got to her feet slowly and smoothed out her dress with great deliberation before she turned and approached the door. Although she was aware of him standing silently by the bookcase that had previously given her so much pleasure, she walked quite steadily. Her head was unbowed; only the violet eyes were lowered, protected by long, thick lashes.

She left the room, closing the door quietly before she made for the stairs and began to mount them unhurriedly. The whole house seemed eerily mute; there was not a sound of life anywhere. She turned the corner into the corridor that lead to her room. She paused and listened before suddenly regripping the material of her skirt tightly and racing along the now gloomy but thickly carpeted passageway to the end door. She turned the handle with shaking fingers and, on entering, felt automatically for the key.

It locked at the second fumbling attempt, her thumb nail splitting and tearing with the strength of her panic. She ran through to the sitting room to check that that door was still locked, then she moved into the room again, backward, as though still anticipating an intrusion despite her precautions. She felt behind her and sat down in the chintz chair she had slept in earlier and gazed sightlessly into her own low fire. One hand moved to cup her face before she bit frettingly at the side of a tremulous index finger. She allowed the heat from the fire to warm and calm her a little and her head fell forward slightly. After a moment she began to remove the pins from her hair. She combed through soft, long tresses with unsteady fingers before her head settled into the chair back. The dead weight of mental and physical exhaustion was sapping her, but she knew it would be some while yet before she felt courageous and secure enough to go through into her bedroom and undress.

Clifford walked back slowly toward the chair he had vacated. He stared down at the empty glass on the table and his hand reached automatically for the decanter, as though to refill it. He withdrew without touching it, realizing that if he hesitated, even for an instant, she would win. His eyes closed and the interminable battle within swayed him on his feet, sexual and vengeful needs raging furiously against the mitigating ache of tenderness and reverence. His eyes located the pearl ring. He looked at it for a moment before his mouth hardened.

He retrieved it and was slipping it into his pocket as he neared the door.

He took the stairs two at a time and as he neared the top, Heath began to descend slowly. Clifford smiled casually at the black man, murmuring his name in greeting, but his pace barely slowed as they passed.

"Can I get you something, sir?" The words trailed at his back as he neared the top.

"No thank you, Heath."

Heath turned on his heel, watching Clifford reach the landing and then turn right into the hallway.

The servant hesitated for no more than a moment before he retraced his own steps with equal speed. He moved to the long corridor and watched, unobserved, as his master walked the passageway.

Clifford had gained almost half its length before his pace started to falter. Then he stopped. He stood motionless for a moment, staring ahead at the end door. He turned slowly sideways, his head thrown back as though something close to the ceiling fascinated him. He stood thus for a complete two minutes before he began to move again; back the way he had just come. He was oblivious to his manservant's presence, and as he returned leisurely, one bronzed hand clenched tight, the fist swinging out abruptly, making hard, savage contact with the wall. Clifford's eyes lifted. Noting the observant black man he gave a vague smile as he passed him.

Heath turned, grinning amusedly at his back. He followed him, a couple of paces behind. "Would you like me to get you something now, sir?" he said again, this time the mocking sympathy quite apparent.

Clifford half-turned towards him and muttered wryly, "Yes, there is something actually, Heath. . . ."

The servant laughed and Clifford sighed ruefully, "Just a decanter then."

Heath turned, scouring the vicinity thoroughly for onlookers before he fell into step beside his master as they walked into the east wing towards Clifford's rooms. He inclined his head deferentially. "Certainly, sir."

Clifford glanced casually sideways at the man. "You needn't call me 'sir' when we are alone," he muttered on a half-smile, "It sounds quite ridiculous."

"Yes, master Cliffuhd," the black man said with droning obsequiousness.

Clifford laughed but his eyes were still preoccupied.

Heath regarded him gravely. "Send her home tomorrow," he coaxed quietly but firmly.

Clifford's head moved once in negation, his jaw gritting and his eyes held steadily by something ahead.

Heath gave a small, disbelieving snort. "Well, if you can't kick down the door and you can't let her go, what are you going to do? Why did you bring her here? To torture yourself?"

Clifford allowed a small dry smile, acknowledging that what he had clung to for ten years and nurtured to an unshakable determination to exact requital was withering already. And no doubt hers was just fomenting.

"We could always go back," Heath suggested with a bright, persuasive smile. "Take her with you. It would be different there."

"You mean I'll manage to be a savage in like surroundings," Clifford challenged, his mouth twisting sardonically.

"No . . . I didn't mean that," Heath denied quickly.

The two men stared at each other and then Clifford demanded wryly, "Why not? It had already occurred to me."

They walked in silence, then Clifford stated abruptly, "I won't be going back. My time there is finished now. The sugar is all but finished too. The East Indies is where to start next, if anywhere." He looked at Heath and offered quietly, "You know you can go back at any time. Or stay . . . it is up to you. But if you stay, it has to be like this between us. I am here for good now, and no one would understand. It has to be this way."

Heath shrugged. "They didn't understand in Jamaica, either," he returned with mild dissent, "but I know then it didn't matter so much." He smiled reassuringly. "It's all right, I know how to be a good servile nigger."

Clifford laughed and threatened softly, "Yes . . . I have noticed. And, if you please, not quite so well in front of Emily. I have got it hard enough there as it is. . . ." His eyes closed as he trailed into silence. He smiled before laughing ruefully and self-consciously. One hand moved to clutch at his forehead as he walked on.

Heath choked a silent laugh, well aware of his companion's embarrassment and unfortunate choice of words. He followed him, comforting in a greatly amused voice, "Do not despair . . . Amanda will be back tomorrow."

"So she will," Clifford recalled without enthusiasm.

They halted by Clifford's bedchamber door. Heath looked about at what he could see of the house, his eyes drawn back toward the magnificent stairwell. "This house is quite wonderful . . . but I'm not so sure it suits you." He glanced slyly sideways at the fair head and Clifford stared at him with something akin to arrogance.

Heath continued, unperturbed, "If you stay in England, I see you more in a little white house—on a hill somewhere." He nodded to himself musingly and then started to back away from Clifford with a neat, mocking bow. "A decanter then, sir?"

Silver-grey eyes watched his retreat. Heath paced backward and with a slow shake of the head cautioned solemnly, "She is very beautiful."

Clifford exhaled heavily, conceding hoarsely, "Yes, she is." He barely paused before adding, with very little irony. "Better make it two decanters—one of brandy and one of rum. And bring two glasses."

147

Chapter Five

Sunlight fell through the chink in the heavy mauve curtains, streaking golden light across the fine dark chestnut hair.

Conscious of the new warmth, Emily raised a slender white hand away from the quilted satin coverlet and her fingers swept through her thick, matted tresses. She felt comfortable and turned languidly in the large bed, allowing the soothing golden heat to gild her face.

Her eyes blinked open reluctantly. After a few abortive attempts to waken herself, she gazed up sightlessly at the bed canopy. Her eyes focused, then stared. She sensed fear shiver along her spine remorselessly once more, and a hand gathered the violet satin cover more tightly to her. She turned her head in the downy pillow to look at the curtains, a roseate flush behind the heavy material heralding a beautiful autumn morning after the night's storm.

She sat up in bed slowly and stared ahead before scanning the room purposefully as though for some sign of disturbance. But everything seemed exactly as it had been just before she had finally given herself to sleep at about two o'clock that morning.

She wondered what the time was, made well aware by the heaviness in her head and the throb behind her eyes that she was nowhere near refreshed enough to tackle another day. She guessed she had not slept for more than five or six hours at the most. She moved back the bedcovers and donned her robe as she stepped toward the heavy curtains and opened them.

She gazed out, her eyes and mind drawn at once to the white house far in the distance, sitting cleanly in its early morning, light-reflecting glory. Emily lowered her eyes to the fresh green gardens where dew graced the verdure. Her gaze roved idly to the stables at one side of the house.

She tensed, her heart palpitating, as she saw first the black servant and then Clifford walk away from the low brick building, each leading a horse. The black man swung into the saddle, mounting the gray stallion easily, as though he had ridden most of his life. He turned the animal's head and looked down at his master. Emily watched him speak, then his face split whitely in an odd, blatantly familiar grin. Bemused by this unexpected, puzzling behavior, Emily watched thoughtfully. Her eyes moved on, to the top of the flaxen head glinting silver-white in the weak sun. Clifford appeared to be tightening the animal's girth, but as though aware of her scrutiny, he turned slightly and Emily knew instinctively that he was about to look up at her window.

She fled to one side of the glass quickly, relieved by her certainty that she had not been observed. She turned back into the room at once, moved to her wardrobe, and opened the double doors, gazing at her clothes. She barely saw the garments and after a moment her trembling forced her to seek the bed once more and sit down.

She had expected him last night; had been sure that he would visit her room to claim the first installment of his retribution and her disgrace. She tried to reason now why he had not but could only imagine that tormenting her with uncertainty and suspense was to be part of the terror. It occurred to her also then that Amanda might possibly have returned from her engagement after all and that Clifford had preferred to seek her company.

Emily rose once more, walked into the dressing room, and splashed her face with cold water from the jug, drying it on the soft, clean towel which she carried, pressed to her cheeks, into the sitting room. The fire was cold and dead now, the ashes gray and powdery in the grate. She sat in the chair beside the fireplace anyway and thought of her parents and Jane.

She wondered if they had missed her, knowing in truth that so far emotional stress had allowed her little time to think of them at all. She reflected pensively on her father and how he fared on this fine, sunny day. She was poignantly aware that he was distraught by his conviction, hers too, that this morning would find her humiliated and broken.

The rosewood escritoire seemed to invite her attention and she looked at it, promising herself that she would write to him as soon as she had dressed. With this incentive, she got up, lighter-hearted, and walked purposefully back into her bedroom.

She selected a dress with little care, eager to be clad now. But as she felt the lightweight cotton material, she realized that it was too flimsy for the autumn country air. She replaced it and fingered through her scant stock of heavier-weight dresses.

The rap at the door went unnoticed at first, then came again with peremptory insistence.

Emily swung toward the noise fearfully, knowing that the brusque summons had not issued from Margaret Phillips.

She moved closer to the door and asked tentatively, "Who is it?"

A woman snorted with impatience, then uttered imperiously, "Let me in, please . . . it is Amanda. I want to discuss your duties today with you."

Emily looked down, regarding her state of undress. She sighed and unlocked the door, standing aside as the blonde woman swept in. The fresh, crisp aroma of moist morning air clung to her heavy traveling cloak. Emily realized then that she must have just arrived back from the Dobsons' and come straightaway to see her.

Amanda closed the door, then eyed Emily from head to foot in lengthy assessment. She stared at the young woman's face keenly. "You look as though you have barely slept, Emily," she remarked with insinuation. "There is more purple beneath your eyes than in them this morning."

She swung away and made a lingering inspection of the room in much the same way Emily had. She probed the bed with proficient eyes and wandered through into the sitting room and scoured that too. Amanda walked back slowly, her ice-blue eyes staring calculatingly at Emily. Emily's interest in her wardrobe increased: she rummaged among the dresses for something to wear, wishing Amanda gone already.

Could you not sleep, Emily?" Amanda demanded abruptly.

Emily grasped the nearest hanger and withdrew a gray wool dress that she knew looked quite awful on her. Amanda glanced at her gown too, half-pity, half-scorn on her features as Emily removed it and laid it on the bed.

"You have not answered me, Emily," Amanda persisted with a hint of menace. "Did you not sleep well last night?"

"I never sleep well in strange beds," came the taciturn reply.

Amanda allowed a brief, ironic smile to touch her face and words.

"How often do you sleep in strange beds? You make it sound as though it is something you do often."

Emily ignored her. To change the subject, she asked hastily, "How was your evening at the Dobsons'? Did you enjoy the cards?"

Amanda smiled, well aware of the attempt at distraction, and said nothing.

"It was such a terrible storm last night . . . I was worried you would not be able to return," Emily added quite truthfully.

Amanda grimaced in obvious disbelief at this concern but agreed, "Yes, it was awful. I had to stay the night, of course; there was no way of traveling in such weather." She paused.

"And what did you and Clifford get up to that was of such immense importance as to prevent you from accompanying me?" she interrogated bluntly.

Emily shrugged, ill-at-ease. "Nothing, really. . . ."

Noting the hard suspicion pinch of Amanda's mouth, she added, "He showed me the library. . . ." Her voice trailed into silence and Amanda's eyebrows shot up almost into her hairline as she exhibited her skepticism.

"All night?" she queried sarcastically.

"We played cards too. The evening was over quite quickly."

Amanda let out a scornful laugh. "You played cards? With Clifford? Well, I need not ask if you won. He plays cards like a professional gambler. Nothing else much to do in the Caribbean at night, except drink and play cards . . . or so he tells me," she finished with an allusive smile.

A light tap at the door had Emily moving, greatly relieved, to open it. She had recognized Margaret Phillips' light summons easily.

Margaret smiled, bunching rosy cheeks as she wished a pleasant good morning to Emily. She entered the room, then hesitated, her smile fading quite conspicuously as she espied Amanda.

Aware of the reason for the housekeeper's waning enthusiasm, Amanda demanded tersely, "Is breakfast served yet, Margaret? I am quite famished after traveling so long and so early."

She received this brusque query with a tight-lipped smile. "You should have set out slightly later, madam," Margaret suggested in silken tones. "I am sure the Dobsons could not have been so desperate to be rid of you as to have set you on the road before six of the morning, and unfed too."

The two women grimaced thin-lipped at each other.

"Of course, they asked me to stay longer—for lunch today—but I have to think of my dear Richard," Amanda informed with a studied selflessness.

Margaret managed to twist her lips even tighter. "How true. And it is just as well you are on hand. I heard the young master as I came from the kitchens, bellowing his dear little lungs out at his nanny. I believe the little chap must want you."

Amanda stared rigid-faced and then tidied a strand of blonde hair beneath her traveling bonnet. "I shall go to him directly. Naturally he misses his mama quite dreadfully."

"I should. . . ." encouraged Margaret expressionless. "I am certain Miss Shaw would not have minded had you gone to see your child first instead of her."

Amanda swept to the door and then swung majestically back toward Emily, proclaiming, "After breakfast, please meet me in the small salon and I shall apprise you of your duties for the day."

Emily merely nodded as the door closed. Then Margaret and Emily looked at one another.

Margaret walked to the windows without speaking and began opening the remaining curtains before moving into the sitting room.

Emily started to slip out of her night things and into the gray woollen dress hurriedly. Margaret returned from the bedroom and remarked evenly, "You probably noticed, Miss Shaw, that madam and I do not get on too well. I mention it because it is hard to ignore when we are thrown together. Of course, we both avoid each other as far as possible, but clashes are inevitable from time to time. She has tried to have me removed from here several times, but the master won't hear of it." The full mouth twisted in satisfaction as she mused contentedly, "He will let her act the mistress in some ways, but not others. . . ."

Aware then of what she had actually given voice to, she colored hotly. "Please excuse me, Miss Shaw. That was most badly phrased. I only meant —"

Emily, well aware of what was meant, nevertheless dismissed lightly.

"Please . . . I had noticed nothing untoward." Her voice sounded strained and she kept her eyes lowered to the small buttons she was fastening.

Margaret threw back the bedclothes so forcefully in her confusion that some of them fell to the floor. She bundled them up hastily, muttering that the chambermaids would soon be at work. She bustled to the door, her large, capable hands digging busily into her pockets. Her eyes lowered, inspecting the contents as though they were of insuperable importance. "Come down to the small dining room for breakfast. It will be served from about now until nine-thirty . . . so when you are ready, come."

Noting caution in Emily's still sleepy eyes, she reassured softly, "Sir Clifford always has his breakfast early. He is gone from the house most days by eight o'clock. Sometimes he is out all day. Certainly he will not be back before noon."

Emily stared at the floor in front of her, realizing by the woman's volunteered information that she had made her avoidance of him too obvious. She smiled without raising her eyes from the carpet, then heard the door click shut softly as the housekeeper left.

A slender finger ran the length of the soft-grained leather. Emily picked up the buffer and applied it gently to the toe of the black shoe.

She let the buffer fall to the table and then collected the soft square of linen. She rubbed the brass buckle, polishing it with one duster-encased finger until it gleamed.

She replaced the shoe in line and picked up the next and repeated the process of cleaning and shining. She mused wryly that versatility was obviously a very important and necessary quality for a good companion. She had already sorted through a box of broken toys for the young master and been told to mend those that were repairable. Emily had managed to salvage none and had merely transferred the bits from the toy box to another, which she had presumed to be for the rubbish.

She had sifted through buttons and ribbons and cleaned mounds of Amanda's less expensive jewelry, which she was sure, judging from the dust it had collected, was never used. On finishing that thankless task, she had been told to thoroughly brush every item of clothing that hung in Amanda's cavernous wardrobe.

The whole morning had passed in such a way. At midday, while Amanda's plump maid waddled off to procure herself and Emily a slice of cold meat and a chunk of bread for what was a rather unappetizing lunch, Amanda and her son had repaired to the dining room for a hot meal.

Emily knew, when presented with the tasks, that all this activity was a deliberate ploy to remind her of her inferior status and servile position in the house. The smile that Amanda had delivered with the shoes made Emily quite sure that every chore was an insult whose effect was being carefully and gratifyingly noted. At one point she had felt affront threaten her temper and composure, but had seen the wisdom in controlling it, knowing that there was nothing she could do to alter her position and that irritating this woman further would simply make her stay at Malvern Hall even more unbearable.

Amanda's dour-faced maid had retired to her room with a crafty chunk of bread and jam and a glass of milk, leaving Emily now alone in a small anteroom that led through to Amanda's bedchamber.

She glanced through the half-open doorway into the soft pink room, noting every flounce and frill of frothy ruched satin and silk, musing that it all looked just as she imagined a french courtesan's boudoir would.

Mrs. Tadworth was rarely to be seen. When not required by Amanda, which appeared to be the norm, she was to be found in her room with her Bible. Her recall from pious learning usually took place when Richard deserved the benefit of her chastisement, the sort that hinted at divine retribution should his behavior not improve forthwith.

Emily examined the scrap of soft white cloth in her hand, noticing the neat hem that bordered it. She was suddenly reminded of the conversation she had held with her mother regarding her dead aunt's contribution in the sewing room while employed as a governess. She lifted the duster, a finger nail skimming the tiny, neat stitches, and she recalled that it was yet possible her tasks could worsen quite horrifically should she be told to sit and hem rags.

She clasped the duster more firmly, considering her fortunes so far and at that thankful moment even beginning to gain satisfaction from the incipient gleam on the black leather.

"What are you doing, Emily?"

She swung round at once, startled by the toneless query.

Clifford was standing just inside the anteroom door. Her alarm at this unexpected intrusion on her solitude and quiet reflection increased as soon as she saw whence it came.

She turned back, rapid-hearted, to her work, aware that he was walking closer. She denied the urge to retort that it seemed quite obvious to her what she was about and merely replied stiffly, "Amanda asked me to clean some shoes."

She polished fiercely at the black leather pump. As he

156

drew close he removed the shoe abruptly from her hand and let it drop carelessly to the table so that it disturbed the neat row she had just formed.

She looked at the discarded shoe for a moment and then reached for it again in a show of defiance.

His hand covered hers, preventing her from lifting it, and she withdrew her fingers quickly.

"Where is Amanda?" he asked, soft yet icy.

Confused and wary of the cold fury she could sense in him, and sure she had done nothing to really merit such annoyance, Emily mumbled, "I do not know." Remembering then that she did, she corrected herself more civilly. "I believe she took Richard for a walk in the gardens."

He turned, looking toward the windows as though he might see her out there, but it was quite clear that from where they stood, all that could be glimpsed outside was sky and wavering treetops.

The bronzed cheek bearing the scar was now presented to her. She stared at it curiously, following the mark from eye to mouth lingeringly as she wondered if it was indeed the wound her father had inflicted all those years ago. So engrossed was she with the thin, pale line that she was unusually slow in removing her gaze when he turned back to her again.

She flushed and looked at the shoes hurriedly, aware that her interest had been noted. In her confusion she absently retrieved the black shoe she had been polishing and made to pick up the duster also.

He took the shoe from her with an exasperated mutter and let it drop to join the others before his arm cleared the table top of all the footwear in one abrupt swing. Emily watched anxiously as the delicate pumps bounced and rolled across the floor.

He turned to her, scanning her face leisurely. "Did you not sleep well?" he asked, concerned. "You look tired."

Emily raised a slightly unsteady hand to her face,

spontaneously touching the blue-mauve shading she knew hollowed her eyes. But she merely replied, "Adequately, thank you."

"What does that mean, Emily?"

Emily looked away from him and at the shoes scattering the floor.

"*I* slept not at all, Emily," he remarked with a quite obvious, amused plea for sympathy, ". . . tossing and turning the night through." He finished with a rueful sigh.

She felt the color sting her cheeks but managed to suggest with sweet sarcasm, "I expect it was indigestion. You probably ate too late and too much."

"No . . . I am sure it had nothing to do with my appetite. . . ." He paused and reflected. "Well, that might have been a rather rash judgment. . . ." he muttered with increased irony.

Aware that her uneasiness grew with every minute that he remained, Emily swung toward the table again. She picked up the cloth and examined the stitching once more. "I am sorry Amanda is not here. Shall I convey a message that you wish to see her?" she offered coolly. "It would prevent you wasting time. I have no idea how long she will be."

"I came to see you, Emily, not her. I guessed you must be here when I could not find you in the main house."

Emily gave no indication that she cared to know his reasons. After a moment he smiled and said, "I thought you might like to come to the Grange this afternoon. You can choose a mount from the stables—"

"I have no wish to see it," she interrupted harshly.

He started to say something else, persuasively, but Emily interrupted him again. "Please . . . I have no wish to see it now."

He watched her for a moment as she stood, head bowed.

"Very well . . . it was just a suggestion; we shall leave it for another day." He walked closer to her and suddenly took her left hand in his, holding it firmly as she made to snatch it away. His free hand went to his pocket and he took out her pearl ring and slipped it onto the third finger. "You forgot this last night."

Emily twisted her hand away quickly and slipped the loose ring off the slender finger. She placed it on the table. "It is no longer mine . . . you know that."

He smiled and admitted softly, "I know I won it, Emily, but it doesn't suit me; and besides, I cannot get it past the knuckle on any finger—it looks quite ridiculous."

He reached for her hand once more, but she put both hands swiftly behind her.

"I realize it would be of no use to you personally," she stated coldly. "Sell it then, or if its value makes it hardly worth the trouble, give it to one of your. . . ." She halted abruptly, the impertinence bothering her less than the vision of something of hers so precious adorning fingers of some notorious courtesan.

She looked wistfully at the small, creamy pearl he was holding between thumb and forefinger. She tried to recall the face of the grandmother who had first owned it but all she could bring to mind was that a small, dumpy woman had once come to dinner and told her not to bolt her food. Emily judged she had probably been about eight or nine at the time and she remembered that shortly after that day the Shaw children had learned that their only surviving grandmama had died of a winter chill.

Clifford looked thoughtfully at Emily before his gaze returned to the ring in his hand. "Will it be better received if I replace it on another finger?" he asked wryly.

Emily was well aware he had slid the ring onto her wedding finger. She simply said tonelessly, her eyes held by the shimmering stone, "I do usually wear it on my right hand . . . and on the middle finger. It is too large for the others."

He held the ring out to her. "Well, put it on, Emily," he urged softly. "There was no proper wager. You never really lost it. I never intended the bet to be taken seriously. It was a joke, nothing more. If you had perchance won, I would not have allowed you home."

She looked up at him searchingly and knew that that, at least, was the truth.

He smiled ruefully at the reproachful look and repeated gently, "It was just a joke . . . no proper wager." He proffered the ring on his open palm. She retrieved it then and slipped it quickly onto the middle finger of her right hand without another word.

He watched her for a moment as she glanced surreptitiously at the pearl ring and polished it lovingly against the material of her skirt. As though just noticing how she was clad in a rough gray woollen dress, he said with a frown, "You look quite awful in that. . . ."

"I am so sorry if my appearance displeases you," she said, pique sharpening her irony. "Unfortunately I have nothing suitable to change into but am, of course, more than willing to remove myself from your sight at once."

His hand closed on her forearm as she made to sweep disdainfully past him.

"I did not say that you displeased me, Emily . . . just the dress. Accordingly I shall arrange for a dressmaker to call as soon as possible. While you are within my sight and within my house, I would prefer you in something more attractive."

"Yes, I do not quite match my splendiferous surroundings—I imagine it must grate dreadfully. But I have no desire for your charity.

"Neither have I any need or liking for something more fashionable. Transparent gauze is most impractical and cold too."

He had smiled during this vitriolic display. He inclined

his head a little toward her. "This is my country house, Emily . . . not a seraglio," he reassured. "I had no intention of dressing you thus." He looked thoughtful and then grimaced in a way that made words completely superfluous. Then he smiled to himself and walked away.

Emily glared at his back. "Amanda has already sympathized with me over my paltry winter wardrobe." she informed him. "She says she is willing to provide me with some of her cast-offs. I am sure I can make do with those the short while I am here."

"Don't be ridiculous, Emily," he chided. "Your shape is nothing like Amanda's." He looked genuinely embarrassed by this gaffe and tempered the unfortunate statement with, "I should imagine."

Emily toyed with the ring on her finger, twisting it back and forth by its shank. She mused acidly that in his sister-in-law's case he need use no speculation at all. "I am sure I can take them in."

"You? Take them in?" he repeated with a constrained laugh. "You would not manage more than one seam before you had ripped the rest apart in a tantrum. By the time they were fit to wear it would be spring and you would have no need of them."

Emily contributed nothing further but merely moved towards the door.

"Come here, Emily," he demanded softly. "You may quit my presence when I dismiss you . . . not before."

She ignored him, continuing toward the door. She was brought up short then by the sound of Richard's lilting tones as the child skipped into the room.

Amanda followed her son. She stared suspiciously and hard-eyed at the two occupants before noticing that the floor was strewn with her best shoes. Her frosty eyes squinted accusingly at Emily.

Clifford's face was set in an expression of bored superciliousness. "Ah, Amanda . . . I have been waiting for you," he drawled.

A coy smile rewarded this pleasing information. He walked closer and as a pastel pump made light contact with his foot, he glanced down and then kicked it savagely and impatiently away.

"Where is your maid, Amanda? And Mrs. Tadworth?"

Amanda was silent.

Clifford suggested with smooth sarcasm, "Perhaps they are resting in their rooms? I suppose it is more than likely and that is why you felt yourself entitled to commandeer Emily to act in their stead. Since they obviously both appear superfluous, I shall dismiss them. I have a great reluctance to pay for things that are not used. I thought I made it quite clear that Emily serves me only. She is here at my sole bidding."

"But Emily offered to help me . . . that is all." Amanda glanced hurriedly and uncertainly sideways at the silent, chestnut-haired girl. "Didn't you, Emily."

At Emily's soft, affirmative response, Clifford's lips slanted. "Amanda, you are a mendacious harlot," he said, cool amusement in his voice, "and my patience and tolerance of having you near me has all but expired. Should I find out that Emily has been working—under any guise, and whatever she may say in your defence— you leave this house the same day."

Amanda's pale complexion whitened. Richard looked up at his mother with wide, tear-filled eyes as he sensed her distress. He sought to cling to one of her hands, but she shook him off.

Emily moved to the child and drew him toward her. Sinking to her knees on the floor, she pulled him onto her lap. One hand held him close and the other caressed his fine, fair hair and the side of his translucent-skinned face. He settled himself on her lap, nestling against her.

"Go to your room and rest," Clifford instructed Emily quietly. "You must be tired and I will expect you to join

162

me for dinner."

"Well aware that he referred to last evening's episode, Emily hesitated before lifting the child away from her lap and rising. Richard clung to her hand, his eyes wide and imploring.

Emily looked at Amanda. The woman managed a weak smile and Emily knew that was permission enough to take the boy with her.

Amanda raised her eyes after Emily had gone and stared at her rigid-faced brother-in-law. She approached him slowly, a determined smile about her mouth, her hips swaying lightly. He stood his ground and she halted close to him and touched a dark-clad arm, tentatively at first, then her hand slipped through, holding him close to her.

"You really are mean to me sometimes. I don't know why I love you so."

He laughed abruptly and moved away from her toward the door.

Amanda's expression became ugly. "I have only to broadcast that this young innocent has been removed from her home and brought here for your pleasure and she is ruined. It would do you no favor either, and it would take more money than I'll warrant you have to buy your way out of such a scandal."

He smiled, but his eyes were perilous and tone likewise. "And I, Amanda, have only to remove you from my house without a penny to your name and set you back in the hovel whence you came, entertaining the dregs of naval life along the docks for a few shillings a time. Never think you will find another wealthy protector to shelter you. For if you cross me—utter one word of which I do not approve—I shall make sure that the rest of your days see you in poverty and probably separated from your son. Richard is a blood relative. I am willing to assume that he is Stephen's son; there is a resemblance and that suffices to protect him. But you are here merely by virtue of the fact that you were once married to my brother and I feel I owe him that much. But my charity depends on your compliance with my desires . . . do I make myself clear?"

She glanced enticingly up at him from beneath lowered lashes. He gave a small, insulting laugh. "No, Amanda . . . personally I can find no further use for you at all."

"But you do want her, don't you." She laughed shrilly. "She hates you; you know that. It shows in every look, every word, every gesture. She is frightened and disgusted by you. Is rape then so much more satisfying for you?"

"I have no idea, Amanda," he replied, "since I have never had to resort to it to get what I wanted — certainly not with you."

She gazed at him unwaveringly, her teeth sinking into her rouged bottom lip to control its enraged quivering, as he left her.

Stringy daisies were laid proudly by Emily's side. She looked up, wiping dark, trailing strands of hair from her face with a muddied hand as she gazed into the pale but brightly smiling young face.

"These are for you and these are for my mama," Richard proclaimed.

Emily looked at the white daisies that were hers and then at the floppy, golden-headed dandelions that the child was saving for his mother.

His small face puckered a little as he frowned. "Mama's flowers are prettier because she is my mama. . . ." He trailed into silence and stared pensively at the two clumps of weeds. He picked up the daisies again and held them and laid the dandelions by Emily's skirt instead. "But I would rather you had the nice yellow ones," he decided.

Emily smiled at him and then murmured, "Well, if you are sure, Richard. Thank you, they are quite lovely."

He inhaled contentedly, holding his breath for a moment with the intensity of his pleasure. He jumped twice on the spot before hopping and skipping back to his basket to recommence filling it with assorted grasses and colorful autumn leaves.

Emily sat back on her heels, watching the joyful child as he crawled about on the damp grass, his breeches filthy already. She smiled at his back, wondering ruefully if she would ever be free of his presence again. But she knew she needed him in her own way as much as he did her. He was welcomingly time-consuming in the interminable days and helped to diminish the loneliness and depression she encountered whilst trying to fill them.

She had been at Malvern Hall now for two months. It was mid-November, yet the days were still quite fine and clear, only the early evenings hinting at the season. She glanced at the pile of withering dandelions; it was not the time of year to see them, though she could remember daisies speckling white into the meadowland near her childhood home right through until Christmas if the climate remained clement.

Her eyes were redrawn to Richard as he gathered russet leaves and stacked them neatly in his basket. She had seen the child every day since that fateful afternoon in Amanda's apartments when her employment as "companion" was brought to an irrevocable close. She had expected rancour from Amanda after the episode but the woman merely seemed to avoid her most of the time or ignore her when they were brought together.

Nevertheless, Amanda was more than willing for Emily to take Richard off her hands and allow her free time to visit friends.

She rarely invited Emily to join her and then only if she was going into the neighboring town to shop.

Having no money of her own to spend, and continually refusing what Clifford offered when he learnt of their prospective trips to the shops, Emily nevertheless enjoyed the welcome break in her monotonous routine.

Clifford asked her constantly to ride with him or visit some notable landmark in the vicinity. He had also tried to persuade her to shop with him in the nearby town. She steadfastly declined every invitation.

She sighed and looked at Richard wistfully. She rarely had a day without him and she knew he was most pleased that she spent so little time away from the house. If she forgot to collect him from the nursery in the morning, he would beg his nanny to bring him to her rooms. He had even on a few occasions, no doubt when refused in this request, made his own way through the lengthy, quiet corridors to find her by himself. Emily knew that the mild affection and sympathy she had felt for the child were growing into much more, and she was unsure whether it was wise to allow herself to become fond of him at all. At the back of her mind always was the caution that should the master of the house realise the comfort she found in Richard, he might deem it time to separate them. She had once or twice noticed him looking thoughtfully at her when she and Richard enjoyed some game or childish joke, and it was enough to sober her good humour at once.

She and Richard would walk in the gardens or play games on the lawns when it was fine. Sometimes, like today, they even helped out with undertaking light chores for the kitchen staff.

Cook needed rosemary for the evening meal, and Emily had gladly offered to procure some. With directions to the herb garden, she and Richard had set out with a gratifying and not easily met sense of purpose.

Emily glanced intently at her basket, wondering if she had enough now for Cook's purpose. "It is Uncle Sir Clifford!" Richard cried, frantically waving.

Clifford and Heath, now acting as groom, were walking toward the stables leading their mounts. Emily stared at the servant in his riding clothes, realizing that the man's versatility must be infinite. He appeared to shadow his master everywhere. He served him at table and must also be his valet as she knew he occupied a room next door to the ones Clifford used.

As Richard's voice piped higher Clifford turned their way. He handed the reins of the horse he lead to Heath and then moved onto the narrow gravel path that wound towards them.

Richard jumped up and rushed along the footway to noisily greet his uncle. He snatched at a tanned hand, swinging it once before letting go and running back to sit close by Emily on the grass.

She mused absently that Clifford's tolerance of the boy seemed to be increasing. One evening, before Richard's bedtime, he had even sat with the boy for nearly two hours trying to explain to him the basics of playing chess. He had not succeeded very well, and Emily had been on the point of suggesting that he instruct him in something more suitable for his age — perhaps dominoes — but she had remained silent and strangely contented by an affinity that seemed to link the three of them that evening.

From the corner of her eye Emily saw the dusty hessian boots approach and then halt quite close by. She gathered together her few things strewn on the grass as though ready to return to the kitchens now.

Clifford stared down at the top of the glossy chestnut head. "Are you trying to put the gardeners out of work now too, Emily?" he suggested drily.

She glanced sideways up at him, knowing that he alluded to the maid and Mrs. Tadworth. Both had been dismissed from his employ the day after he had found her taking charge of their duties. Emily had felt uneasy afterwards, knowing that Amanda had been deprived of her maid and how heavily she relied on having one. But Margaret Phillips had let slip in idle chatter that one of the chambermaids had been drafted onto Amanda's staff because she could dress a good head of hair, and henceforth Emily had not let the matter worry her so much.

Clifford bent abruptly, squatting close to her on his heels. Emily sat back in the grass, away from him, attempting to wipe her dirtied hands on her new skirt. He caught hold of one of her hands and turned it palm up, examining the streaking grime. "What are you doing out here, Emily?" he demanded exasperatedly but with an indulgent smile.

She withdrew her hand quickly and with bad grace. Richard was avidly watching the exchange between them, and Emily smiled at him reassuringly. She lowered her voice and looked away from Clifford as she answered woodenly, "Richard and I were just collecting some herbs for Cook. She is going to use them in the dinner tonight, that is all." She glanced briefly at him before regarding her mucky hands. "Am I confined to my cell today? Is that it?" she inquired with caustic irony and quavering voice. "Am I not allowed beyond the four walls for some reason? Lest I escape, perhaps?" She made to turn away from him further, but his hand went lightly beneath her chin and he forced her to look at him.

He studied her face, his eyes narrowed. "What is the matter?" he asked quietly.

She remained silent for a moment and then the words tumbled out.

"May I go home now?" The query was soft and pleading.

He made no reply and she raised her eyes to his despairingly. "Why are you keeping me here like this . . . for no good reason?"

He laughed mirthlessly, turning to stare out across the fields.

"Why indeed?" he mocked himself savagely.

"May I go home then?"

He shook his head slowly.

"Please, may I. . . ." she whispered huskily as her throat thickened with sorrow.

One of his hands moved to her face immediately, covering her mouth and stifling the rest of the words before sliding to cup her cheek gently. "Why do you want to go, Emily? Have I mistreated you in some way?"

Violet and silver eyes met for an instant as she allowed softly, "No . . . but. . . ."

"No . . . but you think I yet might."

She closed her eyes, feeling them stinging threateningly. "I miss my family. I would like to see them again."

"Are they missing you, Emily? Have you had a reply to your letter yet?"

She winced as the barb wounded. "No . . ." she conceded, humbled, "but I am sure I will soon. The post takes some while, and—"

"I shall arrange for them to visit. Your mother and sister only. They can stay the weekend, if you like."

"No . . . I want to go back to live with them in London, not just see them for two days. I want to see my father as well . . . explain to him that I am . . ." She hesitated, feeling uneasy, then finished lamely, ". . . that I am well."

He gave a harsh, bitter laugh. "God knows I have little enough comfort the night long. But what I do have is the sure knowledge that while you sleep soundly, he is as restless as I; torturing himself until daybreak with imagining the untold scope of my depravity. I won't let you take that from me, Emily. It is little enough to what I had first promised myself."

"But it has been two months," she pleaded softly. "He has suffered enough, has he not? Two months of self-torment." When there was no response, she arose from her heels and onto her knees, so that her face was nearer to his. Bringing herself instinctively closer, she begged with a catch in her voice, "Please. . . ."

His eyes took in the fair face, lingering on a dark smudge by one cheek. His hand came out slowly, sliding into her hair and pulling her head against his shoulder.

After a few restful seconds, calmed by the fingers smoothing her hair, an innate sense told her that persuading him now while they touched might be easier. Pressing herself intuitively closer, she wheedled softly, "please let me go home now."

The hand in her hair slid at once to the back of her head, moving her yet nearer as he responded automatically to her enticement. But she heard the wry laugh, and as he lowered his head to meet hers, he murmured, "No."

The refusal was soft and rueful but quite unflinching. She pulled away and sank back onto her heels at once, chagrined by her shamelessness.

He turned his head away slowly, his mouth distorted, displaying frustration and regret at having been quite so honest quite so soon. After a moment he offered in a controlled tone, "If you are bored during the day you know you can ride. I have asked you several times to join me. We could visit the Grange this afternoon."

She sat silently and he turned back to her with a long sigh that terminated in a rueful laugh and uttered her name in exasperation.

His hand moved to her face as she ignored him still. She tried to shake him off at once, but as her head made an initial sideways jerk, she remembered Richard sitting silently close by. His small, pale-blue eyes were gazing attentively at them both, and Emily forced herself to relax.

Aware of the reason for her lack of resistance, Clifford murmured wryly, as his eyes took in the boy, "I see I should keep the child about me at all times — he seems a useful ally."

He gave her cheek one last light caress and then turned

himself to sit next to her on the grass. He glanced into her shallow basket casually. "Where are they?" he asked mildly.

Emily pointed a grubby finger tersely at the spiky herbs. "Rosemary. The Ancient Greeks swore by rosemary. They thought it had the power to enhance intelligence, if you ate enough of it."

"Thrushcross Grange must have been overrun with the stuff then, Emily," Clifford said. "No doubt you overindulged as a child."

She smiled sweetly, adopting his tone as she countered at once, "Of course, I was most amazed to find any trace of it here at all at Malvern Hall. Obviously it has never previously been much used."

She was cut off abruptly by the weight of his hand at the back of her neck. He shook her lightly, pulling her playfully closer.

Emily fell against him, laughing quite naturally, before glancing up into his face. Most of the humor in the silver eyes had now vanished. They were intense—darkening and, for Emily, infinitely more sinister.

She picked up her drooping dandelions quickly. "Richard picked me some flowers," she informed lightly. "Are they not quite beautiful?"

Clifford's eyes slid slowly away to her gaze. "Indeed they are. Would you like to find me some, Richard?"

The boy nodded importantly and scampered away. Emily watched him as he bent to collect the weeds. "I was quite astonished to see them," she muttered ironically. "I wondered how they dare raise their little golden heads on such an immaculate sward. I was certain all weeds must have been banished from this place long since."

Clifford smiled easily, ignoring the jibes. "That is the way I always remember you as a child . . . sitting on the grass with your hands grubby."

As she blushed he smiled and stared at her more

purposefully. "Nay, rolling on the grass, I should say," he amended. "Usually with your skirt about your waist." His smile strengthened as the blood flooded her face and she started to pick nervously at the spiky rosemary bush close by. He sighed deeply, lamenting, "Such a shame to grow up really. Perhaps we ought now to try and recapture some of our youthful moments."

She swung at him instinctively, the taunt and her intense embarrassment too much to bear. But he had anticipated the blow, and catching hold of the raised arm, he got up, laughing, and jerked her to her feet with him. He brushed the trace of mud from her face with a slow finger, watching the stain disappear before raising his gray eyes to hers. "Just a joke, Emily," he dismissed softly in a tone of voice that made her certain it was nothing of the sort.

She unconsciously wiped muddied fingers against her skirt in her agitation. He watched her trying to clean herself on her new outfit and remarked, "You will soon need another set of clothes."

"I told you not to send that woman to me," she rejoined sharply. "You would insist though; but I never wanted new clothes anyway."

His eyes skimmed her figure lightly. "Well, I did. You look very nice."

She was saved the necessity of thinking of an apt retort by a gleeful Richard returning with his uncle's drooping posy. Clifford received the bunch with a smile and gracious thanks. Richard ran to collect his basket and they all started to return to the house along the gravel path.

Emily looked longingly at the stables as they neared them, tilting her head slightly to see through a half-open door and espy the animals within.

Noticing her interest, Clifford said, "Will you ride with me tomorrow, Emily? You used to have a very nice seat."

He smiled ruefully, keeping his eyes straight ahead.

"My apologies," he corrected himself sternly. "I should say . . . you used to ride extremely well as a child."

Emily muttered frostily, "Well, I have not ridden since we left the countryside. It is more than ten years since. I expect I would now fall straight off. But it would be very nice if you took Richard out on his pony once in a while. He tells me he likes riding it but no one takes him."

"That is his mother's task, not mine," Clifford returned crisply. "Amanda is quite a reasonable horsewoman; there is no reason why she should not spend some time with her own son." He glanced then at the downcast face and smiled in defeat. "Very well . . ." he conceded slowly. "I shall take you both tomorrow."

The wariness in her face must have been apparent, for he added softly, "And nowhere near the Grange if you don't want to see it."

Emily scowled up at him, but he ignored her, turning his head to inspect the horizons with a small smile about his mouth.

They passed the stables and then Emily looked back toward the long, low building. A frisson of excitement shivered through her as she listened to the sound of stamping hooves and smelt the warm, musky scent of the horses. It dislodged pleasant, nostalgic memories and she closed her eyes momentarily, anticipating tomorrow.

Chapter Six

The mare nuzzled warm, moist breath into the palm of Emily's hand as she gently nibbled at another sugary tidbit. The sticky wetness was wiped away absently against her riding skirt as Emily murmured endearments to the animal, her fingers running the length of its bony nose. A pale hand skimmed the velvet tan flanks, then Emily caught hold of the reins and led it toward the slow-flowing stream.

She gazed down into the pellucid ice-gray water, staring until she glimpsed a silver flash in the depths as a fish streaked by. She bent closer, searching for more, but her weight made her sink; her booted feet slid, crumbling away the turf of the sodden bank. Her boots gripped and regripped but she descended slowly and inevitably toward the water until she stepped widely, heaving herself up the grassy bank once more. The night rain had left the ground quite waterlogged, and as she pushed a testing toe into the rich, peaty soil, she noticed, dismayed, the state of her new boots. The dark soil clung quite high at the sides. She endeavored to wipe the soft leather against the grass to remove the worst of it but only managed, in fact, to smear the gritty clods even further along the entire surface of the supple leather.

The mare dipped its head rapidly a couple of times, forcing steaming breath through wide, flaring nostrils. She plodded to the water's edge and her long, graceful neck sank low as she drank from the stream. Emily's hand stretched out, fondling the long, fair mane as she gazed idly about her at the countryside.

She purposely avoided looking at the white house, within a quarter of a mile now, away to the left of her, and she looked instead over the rolling meadowland back the way she had just ridden, seeking the poplar-screened grandeur of Malvern Hall. Her eyes skimmed the upper regions of the building, with windows no more than small silver squares from this distance. She gazed at one in particular, situated in the west wing, where she knew Richard was sleeping, wondering if the child was awake yet.

He would expect her to be there when he finally rose from his afternoon nap; he always did. His disappointment if she failed to return in time normally manifested itself in his nanny being treating to an implacable tantrum.

Emily threw back her head and looked at the sky. The sun was large and fiery but low, dropping to the horizon, and what little warmth it earlier possessed was now gone. She realized the afternoon was passing much too quickly. She knew, too, she should start to return, but could not quite seem to deny herself a lingering half-hour more before returning to Richard and his ceaseless demands on her time.

The mare raised her head slowly from the stream and Emily gazed at the animal fondly, wishing now that she had allowed Clifford to persuade her to ride earlier during her confinement at Malvern Hall. Refusing had been no more than stubbornness and pride, an inability to accept that anything he suggested could be pleasant or well-intentioned.

The day she had allowed him to show her the stables and persuade her to choose a mount had been more than three weeks ago now. She had surprised herself, and him too she guessed, by needing practically no reschooling at all in the basic skills; her childhood learning must have been well ingrained. Clifford had imparted a few tips which she had listened to with a vague superciliousness, but she had been sensible enough to heed them and put them, albeit inconspicuously, into practice.

She looked toward Malvern Hall once more, noticing

the falling orange sun now burning in the top windows of the west wing. She caught at the mare's reins and gave a gentle tug before starting to stroll the river bank with the horse clopping softly and deeply into the soggy turf.

A lightly wooded copse was just ahead, and Emily determined to set it as a landmark, disciplining herself that once reached, it was time to head back toward the Hall and Richard. The first shading oak saplings were regretfully encountered; Emily's head jerked back in alarm as a stridently cawing rook screamed from skeletal branches that veined a pale sky.

She was aware of a more muted disturbance: twigs snapped underfoot. She froze and then swung about, infinitely more apprehensive with this quieter distraction.

A young man stood then from where he had been crouching and examining a basket on the ground. Emily eyed him warily, but noting the caution she felt mirrored in his own eyes, she realized he was as startled by her presence as she was by his. He straightened jerkily and smiled tentatively as he touched his forelock in a respectful manner.

Emily returned a small smile and the man gave another courteous nod. He bent once more, gathering together a fishing rod and the small, rough-woven basket he had been busy with.

Feeling more relaxed, Emily walked a little closer. "I am sorry if I startled you," she ventured pleasantly, feeling disposed to chat.

He merely shook his head dismissively to show that it mattered little. He stood up as she approached and said, with a mild country burr softening the words, "No harm done, miss." His eyes slid to one side of her face as he spoke, watching behind, as though he suspected she might be accompanied. He looked at her uncertainly for a few seconds before admitting, "Actually, I should not be here at all. Neither should you, I think. This is Moore land

176

and as such most certainly out of bounds." He studied her closely as though to judge whence she came. "Are you staying at the Bensons'? Have you lost your way?" he inquired solicitously.

Emily laughed lightly. "Oh, thank you for your concern, but it is quite all right. I am not staying with the squire—in fact I do not know the Bensons at all." She glanced then toward the small, crudely-crafted basket, noticing that it held quite a few inert dun-colored fish. He had apparently been poaching. Aware of her attention, the man flipped the lid over hastily, his eyes vigilant once again, surveying the surrounding countryside carefully.

Emily watched him as he scoured the area thoroughly, judging then that he was probably scarcely older than she herself. His complexion was light but threaded with pink veins and freckled across the bridge of his nose. His hair was light-brown and quite straight, and as he swung his head to the left, still scanning the vicinity for witnesses to his trespass, a lank of fine hair flopped across one eye. Emily glanced at his clothes, noting that they were clean and in good condition but of hard-wearing, workmanlike material. Both the jacket and trousers were of a dark coarse-weave and of serviceable, shapeless style.

He glanced at her uneasily, his green eyes flecked with gold, seeking her reaction. She merely smiled sympathetically and pulled a small face. As though seeing her properly for the first time, he stared more intently, and in a way that stirred a niggling discomfort in Emily. His eyes moved across her features and to her thick dark hair. As she raised her eyes to his once more, a trifle tentatively, he blushed and shuffled on the spot. She realized then, quite surprised, that he was more disconcerted than she in their encounter.

"Are you from around these parts, miss?"

"I am staying at Malvern Hall at the moment."

She wondered how to explain her residence but merely

177

resorted to using the excuse everyone else had been treated to. "I am a temporary companion to Sir Clifford Moore's sister-in-law." She added more firmly, for it was the truth, "Mrs. Moore's previous companion left just recently."

The young man nodded slowly. "I heard that. Dismissed with Jess the maid; Jess is cousin to one of my farm hands." He noted the bewilderment in Emily's face and added quickly, with a tut of self-reproach, "My apologies; I should have introduced myself. I am Jonathon Cross." He extended a roughened hand; Emily placed a muddy glove in his firm grasp and they shook hands.

He swung away then and pointed a finger to the east. "I have a freeholding between Moore and Benson land," he informed clearly, "not a very large farm, but it is mine and I intend staying there," he finished with obvious resolution. He looked away from his acreage and back at Emily. "Are you then Miss Shaw? I had heard from Jess that a Miss Shaw was in residence." He looked at her musingly as he delivered this, and Emily colored a little, wondering what else the garrulous maid had found fit to add to the information to make him look quite so thoughtful.

"Yes, I am Emily Shaw," she admitted softly. "I was sorry that the maid was put off. I hope she has found employment elsewhere."

Jonathan Cross changed weight in the wet turf and then banged his boots into the mud as though to warm the feet within. He looked out across the countryside, stabbing at his toe with the tip of the fishing rod he clasped. "I believe she found work in St. Albans — as a lady's maid in one of the big houses."

"Oh I am glad," she said sincerely. She followed the meandering course of the brook with squinting eyes. "Can you not fish this stream from your own land?"

He laughed with an amount of bitterness. "Unfortunately not. It misses my boundary by about one hundred yards, that is all; and the stretch that is nearest is no use for fishing. I could sit there the day through and never get a bite. Here though, beneath these trees, is another story." He hesitated, then added with quiet dignity, "I very rarely do this. . . " He moved the basket containing the fish indicatively. "Just once in a while when rations get very low and a fish supper will make a nice change from bread and vegetable broth. But I shall be restocking provisions soon and livestock. The chickens are low at the moment — a fox got in and killed the rooster and two of the hens. What with that and the pigs. My sow was sick and transferred the disease to her litter and. . . ." He paused and then looked at the girl standing silently and wide-eyed at his side. He gave a small laugh and apologized with harsh embarrassment, "Pardon me . . . I must be boring you."

He made a slight bow and, touching his forehead deferentially yet again, started to walk away at once.

Emily turned too, leading the mare as she followed him.

She could sense his guilt and discomfort at being caught out by her in petty theft. Drawing level with him again, she asked, "May I walk with you a way? I was just about to return to the Hall. It must be getting quite late now."

"About half-past three, I should judge," he advised as he scanned the empty horizon. Emily looked to the west also. The molten-gold ball had disappeared, leaving no more than a weak yellow glow to colour the insipid winter sky.

They walked on quietly for a few minutes and Emily slanted an indirect glance at the ruddy-complexioned man at her side. He was only a little taller than she herself but broadly built across the shoulders. The hand closest to her, grasping the fishing tackle, was broad and sturdy and seemed unusually thickly covered in freckles and light-colored hair.

Emily looked away and up at the sky and then down to take in the white, angular house they were passing on a diagonal.

"Is that house completely dilapidated inside, do you know?" she inquired.

"I am not too sure. That is Moore land now too. The Windermeres used to live there. I never knew them very well, but they seemed nice enough folk. They seemed happy enough there too. I am not sure how he managed to get them out and so quickly. They had been there some seven years I believe and were by all accounts quite settled. Such a waste of a good house too. It has been empty now this past year or more. Why he should want it is beyond me. . . ." His voice trailed into silence and he looked away from the property deliberately as though to prevent himself saying more.

He gazed instead toward the east and his own strip of land that ran like a small, incomplete barrier between Moore and Benson meadowland. "He has managed to buy practically every acre around these parts in the last year or so," he remarked with more than a hint of sourness. His head lifted. "Not mine though," he muttered quite arrogantly, "not mine." He waited a moment before he continued.

"Not even Sir Clifford Moore is taking what is rightly mine, although he has tried hard enough." He glanced at Emily and added with a nod, "Offered me good prices too . . . I'll say that for him."

"Is it especially valuable land? Is that why he wants it?"

"No. I don't see how it could be. It is just the same as the rest around here. He wants it because he can see it from that palace of his. That is the impression I have anyway. I sense he is the sort of man that desires most things he sets his eyes on." Jonathan looked at Emily keenly, his eyes roving her face before he turned from her determinedly. "Is that a reasonable judgment, do you think? Is that the way he seems to you?" he asked quite harshly.

Emily was silent for a moment, then admitted honestly, "Yes . . . I believe he is, especially where property is concerned. I know he always wanted to own Malvern Hall, even when he was quite young." She felt his green-gold eyes studying her again, speculatively. "I knew him when I was a child," she explained quickly. "We . . . that is, my family, used to live close by here, and of course Malvern Hall always used to belong to the Moores."

In order to preclude any further comment on the subject, she questioned him quickly, "How long have you lived here? I cannot say that I remember your family name from when we lived in Hertfordshire."

He smiled. "My father was only recently a landowner, and I inherited this freehold from him on his death. He was given the acreage by Squire Benson on his retirement. It was a gift after forty-five years' service on Benson land as a gamekeeper. He allowed him it in a strange fit of generosity. Some say he was drunk at the time he made the pledge and afterward wished to withdraw from the undertaking. But he had given my father it in front of others and I suppose he felt obliged to keep face and lose the land. Anyway, he gave it to my father, but by then he was too old and arthritic to do much with it. I have worked it for these past five years and now it is mine. My father was dead within two years of his retirement and I live there now with my sister Lucy. My mother was dead within a month of Lucy's birth—eighteen years ago now." He breathed out with troubled recollection, "Lucy . . . ." He glanced at Emily's puzzlement and laughed. "My sister will be wondering where on earth I have got to," he clarified. "I told her I would be but an hour or so and that was just past midday. She frets when left alone for too long." His pace speeded up a little and Emily increased hers too.

"I am sorry . . . I have made you dawdle," she said anxiously.

He made a slight, chivalrous denial. "Perhaps you would like to visit," he suggested amiably, "if you are in the vicinity. I am sure Lucy would like to see you and perhaps take tea, if you have the time." He halted abruptly and looked embarrassed again as though judging he had presumed too much. Emily started to thank him and say that she would like to have tea, but he spoke over the words awkwardly. "Do you know anything of farming, Miss Shaw?"

"Very little, I'm afraid. I have lived in the city for more than ten years and have forgotten most of what I knew of country life."

He looked at her more purposefully and she knew he was about to impose some inquisition on her childhood in the neighborhood. But his eyes shifted past hers abruptly. Emily noted the wariness re-establish in the greenish eyes before his face set grimly, his lower jaw jutting defiantly.

Jonathan glanced at the basket and fishing rod in his hand, and for a moment Emily was sure he was about to drop them to the ground. She turned slowly to look at what disturbed him so.

Two men on horseback were shadowing their progress, slightly behind as though they could have been there for quite some while. She recognized them immediately. "It is Clifford Moore. Will you be in trouble for fishing on—"

He did not allow her to finish. "Oh, yes," he muttered acridly. "He could have me prosecuted for it, had he a mind to. Even for just trespassing on his land . . . and no doubt he will. I fear we do not like each other and he has now caught me quite red-handed."

Emily noted his head spin rapidly from side to side as though looking for some avenue of escape. Then, as his gaze became constant, she knew that the men were now approaching them. She turned swiftly, watching them descend the slight hillock and ride toward them.

Emily glanced hurriedly back at Jonathon, knowing that she desperately did not want this pleasant young man to be in such trouble just for procuring his dinner for that evening. "Where does your land begin?" she whispered. "Is the boundary close by?"

"I am afraid not," he disappointed her. "It is too far to run. He has most definitely caught me red-handed. It is my own fault, I should not have tarried so. I am usually gone in a flash."

Emily bit her lip. "I am so sorry. It is my fault. But for me you would have been home by now."

She was aware of the snort and stomp of horses being reined in close by. Both she and Jonathon slowed their pace and then halted, unable to ignore the presence of their unwelcome escort further.

Emily swung about slowly, her eyes seeking Clifford's. She looked past him to note that Heath had halted some way off—a respectful distance, she judged sourly, it would be termed.

Clifford's granite stare lit on the man shifting restlessly by her side.

Jonathon harrumphed nervously in his throat and Clifford's mouth tilted a little as he recognized the younger man's disquiet. Silver eyes traveled the length of Jonathon's rough woollen jacket to his clasped hand. The rod and basket jerked against Emily's leg as Jonathon involuntarily acknowledged the interest they were arousing.

"Have you been fishing on my land again, Cross?" he asked with amused tolerance.

Jonathon cleared the hair from his eyes with an abrupt sideways jerk of his head. "Yes, Sir Clifford." The title was emphasized but without any sense of deference and in a tone that was as uneasy as it was brash.

"Catch anything?" he asked interestedly. Aware that this

casualness could veil ill-humor and that it had been encountered before, Emily hastened to interrupt Jonathon's next words. "No . . . no he did not. He . . . we were there barely a half-hour. I had no idea it was not allowed or, of course, we would not have. It was my idea. I used to like fishing. . . ." She faltered and gazed up at him appealingly, knowing that his memory of their angling in this very stream years ago would be no less vivid than her own.

Emily was aware of Jonathon Cross glancing from her to Clifford with increasing surprise and interest.

Emily relieved Jonathon of the rod. She examined it carefully, then said lightly, "We made this from an oak branch and a bit of string." She held it out for inspection and smiled at Clifford. "Quite serviceable, don't you think?"

Clifford nodded slowly, sardonic humor cooling his narrowed silver eyes until they looked icier than the washed winter sky.

"No doubt you wove the basket from water rushes in about ten minutes, Emily. I know your handicraft skills are quite exemplary."

His cutting sarcasm made Emily look away and bite at her lip. She knew then that he was in no way fooled or swayed by her pretended involvement in the crime. "But we meant no harm," she persisted firmly.

Had she believed that Jonathon Cross may, through gallantry, deny her involvement in the poaching, she was mistaken and disappointed. She was acutely conscious of his silence, only the intermittent twitching of the hand that held the basket against her arm making his presence and his agitation known to her.

The white stallion stamped restlessly and Emily noted that Clifford checked the animal with unmerited and unusual savagery. Her eyes were drawn at once to the animal's mouth and a soft gasp of protest escaped her.

She glanced back fearfully at Clifford, knowing then that his fury was in no way tempered or abated by her tale. He stared at her steadily and she looked away and fiddled awkwardly with the string hanging slackly from the make-shift rod, winding it slowly about a slender finger.

"Well, if there is nothing in the basket, Emily, you certainly will not mind me inspecting this feat of manual dexterity."

She walked closer, and gazing up challengingly. proffered the rod. He took it from her with a smile. "I meant the basket, actually, Emily. Get it for me."

She did so and walked back, looking up defiantly once more. He lifted the lid just momentarily and glanced within before letting it fall back almost immediately.

He stared at Emily again with a mingling of hard amusement and threat. She returned the gaze unwaveringly for a few seconds before looking away from the cold eyes.

"I caught them all . . . every one," she said.

"How many?" he asked softly.

She looked down for a moment, trying desperately to recall how many fish she had glimpsed in the basket. Jonathon was now slightly behind her and she made to sway casually sideways. Clifford stooped in the saddle, his hand swiftly arresting her face as she tried to turn for furtive aid.

She gazed up into the gray eyes boldly again. "I cannot now remember. Three or four, I think . . . I did quite well. I gave them to Jonathon for his dinner tonight. For him and his sister to eat. Of course, if you are equally as desperate for a meal on your table this evening, I am sure he might share them with you."

She felt lean fingers tighten on her face, just slightly, and then he released her with a light flick and a smile that made her shiver and back step at once.

Clifford looked across at the silent, immobile young

man. "You should have accepted my offer for the land when I made it. I had heard you have been having a run of bad luck. Accordingingly next time I bid for the freehold, the price will be considerably less."

"I will not sell," Jonathon said, "now or in the future, no matter my circumstances. You will never lay hands on what is mine."

Clifford merely smiled and remarked evenly, "We shall see."

There was a short pause before he said, with complete change of subject and in a cordial tone, "Well, as you seem to have found a kindred spirit at my home, Cross, perhaps you would like to call — with your charming sister, of course — at some time in the near future. I am sure Emily would be pleased to receive you. In fact, I am thinking of holding a social evening quite soon . . . to meet some of my immediate neighbors. I feel it is high time I introduced myself properly. I hope you and your sister will be able to attend." Emily stared at Clifford as though unable to believe that the offer had really been made. Jonathon stuttered some incoherent reply.

"Good," Clifford said. Jonathon turned to Emily and made a slight bow. "Miss Shaw," he murmured courteously, gratitude and amity plain as his gold-green eyes met hers. He turned and nodded stiffly to Clifford also, murmuring his title and name with slightly more civility than previously.

Clifford held out the fishing tackle with a mocking smile. The younger man took it swiftly away.

"Enjoy your meal, Cross," Clifford called after him.

Clifford's gaze moved from Jonathon's figure to Emily's. She hastily neared the docile tan mare, patiently cropping grass still, and made to mount her.

Clifford swung out of the saddle and was with her in two strides. One hand went to the bridle of her horse, preventing it from moving, and the other to her elbow. He jerked her round roughly to face him.

"You lie to me too often lately, Emily, and mostly on others' behalf. Why is that? Do you believe perhaps you can soften my anger?"

Color flooded her face at the quiet reprimand, but it was the hint of truth in the words that confused her most.

"I don't know what you mean. I have been fishing and I did catch those fish," she said.

"If you are telling the truth, why can you not look at me when you say so then?"

She rectified that with a glare.

His eyes lifted reluctantly from her face and to the young man some way off. "He is still trespassing on my land," he informed evenly. "I could yet stop him and find out the truth of it . . . and very easily."

"No," she persuaded softly.

Gray eyes raked her face. "Why not, Emily?" he queried with treacherous gentleness. "What is he to you?"

"I have only just met him today. We only talked and. . . ." She trailed into silence, knowing that there was nothing else to add, because in fact they had done no more than that.

She felt the fingers on her arm grip her as he repeated with a softness that cut, "And . . . ?"

"Fished . . . that is all. We talked and fished. He told me of his farm and his sister while we fished."

"So . . . you have found yourself a friend then, Emily," he observed slowly. "Is that why you never ride with me lately."

"No." The denial was immediate but her gaze lowered beneath the suspicion in the attentive silver eyes. "I like to be on my own . . . I like to ride on my own . . . that is all. I have told you I met him but an hour or so ago. How could I have. . . ?" She paused, knowing that she was becoming agitated. She gave up trying to be defensive and attacked instead. She raised her eyes, inquiring caustically,

"Am I allowed to have a friend? Or am I now to be punished for my unspeakable audacity in enjoying another's company for a short while?"

Clifford's eyes moved across her features, lingering on her mouth. "Oh, friends are allowed, Emily; friends are allowed," he granted, but in a way that made her uneasiness increase.

He released her and moved back to the white stallion. She mounted the mare automatically and, aware that he was waiting for her, nudged the horse forward and rode back to the Hall, with him — and Heath some few yards behind, in total silence.

The cheval glass pivoted on its axis. Emily shrugged her shoulders, turning herself sideways to inspect the back view of the amethyst silk dress. She altered position to examine the other side, noting that the material looked as new: Margaret had certainly made an excellent job of cleaning and pressing it.

Her eyes ascended leisurely and thoughtfully, scanning the creamy-pale skin of her neck and throat, before rising further to gaze critically at her face. She rubbed at her cheeks a little to bring some color to the high, prominent bones, then bit at her lower lip to increase the redness there too.

She knew without any trace of conceit that she looked attractive and that she could always look as beautiful and well-groomed as she did tonight if she would only spend some time on perfecting her appearance instead of merely keeping clean. Her resistance to ever capitalizing on her good looks had been a constant source of disappointment to her mother and a bone of contention between them.

Emily moved away from the mirror as Amanda's imperative summons sounded on her bedroom door.

The blonde woman rustled in and Emily caught her

breath at the sight of her. Any satisfaction she might have felt at her own appearance diminished as she gazed at this epitome of cultivated elegance and composure. Blonde curls were piled high at the back of Amanda's head, a few single ringlets teased free to drape softly against her white nape. Her dress was of a much deeper blue than she customarily chose, and as Emily stared at the usually light eyes, she discovered that they looked almost as vivid as the peacock gown Amanda wore. On closer inspection she noticed the subtle shading across Amanda's lids, smudges of color enhancing and deepening the blue of her eyes; her lips were darkened with rouge.

"You look absolutely stunning, Amanda," Emily breathed.

Amanda smiled as though the compliment was noted but quite unnecessary as she had already drawn the very same conclusion.

Amanda assessed Emily's violet-clad figure lengthily. "You look quite presentable also, Emily," she rejoined begrudgingly. She studied the amethyst dress with a frown. "But have I not seen that gown once or twice before? Have you no other to wear? I am sure if I remember it others must too."

The amethyst silk was smoothed automatically as Emily shook her head. "No, it is the only suitable evening dress I possess. The others are ridiculously out of date. Besides, I am sure my mother and sister will not mind me wearing it yet again. And the Bensons and Dobsons — well, I have never met any of them before, so. . . ."

Amanda stroked the peacock blue taffeta of her own gown with white fingers. "You should have asked Clifford to buy you a new one," she hinted slyly. "You know how very generous he can be."

Emily turned away and walked back to the cheval glass, rearranging a ringlet by her ear. "I had no need to ask," she replied a trifle haughtily. "He offered and I told him

189

that I did not wish for any more new clothes. I have no need for ball gowns, for I socialize little, and very soon I will be going home."

Amanda met Emily's eyes in the glass. "Will you indeed? How do you know?"

Emily shrugged. "I just know, that is all. It must be time soon, I know it must. There is no reason for him to be keeping me here like this. All I do now is annoy him and cost him money in my keep. He will realize that soon, if he does not already, and be as glad to be rid of me as I will be to go home to my family."

Amanda approached slowly with light, whispering steps, the light-spangling dress shimmering about her. She looked at Emily's face in the glass for a moment.

"You are far too pale, Emily; quite wan." She opened a small evening pouch that hung from one shapely arm and took out a small pot. "Just a little dab of this, I think. It will make you less cadaverous. I know Clifford likes his women a little less hauntingly fair — I am sure Jonathon Cross must find a little blush more attractive too."

Emily started to protest, but Amanda dabbed a small amount of rouge on a cheek bone and blended it quickly. Emily watched, transfixed, as the flush brought one side of her face to life.

Amanda repeated the process on the opposite cheek. Emily allowed her to this time, noting, fascinated, that the simple trick had made her adopt some of the poise she had just admired in Amanda.

The color was dabbed evenly across her mouth, and then Amanda stood back to admire her handiwork with a contented smile.

"There . . . your mama will hardly recognize you, so sophisticated do you now look. I am sure that our young farmer will be totally smitten."

Emily stared entranced at the vision of sophistication gazing back at her from the glass. She looked more than her twenty years now, she realized; and she was not entirely displeased. She turned her head from side to side and examined her strangely captivating reflection. Remembering then the hint in Amanda's last words, she demurred hastily, "Jonathon and I are merely friends, nothing more. We meet sometimes during the day and ride or chat when he has a free moment — which is not very often. And his sister seems very . . . pleasant," Emily added rather lamely, none too sure that the description was accurate.

She had met Lucy but twice, and although the pretty, titian-haired girl seemed reasonably amiable, there was a sharp watchfulness about her when Emily and her brother conversed or laughed that had made Emily uneasy. She had attributed this at first to the fact that the young girl might merely be timid and withdrawn and resent her brother — her only relative — being attentive to other females. But this theory had soon been dispelled. Emily had henceforth transferred her friendly attention to a young farm hand, but instead of easing the tension in the small farm kitchen, this had elevated Lucy's sullenness to new heights.

Emily had then realized enough to guess that any male attention diverted from the young lady of the house was likely to cause the sulks.

Lucy would be present tonight, as would Jonathon; she expected the Dobsons and Squire Benson and his family too, with no doubt some others from the neighboring villages. There was a nervous flutter in the pit of her stomach at the prospect of meeting so many new people, but it was the anticipation of seeing her mother and Jane again that really excited her.

Clifford had been true to his word regarding their promised visit. When last in London on business, he had returned within a couple of days with a letter for her that she had immediately recognized as bearing her mother's lofty script.

The letter had conveyed Isabelle's apologies for not having written sooner. She imparted, and with a total lack of compassion, that her father's health was worsening and thus had become more time-consuming for her. But the stress for the delay had been excused by an infinitely more important and pleasing diversion.

A young wealthy earl had been paying avid attention to Jane over the past months and now very serious attentions were intimated. His name was undisclosed, but her mother implied in the letter that all would be revealed when she visited Malvern Hall.

The gentleman in question had a country estate, and Jane and her mother had been kept away from London and other commitments by a stay in Surrey as his guests. The expected outcome of this courtship was not stated, but Emily could tell from the glut of adjectives in her mother's prose that she was excited and no doubt banked on having, at some time in the new year, a countess for a daughter.

Emily had smiled wistfully to herself on reading this. There was much about the exciting state of Jane's future; less about the dreary dismal condition of her father; and even less yet about herself. She had expected a little more than but one line inquiring of her own health and happiness, and this penned in such a way that required no immediate reply . . . if any at all.

This same letter that Clifford had produced from his pocket on arriving home had been accompanied by a gift for herself from him. It was a small volume of verse, translated from Arabic, which he had handed over with a dismissive remark that it was just something he had chanced upon whilst browsing in a shop and thought she might perhaps find a use for. Thus randomly given, it had been deemed by Emily more than superfluous a gift to decline. She had thanked him formally, implying graciously that it certainly pleased her, and then taken it to study in her room. She had soon discovered, and within quite a short time, that the book was of limited edition and, on perusing the quality of the print, paper and leather binding intricately tooled with gold, quite obviously expensive. Its text she had found equally as rich, if disquieting. It was the poignant tale of a young man and girl growing from childhood friendship and devotion to adult love.

As allegories went, she recognized this one well enough. She had thanked Clifford again for the book that evening after dinner, watching him for some sign of mockery. But he had merely smiled thoughtfully, and then again reduced her discomfort and inclination to return it by decrying its significance with his vagueness, as though ignorant of its content.

"I am sure you have not listened to a word I have spoken."

Emily's eyes focused on Amanda's reflection in the mirror. She turned hastily to smile apologetically. "I am sorry . . . what was it you . . . ?"

Amanda laughed slyly. "Who were you dreaming of? That young man from across the fields *is* rather good-looking, in an earthy sort of way, isn't he," she hinted.

Emily merely smiled and turned away. She moved to the window and looked out into the darkness, craning to see round the side of the building towards the wide graveled drive that wound to the great entrance door of Malvern Hall.

"I wonder if Mama and Jane have arrived yet. I have been expecting them since midday. Mama did say in her letter they would arrive for lunch if they could." She swung back into the room with a sigh. "If they are not here soon, they will barely have time to dress for this evening, let alone freshen themselves after the journey. I expect the other guests will be here by seven o'clock. I hope they arrive safely . . . and soon."

Amanda swept to the door. "Well, are you coming down? I really ought to make sure that all those servants who have been darting about the day through have done a thorough job. I am hostess tonight, you know," she added self-importantly.

Emily did know, but she managed to look reasonably impressed and congratulatory. "I will be down in a few moments," she said softly.

Amanda shrugged easily and then closed the door quietly as she left to greet any early arrivals.

Emily turned back to give her appearance a last cursory inspection in the glass, and then she thought of Richard. She wondered if he was yet abed, realizing she should have asked Amanda if her son was asleep. She usually visited the boy at night to wish him pleasant dreams, and she decided to go to him now, before the evening entertainment commenced.

She vacated her room and walked slowly toward the stairs. Her pace slowed as she espied Clifford walking, deep in smiling conversation, with Heath, from the corridor directly opposite hers that led to their rooms in the east wing.

Emily realized that they were going to reach the stairs at approximately the same time. She did not now avoid him quite so rigorously or purposely as she once had, yet she never actively looked for him either.

She was aware that her fear and resentment of him were wearing away—quite worryingly so—because he was providing her with nothing for them to feed on. She had so far had no cause at all to complain of his treatment of her; in fact, she was clothed and fed better than she had ever been in the last ten years. Yet the antagonism remained, although she sensed, also worryingly, that it stemmed from something other than dislike.

Both men had noticed her, and after a further exchange

of words, Heath speeded up toward the stairs, leaving Clifford behind. The smart gold and blue-liveried servant descended the stairs lightly after a brief, courteous nod her way.

Emily watched Heath disappear from sight before looking once more at Clifford. He reached the stairhead first and halted, waiting for her. She drew closer but reluctantly for some reason, wishing he had gone ahead.

She was conscious of his eyes surveying her from head to foot and then settling lingeringly on her face. He remained silent, but his hand went to a pocket of his dark-wine velvet jacket. He produced a handkerchief, which he proceeded to shake open carefully and leisurely.

His other hand moved toward her casually and then jerked her abruptly close. A handkerchief-covered thumb wiped the rouge from her mouth swiftly and none too gently, before she had the sense to try and stop him. She endeavored to twist her face free, but his grip tightened, his hand moving from her elbow to lose itself in her hair as he held her head still and removed the last traces of make-up from her face.

She shook her head savagely, trying to rid herself of him, and some of the carefully prepared ringlets dropped loosely around her face. He released her slowly and stood assessing her for a moment before he concluded, "There . . . you look more like a nice, innocent young lady and less like a Haymarket doxy now. Amanda's idea, I have no doubt."

Emily stood rigidly, shaking with fury and mortification, her fists clenching as though she itched to use them.

He smiled, his eyes roving the trailing dark hair as he advised, "I should go and neaten yourself, Emily. Wash your face and tidy your hair. It is fortunate I saw you before your mother did. No doubt the poor woman would have been completely distraught, wondering what on earth her daughter had been through while under my protection, looking as she did more like a harlot than a lady's companion." He emphasized quietly, "For that is what you are tonight, Emily, in front of our guests." He shook his head. "What would your poor mama think!"

"Probably exactly what she thought when I first came here . . . I doubt she would fret," Emily returned impetuously. Her eyes lowered as the humor in his eyes hardened.

"Well, we both know that any such improper imaginings were quite without foundation, don't we, Emily?" he murmured.

"I shall go back to my room and I shall tidy myself and I shall reapply some of the rouge you have just deemed yourself entitled to deny me," she rejoined haughtily.

"I should not, Emily," he counseled softly, "or I will be forced to remove it once more and probably in front of our guests next time."

She glared at him, seething inside at his arrogance and presumption.

"You do not need it, Emily," he said. "It looks ridiculous because you have no artifice to carry off the deceit." His eyes perused her features slowly, his finger moving away from her face and to the mahogany hair, winding a loose, spiraling curl around the length of it. "You are quite beautiful without any such aid." His hand dropped away from her abruptly. He began to descend the stairs, throwing over his shoulder a remark which had her fleeing back to her room. "By the by . . . your mother and sister have now arrived, so Heath informs me. . . ."

The glass of punch was proffered and Emily received it with a smile. She murmured thanks as Jonathon reseated himself by her side with a similar drink for himself and a charming smile for Jane, who was seated the other side of Emily.

196

Jane returned the greeting shyly and then looked at her vivacious sister. It was hardly the Emily she remembered in London who used to shut herself nightly in her room to read. She eyed the refilled glass of punch in Emily's hand. "Do you like that, Emily?" she asked interestedly. She wrinkled her nose, "It looks most terribly strong."

Emily laughed gaily. "Oh, I assure you it is not. It tastes just like . . ." She took another long sip and savoured consideringly, "Just like a mixture of lemonade and cherry wine," she declared. "Not that I have ever drunk punch before, but I do believe that is a good description of this one." She looked at her sister with a smile.

"Are you happier here now, Emily?" Jane inquired quietly. "You were so set against coming, and yet when I first saw you, when we arrived tonight, I thought you looked quite composed . . . almost content."

Emily said nothing and kept her eyes on her glass. She inclined her head so that her lips touched the rim once more and she sipped. She was drinking far too much of it, but she didn't care.

Jane looked about her, examining the drawing room with slow appreciation. "I do not see how anyone could fail to be happy in such a house as this," she sighed. "And to think you could have been. . . ."

"How is papa? Mama stated in her letter that he is unwell," Emily interrupted stridently, drawing a curious look from Jonathon.

Jane looked taken aback at this brusque query. "I believe he is improving a little," she replied.

"Did he want to come tonight?"

Jane shook her head. "He wants to see you, but not here. He sends you his love, of course, and I have a letter for you in my bag upstairs." She paused and looked around again, the magnificence of the room capturing her interest once again. "I do believe this house is even more distinguished than Sir Clifford's London mansion . . . where we were guests that evening."

Emily turned to look at her sister's pink and white complexion. She held out her glass. "Do taste this, Jane. It is so sweet and I am sure you would like it."

Jane took a dainty sip of the mixture with a delicate screwing of her small nose before she returned the glass.

"You look most beautiful tonight, Emily," Jonathon murmured in a hushed tone and with his customary awkwardness. "I am quite glad now that I allowed you and Lucy to persuade me to come. I did not want to, you know, because of. . . ." he hesitated. "Our host?" Emily offered.

Jonathon smiled. "I have never seen you look quite so lovely," he said.

Emily accepted the compliment with a smile that was almost coquettish before she turned back into the room and scanned the other guests. Her eyes were drawn to the girl in the emerald-green dress — her shy gallant's sister. Lucy was standing with Clifford, listening limpid-eyed as he spoke. Emily wondered sourly how she had ever excused the girl as timid or shy. As she watched, she saw that both Miss Clara Dobson and Miss Stella Benson were vying furiously for his attention as well. They smiled frequently at him and very little at each other. It was enough to make Emily feel ill.

Though she murmured appropriate responses, Emily's mind was not on the trivialities that Jonathon and Jane were discussing.

"I do believe, Jonathon, that your dear sister is looking for you. I expect she is quite famished . . . or perhaps keen to take a turn around the dance floor. Why do you not take her," she suggested in a honeyed tone, "and Jane and I will join you later. We have such a lot of girlish gossip to catch up with."

Jonathon rose a trifle reluctantly, and with a smiling,

neat nod for both Jane and Emily, went to join his sister.

Emily turned to Jane. "Now do tell; what is all this Mama has hinted at in her letter? All this talk of earls and serious intentions?"

Jane blushed. "I . . . I think I am not being over-optimistic in saying that it is quite true, Emily. We have recently been house guests of. . . ." she hesitated coyly.

"Go on," Emily prompted.

"The Earl of Creighton."

Emily's smile faded a little. "The Earl of Creighton?" she said incredulously. "Surely he is older than even sprightly Mr. Rochester––he of the gammy leg who was once so keen for you. I believed from Mama's letter that he was a young man."

Jane looked rather put out. "Well, he is young––for an earl," she countered, "I believe he is not yet forty-five, and without heirs. He is very taken with me too, I think." She colored at the immodesty and asked anxiously "Does that sound very vain, Emily?"

"Of course not. Anyone would be taken with you. Are you fond of him?"

Her sister's color heightened further. She raised her chin. "Yes, I believe I am," she said.

Their tête a tête was cut short by the appearance of Clifford Moore.

"Your mother was just looking for you, Jane," he said.

"Oh, I expect she wants to introduce me to her new friends . . . excuse me, please."

Emily's hand found her empty glass. She offered it to Clifford. "Would you care to refill this for me," she asked sweetly. "I have a frightful thirst this evening."

He took the glass and replaced it on the table. "And I have a most frightful temper this evening," he returned with quiet force.

She raised mock-inquiring brows at him and then gazed past him with glazed eyes "Why . . . I do believe your girlish companions are looking for you," she remarked dulcetly. "They appear to be creeping this way *en masse*. I think perhaps I might like to dance with Jonathon after all."

She made to get up, but his hand gripped her wrist below the screening table, keeping her in her chair.

"And I think, Emily, it is high time this evening that we had a little talk."

"About what?"

"About your behavior. Nice young ladies do not down glasses of alcohol as though their life depended on it. Neither do they flirt quite so openly with the neighbouring farm hands."

"He is a farmer, with his own land and . . . and you are just jealous. . . ." The accusation out, she faltered and stared at him as though uncertain in her tipsy confusion whether she had really given voice to it or just considered doing so.

He gave a small, hard smile. "Very likely," he admitted quietly.

Miss Benson had edged her way toward their table with her friends. Ignoring Emily completely, she smiled at Clifford. "This house, Sir Clifford, how absolutely marvellous it is!"

He thanked them tersely, then made a laconic excuse for their departure to the newly arrived ladies.

"But where are we going, sir?" Emily said loudly, "I believed my chores finished for the day."

"You were mistaken," he returned through his teeth.

Emily obediently allowed Clifford to lead her from the room, his hand firmly on her wrist.

They made their way past the throngs of guests, out into the hallway, and finally into Clifford's study.

He released her as soon as the door was closed, and Emily walked into the room slowly, but breathing rapidly. She neared the fire and then stood and rubbed her hands together to warm them, observing quite cordially, "It really is getting most cold and damp now — I suppose that is because winter has come at last."

She gazed up at the high mantel shelf above the fire and noticing a brandy decanter, her hand stretched up for it automatically.

A tanned hand came from behind, moving the glass bottle and placing it on a ledge yet higher, out of her reach. The hand lowered, touching her shoulder and making to turn her round to face him.

She tensed instinctively, attempting to shrug him off, but he was unyielding. He moved her about slowly and firmly and stood studying her with unsettling steadiness.

An imposing grandfather clock in one corner struck away the timeless moments of the echoing silence, and then Emily looked up into the attentive silver eyes. She asked with genuine concern, "Do you think the war will end soon? I read in the paper that it is generally held that Wellington has the Grande Armée on the run. And West Indian sugar prices have shot up . . . because of the expectation of peace. Did you know that?"

He smiled in exasperated humor before answering solemnly, "Yes, Emily . . . I did know that."

"Yes, you would know that. Of course, you would know that. No doubt this evening's little extravagance is courtesy of the fact."

"I want to announce our betrothal tonight." It was a statement uttered softly but with absolute resolution.

Emily's stomach lurched. "And I want to announce to my mother that I will be returning home with her when she goes tomorrow," she said.

"Well, I am quite sure my announcement would be better received, Emily," he argued gently.

She was silent, knowing well enough the wounding truth of those words.

"Now how are we going to reconcile these two desires,

Emily? It seems to me that the one most definitely precludes the other. You see, I think of Malvern Hall as your home now. I also think I am right in believing that my wishes have precedence," he reasoned softly.

She was aware of the muzz in her head and the throb blurring her vision, but it was the hand, light and warming on her shoulder still, that bothered her the most. Her tongue wetted her top lip. "Why do you want to marry me now?" she asked suspiciously. "You know you do not have to; you know that I will make a most terrible wife."

"I have no idea really, Emily. I agree it seems at times quite absurd."

She glared up at him then, illogically affronted. "Well, I do not find anything humorous in this at all," she declared haughtily.

Lean fingers caressed fragile shoulders beneath the violet silk gown, moving her subtly closer. "Neither do I, Emily. I apologize for being facetious," he murmured with a tender smile.

His fingers caressed the bare skin of her throat, while drawing her so close she could feel the pressure of one hard thigh against her own slender leg and hip. She was conscious of his head nearing hers too, his mouth brushing her cheek gently as it progressed toward her mouth.

She pulled away jerkily and gazed up at him with large, wide violet eyes. "I cannot marry you. I have no wish to every marry anyone. I hate the idea of being tied to someone else . . . belonging to them . . . not only you." She flushed, knowing the mitigation sounded insulting.

"But I would belong as surely to you, Emily," he pointed out.

"No, it is different for a man. Your life would still be your own and I would know little of it, and not be expected to."

He looked penetratingly at her for a moment. "Are you accusing me of adultery, Emily?"

She flushed. "No . . . of course not. I was merely theorizing, in general terms, of the way marriage is. It is not just what has passed between our two families, although when I think of my father. . . ." She bit her lip and tried again. "But I was very sorry to learn of your mother's death in the poorhouse, truly I was, even though I never said so before. I always liked her."

"She liked you too, Emily." He watched her thoughtfully for a moment. "What have you heard of her death there?"

Emily toyed with a pleat in her skirt, creasing it first one way, then the other. "I know she died of an illness, a brain fever, and that it was probably due to the insanitary conditions there and the lack of food. I am truly sorry she perished in such a way. Is that what happened, wasn't it?"

"Yes, Emily . . . it is. Now tell me again why you can't marry me . . . and give me a proper reason this time, Emily."

She shook her head. "I really don't know why. If I were like other young ladies, I would be pleased and grateful. But I seem to dislike most men. I would rather be with my family . . . or alone, perhaps. I find it difficult to explain. . . ." She trailed into a final awkward quiet, and he watched her in her agitation for a moment, his eyes dark and brooding.

He stretched out a hand to her. She withdrew at once.

"Are you frightened of me?" he asked. "Do you still think I might hurt you?"

"I think we ought to go back," she remarked briskly. "Your guests will wonder where you are. Some might want to leave soon and not be able to find you." She walked away from him.

Clifford watched her as she roamed the room aimlessly, her fingers brushing along every available surface as she traveled the perimeters. He walked to the door, but although he knew she was anxious to leave the room, she waited until he opened it before nearing him again.

He half-closed the door as she came within reach and the backs of his fingers caressed her cheek. "No more glasses of punch, Emily. I would hate to see you slide beneath the table in a drunken stupor. I believe it might upset your mother also. Two inebriates in the family would be too much even for her sensibilities."

From Emily there escaped a small, acknowledging smile, and then he opened the door wider.

She walked calmly back to the drawing room with him, and as they entered they moved in different directions. She was aware of a wistful melancholy edging in on her, but her smile returned as she saw her mother look up.

Jonathon accosted her fist, with Lucy clinging to his arm. "Where have you been, Emily? I have been looking for you everywhere."

"Oh, I have just been for a breath of air . . . I felt a little faint."

Aware that she could no longer ignore her mother, who had been contorting her neck and raising and dipping her head in an effort to draw her attention for some minutes past, Emily excused herself.

She smiled at both Mrs. Dobson and Mrs. Benson who, she reflected idly, had not appeared to stir from those precise armchairs the whole night long. She settled into a seat close by her mother.

Isabelle smiled promptingly at her eldest daughter and raised her eyebrows optimistically while Emily merely gazed about the room, Isabelle informed her a trifle flatly, "Your sister has gone to join the dancing. A rather elegant looking young man in a green jacket. . . ."

Emily interrupted quietly, "Yes, I saw them, mama . . . just a minute ago."

Aware of her mother's eyes still staring at her with relentless monotony, Emily turned and returned the gaze.

"How is papa?" she asked evenly.

The query deflected her mother's shrewd imaginings at once. Isabelle shrugged, her pale-blue eyes now more intent on distant horizons as she remarked quietly, "I suppose he is as well as a man that drinks as much as he does can expect to be."

She sighed heavily and fiddled with the ivory handle on her fan, then continued in the same barely audible murmur, "He drinks morning, noon, and night now, Emily." Noting her daughter's distraught, fierce face, she cautioned, "But before you begin to level accusations at our host for bringing him to that miserable condition, remember this: he was practically doing as much before you were ever removed to this house. I admit so freely now because I am past wanting or needing to cover for his dissolution to you or Jane. You have both been made very rudely aware of it, and by his own hand. . . ." She paused reflectively, remembering the game of cards he had lost, and added drily, "No pun intended, of course. But as I was saying, Emily, he has embarrassed both Jane and me recently. We have been utterly mortified by his maudlin self-pity — worse still, in front of influential guests." She sighed with recollected mortification. "I am hoping he will consent to leave us in peace soon . . . go off into the countryside somewhere, ostensibly to convalesce. Perhaps even travel abroad — a sunnier clime might do him some good and —"

"And you too, I take it," Emily finished with quiet bitterness. She stared censoriously at her mother. "It would benefit you and Jane, would it not, if he and his unpleasant habits were as far removed as possible? At least until the earl is bagged."

"Emily, really . . . ."

"Is George aware of any of this?"

"Of course not!" Isabelle breathed out, aghast. "I have written to him, informing him that you are staying with

205

friends. How can I disturb him at such a critical time in his life? The war is at a crucial stage now. If he knew of our plight, he would feel obliged to come home, I know he would. How would that look to his superiors?"

Emily challenged in a hard yet forlorn tone, "It has been a critical time in my life also, Mama. At times, I think you forget that you have three children."

"Yes . . . I own I don't worry as much about you, Emily," Isabelle consented. "You have never needed me as the other two have. You are always quite happily self-sufficient. Even now you have managed very nicely on your own once again." Her eyes raised then to Clifford standing, laughing and at ease, in the center of the room with a group of acquaintances. She sought the dark, smiling face and murmured, "I can do nothing now for you, Emily, except give you advice you refuse to take." She turned to look at Emily then. "You are obdurate and always have been. I have only ever known you to heed one person than yourself." She looked forward purposefully at Clifford again. "He wants you still; you must know that. Even I can tell that, and I have been here but a matter of hours."

Emily swung her head savagely away from Isabelle. A hand moved to smear away the wetness along her lashes. "You have not thought to ask how I fare, Mama," she accused fiercely. "Do you care how I have been treated since I have been here? Did it ever once bother you that I might have suffered all manner of indignity whilst installed in this supposedly dignified house?"

Isabelle looked at her daughter and answered quite honestly, "I own I did, while in London, fret that he might have abused you. But when I saw the way he looks at you, I knew my anxiety was unfounded." She looked her beautiful daughter over from head to foot, then smiled, satisfied. "You are blossoming, Emily, more lovely than ever and most definitely healthy. His company seems to agree with you."

Emily changed the subject. "Where do you expect Papa to obtain enough money to pay for some extended convalescence? Even a stay in the English countryside will be beyond his means."

Isabelle dismissed the obstacle with a brisk laugh. "Oh, I do not expect him to raise the money any more than I expect him to raise any objections when I suggest it to him. I am quite satisfied he will be more than willing to go when I present him with the opportunity."

"But where will the funds come from?"

"Oh, I have my sources, Emily, never fear."

Emily regarded her mother curiously, noting that her color had risen a little as though caught out by someone in a guilty thought.

Emily's eyes scanned Isabelle's flushed face hastily. "You would not . . . could not ask Clifford," Emily protested, horrified.

"And why not?" Isabelle challenged softly, yet with a hard glint sharpening her blue eyes. "I am no longer as proud as I once was. Did you ever consider how we were surviving at home? You knew we were poorly off. Even without what your father owed to Sir Clifford, he was already badly in debt." She paused, then asked drily, "How do you think Jane could have drawn the interest of an earl, had I not been able to clothe her decently and allow her to socialize with people of quality? The first time Sir Clifford was in town, I requested he visit. Fortunately, he had offered me a loan before I had found the gall to broach the subject. Thank Heavens he was gentlemanly enough to save me the humiliation of asking for money."

Emily stared silently at Isabelle's red cheeks.

"Don't look at me that way, Emily," her mother entreated, twisting her hands in her lap.

But Emily had already turned away.

Her eyes rose, reluctantly seeking the man who had, in a matter of months, destroyed her family. Emily felt distress and humiliation heat her eyes, the dark face and pale hair wavering as her vision blurred. She was making to get up and leave when she saw he was coming toward them.

Isabelle's hand covered Emily's on the arm of the chair as she tried to stand up. "You wait for a while," she muttered. He has barely spoken to me the night long. But with you close by, of course, it is a different matter." Isabelle's pale eyes darted from Mrs. Dobson to Mrs. Benson and she smiled to herself. "I know these two ladies have been waiting for a chance to charm their host also. I am sure I might manage to beat them to it."

Clifford bowed and greeted the grouped ladies courteously before requesting the pleasure of sitting with them awhile.

The insistence that he indeed do so issued forth immediately and with gusto from the trio of middle-aged ladies present, but there was not a word from Emily.

Mrs. Dobson enthused vociferously, just beating her like-minded companion to the compliment, "What an absolutely splendid residence this is now, Sir Clifford. Who would have thought it possible to restore it to any such brilliance! Far greater than I ever knew it when your father was alive." She loosened her starched collar from her neck, puffing slightly with embarrassment at having mentioned the taboo topic.

Clifford merely smiled and murmured polite thanks and his pleasure that his house found favor with them.

Mrs. Benson, deeming it her chance to shine, following her fidgeting friend's gaffe, remarked admiringly, "The West Indian sugar trade must indeed be a profitable business to deal in, Sir Clifford, if it allows you to perfect such an exquisite residence as this. And by the look of things, with no expense spared at all."

He smiled blandly. "Indeed it was, Mrs. Benson," he countered smoothly. "But I have no further financial interest in Jamaica now. My business affairs are all diverted into other commercial areas: shipping, warehousing, banking. The West Indian sugar trade, I believe, is now coming to an end and will be superseded by cheaper imports from the East Indies. Pardon me, I did not mean to go on so." He hesitated and then added with soft irony, "I have to tread warily, lest I upset those who feel perhaps I have come by my money misanthropically, having stolen the bread from the mouths of starving wretches."

The mild taunt found its mark. He smiled at Emily directly and with such obvious intimacy that all three matrons present eyed each other with increased speculation.

"If you refer to my attitude, sir, I would be more likely to accuse you of extracting the breath from their mouths," Emily remarked distantly. "I understand that it is not uncommon for slaves to be worked until they drop dead. Accordingly I would never have accused you of erecting a palace out of bread or sugar but rather a mausoleum of blood."

Isabelle closed her eyes in exasperation while the other two ladies gawped.

"I had no slaves, Emily," Clifford said evenly. "Every man, woman and child that has ever worked for me — white or black — has been free and fairly treated."

Emily gazed at him, dislike and disbelief vivid in her face.

Isabelle attempted bravely to break the tense atmosphere. "And how is your young nephew, Sir Clifford?"

"Well, thank you," was the civil reply.

Mrs. Dobson grimaced a peculiar smile in Emily's direction. "Is Mrs. Moore keeping you pleasantly occupied now you are her companion here at Malvern Hall?" she inquired. Without waiting for Emily's reply, she went on. "I should imagine Mrs. Moore is scarcely older than yourself. Do you enjoy having such a lovely young mistress?"

"Not as much as Clifford does," Emily said acidly.

Mrs. Dobson's pink cheeks turned purple.

Clifford, deciding matters had gone far enough, informed Emily curtly that in view of her obvious fatigue, she might retire for the evening.

Emily stared at him unblinkingly, mesmerized by the strange mix of menace and sympathy that darkened the silver of his eyes to jet. At another time she might have resented being dismissed — sent to bed like a wayward child. At the moment, though, she felt only a dull sense of gratitude to be able to make her escape.

After saying goodnight, she crossed the hall and mounted the stairs unhurriedly, the music ebbing and flowing beneath the laughter and conversation, strains of a light march marking her ascent.

Emily entered her room quietly, shutting the door slowly and locking it carefully before moving to the dark, undrawn window. She gazed out into utter blackness in the direction of Thrushcross Grange, closing her eyes as she imagined its clean, white lines. She opened her eyes reluctantly.

She moved to the rosewood bookshelf and selected a book, then retired to the chair by the low, smoldering fire.

Chapter Seven

Emily's head snapped back sharply, away from the book she stared sightlessly at. She had been expecting the noise for so long, anticipated it a thousand times yet it now so startled her that blood pounded heavily and deafeningly in her ears and she could not be sure if she had really heard anything at all.

Her fingers whitened on the book in her lap. She sank back into the chair with silent, heart-stopping stealth, pushing herself securely into the cushions.

She looked quickly at the fire as some of the coals gently shattered and white-grey embers flaked into the grate. At the sharp double rap on the door the book fell from her lap to the floor with a loud thud.

Well, Emily thought, pretending she was asleep was now out of the question.

"Who is it?" she called.

"Clifford. Open the door." The command was quiet and yet absolute.

Her hand rose clumsily to the shelf by the door fumbling for her key. She inserted it in the lock, turning it with inflexible fingers.

She moved at once away and to the wall as the door opened.

He closed the door, relocking it before removing the key. His eyes rose to look at her standing just to one side of him, backed against the wall.

Although she realized it hardly mattered now, she asked in a hoarse murmur, "Haven't you got a key?"

"Yes, I do have a key. But I wouldn't use it unless I had

211

to," he replied, amused.

He placed Emily's key onto a chest of drawers close by her bed.

"What do you want?" she asked awkwardly.

He walked slowly toward her, halting barely a few paces away, and she flattened herself further against the wall at her back.

Emily's eyes were silently appealing as they met the mercurial ones of the man opposite. But his ruthlessness was as glaring now as it had been earlier that evening when he had dismissed her to her room.

"What time is it?" she asked.

"Half past one."

"Has everyone left now?"

"Yes . . . all that were leaving have gone . . . at last."

His eyes lowered to her dress, sliding the length of her slender form with blatant appreciation.

"I would have been here sooner . . . I see you were expecting me," he remarked with a hard smile.

"You're wrong. I wasn't expecting you at all."

"I suppose you always retire for the night fully clothed then, Emily?" he asked relentlessly.

"I was reading . . ." she faltered. "I was about to go to bed when you disturbed me."

The cruel smile strengthened contentedly. "It seems my timing was perfect, then."

Frozen, wide violet eyes slid away from him and to the dark, sombre window that could be glimpsed past his shoulder. Her eyes were held by the ebony glass. "My mother is asleep upstairs . . . and Jane," she whispered.

Her eyes shifted back to his then, entreaty emanating from her so forcefully that it was almost tangible. But his mouth only twisted mercilessly. "True . . . but they don't appeal to me in the same way you do, Emily."

Thick, dark lashes shielded her eyes as she blinked slowly. "I could scream," she threatened shakily,

". . . wake the whole household. There are other guest staying overnight too."

Her eyes darted back to his quickly and keenly, but she could tell that he was wholly unperturbed.

"But not on this floor. Scream away. I am sure there must be many among them who are aware of your unsubordination and are expecting it . . . if they are not already deep in some wine-soaked slumber. Such insolence never goes unpunished, and this is my house and here I am law. It is for me to choose what form retribution takes and for others to wonder. If they do hear, it will provide them with little more than a week's worth of speculation and gossip."

He stared unflinchingly at her pale, tense face and wide, glossy eyes, where tears were dammed behind shock and fear. He smiled, but his eyes were as cold and dark as the undrawn window behind him. "There are no knights in shining armour, Emily," he mocked. "Well . . . perhaps just one—but he left some hours ago with his sister."

Emily swallowed. "Please . . . you cannot . . . not with my mother in the house . . . please. . . ."

He moved closer, one hand snaking out to hold her face abruptly. His fingers slid soothingly against her jaw. "Why should I not, Emily? Is it not now my turn to mock and humiliate? You have insulted and provoked me beyond patience more times than I care to recall over the past months, yet I have borne it very well I think and never once retaliated. In private, perhaps I will choose to tolerate it, but not when you do so brazenly and in company. Not when you have made it this obvious and this public."

"I alluded to nothing that was not true," Emily said defensively.

"It is no longer true. It has not been true for quite some time."

"Please leave me alone. I am sure Amanda would be

prepared to accommodate you tonight, if your lust is ungovernable, and much better than I ever could." She paused before adding with bitter humility, "I know I behaved very badly this evening and am neither proud nor pleased of myself. But had you never treated me as though I were a trollop perhaps I would never have begun to act like one."

She attempted to prise the long hard fingers from her wrist but could loosen not one. He caught hold of both small elusive hands that strove so desperately to evade him. He jerked her away from the wall now too, back-stepping into the room and moving her with him.

"When was this, Emily? Come, tell me . . . when did I treat you like a whore?" he asked with deliberately exaggerated bewilderment. "I am sure I should have remembered . . . for there was I, thinking all the while that it was merely a dream I have."

Her eyes flicked past him to the bed, noticing that it was now no more than a few paces away, and she fought to escape him in earnest.

His hands released hers abruptly and moved to her arms, sliding up the length of them caressingly, his thumbs brushing silken skin with slow, circular strokes. He jerked her fast against him, one hand moving to the small buttons that fastened the back of her amethyst silk dress while the other restrained her, keeping her close.

She was aware of the thin straps of material on her shoulders loosening and she stopped fighting him and struggled instead to keep herself dressed.

His hands were at her shoulders now, easing beneath the silk, and as she felt the gown sliding inexorably away from her, she beseeched brokenly, "Please, Clifford. . . ." He lifted her past the gown that cluttered her feet as he started to move backwards again. His face lowered, meeting her bare shoulder, warm breath fanning her chilled skin and making her shiver uncontrollably.

"Please, Clifford . . . what?" he said tauntingly. His mouth found the sensitive crease between neck and shoulder, worrying tantalizingly until a light moan escaped her and her head swayed to rest against his. He smiled into her neck, satisfied. "Please Clifford, don't leave me?" he suggested softly. "I'm sure you could say that, Emily . . . you did once before. Say that and perhaps I might be gentler than you deserve."

A sob tightened and then broke painfully in her throat. Her fists went against his shoulders, but she made no further futile attempts to free herself. "I am sorry, truly," she choked out humbly. "I am sorry for insulting you. I'm sorry for everything that's happened to you."

She raised her eyes. She ceased straining against him or pleading as she watched the wine velvet jacket drop to the floor. The free hand that was not restricting her and moving her with him went at once to his shirt; deft, dark fingers unfastened the buttons swiftly before one arm shook sharply and the shirt was half removed too.

The smooth, dark skin of his shoulder pressed against her face as he shifted position, his naked side moving closer to hold her as he removed the clothing from his other arm with abrupt impatience.

She knew at that moment that he had no intention of letting her go, however much she lowered herself and begged him to do so.

He pulled her toward the bed, his hands at the front fastening of her thin camisole, and this time she went with him silently and without resistance.

The camisole loosened and her hands flew spontaneously to clutch it together over her breasts. A vestige of cold reason emerged from her terror. "May I go home tomorrow?" she asked.

She looked up only to see intemperate desire and raw excitement darkening his eyes.

He remained silent.

She tried to recall how it was that she had managed to bring him to such tenderness earlier that evening when he had mentioned their betrothal. He had wanted her then — and she had known it — but with a gentleness she now would have deemed this brutal, half-naked stranger incapable of ever achieving.

Perhaps if she pretended to want him. She raised her head, swaying toward him intuitively.

The lure worked at once. His mouth covered hers with immediate bruising sensuality and, although she steeled against it, she flinched, jerking in his hold before tensing to rigid acquiescence.

His mouth relinquished hers abruptly, sliding to rest against her hair. He cursed himself for his impatience. When he turned back to her, soft, warm lips caressed against the inflexible solidity of her cold mouth. At his sudden gentleness, a breath caught in her throat. One of his hands skimmed the naked hollows of her throat, the backs of his fingers lightly brushing the swell of her breasts above the camisole top that she still clutched at so tightly. They stroked to her face, long, lean fingers spanning and maneuvering her jaw slowly until her mouth parted a little into the leisurely kiss.

She was half-aware of traveling backward again until her legs touched the bed.

Emily shuddered, sighing relief and contentment into the enthralling kiss that subdued and seduced. Soothing, reassuring fingers smoothed her face and hair and the last of her loose curls dropped, with a little help, to sway against her shoulders.

In naive gratitude for what she was sure was now forbearance, she pressed closer, knowing that if only she could contain the extent of his lust and revenge to this she could bear it, and quite easily.

She squirmed in his grip a little as his weight bent her

backwards, twisting herself sideways to the bed so that she felt less vulnerable. But her arms raised, touching his shoulders as though offering some solace for her objection.

She tumbled backward suddenly, cushioned by the yielding covers on the bed. Before she could control her breathing enough to scramble upright, she felt his weight check and obstruct her. His mouth was on hers again, and at her throat and neck, seducing relentlessly until all the advantage she was sure she had gained was lost in an ephemeral, enraptured moment. One of his hands lowered, the palm just grazing across her breasts in a subtle, tormenting caress that had her curving instinctively toward him even as she strove to push him away.

At that moment she realized she had lost her camisole and the rest of her undergarments without even being aware of what had become of them.

One of his hands removed to himself and she realized that he was undressing.

He moved away from her and sat on the edge of the bed. One foot rose casually to rest on the opposite knee as he started to take off his boots. Emily heard the black hessian boots thud to the floor before he stood up, his hand lowering immediately to his trouser buttons.

She grasped hurriedly at the edge of the quilt and pulled it to cover her nakedness. She raised up onto her knees and edged towards the side of the bed away from him. He was sitting again on the side nearest the door, and her eyes were drawn to the key, visible on the chest of drawers quite close by him.

He turned to look at her and she gripped the violet cover to her more tightly. She glanced swiftly away from the mocking key and at the wide space of bed that gave her relative safety at the moment.

"Emily. . . ." He murmured her name softly and held out a hand to her, and she knew then that he was offering her what she had wanted so desperately before: a little affection and an amount of gentleness that would only be exchanged for her submission.

She knew too she must salvage something for herself from this violation; that he should not completely destroy her pride and dignity and win outright. She looked at him with wary, frightened eyes but bargained coolly, "You must allow me to go home then tomorrow."

"You are not in a position to make demands," he corrected quietly and clearly.

She moistened her lips. "You must . . . it is not fair otherwise. Please . . . if not for me now, then for how you liked me once." Hot, sharp tears stung her eyes as she coaxed softly. "I know you did . . . everyone tells me so. Mama and Nanny Greg too. . . ." She hesitated and then, in a desperate bid to stall for time she added, "I forgot to ask Mama how Nanny is! I hope she is well and—"

The words were cut off abruptly and she recoiled hastily out of his reach as he made a sudden, sly lunge for her. She got off the other side of the bed carefully and stood shaking and with the cover grasped about her more securely still.

His outstretched hand dropped to the bed to rest. His head inclined a little and he gave a small, frustrated laugh. "Emily!" he threatened exasperatedly.

He looked up at her then, the inexorable need hardening the amusement, and she could tell that his patience was now ended. He raised one hand beckoning authoritatively. "Come here," he demanded softly, yet with implacable determination.

She shook her head, barely able to move it in her trepidation, but some of the tousled hair stuck to her face with the slight movement. She repeated entreatingly, "Say that I may go tomorrow. You need not promise, for I know that you will not go back on your word. And I will not go back on mine. I will lie down and not move until you are finished — I swear that in case you do not believe me as I do you."

His eyes closed slowly at her words and he murmured her name on a soft, sadly frustrated breath. When he looked at her again, she realized that she had somehow, finally, managed to move him. She gazed at him unwaveringly, her teeth worrying first at her top and then her bottom lip as she watched him without blinking, trying to recall how she had achieved it. For she could see now that some inner conflict was making him grimace his exasperation and turmoil at the ceiling. One of his hands went suddenly to his face, the long fingers sliding and pressing to the bridge of his nose as his eyes closed once more.

She frowned doubtfully, the grip on the violet cover loosening a little as she waited nervously, barely breathing.

He was across the bed and with her so abruptly and swiftly that the movement was almost inperceptible and gave her no chance even to think to evade him. His hands stilled the violently turning head, tilting it back so that their eyes merged and strained. His tore away, roving her face lingeringly for a moment before once more seeking the wide, dark-violet eyes that pleaded and reproached and attempted to freeze his desire. But the need was ten years old and too long repressed and now inevitable.

His thumbs slid against the satin skin of her face, tightening a little as the words formed but stuck in his throat as he realized how false it would sound at such a time.

"I love you, Emily!"

The soft, vehement declaration was out. But he watched mortification lower her eyes and heat her face and knew that, for her, the admission was calculated; no more than a blatant, selfish lie, and that he could not have insulted her more. His mouth touched hers with tender, pleading persuasion, the same artful skill wooing and subduing her now that had before. Sensing capitulation threatening already, her hands rejected him furiously and in panic. He took them behind her back, moving away from her a little so that the cover held between them dropped to the floor. He eased her once more closer, sliding her nudity against his as they turned so she was backed against the bed. As they lowered to it this time she knew there was no further escape.

The tears she had been unable to weep previously in her defense now welled up as she realized her ultimate defeat. The wetness slid between their faces and she tasted the salt and sensed it burning her bruised mouth.

His hands and mouth lowered, away from her face, commencing a lingering, gentle exploration of her body. They stroked seductively until her breathing became as erratic as her tolerance of it. She lay quiet and gasping shallowly at one moment and protesting silently yet with vicious force the next.

Iced fire kindled, burning and chilling her simultaneously. It pervaded deep within; an untasted, aching core of heat and sensations making her breathless submission start to outlast the bouts of savage resistance.

One of his hands slid slowly to her hip, caressing as it descended covertly to her thigh. But the first subtle touch was enough to make her fold up against him in outrage, her head twisting away and her hands flailing at him in objection.

His hands raised, returning to her face to soothe and reassure and keep her mouth available. He forced her back into the bed with draining, treacherous kisses; his enticing magic captivating, keeping her tacitly acquiescent to his persistence. His fingers tantalized and teased with infinite patience and artifice, sliding leisurely and lengthily, well into the night.

The heat became unbearable, like summer sun hot on her face and body, and she writhed against the sweet torment. Her hands lifted finally, away from the sheets and to her face, as though to shield the light from her eyes. But they found the golden head instead and slid into thick blond hair. Her arms wound about his neck, crossing at the back of his head. She clung fast, raising herself against him, holding him tightly to the throb expanding and chafing her.

And then she told him not to leave her.

His mouth found hers again, and this time it parted readily, following every moment of his greedily, even as ultimate pain made her gasp. But it came so lingeringly and was so needed that it evoked no more than a low moaning and sighing. Her panting heightened as each abrasive movement contracted her slowly, tighter and tighter, until the tension spun off spiraling away from her too rapidly and yet in slowly sapping waves that made her jackknife against him again for support.

His head dropped forward, resting against hers and she felt a warm, hissing exhalation closer to her ear as his movement lessened and he relaxed against her.

Emily's breathing became slower, more even. Her eyelids flicked up and she gazed past the pale hair closer to her face and at the strange, shadowy patterning on the ceiling. She stared at it unblinkingly, sensing the warmth and lassitude receding already. She closed her eyes tight again, trying to cling to it and hide as glaring truth and chilling reason crept pitilessly and belatedly upon her. She convulsed lightly as she swallowed, attempting to prevent the thickness forming in her throat.

He stirred, but then rested back against her, only his hands moving, losing themselves in her soft, tangled mass of hair. He held her close, turning his head to nestle against hers.

Emily swallowed jerkily and opened her eyes. She watched disjointed, spidery movements on the ceiling, absorbed as all her life and family seemed to form, floating and flowing in fluid, spectral shapes.

She was sure George stood there, handsome in his hussar's uniform, with a French girl on each arm. Her father wanted one too, but George offered him a decanter instead and he smiled and seemed content. There was a brick fireplace in a room that she dimly recognized and a small, dark-haired woman she thought she knew was sweeping out the grate. She turned toward Emily then, and Emily wanted to smile and greet her, sure she was benevolent, but the empty eye sockets and fleshless bones gaped horrifyingly. She twisted her head savagely away, crying out, terrified. But the vision was oddly fascinating. Her head swung back and she watched her mother play the piano and sing quite sweetly, yet with no noise, by an open window while a small, frail girl shuffled dead leaves neatly in a folder. Her delusion drifted on: a fair-haired youth stood holding the bridle of a jet-black stallion. He turned slowly and laughed at her.

Emily moaned in anguish, her head boring into the bed as she denied the scene, but it merged, colliding and spinning about, mocking her in colorful fragments. She screwed her eyes tightly and then opened them, startled, aware that a man had spoken her name. She stared up searchingly at the ceiling once more, but the pictures had gone.

She wondered quite sanely if perhaps delirium threatened simply because she knew her mother was in a room directly above and had guessed what went on below.

Her eyes roved as though she might indeed see the woman asleep up there if she explored carefully enough, perhaps even peering down at her. She raised a hand to her mouth to stifle a crazed laugh as she realized that if her mother could see her at this precise moment, she would, of course, approve. For Emily was now being sensible . . . sensible as she ought. Her hand spread to cover her face fully. Her mother would be most grateful too for this discipline . . . this punishing degradation . . . for it no doubt left her entitled to ask for yet more money before she left for home tomorrow. More money for more clothes, for Jane needed something beguiling to ensnare an earl; perhaps nightdresses in some flimsy, alluring style. Her mother could dress Jane in them and tempt him but say it was for her trousseau — never again to be worn until after the wedding.

Another hysterical laugh lurched out, throwing her against Clifford. He was back from her a little now, watching her with dark, unwavering eyes. But Emily sheltered in her dream, with her family, until the culmination of her visions became too much for her ravaged, saddened mind to bear. She raised her other hand, away from the dark shoulder she quite unintentionally tore at with her nails, and she covered her face with that hand too and she laughed and laughed.

She laughed until tears soaked her face and ran into her hair and ears and onto the fingers that attempted to shield her derangement. She laughed until she wept with such tearing force that she was unaware that he moved away from her and went to sit on the edge of the bed. His head turned away to the wall, remaining so for an age, before it dropped low, held in hands that pressed at his eyelids.

Half-aware of her loneliness now, she turned sideways toward the dark window, away from him. One hand reached for the pillow slightly above her head, drawing it close, and she cuddled it to her in a way she had often done as a child when frightened at night. Her knees moved up and her head down to meet them, burying in the clean white softness of the pillow, and she cried until exhaustion left her tearless and spent and finally so apathetic that she was unaware and uncaring that he had left the room.

Margaret looked at Emily anxiously, suggesting, "Shall I find you some laudanum? That might help."

Emily turned away from the window slowly and attempted to smile. "There is really no need. It is just a headache—a chill I expect. The weather is so cold now; I have taken a chill while riding."

Emily looked at Margaret Phillips more penetratingly, wondering how much the woman had guessed. Perhaps she suspected that what ailed her was no more than slight physical malaise.

Margaret had cleared the bed of sheets that morning but said nothing, although Emily knew the bloodstains were obvious. The housekeeper had busied about at her tasks, removing the soiled linen herself instead of allowing the chambermaid the chore.

"Your mother and sister will be leaving soon," Margaret advised softly. "You will want to see them off, won't you?"

Emily nodded slowly. "Are they downstairs now?" Remembering then the other guests, and sure she could not face anyone else, she asked, alarmed, "Have all the other overnight guests left now?"

"Yes; most left quite early. I was expecting some to stay, I must admit . . . and for the whole weekend. I had bought joints of meat and fowl . . . masses of vegetables especially for them." Margaret shrugged. "Heaven only knows what he said to them to get them out so early. Yet he did. I heard him say to Frank Dobson before the man had finished breakfast. . . ."

Emily turned away and approached the window. "Are my mother and sister ready to leave now?" she asked gruffly.

"Yes. They are just taking some tea in the small salon before setting off. It is well past midday. If they do not leave soon, they will never reach London before nightfall."

"I shall come down now then, Margaret."

The woman nodded that she thought it was best. "And when Sir Clifford is back, young lady, I shall ask him to send for the doctor," she advised briskly. "In all the months you have been here I have never seen you look so peaky. We don't want you confined to bed now, do we?"

"There is no need . . . I have already said . . . it is nothing." The rebuff was grated out immediately.

Margaret stared, clearly hurt that her solicitude had engendered such hostility. She murmured some brittle, short apology and made to leave the room.

"I am so sorry, Margaret. . . ." Emily breathed the words quickly and faintly, as the extra, unexpected stress brought spontaneous, blinding tears to her eyes once more that morning. She stifled the uncontrollable sob that choked out with them with the back of a swiftly raised hand.

Margaret was comforting her again in a second; soothing and placating with an arm around the slight, quivering shoulders.

"There . . . not to upset yourself, miss. We all get these bouts of low spirits." She glanced meaningfully at the stripped bed. "It is a monthly curse, all right, no doubt of that," she muttered sympathetically.

Emily smeared the wet from her eyes and shrugged the woman away, but gently. "Ask my mother to wait for just a little while longer; I will be down shortly," she murmured.

She was aware of Margaret nodding and smiling kindly, and then the door closed. Emily went wearily to study her face in the mirror. She knew she could manage to disguise a little of the pallor in her complexion, but it was her eyes that betrayed her. They were red-rimmed and swollen from crying and lack of sleep, and the bruising below them was livid.

She moved to the jug by her bedside and, dipping the cloth back into the icy water yet again that morning, she once more held the cool salve to her aching eyes.

Isabelle Shaw rose at the sight of her eldest daughter. "Ah, there you are at last, Emily," she announced, relieved. "Jane and I really have to be on the way and very shortly if we are to reach London before—"

"May I come home with you today, Mama?" Emily interrupted quietly as she walked closer.

"You know you cannot, Emily. How can you come home with us now? You are not ready . . . packed . . . anything," her mother dismissed tersely.

"I need nothing, Mama. The rest of my things can be sent on."

Isabelle bent and retrieved her hat and gloves and began donning them nervously. She turned quickly to Jane and urged stridently, "Now do come along, Jane. We have to be ready for callers this evening. You know the earl realizes you will be home later today. He might visit; it would not do to disappoint him."

Jane was lightly on her feet in a trice, with sweetly delivered apologies. Both Isabelle and Jane Shaw started towards the door of the small salon.

Emily followed a pace or two behind as they crossed the large entrance hallway and made for the great double doors which were slightly ajar.

They descended the narrow tiers of stone steps to the graveled, circular drive. Isabelle, noting the coach-and-four waiting, with groom and driver ready, touched light gloved hands to her elder daughter's shoulders and skimmed either side of her waxen face in a brief kiss of farewell.

"Let me come with you . . . please, Mama." Emily's voice cracked on a low, plaintive note.

Isabelle's hands tightened on her daughter's arms and then she drew back to look at her. "I cannot, Emily." Isabelle sighed and a gloved finger touched one of Emily's cold, white cheeks. "Sir Clifford made it very clear this morning, when he took his leave of Jane and me, that he expects you still to be here after we return to London," she said quietly. "Perhaps not quite so bluntly as that. In his own subtle way: he told me that we were welcome to visit you here again and quite soon. The signs are there, Emily, and I cannot ignore them, you know that."

"I care not what he says or threatens, Mama. I have to go with you now . . . today . . . please."

Isabelle's hands dropped away. "We could yet be turned out onto the street, Emily," she said. "And he will do it if we attempt to cross him. He does not bluff . . . you know that well enough."

She looked over her daughter shrewdly once more, absorbing the controlled distress and ashen, spoiled face, but her eyes hardened. "If you have been insubordinate the whole time you have been here, no wonder you are not happy."

Emily remained silent.

Isabelle turned away and to Jane. The girl came closer at once, abandoning the stamping, shifting horses that threw steaming breath after her as she ceased petting them.

She kissed Emily's bloodless cheeks lightly. She pulled back a little as the sisterly response was not as enthusiastic as she had expected and looked at Emily with frowning perplexity.

"What is the matter with you, Emily? You are so wan today. Are you sickening for something, do you think?"

Her mother cut in quickly, steering Jane by the arm towards the coach, "She is overtired — all the excitement of yesterday evening and a restless night."

Thread veins in her pink cheeks dilated, her complexion

227

flushed with a vengeance; and for a moment she avoided both daughters' eyes carefully.

Isabelle urged Jane to mount the coach at once before turning back one last time to Emily.

"Please, Mama . . . I beg you to take me home."

Isabelle looked at the gravel underfoot and the toe of a calfskin boot ground savagely into it. "No," she insisted remorselessly. She gazed at Emily, unsmiling. "I expect very shortly to hear some news from the earl. With you in evidence, of course, it might well never come. You would be an unwelcome distraction at this time, Emily. Your beauty always outshines Jane, you know that very well. Should the earl see you, all would be lost, for his interest is sure to deviate. Naturally, you would reject him. He would then go elsewhere—to pastures new and more welcoming—and Jane would be utterly forgotten. It wold just not be fair, you see."

"If his affection is so fickle, then he does not deserve Jane," Emily remarked quietly and contemptuously.

"All men's affection is fickle, Emily," Isabelle rasped with a sour laugh. "The trick is to retain it just long enough to get them to formalize things. After that, sometimes it is as well to encourage their faithlessness. Men can be quite brutishly unpleasant in their habits." She looked at her silent, subdued daughter and added softly, "I fear I need not stress that fact to you today."

She turned to mount the coach and then hesitated and waved away the groom who had sprung close immediately to assist. She glanced back at her elder daughter and informed with a small, wry smile, "If it is any consolation, Emily, he looks more wretched than you do this morning, and it sits badly upon him. Arrogance suits him better." Isabelle gave a short laugh. "Do you remember, Emily . . . the day I told you you could hurt him?"

Emily said nothing. She stared sightlessly into the distance.

Her mother gave another crisp laugh. "You are definitely winning, Emily. What I would like to know, my girl, is how you manage it with that attitude." Isabelle settled into the cushioned seat and raised a gloved hand in salute. The footman shut the door firmly and the coach was swaying away in a moment.

Emily heard Jane call out sweet farewells to her, but she turned away at once and walked back to the steps.

Unwilling to reenter the house just yet, she wandered toward the gardens. She roamed for an hour or so in the chilling air, cold and with gnawing hunger pangs, yet unable to go in until her constant vigilance alerted her to two approaching horsemen; then she returned immediately to the house and her room.

"The master requests your company at dinner, miss."

Emily did not look away from the book she read, merely returned quietly, "Thank him for the invitation, Margaret, but I am afraid I want no dinner. Perhaps you would convey that and perhaps also you would be kind enough to bring me some of the laudnum we spoke of earlier. I believe I might need some after all."

As she finished speaking she looked away from the book and at Margaret.

The woman stared at her, her concern plain in her eyes. "Would you like a sandwich? Some cold meat . . . cheese?" She paused and then tempted with a wrinkling of her snubby nose, "How about a nice veal and ham pie?"

Emily managed a weak smile. "Nothing, thank you, Margaret. Just the laudanum."

Margaret nodded slowly and made to leave, then turned back. "Only a small dose, mind," she cautioned, "It never does to take too much of the stuff."

Margaret poured a small draught into a tumbler and then uncovered the linen-shrouded tray she had brought with her, protesting with a smile, "It is only a light snack.

I thought to bring it just in case you feel a bit better later and are peckish. You might want something to nibble at."

Emily gazed at the tray laden with tempting tidbits, knowing that Margaret had gone to some trouble to prepare the delicacies. She smiled her gratitude but reached only for the proffered potion and drank it down quickly. The bitter taste made her gag as it clung to the back of her throat. She quaffed deeply of the glass of water that Margaret held out to her, swilling her mouth with it before swallowing.

"Did you tell him?" Emily faltered and quickly rephrased the query with slightly more civility. "Did you convey my message, Margaret, that I would not be down?"

Margaret glanced sideways at Emily, seated on the edge of the violet-draped bed. She nodded confirmation and when Emily said nothing else, offered, "There was no further message. I suppose he and the madam will eat alone."

Emily recognized the slight sneer in the woman's voice as she referred to Amanda. She rose and walked to her wardrobe, starting to unbutton her dress. "I think I shall retire now, Margaret."

The housekeeper replaced the glass on the tray and moved swiftly to aid Emily in unfastening the small pearl buttons at the back of her dress.

Emily felt her thick, strong fingers fumble clumsily at the fastening. She felt a melancholy urge to laugh at the way this capable woman struggled to undo similar hard buttons like the ones that had given her no protection at all last night. Conscious of where her musings led, she closed her eyes and tried to shut her mind likewise. She concentrated on the tray that Margaret had brought for her, and the food on it, although she knew she felt like eating nothing.

She opened her wardrobe to hang the dress, as Margaret bade her pleasant good nights, and Emily saw at once her amethyst gown. She took it out slowly and looked at it. Apart from being rather creased, it was in exactly the same condition as it had been when she had donned it early yesterday evening. She smoothed the cold material with a shaking hand and then pushed it abruptly right to the back of the wardrobe, knowing she would never wear it again.

She walked to the door and locked it, replacing the key on the shelf before she moved to the bed and sat on the turned-down covers. She uncovered the tray again idly, drank a little of the milk, and ate half a treacle biscuit before letting the remainder drop back to the plate.

She got into the cold bed sensing a welcome, comforting drowsiness. It crept upon her, making her head sway lightly yet feel weighted. She closed her eyes, wanting to hurry to the promised oblivion. Her numbing head sank into the pillow and she allowed her body to relax as what was left of her awareness clung to the comforting notion that should he come to her again tonight, she might neither hear or know.

Chapter Eight

The sketch completed, Richard hung his small head first one way then the other in consideration before rising and taking it to show Emily.

She moved her hands quickly to shield her own picture, as he approached, and then shook her head at him. "Not yet . . . I have not finished mine."

The boy giggled and ran closer, and started to circle her dizzyingly as he contorted his neck to try and glimpse the outline beneath her splayed fingers. He tired of the game quickly. Clutching his drawing still, he went to the large floor-to-ceiling windows that surrounded his nursery on two sides and overlooked the gardens of the west wing.

Emily looked up then too, following the boy's lead, gazing through the windows at the crisp white snow blanketing the ground. It was well into January now and bitterly cold outside, although the nursery was warm and relatively draft-free.

"Come and see what I have drawn, Richard," Emily coaxed.

Richard sauntered closer with studied nonchalance, feigning disinterest. He circled her desk, his head inclined, examing the sketched outline of a large house with three chimneys that smoked.

"Don't like it . . . mine is much better than that," he shrilled.

"Let me see then, Richard," Emily persuaded patiently.

He shook his head forcefully and immediately crushed his drawing into a ball and threw it to the floor. He rushed towards her sketch on the desk and grabbing at it, ripped it almost across. He ruined that too and then threw it to skid closer to his own discarded artistic endeavour.

He jumped on both tight wads of paper and started to slide them beneath his feet before skating against the polished wooden floor with them. He glanced up at Emily and smiled brightly, his tantrum past, and now pleased with this unexpected entertainment he had made for himself.

He ran to the window once more after about five minutes of joyful slipping. He watched, laughing, as a flock of starlings attempted to alight on the soft white snow.

Emily slowly approached the crumpled paper. She went down on her knees and retrieved them. She smoothed out hers first with painstaking care and then Richard's: a crudely drawn snowman with a hat and scarf and a bird perched atop its head. She sat back on her heels and looked at them both, realizing then that she had omitted to provide her house with any windows or doors and that the chimneys smoked so blackly that the charcoal had powdered.

Richard forsook the window and the starlings abruptly and ran towards the doorway, singing out with happy astonishment, "It is Uncle Sir Clifford come to see me in my nursery."

The information was so unexpected and so daunting that it took Emily a moment or two to properly absorb it. A finger went to rub absently at the black smoke billowing from her rather hazardous-looking chimney before her head raised swiftly and she turned with sudden consternation towards the door.

Richard rushed towards the long, hard legs with some force, arms outstretched. Before he made heavy contact, Clifford had swung the boy off his feet and high into the air. He placed him back lightly on the ground and slightly distanced from him.

He walked further into the room, his eyes immediately with Emily, rather than with the small boy who clutched twistingly and tenaciously at his fingers.

Emily knew that the dark boots had drawn level, but some distance away, to one side of her. She turned from him at once, facing the opposite wall, and gathered the pictures from the floor, the blood pounding within so fast now that her breathing threatened to choke her.

She had not spoken to him for so long, not since he had left her room at dawn nearly two weeks ago.

The first week had found her leaving her room little during the day and then only when she was certain he was away from home. The evenings were invariably spent eating and reading within her own small sitting room.

The second week she had ventured to the west wing most days; sometimes spending a few hours with Amanda if the woman had nothing better to do than mope about her apartments when the weather was too inclement to allow her out to shop or visit friends.

Emily had apologized to Amanda for her rude comment as soon as possible with quiet dignity. Amanda had merely smiled and looked completely unconcerned by the whole affair . . . almost, in fact, as though the allusion concerning her and her brother-in-law did her more credit than harm.

Richard's nanny was only too happy to relinquish charge of her small treasure to Emily for a few hours and remove to her room to recuperate from the stress of continual frantic activity or tantrums. Thus Emily was with him in his nursery now, until the woman returned to take him for his nap.

Margaret still arrived at the same time each evening to advise her that the master of the house requested her to dine with him. Emily's answer was always the same, and he had never insisted that she do so. In fact, so used had Margaret become to the fruitless mission that she would now merely knock and poke her head around the door. Emily would simply shake her head, with a small smile of greeting. Margaret then retreated, closing the door softly, without either one of them needing to utter a word.

But for this constant evening ritual, Emily would have imagined that he was avoiding her as studiously as she was him. She rarely saw him, and if she did glimpse him at a distance, it was enough to make her find some pressing errand that took her immediately and swiftly in the opposite direction.

But she had shut her mind completely to the reason for this frantic evasion; she had allowed no further conscious thought of it, as though it were merely a nightmare she would only allow herself again to meet when asleep and unable to prevent it.

But now, with him close again, she could sense all the degradation of that forced intimacy, her subjugation crowding upon her with draining intensity.

Emily gazed sightlessly at the two battered drawings in her hand, aware of the straining silence that nevertheless hummed with Richard's idle chatter.

She rose carefully from the floor and turned away, recrumpling the papers in her hand and carrying them with her as she made for the door.

She was conscious of Richard's high, clear chatter

trailing into quiet at her wordless withdrawal. "I shall come back later, Richard. After you have awakened from your nap," she reassured him faintly.

"Don't go. Emily . . . not yet," Clifford cried.

She faltered at once at the soft, pleading words, acutely sensible now of his authority and her new regard for it. She did not turn but merely toyed, unsteady-fingered, with the papers she clutched.

"How are you, Emily?" he asked in a husky, concerned voice.

As though one question and answer gave her leave now to remove from the room, she approached the door again. "Well, thank you," she replied quickly, with cool civility.

"Emily!" The imperiousness conflicted with the sharpening entreaty in his tone.

Emily hesitated.

"I have heard differently," he murmured with more control. "That you have not felt well since—" he broke off abruptly. When he spoke again the hoarseness was back. "Since I spoke to you last."

Emily blinked and swallowed. "I am well, thank you," she repeated with the same toneless formality.

He moved to lean against the door by which she had intended leaving the room. The silence protracted again, and aware of him studying her relentlessly, Emily turned back into the room, her eyes seeking Richard.

The boy was fully and contentedly occupied now with a fistful of candy, and Emily knew at once whence it came and why.

"Margaret tells me you take laudanum nightly."

Emily looked down slowly at the floor, her face heating. "I will not if I am not allowed," she yielded at once. "I had not realized it was rationed."

"Why do you need it?"

Emily's eyes moved from the child relishing his sticky fingers and returned to the crushed papers she still gripped. "It helps me sleep . . . because my head aches," she added quickly to this.

"Every night?"

Richard licked his thumb thoroughly before suggesting in a helpful way, "It is probably because she cries so often. My head always hurts when I cry. It aches and aches and mama tells me it serves me right for bawling so loud. But Emily hardly makes a sound . . . so perhaps it does not serve her right."

Emily approached the doorway again hastily and purposefully. Clifford shifted slightly from the door frame to the space between it, making it impossible for her to leave without pushing past him or asking him to move.

"Do you cry still, Emily?" he asked with a raw softness.

"I have to go now," she mumbled almost inaudibly.

"No. I have seen nothing of you for two weeks. Surely ten minutes within my company is not now quite so hard to bear." The words were coarsened by the intensity of the request. He stretched out a hand spontaneously to touch her, but she jerked backward before looking swiftly at Richard. But he was better interested now in the new stick of sugar candy that he chewed, and he smiled up at them both with bright enjoyment.

Emily walked away then, back into the room, unable to be so close to him longer. She stood by the large windows and watched, her face turned up to the heavens, as the first obliterating flakes of that day's grayish snow descended from the leaden skies.

Clifford moved back into the room and stood by the window, slightly behind her, and she knew that he could still, if he wished, reach the doorway before she could.

She could sense the force of his scrutiny distressing her further, and she turned away from him completely and paced the length of the room slowly and hot-eyed. She gazed out into the desolate, cool whiteness, wishing despairingly that Richard's nanny would come and take him to his bed, giving her the distraction she needed to be able to escape to her room.

She shut her eyes and tried, likewise, to shut out Richard's noisy enjoyment of his sweets. Every pleasurable sound seemed to sigh and moan softly about her head in a way she remembered she had done, heightening her own humiliation by making it audible while his lust had remained so controlled and so quiet.

The noise seemed to expand, drumming within her throbbing head, and she swung about abruptly and looked at last into silver eyes that watched her closely.

"Will you come down tonight and have dinner with me?" he asked, his eyes watching her intently for reaction.

She said nothing, but simply bit at her trembling bottom lip.

"Please, Emily . . . I have tried to be patient," he persuaded softly. "And I don't want you to lock yourself away any more or secrete yourself in odd corners of the house for another fortnight."

The insinuation that she had hidden from him, true as it was, made her retort swiftly and hotly, "I have not done so."

He smiled, pleased at having elicited some response from her at last. "All right . . . you have not," he conceded indulgently. "Will you dine with me tonight then?" The continuing silence prompted him to reassure gently, "Please, Emily. It is all I expect . . . just to see you for an hour or so a day . . . nothing more, I promise. If you say you will, I will believe you not to shut yourself away. . . ."

Emily stared at him then as the tone of the words stirred heartrending memories. As though he recognized it too, he gave a rueful laugh, and a hand moved to rub at his eyes slowly as though in fatigue. She noticed then for the first time that he did indeed look weary and his skin paler. He seemed less well groomed also. It was hard to pinpoint the cause, for he was clean: the silver hair was bright and well-kempt, but it appeared closer to his collar and eyes now. His attire was different too: less sartorially immaculate, yet not exactly untidy.

She looked back at his face, and as their eyes met and held for a moment, she knew instinctively that she could leave now without fear of being stopped. She moved slowly toward the door again, and as she passed him he made no attempt to touch or halt her. His eyes closed and as she walked out into the corridor, he called after her with pleading command, "Emily. . . ."

Margaret backed carefully into the room carrying the tray and pulled the door behind her. She turned slowly and, eyes still with the meal she bore, approached the sitting room table.

She placed the tray down safely and then walked through the dressing room and into Emily's bedroom.

She began to speak and then stopped short and stared.

Emily looked up at her from where she sat at the dressing table and smiled at the woman's astonishment.

Margaret laughed and stated frankly, "So you are going to join him tonight then." She cocked her head to one side and assessed Emily admiringly. She was in a new dress that she had never worn before. It was of fine scarlet wool with small bead buttons running from the waist to a high collar. Margaret's appraisal moved approvingly to the newly washed and softly curling hair. She nodded her liking for the overall effect. "And the only day I think to bring a tray for your supper without asking you first," she remarked with mock self-reproof.

Emily stood up slowly, the faintheartedness making her say at once, in a relieved tone, "Oh well, if you have, Margaret, then I shall eat here. It matters little; I just thought that as I feel slightly more. . . ." She hesitated, unable to put into words exactly what she did feel. She smiled vaguely at the plump woman. "I believe I just felt like removing from this room tonight for a few hours . . . that is all."

"And about time, too, miss, if you don't mind me saying so." Margaret beamed and added good-naturedly, "I was beginning to think that you and the master must have had words. . . ." She gave a slight cough to cover this indiscretion and fumbled in her pockets.

"No . . . it is quite all right, Margaret. As you have brought the tray, I shall remain here," Emily mumbled at once. She raised a hand to press at her temple, well aware of her cowardice as she faltered, "Besides, I think my head is beginning to ache a little again."

Margaret walked away from her then and approached the sitting room. She reappeared carrying the tray and walked steadfastly toward the exit with it. "You are not eating this tonight, young lady," she stated firmly. "I am taking it straight back to the kitchens. It is stone cold now anyway," she informed with a lugubrious shake of the head as she stared down into the steaming dinner plate.

Emily started to protest but Margaret opened the door with one hand, balancing the tray skillfully in the other. "I shall inform Sir Clifford that you will be down in five minutes," she advised with a determined nod. Before Emily could demur further, the housekeeper had gone, bearing the dinner with her.

Emily returned to the dressing table, sat down, and studied her face in the mirror. She looked pale still, but, as she critically assessed her appearance, she knew she also looked attractive.

She turned dejectedly away from her reflection. Her stomach gurgled hungrily and she thought of her lost meal, silently berating herself for ever having decided to divert from her new and secure routine.

It had not been so much his request that she eat with him that had swayed her to do so as much as the need to escape the oppressive silence of her room and her own company. She liked her solitude and guarded it jealously at times, but she also liked, from time to time, to have company. The prospect of eating a proper meal and perhaps chatting for an hour or so, even with taciturn Amanda, was suddenly quite ridiculously tempting.

Emily opened the door to the small dining room and walked in slowly. Her eyes roved, seeking Amanda's comforting presence. She was not in the room and Emily glanced at once towards the table, noting silver gleaming at two table settings. Whether Amanda was merely late, and there was no place yet laid for herself, she could not be sure.

She inquired politely, "Is Amanda coming down?"

"Amanda is not feeling well. She is eating in the west wing tonight."

The skepticism must have been plain in her face, for Clifford moved away from the hearth and toward her as though to stop her leaving. "Don't go, Emily," he appealed. "I shall send Margaret with a note — see if I can persuade her to join us for an hour, if you like."

Emily realized then that he probably spoke the truth about her absence; it was unlikely he had deliberately barred her presence tonight. He had after all had barely ten minutes to arrange it. Insisting that he fetch her would merely display flagrantly that she feared being alone with him.

Emily walked toward the table in tacit acceptance of the situation. As though to break the ice, he asked conversationally, "Did you want to speak to her about something in particular?"

"No it was nothing."

Emily allowed her hand to touch the silver set on the table and then slide against the high-glossed, honey-colored wood that slipped beneath her fingers.

"You look very pretty tonight, Emily."

She glanced up at him tentatively, one hand moving spontaneously to the red dress. "Thank you," she replied distantly.

Silence ensued; conscious that he was still looking at her, she flushed and added remotely, "It is one of my new dresses . . . one that you paid for. . . ." She halted abruptly, looking hastily back at the polished table, wondering why she had mentioned that when she knew it would make her feel uncomfortable.

He smiled slightly at her bowed chestnut head. "Well, it nevertheless looks very nice, Emily," he remarked with light irony.

Strangely uneasy with this polite exchange of innocuous remarks, Emily turned abruptly and gratefully as she heard the door open. Heath entered briskly and in a most unservile manner, Emily thought, although he was dressed as usual in his neat black uniform. He swung into the room in a way that made Emily sure he was about to speak at once. But having absorbed her presence as dark eyes swept the room encompassingly, he remained quiet and unruffled. His eyes lowered calmly and immediately. "Miss Shaw," he murmured with customary courtliness.

Emily returned his name in cordial reply. He moved at once to the table and held out a chair. Emily sat down with a smile of thanks.

She watched his sober, broad back retreat from her.

Clifford had already seated himself. His silver eyes raised blandly as the man approached. For some ridiculous reason as the two men looked at each other Emily was sure, although Heath had his back rigidly turned to her and made not a sound, that the servant was smiling at his master.

Emily looked curiously at Clifford, watching his eyes lower and his jaw set almost imperceptibly before his eyes sought hers.

Finding her gazing at him quite openly, he smiled in a way that made her blush. Her eyes were then once more with the table silver, and a slender finger ran the length of a gleaming fork.

More servants filed into the room to serve the first course. Emily looked at the hot, appetizing soup and felt her hunger roll hollowly in her stomach. The staff withdrew. Emily tasted the soup almost at once, her hunger uncontrollable.

"You look as though you have lost weight. What have you been eating these past weeks? Little, I'll wager."

She kept her attention with her soup plate. "I have eaten well enough, thank you." Stubbornly she laid her spoon against the half-empty plate, indicating she had finished.

He raised his eyebrows but said nothing. She clasped her hands in her lap and looked at the fire to one side of her while he finished eating.

The second course was brought in and Emily ate all the dainty slivers of smoked fish. It occurred to her that the fish might have come from the stream that ran through his land, and she was almost tempted to ask him. She discarded the notion hastily, knowing that resurrecting any memory of old scores would be pure stupidity.

Heath returned bearing the joint of meat for the main course. Emily once more had the absurd impression that some aura of amusement accompanied him although his decorum and attitude to her and to his master were impeccable.

The dinner served, he turned to Clifford with a slight, stiff bow and a discreet cough. "May I assume, sir, that we will not now be going into town this evening?" he asked.

"Yes, Heath, you may," he answered in an equally bland voice.

"Thank you, sir."

The servant retraced his steps a little and then paused. As though to be certain he was perfectly clear of his master's express wishes, he added tonelessly, "We will, in other words, sir, not be riding tonight."

Emily watched them as she ate slowly. She listened to this curious exchange between master and servant, wondering if the slightly equivocal air she could sense was merely her imagination.

Clifford looked up at the man this time. His eyes skimmed immediately to Emily, noting her steady observation. "That is correct, Heath," he replied mildly but through lips that moved little.

He stared expressionlessly at the black man for a moment, and then his mouth thrust very slightly in an odd smile. "But should you wish to . . . ride into town . . . you have my permission," he grated with a quite obvious and unusual show of munificence that was condescending in its excess.

The servant bowed exceedingly low this time as he murmured gratefully, "Why, thank you very much, sir."

He straightened. As Emily gazed unwaveringly at the side of his face, she noted full, dark lips curve upward very slightly. He turned and walked to the sideboard and busied himself.

Emily remembered her dinner then and cut into it, but her eyes returned as though magnetized to the dark-clad figure as he worked quietly.

Clifford, his dinner forgotten, gazed astutely at her. "That will be all, thank you, Heath," he said evenly.

The door closed quietly. Emily looked at Clifford, openly returning his attention. "If you have to go out tonight, please do not feel obliged to stay here because of me," she said. "I was intending to return to my room directly after dinner."

"I have been wishing this past two weeks or so that I had provided you with accommodation a little less comfortable and attractive; perhaps then you would spend less time within it and more time with me. You surely cannot be tired still: you must have slept and rested more in the past weeks than I believe I manage in six months."

She frowned, nettled. "I have not slept that well, and I still feel. . . ." The words faded. She looked away from the silver eyes that regarded her so relentlessly and cut into her meal quite ferociously.

"Still feel what, Emily? Surely you never feel anything . . . not with the laudanum drugging you nightly." He paused for barely a moment. "But that is why you take it, is it not? To anesthetize you in case. . . ." He broke off without finishing the sentence, his jaw gritting slightly. "I do not want you taking it again," he instructed in the same light, impassive tone. "I have already told Margaret as much; please do not ask for it."

She looked up then, uttering defensively, "I merely said that should you want to go out tonight—"

"But I do not want to, Emily," he interrupted with a soft smile. Silver eyes roamed her face leisurely. "I want to stay here with you."

Their eyes held for a moment.

The dessert dishes were brought in and laid along the length of the table once they were both served, the servants again withdrew. Emily wondered if the enigmatic Heath would put in another appearance and puzzle her further. He did not and she felt oddly disappointed by it.

"Why does Heath have your name?" she asked. "Is it some sort of brand of ownership?" She chilled a little at the rash choice of words and amended quickly, "I mean a badge of ownership."

"Not many people make the connection—that his name is a synonym for mine. He chose the name himself. His

245

parents were dead when he was a baby and he grew up without ever having been called by a name of his own." He paused and looked reflective.

"I think he was known by his mother's name for the most of his early life—before he joined up with me—something like 'Marje's boy.' I believe that was his mother's name, but it is so long ago now." He smiled at her and related, "Anyway, he asked me what Clifford meant, but I had not the vaguest idea, so we got to Moore. I told him it meant 'heathland' and described that to him. He liked it and decided he would be 'Heathland." He looked at her and gave a slight grimace of mock relief. "But I managed to get him to shorten it slightly."

Emily gazed at him thoughtfully and wide-eyed, keen now to learn more. She asked quickly, "And how is it that he speaks English so well and so correctly. Has he had some education?"

"Yes, he is educated. He is an extremely adept clerk, actually. In Jamaica he worked for me in that capacity—keeping logs and financial records. He does here too for that matter."

"Who has taught him then?" She looked at Clifford eagerly and asked, "Did you?"

"Some . . . most, I suppose. When I arrived in Jamaica he was up for sale and I had just enough money to buy him. He was fourteen and I was just eighteen at the time. Some enterprising planter had noticed his intelligence and started to educate him. He was put to work with the office papers. Well, it saved his master needing to pay a white man to do it. Fortunately enough for me, when he came to sell him there was not much call for an educated black. They make planters feel uncomfortable. They want slaves to be heathen and illiterate, fit to work the fields, not sit around indoors rifling through books . . . and worse still, understanding them. I managed to buy him very cheaply and he has been with me ever since. He reads widely — more than I do. Probably not as much as you do though, Emily," he mocked tenderly. "He is accomplished in several disciplines — history, geography — and he reads well in French and Latin, apart from English, of course."

"Why did you teach him so much? Is he now some quaint novelty for your friends to gawp and laugh at?"

"What friends, Emily? It cannot have escaped your notice that I have very few. I rarely invite anyone here. No one stays for any length of time. It is a conscious choice; I dislike people constantly about me, especially those that seek me out for the same mercenary motives as I do them from time to time. I need other people just when they can help provide comfort and security . . . and now that I have money enough, less and less. Heath is probably the only true friend I have, and when it comes to spiritual fellowship. . . ." He gazed at her intently and then murmured, "Never mind." He recommenced briskly, "I have told you before that I keep no slaves, Emily. I never have. I bought my work force in Jamaica, it is true, but the moment they were mine, they were free. In fact, my consideration for them made me unpopular with the other planters throughout the West Indies, not only in Jamaica." He paused and then laughed, amused. "That is a slight understatement — my assassination was high on the list of many a planter's priorities. But in a way it was sheer economic sense to treat labor well. They never saw that — equating well-fed, amenable blacks with increased profit."

Emily sat mute, mulling over all this fascinating detail.

"We had heard you were dead. I believed it to be true," she uttered quite tonelessly.

"My apologies," he rasped sarcastically, "I fear I am disappointing you too with my continuing health and well-being. No doubt the rumors began after a run in we had with the French merchant ship. Times of war are always ripe for exploiting a spot of privateering. I had my own ships and it seemed foolish not to use them to capacity at all times. We used to relieve the French of some of their valuable cargoes. The Americans too at times. But they were quite good customers and I never liked to upset them too much," he added with a dry laugh. "Unfortunately, on one occasion a French guard practically relieved me of my life—I was impaled on a bayonet. Luckily I had Heath about me at the time or no doubt I would indeed have perished." He watched for some reaction but could discern none. "Has your sympathy for my black savior just rapidly diminshed, Emily?" he jibed sardonically.

She ignored his husky taunt. "Did you keep what you stole?" she asked. In fact she was quite awe-stricken, although she was managing to suppress showing it.

He smiled at the implicit condemnation. "Yes, mostly. My wealth not only derives from Jamaica and the sugar plantations but from smuggling and privateering and all sorts of suspect enterprise. In all I expect the latter probably provided me with more than the former, but no matter now."

He drained his wine glass, then added conversationally, "I kept most of the seized cargoes, but not all. Food supplies were sometimes diverted to Wellington and his troops. Feeding his army seemed like a nice, loyal thing to do for King and country, and of course it ensured me a friendly welcome home . . . paved the way. It was sensible as some of my erstwhile rival neighbors in Jamaica were returning home at about the same time. We see fit to ignore each other now too. It suits me. But it is always wise to have influential friends when starting afresh somewhere, and Wellington is certainly that. The Prince of Wales as he then was, was also indebted to me for my patriotic spirit . . . not to mention the money I lent him."

Emily sat in utter silence for about five minutes, toying

with what was left in her dish. Her spoon stirred round and round. She tried to assimilate and judge the truth of all she had heard. She looked up then at his face, her eyes drawn to the mark below his eye. She realized now that as his tan faded, it was much less noticeable. She swallowed, then asked in a rush, "That mark—the scar on your face—did you come by it in an incident abroad?"

"No, Emily," he said with quiet bitterness. "I came by that in an incident in my youth, while still in England's green and pleasant land."

Emily sensed her color rising and her uneasiness increasing. "These loans you make—you appear to be supporting quite an amount of London society. What sort of interest do you charge?"

"Enough to make it worthwhile," he returned immediately with an impenitent smile. "Your mother told you I have given her money. I thought as much. When was it? The night. . . ." he halted abruptly, his head jerking away. He stared silently into the fire to one side of them for a moment. "Why did you not ask me about it? Why assume it had to be for some sordid motive?" he challenged softly.

Emily's interest in her dish seemed to increase.

"I thought it would please you. I can give them nothing, if you prefer, Emily. It matters little to me how they go on."

"Yes . . . that I can believe," she uttered coldly. "I believe you are unprincipled indeed," she judged quietly, as though summing up all she had learned of him with that conclusion.

"Indeed," he agreed softly, "and it has helped me survive and prosper and if I am corrupt then I am not alone. You will find others more mercenary than I and with far less reason for being so. Your mother would have sold you to me quite unconditionally for a lot less than was actually tendered. It was I who offered you some

249

honor."

Emily glanced up, fierce-eyed. "You gave me nothing you would not take back," she choked.

He gazed at her tenderly, wounded as much as she by her humiliation and pain. "We have not all got your integrity and virtue, Emily," he said gently. "Some of us succumb to temptation and vice . . . but it does not mean that we are not sorry for having done so and would not wish to apologize."

"Apologize for what?" she demanded in a whisper. "The temptation or the vice?"

He was silent until she glanced up tentatively. "The weakness, Emily," he admitted softly, "for I could never in truth say I regretted the deed."

After a few moments of throbbing silence, he changed subject abruptly. "Do you believe me when I say I have no slaves, Emily?"

She shook her head slowly.

"Why not?"

"It is just hypocrisy, fine words," she accused shakily. "You have enslaved me, and when I tell you I wish to go home, you deny me."

"That is because I need you. You are the soul you say I don't have; and it is true, Emily, for without you. . . ." He paused and looked up at her but she sat quite unmoved. "Perhaps I left it with you . . . for safekeeping ten years ago . . . while I went to hell and back. Have you finished?" he tacked incongruously onto the end.

She glanced at her half-empty dish and murmured, "Oh, yes . . . thank you."

He rose abruptly and Emily got up equally quickly, making him halt halfway along the table toward her. "Will you sit with me in the library? Just for a while?" he requested.

"No, thank you," she said, approaching the door swiftly. He walked toward it too and reached it first.

Emily barely faltered. "Good night," she murmured tremulously, her hand reaching out for the door handle.

He clasped the outstretched hand before it made contact. She gasped as his free hand slid behind her head, easing her closer and caressing it soothingly. "I only want you to sit in the library with me just for an hour," he reassured hoarsely.

She shook her head once but otherwise remained rigid against him. "Half an hour?" he coaxed softly.

There was no response from her at all this time. He inclined closer, suggesting wryly against her hair, "Ten minutes?"

Large violet eyes then raised to his cautiously and she made a tentative movement to free herself.

He released her at once and she back-stepped a little way into the dining room.

She wanted to refuse him again, but the library was enticing as was, oddly, spending a little while longer in his company.

"Ten minutes only," she capitulated slowly.

He smiled acquiescence and opened the door for her.

"Where did all these books come from? I have never seen so many," Emily declared. The library's magnificence still had the power to awe and her eyes roamed the shelves in slow fascination.

Clifford stood some way along the room from her, perusing some almost illegible title with narrowed eyes. "About half were locked away in trunks in an attic room upstairs. They were obviously overlooked when everything else was sold off. Ridiculous really, for some are quite valuable." He smiled to himself, satisfied, before muttering, "Somebody's loss has been my gain." A long, lightly tanned finger went to touch the flaking gold lettering of the book he studied. "The others I bought when in England again." He looked up at her then, remarking with casual irony, "Heath was pestering for a few books to read."

"How did you manage to reclaim the house?" Emily asked quite interestedly. "Someone must have owned it after your father's death. Who did you buy it from?"

"The bank had seized it and were holding it against their debts. They had no need of it but had never sold it on — to my inestimable good fortune. Had they done so, it would have made it that much more difficult to reclaim."

"But certainly not impossible," Emily mutterly acidly.

He selected another book at random and glanced at the title. "Nothing is impossible, Emily," he informed evenly, "not if you have money enough. Everything is purchasable. That is why I always intended making myself rich — so that nothing was ever beyond my reach. Well . . . that is what I foolishly supposed," he ended wrily.

Emily touched the mahogany bookshelves. "And what of Thrushcross Grange — how long have you owned that?"

"About a year or so. I bought it when I arrived back in England."

"Jonathon told me there was a family in residence. What happened to them? Did you force them out of their home just so that you could tear it down or let it decay and further this insatiable. . . ." Emily bit her lip immediately as though to physically quieten herself as she realized how perilously her new, mannerly conduct wavered.

"I paid them quite handsomely for it, Emily," he answered levelly, "and they knew it. Once the sum was agreed they were extremely keen to sign the documents and relinquish all rights."

Emily's dark head bowed a little, loose curls brushing the collar of her scarlet wool dress. "And what have you done to it? Is there anything of it left inside?"

He walked the length of the shelves to stand close. He smiled as she glanced nervously up at him. "Nothing, Emily. I have done nothing to it." He laughed ruefully.

"Well, perhaps that is not quite truthful," he admitted with a small grimace. "The first week I had it I smashed every window in the place. Very juvenile, I know. Heath thought I had gone mad. But it made me feel so much better. Apart from that its condition is reasonable. There is nothing wrong at all that cannot be put right — should I at sometime wish to do so." He paused, then coaxed softly, "Let me show you tomorrow."

"I am not sure that I wish to see it again. It would disturb too many memories that are now best left alone."

He smiled wryly. "Yes, for me too," he admitted. "Yet sometimes now I feel I have conquered the worst of them and the others — those that include you — I like to dwell on."

He reached out slowly and touched her face very lightly, just skimming the cheek closer to him. She closed her eyes for a moment. Then she moved briskly away along the line of books as though a volume two yards away interested her greatly. She picked it out at random and took it to an armchair. She sat down by the fire, studying it, relieved to find that she had in fact, made a good choice: it was *Ivanhoe*.

She had read barely the first paragraph when the library door opened. Heath walked in. "I shall be leaving soon, sir. Is there any message to be conveyed in your absence?" As he straightened, his liquid brown eyes met Clifford's the amicable teasing recognizable to Clifford alone, although Emily was regarding him just as steadfastly.

"None at all, thank you," he responded. He opened the door for Heath in a way that looked strangely civil. Yet as the servant made to leave the room, Emily was sure she noticed one swift hand come out and make contact with the dark, cropped head.

As Clifford returned toward her, she stared, shocked.

"Did you hit him?" she demanded, aghast.

He grimaced, shrugging bewilderment and then swung back to look thoughtfully at the door Heath had just left by. "I don't think so, Emily . . . did I?" he inquired of her in a bemused tone.

She glowered at him skeptically for a few moments. But he looked guiltless; quite unruffled. She flicked through the pages of her book and then glanced up at him again, suspiciously and penetratingly.

"Read to me," he suggested quickly. "Just a few pages . . . please." He smiled at her with undeniable charm and she half-smiled back. She looked at the book in her lap, then started to read quietly from the first chapter.

She read to the bottom of the page and made to turn it. On glancing across at him, he encouraged softly, "You read very well. I thought you told me otherwise."

She colored a little.

Carrying a glass of brandy, he approached her. He pulled her out of the chair and sat in it himself. "Sit down beside me, Emily." he ordered mildly, "So I can see the book as you read and look at the pictures."

Emily sank obediently to the carpet beside the chair. "But there are no pictures in this book," she protested solemnly.

He pretended surprise, then laughed and a hand came out to caress the soft dark head. "Never mind . . . I shall imagine some," he teased gently.

She turned then and laughed too. As their eyes met and clung, something in the way he looked at her made her determined to study her reading again.

His hand moved to her face, turning her back, but she slipped free of his clasp hastily and raised the book in her hand as though to begin reciting. He removed the book from her and let it drop to the carpet by her side. The back of one finger brushed against her cheek as though to gain attention as he murmured her name softly.

She picked up the book again quickly and opened it,

but before she could properly see the text, he tilted her head and touched his mouth to her forehead. She remained quiet and his hand slid behind her head and into mahogany hair as he moved her nearer to him. His mouth lingered at her face, descending to just brush her mouth lightly a dozen times.

She leaned back a little from him. "You could still go with Heath if you want," she encouraged breathlessly. "I am sure he has not got far. You should have gone, really."

"Why should I do that, Emily?" he queried quietly.

She shifted away from him further and her tongue tip came out unconsciously to travel the path his mouth had just followed. "Well, it must have been important," she reasoned. "Why else would you arrange to go out in such weather — with snow on the ground. You might never get a carriage through though, I am sure."

His eyes were flinty and wary and, aware they might betray him, he looked at his glass. "It was not important . . . not at all."

"Where has he gone to tonight then, in this snow? Why could it not at least wait until daylight?"

Clifford raised the book in her hand, urging huskily, "Read to me some more, Emily." The book dropped slackly back into her lap. A niggling suspicion knotted her stomach.

"Why has he gone to St. Albans in this weather?" she persisted gravely.

"He has a friend there — a black servant he has become acquainted with; they enjoy each other's company."

Emily smiled then and sighed lightly as she relaxed against his chair. "Oh, that is nice. Is he from Jamaica as Heath is? They will have a lot in common."

Clifford's eyes lowered to the glass of brandy he held. "From Canada, I believe," he informed evenly. "I am not sure of which generation or whether born there; I assume so."

"It is very good of you to allow him a friend and one so suitable." Emily smiled up at him softly. "Did you find him and introduce them to each other?" she asked with bright approval.

The brandy glass rose slowly to his narrow mouth and he smiled neutrally before drinking lengthily.

Emily was gazing up reflectively at him now and she shut the book in her hand, relishing this new topic. She leant slightly closer, resting heavily against his chair. "What does the man do?" she asked most attentively.

He shrugged noncommittally and raised the drink to his mouth once more, downing the rest in one swallow.

"Do you always accompany him then?" she interrogated steadily. "Is he not usually allowed to go alone for some reason to visit his friend? It is very good of you to—"

The light-bronze hand moved swiftly, covering her mouth. He laughed shortly. "You tend to talk lengthily, Emily, on the most tedious topics," he chided. "Now, before I fall asleep from sheer boredom, tell me what you have been doing with yourself these past weeks."

She felt his hand slide from her face to her neck and rub softly, almost platonically. She leaned closer, turning unconsciously into the caress. Her head fell slightly to one side as she tried to remember something of interest that she had actually done in the monotony of the past weeks.

She could think of nothing at all and her mind drifted back to Heath ploughing through the snow to his comrade. "I suppose if he is not as educated as Heath it must be difficult for them to find common pastimes," she declared soberly. "What work does the man do?"

Large violet eyes gazed up trustingly into his tense, unsmiling face. "She is a lady's maid," he apprised quietly. "She returned to England with her mistress when the war threatened there last year and they now live in town."

He watched bright eyes cloud a little in wonder. She

frowned, mouth aslant, as she considered this unexpected news and how it related to what she already knew. Realization dawned slowly. She glanced at him with undisguised hurt sharpening the violet of her eyes before looking away quickly. "Oh, I see," she murmured coolly.

A hand came out immediately to keep her close but she flinched away at once. His eyes closed and his head dropped forward momentarily in despair. He gave a small, bitter laugh. "What do you see, Emily?" he asked with grating irony. "Come, tell me what you see. That I am human and need female company sometimes? You cannot see that, can you? All you can see is some selfish, rapacious whoremonger. . . ."

Emily made to rise swiftly, away from him, but his hands came out, fastening at the tops of her slender arms, holding her still and close to him. "Ask me not to go there again and I will not," he muttered hoarsely.

She looked up at him then, wintry eyes blazing with a torrid scorn. "Why should I do that?" she asked sweetly. "It is no concern of mine where you go or what you do. If it was not there it would be somewhere else, so—"

"Yes, where would I go, Emily, if not there?" he cut in despairingly, his sarcasm matching hers. "Perhaps where I want to be. But that would never do, would it? You have not much liking for men in general, have you, and none at all for me in particular. And yet if I believed that—really believed it—you would be back with your parents now and I would be back abroad somewhere. It is what I feel for you now you have no liking for." One hand moved from her arm to her face, attempting to soothe her, but she swung away from him savagely.

His hand moved back to her shoulder, controlling her continually until she ceased straining to get up and remained rigid, with her face averted.

He bent his head closer to her. "I am nearly twenty-nine now, Emily, not seventeen," he murmured in a tone that pleaded for compassion. "And you are no longer a child. You are twenty and a woman, and when you allow it, you you can feel for me exactly what I do for you; we both know that."

She swung a hand at him abruptly at the words, crying out raucous denial as she pulled herself back from him. He jerked her yet closer, so that her head was but inches away from his. "I want a wife now, Emily, not a playmate. I want to lie with my wife and love her."

The softly worded plea achieved nothing other than to make her renew her attempt to free herself. This time he allowed her to do so. She stood up quickly, backing away and smoothing her scarlet dress with trembling hands. She taunted in a hard, shaking voice, "Well, I should ask your Canadian friend to marry you then. Or perhaps Miss Dobson or Miss Benson. Or go to London, where the choice would of course be quite phenomenal . . . quite baffling, I am sure. But somewhere one must appeal to you. For a short while at least, until you found yourself bored and scouring the neighbouring countryside towns once more for some purchasable new friends. How long did Amanda manage to charm you? Not that long, I should imagine — and she within such easy reach too . . . so available when the weather is inclement."

She swung away at once and walked to the door, then faltered as her rudeness crowded terrifyingly upon her. She turned about slowly, retracing her steps a way, reasoning coldly that it would be best to know before she went to her room.

"Have I been insolent tonight?" she asked in a quiet, unsteady voice.

He remained unmoving for a moment, staring at his clasped hands, then stood up. He walked toward her. "I believe you have, Emily, yes."

She sensed the panic pervading her as it had once before. She forced out humbly with her eyes lowered, "I

258

apologize. I did not mean to insult you or pry into your affairs. . . ." She felt her face sting with the stupid choice of word and faltered immediately. "I know I speak rashly sometimes and without due consideration."

His hands moved to draw her close.

She tensed and closed her eyes, but as her palms strained spontaneously against his shoulders, he let her go.

"I want you to marry me, Emily."

There was no reply to the soft, vehement request, but she looked up at him.

They stared at each other for a moment until desire started to flicker, then flare uncontrollably in his eyes. She recognized the darkening eyes and taut, intense face too well. She turned her head abruptly and stared at the book shelves close by, making no move to leave the room.

He watched her holding her fear in check with silent dignity and any indecision had gone. He walked the few steps to the desk in the corner and opened it. He approached her again, standing in front of her for a renewed, conflict-ridden minute. His fist raised, opening to reveal a key identical to the one in her door upstairs. Emily gazed at it for no more than a second, then neared him to take it. Their hands touched as he relinquished the key, and he clasped her wrist as though he might pull her close again or take it back. But he merely raised it a little, looking at the small, curled fingers that imprisoned the key so tightly before he smiled and let the hand drop. As he turned away he bade quite normally, "Good night, Emily."

Heath entered his room, whistling softly and with a contented, reflective smile about his lips.

He walked into the dimly lit bedchamber, about to close the door. "You still up?" he managed before the blow knocked him backward into the door, slamming it noisily.

He regained his balance instinctively and swiftly, one hand at his bleeding mouth. He pushed himself away from the door, launching himself at his assailant spontaneously, fists raised.

He slammed back into the door again, both hands moving to comfort each side of his face now. He removed his hands from his jaw momentarily and held them out. "Fair enough . . . I give up," he muttered, with not wholly mocking defeat.

He slid down the door and sat on the floor, kneading and wobbling his chin gingerly.

He glanced sideways up into vicious gray eyes. "And what was that for?" he demanded, pained.

Clifford back-stepped a little, but his hands were still clenched rigid at his sides. He repeated sarcastically, "And what was that for? That was for . . ." he mimicked in Heath's placid, servile manner, " '. . . we will, in other words, sir, not be riding tonight . . . Is there any message to be conveyed in your absence, sir?' "

Heath allowed a snort of disbelief. "You have never waited up until three in the morning just for that," he scorned.

Clifford smiled and swore unpleasantly. "What the hell else is there to do?" he sneered savagely.

Heath pushed himself upwards, sliding his back along the door again. "Sleep?" he ventured with mocking inspiration.

Brown eyes scanned the harsh-faced man shrewdly. "Sorry," he said quietly, "it was just a joke—"

"I am not laughing," came the frustrated rejoinder.

"But what could she have made of it? An innocent like that?" he challenged.

"Innocent . . . yes; stupid . . . most definitely not," Clifford muttered drily.

They stared at each other in muted hostility for a moment.

"You told her, didn't you?" Heath suddenly accused in an astonished voice.

Clifford swung away from him then and walked toward the low fire, his hands thrust deep into his pockets.

Heath followed him slowly, one hand still stroking his face. "Why did you tell her?" he asked, quite interested now by his friend's eccentricity.

Clifford was silent for a moment longer and then he laughed, relaxing a little. "She asked where you had gone to," he said simply.

Heath emitted another derisive snort. "Oh, she asked," he emphasised for himself witheringly. "Well, I have heard you lie before. I know you can do it if you try . . . and very well, too."

Heath watched him in his despair. "Fool," he berated harshly. "You should have come . . . you know that; and then we would both now be ready for sleep."

A black hand dug into his coat pocket and produced a scrap of white. He held the letter out. "She was not pleased," he cautioned with a mock-ominous shake of the head.

Clifford looked at the note and then away, making no attempt to reach for it. Heath wagged it a little, disdainfully, indicating he had no use for it either.

Clifford took the small letter and looked at it for a moment before dropping it carelessly into the burning coals.

"I don't pay her to write me billets-doux," Clifford dismissed sneeringly.

Heath laughed shortly. "Well, what do you pay her for? It is all she has done for you in a while now."

"Very true. Perhaps tomorrow I should remedy the situation . . . make up for lost time and money."

Clifford walked past him to the door, the pleasurable

prospect forgotten already. "Those cottages — the ones by Baker's End — did you remember to —" He got no further.

Heath assented soothingly and with a wry smile. "Yes . . . of course. When have I ever let you down?"

Chapter Nine

"I am so sorry, Margaret, I just could not seem to get out of bed quickly enough." Emily was holding a cloth to her mouth as she spoke, and the words were muffled and slightly indistinct.

"Not to worry, my dear," Margaret soothed with a concerned smile. "It is not your fault. How can you help feeling so poorly?"

Emily got off the bed and Margaret stripped the vomit-soiled sheet and pillow case. "I shall get this changed straightaway. Are you to dress and come down for breakfast?" she inquired sympathetically.

"I do not think I can eat anything at all, Margaret. I have no appetite lately, since I have been feeling so nauseated."

Margaret gathered together the linen just as the knock sounded on the door. Emily moved to it wearily, recognizing Amanda's treble tattoo.

She opened it a little way, peering round from behind it. Amanda pushed, irritated, at the door, widening the gap with an impatient huff. "Are you not dressed yet, Emily?" she demanded, exasperated. "I thought you wanted to come with me to town this morning, and you know I wanted to make an early start. I have to be at the dressmaker's at midday. It really is too bad."

"Miss Emily is not feeling well," Margaret interrupted

protectively. "She has been sick twice this morning, and I don't think she should be going anywhere."

Amanda's eyes darted Emily's pallid face sharply before they regarded the nightdress-clad figure assessingly.

"I am sorry, Amanda," Emily sighed with regret. "I was so looking forward to it, but I am sure I could never manage to face the journey. I will feel nauseated again; I have felt this way every morning this week."

Amanda's eyes sought those of the housekeeper spontaneously and she noticed a spark of interest narrow the brown eyes too. Both women increased their attention to Emily, now sitting on the edge of the bed with the billowing white nightgown puffed around her.

Margaret seemed about to speak to her, but as though unable to find the right words to use, she shifted uneasily. "I have felt quite strange too this week," Amanda announced suddenly. A hand moved to her rounded abdomen and rubbed easingly. "Quite queasy . . . I have been sick once too," she added emphatically. "That pork we ate on Monday tasted a little peculiar, Margaret."

The housekeeper's attention was diverted from uneasy musings at once. "That was fresh," she bristled, ". . . as fresh as meat can ever be, and the master ate it too. Sir Clifford has not complained of sickness, but never fear — I shall check. I shall ask him how he feels the moment I clap my eyes on him."

She bundled the linen into a corner and made for the door purposefully. Amanda soothed, "Don't be so silly, Margaret. I must be mistaken then if others who ate it feel well. It is just an odd coincidence that Emily and I should both feel bilious."

Margaret glowered at her still, not entired placated.

Amanda smiled with rare charm, offering generously, "Please, Margaret, don't let us keep you from your tasks any longer. I am sure the efficiency of this household has everything to do with the rod of iron you wield over the girls. I imagine you keep them continually on their toes. Should they believe they can, they will be skulking off to idle in odd corners."

Now befriended, Margaret stated emphatically, "And that is a fact, madam, I can tell you. Why, only this morning I caught. . . ." She broke off, sensing some ambiguity in her old adversary's flattery. Nevertheless, she managed a cautious smile before glancing softly at Emily once more, "I shall come back in an hour or so, miss, and see how you are getting on," she promised kindly.

Amanda endorsed pleasantly, "Yes, I should, Margaret. But not a word to Sir Clifford, now. You know he frets if one of us young ladies is indisposed—you know he does."

Margaret gave her a speaking look, eyebrows slightly raised, that intimated she felt herself privileged to know nothing of the sort. She withdrew with another perfunctory smile for Amanda and a heartier one for Emily.

The door closed and Emily looked at Amanda again. "I am sorry, Amanda," she apologized with a woeful shake of the head. "I really wished to go with you, but—"

Amanda dismissed the rest of the words with a thin smile. Her frosty blue eyes scanned the shape below the loose nightrobe quite openly and in a way that made Emily draw it unconsciously closer.

"How long did you say you have felt this nausea, Emily?"

"Just this week, I think, perhaps at the end of last week, too. It is just a strange sensation more than sickness. I have hardly vomited at all—only today."

"Do you feel strange anywhere else? Any pains or suchlike?"

Emily looked up then and frowned at this unusual and puzzling concern.

"Well, I have. . . ." She hesitated and then shook her head and shrugged. "No, not really, nothing specific."

"Have you put any weight on?" The query was just as

concise and swiftly posed.

Emily regarded Amanda searchingly. "Yes, I think so," she admitted slowly, "but only . . . ." She paused and then shrugged again, a trifle embarrassed.

Amanda smiled at her confusion and assisted with, "Only about your bosom, I'll wager."

Emily looked up sharply at the astute comment. Amanda moved to Emily and pulled her upright from the bed. As the nightgown fell close to her body, the blonde woman eyed the increased curvaceousness. "Do you feel sore there too?" she inquired clinically.

Emily nodded, her face set now, apprehensiveness stealing over her. She followed Amanda's eyes nervously as they lowered to examine her lightly rounded stomach.

"How many months have you missed?" The interrogation was curt and sharp.

Emily stared at her, stunned for a moment by her audacity. "How did you know that?" she demanded, astonished.

Amanda smiled tightly, persisting adamantly, "How many months have you missed, Emily?"

"Two."

Amanda walked away a little and to the window, and she glanced out for a second before swinging back to face Emily. She smoothed her smart black traveling skirt and then smiled, but her blue eyes remained as cold as the spring morning. "So . . . he claimed his revenge after all. How many times?"

Emily stared at her dully, then started to voice her perplexity.

"Was it just the once?" Amanda interrupted harshly, tidying her blonde curls with a rigorous hand. "Has Clifford been to you at night just the once?"

Emily stared at her, then blood suffused her face as Amanda's meaning penetrated. She swallowed and simply nodded.

"The night you insulted him . . . us . . . no doubt. Was that it?"

She watched avidly as Emily assented silently.

Amanda rasped out on a brittle laugh, "With guests here too? He is quite the most. . . ."

She made no attempt to finish her assessment of her brother-in-law or his recklessness.

"Well, miss, I do believe you are pregnant," she bit out, tight-lipped. "He has bestowed living proof of his persecution and how it will gratify him."

Emily stared blankly as the words were snapped out. "Pregnant?" she repeated stupidly. "How can I be? It is spiteful to suggest such a . . . such a base thing." She turned away, hurt and bewilderment plain in her face. "Please go now, I want to dress," she ordered woodenly.

Amanda approached her swiftly and, snatching at a slender wrist, jerked her round. "God . . . did your mother tell you nothing?" Amanda hissed. "Surely you realize how babies are made—a man and a woman and a bed, and in this instance, an amount of lecherous vindictiveness."

Emily stood rigid then. As the horror was absorbed, she whispered, appalled, "Surely not. He came here but once. It was only once." The words were desperate, her eyes pleading with Amanda to make the terror go away. Amanda's face merely hardened as did her rouged mouth into a slight sneer.

"Oh, once is quite enough, Emily."

Amanda stood thoughtfully for a moment. "But then you have seen Jonathon quite a lot these past months—since the snow cleared," she muttered reflectively. "You seem inordinately friendly with that young man. Has he ever . . . ?"

Emily spluttered into her words as her face reddened and more with anger than uneasiness, "How can you intimate such a thing . . . that Jonathon would . . . ?"

Amanda laughed into the outrage, "I know it sounds ridiculous, Emily, for he certainly is one of the most soppy males I have ever come across. But then, sometimes it is the most seemingly innocuous men that do the most harm." She laughed with more sarcasm. "Which theory is, of course, hardly borne out in the case of our lord and master here at Malvern Hall. Harmless he certainly is not."

Emily gazed at her unable to take any of this in, and Amanda grated out dismissively, "Oh, never mind."

Her eyes moved back to Emily's shocked face, now tautened by grief and panic. She cautioned in a vehement whisper, "Well, if I were you I would not tell him . . . ever."

Emily wetted her parched lips and swallowed painfully. "What shall I do?" she asked desparingly. "How can I ever return home now? Even if he were to allow it . . . perhaps he will now. Do you think he will now? Now that I am totally disgraced?"

Amanda neared her slowly, saying, "You really have no choice, Emily, but to try and rid yourself of the child. I know someone, but in London. We would need to travel there."

Emily turned away feeling harrowed, a bubbling nausea churning in her stomach and rising in her throat. She closed her eyes and breathed deeply. "I shall tell him," she declared shakily. "It is his fault. Why should I not tell him?"

Amanda shrieked a malicious laugh. "Why should you not?" she mimicked tauntingly. "Because I believed you would not want to gratify him quite so much by the news of his utter triumph and your utter disgrace, that is why. Do you think he will be chastened by the news, feel some sort of pity or remorse for you? You could not be more wrong. Nor could you satisfy his sick vengeance more." She paused and looked into staring violet eyes. "You are following his mother's life closely; he has plotted that you do so, and it pleases him greatly that you should suffer as she did. I thought you realized already that that was his motive for bringing you here: to humiliate and degrade you in the manner his mother was humiliated and degraded at Thrushcross Grange."

Emily shook her head and declared weakly, for she felt emotionally drained now, "That is a lie . . . a vicious rumor that was spread about by evil-minded gossips. The Moores were servants at Thrushcross Grange, it is true, but none of the rest was. It was malicious falsehood. My father would never . . . and it was hardly any of our fault that Mrs. Moore died. She might have done so in any case at that time in her life had she never lived with us at all. She could have contracted illness anywhere—"

Amanda broke into this shaking defence with a choking laugh, blurting out contemptuously, "You fool. Why do you think she died? Have you really no knowledge of it, or are you just faking this idiocy?" She gazed scornfully at the white-faced girl. "Very well . . . I shall assume that you do not know, although I should have imagined Clifford would have told you; and enjoyed regaling you with every sordid detail. And trust me . . . I lie not. I have no reason to, and neither had Stephen when he told me of it. But you can always ask Clifford, if you dare."

She halted and smoothed her skirt, picking at a speck of lint that marred the dark perfection. "Katherine Moore was evicted from Thrushcross Grange with Clifford because she was pregnant. It was your father's child. She had been seduced by your father practically as soon as they were resident at Thrushcross Grange, and he kept her there not only to labor but as his mistress too. She told him of her pregnancy, and to protect himself and deny any tale she might tell of his debauchery, he concocted some ridiculous story that she had stolen a brooch. He wanted reasonable grounds to dismiss her and Clifford, to

269

get rid of them quickly, for no doubt in six months' time, the evidence of his lechery would have been only too plain, would it not? And not quite so easily explained away, and his wife perhaps not so gullible to silly tales."

Amanda paused and smiled at Emily's dazed countenance. She continued with malicious satisfaction. "They went to the poorhouse. Katherine Moore started premature labor after about three months spent there, I believe. Hardly surprisingly, I suppose, when you take into account the prevalent conditions — filth and squalor everywhere, and lack of food and warmth. She died eventually, after a day and a night of agonizing labor. The child was stillborn after she had screamed and writhed in pain with the child stuck in her hips for more than twenty-four hours, and Clifford with her throughout. He stayed with her until his dead sister was born; brought belatedly into the world by some filthy-handed slut who was soaked in gin and barely knew what she was about."

She glanced slyly at Emily. "He would have had a sister. You too, you would have shared a sister."

She stared at Emily, noting impersonally the silent tears wetting her ashen cheeks: Emily moved her head once in mute, dead-eyed refusal of what she had heard; Amanda laughed. "Oh, yes," she mouthed smugly, "every word of it is true, every one; and perhaps there is more that I know nothing of. But it matters little what I know, for Clifford knows everything, and it is he that has brought you of this, and deliberately. That is why I say you will content him beyond anything by announcing that you are with child."

She spun away from the silently crying girl, musing aloud, "It is quite uncanny the way your life is following hers, and yet he did plan it to . . . perhaps your death also. It would requite his mother's death — you cannot deny it. Perhaps he might even, if you let him know of this, turn you out to some hovel somewhere — just to give the likelihood a better chance. Considering his mother's plight, I expect he would deem it condign."

Emily closed her eyes, remembering now quite remotely that he had indeed used just such a word to her father when intimidating him into acceptance of his terms, all those months ago when she had been safe still, at home.

She remembered more recent times when they had sat in the library together after dinner, browsing through the books. She could not deny that she had often looked up to find him scrutinizing her figure, but without any obvious lechery. It was more as though he merely assessed it for change, and he would ask casually how she felt, whether anything ailed her.

Emily closed her eyes once more, as though futilely trying to exclude some of the nightmare. "This place you spoke of, Amanda, where is it exactly in London?" she asked hoarsely.

Amanda gave a brief smile and waved a dismissive hand. "Oh, I know it, never fear. I will see if we can go there next week . . . perhaps for the weekend. I shall ask him if we may. I am sure he will allow it. I can explain that we have to shop there and visit a friend of mine."

"Surely he could not be that duplicitous . . . surely not," Emily reasoned despairingly. "Why would he ask me to marry him? Why would he do that if he wished me dead? He did not need to ask."

Amanda stared at her, listening avidly, pinch-mouthed. "It is a way he has with women," she lied immediately and malevolently, ". . . a selfish ploy to keep them doting until he is ready to discard them. He promised affection and loyalty to each. I should know; he promised me that he loved me and would marry me when I was his mistress and look now." She gave a small, miserable laugh. "I live with him here, willing to share his bed even now because I still love him, and he treats me worse than the dirt beneath his shoe. You have heard how he speaks to me,

Emily; you know I do not lie." She paused, then sighed out wistfully, "He comes nowhere near me now, Emily, and has not done so since we returned here from London. Yet just weeks before we had been lovers. Now he prefers to visit some harlot in town."

Blue eyes darted to assess the tear-streaked face. "And it would be the same for you, Emily; you know that, don't you?"

Emily made not a sound or gesture but merely stood tensely.

"Did you know he goes awhoring in town, Emily?" Amanda asked coarsely. "He has a . . . friend who owns a teashop in St. Albans. He takes that black man with him too; even paying for his pleasure with some black slut of a maid. Now who would have believed that of such a mean bastard?" She halted then, and her white hands clung together, grasping tightly. She rectified shrilly, "No . . . I must be fair. It was the wrong word to choose, for it makes him sound ungenerous with his payments, and he has ever been free with his money. I cannot complain there. He has never stopped my allowance or even lessened it, and yet he claims nothing in return." She halted abruptly and looked at Emily. "So what do you think they are doing at this genteel establishment at ten o'clock at night, Emily? Taking tea?" she sneered. "I'll warrant they are taking something else entirely."

Emily turned away utterly exhausted. She groped her way along the mattress as though she would collapse and then sat on the side of her bed.

She remained silent, numb now to any emotion at all. Amanda took the quiet to mean further counseling was needed. "He hates you, Emily," she stated, affecting concern and sympathy. "He hates all of the Shaws, and in a way I believe in that he is justified. For to witness what he did, and of someone he loved, and to be able to do nothing to alleviate her agonized suffering, must have been torment indeed. I should imagine it might have addled his brain somewhat, for I am sure he is no longer capable of any human feelings. Certainly he cannot love, even though he may indeed at times profess to do so."

Flinty blue eyes gazed fixedly at the still vacuous-faced girl. "Do you believe what I have told you, Emily?" Amanda demanded with soft sweetness.

Silence ensued and Amanda approached the bed, bending close to Emily, their heads barely inches apart. "Do you believe what I have told you, Emily?" Amanda repeated more firmly.

Violet eyes focused at last on fine, fair skin and piercing, shrewd blue eyes. Emily nodded slowly and one hand went to smear the wetness from her cold face. She started to rise away from the bed, and Amanda was forced to retreat from her a little to allow her passage.

She walked to the wardrobe and her hand went automatically to remove a gown. She began to unbutton her nightgown, preparing to dress as she said with quiet grace, "Thank you for telling me, Amanda. If you could arrange that trip to town I would be most grateful."

The knock came again. Emily looked away from the flaming coals in the fire, rose from the chair, and walked to open the door.

There appeared to be no one about, and she widened the door with a light, melancholy sigh, wishing that Richard had chosen another time for his games, for she now felt so little like participating in them.

She stepped out into the corridor a bit, about to call the child's name, when she half-turned and saw him.

Clifford moved away from the wall he had been resting against and moved toward her doorway. He leaned casually against the door jamb, making it impossible for her to reenter without removing his obstructing arm. Her eyes lowered at once. She sensed her body icing in fear and hatred, but she remained composed and merely stared past him, back into her warm sanctuary.

"Have I upset you in some way?"

Emily shook her head just once, her face emotionless.

"What is it then? Why have you been shutting yourself away for days past? I believed we had got over that once."

She looked up briefly with cool, dispassionate eyes. "I have felt ill for a few days," she excused herself tonelessly. "It is just a recurring indisposition." She paused and then said with barely a stutter indicating her embarrassment, "It comes once a month."

She felt a flush of traitorous colour warm her face at the lie, but she knew it was of immeasurable help for what it implied of her health and condition.

His mouth set slightly in consideration before his eyes flicked inconspicuously, yet estimatingly, the length of her figure. As Emily guardedly watched the appraisal, she was sure he knew that she lied and why.

His eyes moved back to hers leisurely, staring relentlessly. Hers dropped away almost immediately. "I shall get the doctor to you," he resolved quietly.

He made to turn and Emily realized, agitated, that he meant to do so straightaway. She caught at his arm, swiftly halting him. "No . . . please, it is nothing," she demurred hastily. "I just want to be by myself today, not with anyone. Not with Richard or Amanda . . . and not with you."

She sensed tears threatening and a hand raised to shield her face in a pretense of soothing her head. "May I have some laudanum tonight . . . for my headache?" she requested quietly.

He nodded and then said evenly, "Amanda tells me you two want to shop in London next week." The words were slow and unstressed, but Emily was sure there was an undercurrent of suspicion.

"Yes, I would like to very much," she murmured.

He nodded thoughtfully. "Very well. I shall accompany you. It is time I checked on my house there and tended to a few other matters."

Emily felt guilt and uneasiness color her face, certain now that he knew. His hand came out, touching one of hers, gripping hard as she tried to withdraw from him at once. "Come and sit downstairs with me . . . just for half an hour."

Emily allowed her cold, weak fingers to rest in larger warm ones as she prevaricated, "I did not think it was you. I expected it to be Richard, come with his nanny to say good night. I believed you always to be out on Wednesday evenings." The words faded away as she realized what she was alluding to and her fingers squirmed spontaneously in his to free themselves.

His clasp strengthened, his thumb caressing the back of her hand soothingly. "My lust appears to be governable tonight, Emily. I have no need to go elsewhere," he murmured with very little irony.

She looked up at him then. For an instant the sadness and horror of the past days, which had taught her so much of their families' pasts, all of which she knew now to be true, gathered and mingled heart-breakingly in her face and eyes. He pulled her against him abruptly, murmuring her name huskily as his arms enclosed her tightly. His face leaned into the dark hair as he swayed her gently in his arms in mutual comfort and despair.

She nestled into him at once, clinging to the warmth and security for a moment before remembering that she could not find those in his arms. She pushed him abruptly away, one hand moving swiftly to wipe her eyes. "May I go into my room now, please? I feel quite sick again," she said coldly and deliberately.

He gazed at her in utter silence for half a minute or more, the anguish in his eyes unseen, then turned suddenly and walked away.

Emily approached her door and entered, shutting and locking it before returning to the chair by the fire.

Emily watched Jonathon's muscles ripple and bunch beneath the straining calico shirt as he knocked stones into roughly uniform shapes.

She peered over the top of the slowly forming section of wall that her friend was painstakingly erecting. As he looked up and grinned at her, she smiled sleepily, then yawned.

She watched him toil with strange pleasure, wondering why it was that regarding others at monotous work had such a soporific power over her. It had been the same at home when she and Jane had sat together in the parlor and Jane worked lengthily and diligently at her sewing. Emily would study her deft fingers at first with alert intent and some degree of admiration for the seemingly effortless talent and patience that accompanied it. But within a short while, her eyelids would begin to get heavy and her gaze would glaze as the flying fingers and air of quiet industry drugged her.

Jonathon brushed down his rough work clothes abruptly, breaking this incipient trance. He turned and smiled. "Are you ready to ride now?" he asked.

He did not wait for an answer, adding wryly, "But just for a short while. Lucy is a little under the weather at the moment. She has been coughing the night away for more than a week now."

He gazed past her shoulder and into the distance, and Emily noted his greenish eyes harden. "I see my wealthy neighbor is in fine fettle though, this sunny afternoon," he muttered. Gold-green eyes shifted slowly, following the motion of the two horseback riders.

Emily noted that his eyes were now stationary. "Are

they coming this way?" she inquired immediately without turning to see for herself.

Jonathon shook his head slowly, a lock of thick brown hair falling across his brow. "No. They stopped for a while; he has seen us but obviously deems us of little importance today. They are carrying on toward the Hall."

Emily nodded slowly in grateful acceptance of this news. "Come, then," she urged Jonathon enthusiastically. "The wall is finished and I have been most patient in waiting for you. Now let me see you jump it as you boasted."

Jonathon smiled and then, wiping his hands thoroughly on the cloth he kept in a pocket of his work jacket, he donned the garment quickly. He moved to his dappled stallion and mounted the animal.

The tan mare was placidly cropping grass quite close by. Emily moved to mount her. The stallion backed off slowly and then Jonathon spurred the animal forward toward the waist-high pile of stones he had just erected. He cleared it easily and was riding into Moore land at a gallop. Emily stared after him, then collected her drowsy thoughts enough to laugh and give chase.

Emily caught up with Jonathon as he purposefully slowed, allowing her to do so. She smiled breathlessly as the cold spring air tingled effervescently in her nose and throat.

Jonathon narrowed his eyes, staring back the way they had come. He considered his newly built section of wall far away in the distance now. He cocked his head to one side and murmured judiciously, as though the subleties of his handicraft were well within eyesight, "Yes, I believe I am quite pleased with my stonemasonry."

Emily grimaced her doubt and he laughed and walked his horse closer. His eyes were grave now as he solemnly informed, "Moore was over this week, asking again if I would sell to him. His price is much more tempting this time. He has increased it by half as much again. It is a good deal more than the land is worth, I am sure of it."

Emily's hand moved to touch her saddle. She traced a design on the dark leather. "I would hate it if you moved away from here," she sighed wistfully.

"And, of course, I would miss you too, Emily," Jonathon admitted softly. "But I have to be rational and think of Lucy as well as myself. If it were just me I would tell him to go and. . . ." He halted and flushed. "Lucy sees so few people here," he hurried on briskly. "She will never meet any suitable husband, and I want better for her than some oafish farmhand," he muttered with quite an amount of patronizing derision. As though aware then of his arrogance, he colored once more.

After a silent moment he decided slowly, "I think if he is willing to pay, then I shall move on. I have not refused him outright this time. I said I would null it over." He smiled at Emily, informing brightly, "I have thought of shopkeeping somewhere. Do you see me as a shopkeeper, Emily?"

Emily merely gave him a small smile and a shrug.

Jonathon looked out over the meadowland, first toward his own farm and then in the direction of Malvern Hall. "I hate the idea of him having it, though, because I know he wants it so much and that I will be yielding to his wishes. Yet . . ." he smiled with an amount of malicious satisfaction, "yet, the idea of selling to him and at such a grossly inflated price is almost recompense."

Emily smiled, understanding his spite. "You must look after yourself and your sister, Jonathon. If that means trying something new and more profitable, then . . . but I would hate it so if you left."

"How long will you be staying here, Emily?" Jonathon asked, watching her intently.

"Not too much longer now, I think," she said. "My sister is soon to be betrothed. It is all arranged, so my mother tells me in her last letter. I should imagine once that is settled I shall return home." She knew further explanation was called for and informed quite truthfully, "It is quite a financial burden, you see, for everyone to be at home. It was deemed best that someone seek employment for a while. I had considered joining a household as a companion or a governess for some time before I actually did so." She fell silent and looked at the countryside for something distracting to talk about.

Jonathon leaned across at that point, his hand touching hers lightly. He gripped it eagerly then, choking out, "I have been meaning to say . . . I mean that for some while now, Emily, I have—" He flustered to an abrupt halt, his cheeks more ruddy than Emily had ever seen before. He recommenced in a rush, "I know you seem quite settled working as you do for Mrs. Moore. I know you have a good life there. There cannot be many working in such a capacity that enjoy the sort of life you do. But . . . well, I just hope I am right in thinking you would not want to be so employed all your life. You have to think of yourself too, Emily, and of your future. . . ." he hesitated and then blurted out on a huge breath, "Please excuse me, I have no right to talk so. I have nothing to offer. . . ."

Emily grimaced amicably. "What on earth are you on about, Jonathon? It makes no sense," she chided good-naturedly.

"Forgive me . . . I thought as much too," he mumbled stiffly with a jerking nod of the head. He moved the horse away suddenly, and Emily's gaze followed him as he prodded the stallion into an immediate canter in the direction of the stream.

Emily urged her mare forward more slowly, feeling the strange nausea starting up in the pit of her stomach.

Jonathon wheeled his horse around in a wide arc and returned to her side, pulling the horse to a rather jerky halt. He reined in, and then, as though he had contained the words within his mouth the whole length of time it had taken to return to her, he gasped, "Will you marry me, Emily?"

Emily stared, speechless, into his flushed face. She managed a small uncertain smile and made to utter something.

He interrupted, "I know I have no right to ask you. You come of a good family, although I realize you have all been hounded by misfortune lately and your father's financial position is not at it once was. But if I accept Moore's offer for the land, we might then have enough to start a new life, you and I, in the city somewhere. We could go to London and buy a suitable premises and set up in a shop."

Emily looked uncertainly at his ardent, youthful face.

Reading her skepticism, he declared with some arrogance, "I am almost twenty-four now, Emily, not a lad. I know I look younger than my years, but I am hardworking."

"I am sure you are, Jonathon . . . I never doubted that for a moment." She stared down at the leather gloves covering her fingers. She flexed them slowly onto the saddle, trying to elucidate what could be gained from this new and unexpected situation. The knowledge of her spontaneous mercenariness as she tried to weigh advantages and disadvantages made the blood flood her face just as hotly as it did Jonathon's.

Perhaps thinking that maidenly modesty might be the cause of this most becoming roseate flush, Jonathon leant across and tenderly took a gloved hand in his.

Emily allowed him to hold her hand and even gripped it a little in fondness. "You know so little about me, Jonathon. There may be things you might not like—"

"Impossible," he interrupted passionately. "I worship you, Emily, I think I have from the moment I first saw you, with all your riding habit covered in mud, when I was trespassing on Moore land." He gave a hoarse laugh and added ironically, "Much like now, of course."

Emily smiled at him, and the calculating reason started to whir within her brain once more. Marriage to Jonathon, she knew, could provide both her and the child she carried with respectability and protection from any further malice or persecution. Some comfort from a friend and from a modest home of her own might compensate for the fact that she did not truly love Jonathon, although she liked him and felt at ease in his company.

Taking her continued silence to mean further persuasion was needed, he murmured ardently, "I know we could be happy, Emily, and should you agree, I will accept his offer and we can marry and move away at once. I know you have no more liking for him than I do."

Emily gave a small, pensive smile. "I shall have to think about this, Jonathon. I had not realized you felt this way—I hadn't an inkling." She bit her lip a little. As logic once more predominated, she added slowly, "Also, I might have to ask his permission. While my father is . . . unwell, and he has been unwell for some time now, Sir Clifford has been acting almost as guardian to me." A spontaneous laugh escaped her as she muttered bitterly, "In principle, if not in deed." Jonathon looked at her quite sharply and she added quickly, "I would not be surprised if I am his legal ward."

The granting of permission was forgotten momentarily as Jonathon clasped her hands tighter to him and looked down at them cherishingly. He murmured, "I never in my wildest dreams expected you would entertain my proposal at all . . . oh, Emily."

Emily withdrew her hands a trifle abruptly. "You should not idolize me, Jonathon, or adore me so, for I fear I will only disappoint you."

He merely shook his head in mute refutation of this

quiet statement, his eyes now quite amorous.

"I really should be getting back now," Emily said quietly, her conscience still bothering her. "Thank you for asking me to marry you. I am truly honored . . . but there are things I need to consider."

"Of course," he murmured solemnly.

Emily turned her horse and started to ride back to the boundary of their estates with Jonathon slightly behind her this time. They parted quickly and with few words. As Emily rode toward Malvern Hall, she felt her wretchedness increase. She tried to estimate whether she would ever be able to carry off the deceit well enough to trick Jonathon while fully aware that she carried another man's child.

She forced all the muddled, anguishing troubles from her mind and thought instead of Amanda. Amanda would know what was best; she was sure to.

Emily watched surreptitiously as Clifford returned his gold watch to his pocket. He drained the last of his wine and then replaced the thin-stemmed crystal goblet on the table and sat motionless, staring into the fire.

She was dining downstairs tonight, having determined to speak to him about Jonathon's proposal.

They were dining alone. Amanda had been out the whole day and had not returned from a visit. It was assumed she would now spend the whole evening abroad.

No opportunity to speak to Amanda on this new situation had therefore presented itself. Emily mused on the development more calmly and rationally now, realizing it was probably best. The problems were hers and ultimately she knew she would have to deal with them alone. She felt ill-at-ease confiding any personal details to Amanda and trusted her little, although she knew she had not lied to her about the truth of her father's involvement with Katherine Moore.

One of her hands went to touch tentatively at her stomach, below the shielding table. It traveled curiously, her fingers exploring gently as though she could perceive by touch what lay within. She thought of babies — crying, demanding to be fed and cleaned no matter their sex — and her hand sprang away from her belly. Her head jerked up to stare at Clifford again.

He seemed just as oblivious to her now as he had been when she had joined him that evening. He had been polite but formal and quite impartial throughout the meal. There was no indication that joining him tonight either pleased or vexed him.

Their conversation had been limited to a brief observation he had made that the bruising on the fetlock of Richard's pony appeared to be healing well. Emily had reciprocated with a comment on the fine weather, but apart from that the entire mealtime had passed in silence.

Perplexed and oddly disturbed by this change in him, Emily had found herself looking up at him quite openly several times, hoping he might be tempted to talk further. But he appeared impervious to her. When he was not eating or drinking, he seemed more interested in musing thoughts of his own that kept his eyes constantly on the warm, orange glowing coals in the grate.

This new disregard for her presence nevertheless reassured her in a paradoxical way, for it had removed the last doubts she had harbored that he would refuse Jonathon's proposal out-of-hand. He seemed now so totally indifferent to her that she realized he would be unlikely to raise any objection to her marriage to a peasant farmer. Her hands gripped together in her lap and tightened. No doubt it would gratify him greatly, if anything, that Squire Shaw's daughter was to be the wife of a man who was barely financially solvent and whose parents had both been servants practically their whole lives through.

Her fingers twisted, and as the continuing silence washed over her and the atmosphere remained as dead, she sensed a strange, aching hurt. She realized he might be ignoring her out of contempt. Perhaps he had indeed guessed she was pregnant and that she would be of no further use. Perhaps he would henceforth ask her not join him at dinner . . . or anywhere else, for that matter. He might be planning to send her home, to disgrace them all. She knew well enough that all Jane's marriage plans would be utterly destroyed if just one murmur of her shame touched them.

She started from her haunting reverie as she heard him murmur something. He rose, obviously having taken his leave, and their eyes met briefly. She stared at him avidly but his attention was gone; there was a terse, parting nod directed her way as he made for the door.

It closed quietly as he left the room, and Emily dropped her head forward once more to gaze at the unsteady, intertwining fingers in her lap. She knew suddenly and with startling clarity that Jonathon was indeed her only hope.

She also knew she would have to ask for permission straightaway, for if this coldness he now displayed for her increased any further, she might never again find the fortitude to approach him.

She hesitated barely a moment longer and then rose from the table and quit the room.

She walked the length of the corridor, instinctively in the direction of his study, feeling it was most likely he had gone there. She walked tensely, trying to steel some courage and make her brain recite the rehearsed speech. She had previously believed she had it memorized, but now words tried to lose themselves in odd corners of her mind.

She clenched her fists, wishing she could instill the same steadiness into her trembling limbs. She turned the corner of the corridor into the massive reception hall, her eyes downcast, and then came upon him suddenly and quite unexpectedly.

He was standing by the large hall table, over which hung a massive and beautifully scrolled mirror. He was obviously readying himself to go out, for he had on a dark overcoat that hung open as he made some adjustment to his cravat in the mirror.

Emily glanced about the hall nervously. Her attention was arrested by the silent, dark figure of Heath, also dressed to leave the house, standing by the great oaken double doors.

Her attention swung back to the sparkling glass, and she saw Clifford's eyes on her now and realized he had seen her reflection in the mirror. Silver eyes lingered briefly before they returned, as did his hand, to the gray silk, and he folded it once more with slow deliberation.

He turned casually, picking up leather gloves from the table. He gave her his attention then, his gray eyes completely impassive. She felt herself numb completely as he raised casually questioning brows which lazily inquired of her what she wanted.

Emily stuttered hastily, "I . . . I wanted to speak to you . . . about something. . . ."

He glanced down at the soft leather gloves he held, then back at her. "I am just on my way out," he informed coolly. "But if it concerns, yet again, your wish to quit my house, I believe we have nothing further to discuss. You are already aware of my answer and I would that you trouble me with the matter no more."

Emily stared at him, sensing his aloofness in manner and words freeze her further.

Her eyes shifted uneasily and uncertainly to Heath, but the man stood immobile, without a trace of amusement today in his attitude or in the atmosphere.

She looked hastily back at Clifford, sure now she could

285

sense just how greatly she irritated him. She made to utter something quickly, desperate to get finished and away from him and back to her room. She faltered as she realized she was talking utter rubbish.

"I am afraid this will have to wait, Emily," Clifford stated levelly. "I really have to go. I am late already. I was expected in town some time ago." The implication was deliberate and unmistakable, and as their eyes met and held, she knew at once where he was going and that he intended she should.

Pride and hurt engulfed her, but she resolved to finish what she'd begun. "It is important; I would not have bothered you else," she uttered with a remoteness that now equaled his.

His jaw set slightly as she sensed the return of her pride and composure. His eyes narrowed, a ruthless mockery incipient. "Well, should you prefer I stay here with you tonight, Emily, I expect I might be persuaded." He murmured with deliberate insinuation, "We could discuss any number of things the night long, should you so wish."

Emily felt her face sting hotly, mortified to realize that she indeed wanted him to stay with her, despite knowing that he would then expect her to provide equal entertainment to that which he was about to forgo in town. Her eyes lowered and she remained silent.

His mouth twisted and he gave a hard laugh. "I thought not . . . in which case, I have no further time to spend with you right now."

He turned away from her and moved leisurely towards the servant. Remembering then why she had sought him out, and the urgency of the matter, she followed a few paces. "Well, might I speak to you in the morning?" she called appealingly. When he remained silent, she reiterated huskily, "It is most important."

He hesitated then and as though something had just occurred to him he swung back towards her abruptly.

"Does it concern your health?" he demanded softly yet imperatively.

She shook her head, her eyes gazing at him beseechingly and with a directness hitherto unknown.

He returned the regard for a moment and then bowed his head suddenly to look at his polished shoes. "I really have to go now, Emily," he informed with toneless civility, "and I am not sure that I will be back before late tomorrow morning, perhaps even the afternoon. Should the matter still need my attention, you may look for me then."

He turned away with a small, unfeeling smile.

Clifford appeared unaware of Heath as he left, merely passing the man without a word. Emily's eyes moved to the servant and she looked at the grave-faced man for a moment with the same intensity with which he regarded her. Then, with a vague air of melancholy, he turned and followed Clifford out into the night.

Aware of being steadily watched, Clifford's mouth thrust slightly in a wry smile, anticipating the light mockery in Heath's eyes even before he turned toward him and saw it.

The two men gazed wordlessly at each other for a moment, then Clifford turned back to the coach window, the amusement still in his face as he looked out into the sombre night.

"Enjoying yourself, Heath?"

"Immensely, sir."

Clifford's smile deepened at the dry response and he said with alacrity, "Good . . . good. Nothing like a country drive to heighten the senses."

"In darkness? At ten o'clock at night? And in perishing cold weather?" Heath countered sarcastically.

Clifford laughed and gazed through the window more

purposefully. He breathed deeply of the wood-scented dusk air. "Fresh air . . . the call of the tawny owl in the still night . . . the rustle of the breeze in the leaves . . ." he enthused lightly.

"There are no leaves — not yet," Heath interjected with increased irony. "You shall need to wait a few months more before waxing lyrical over them."

Clifford turned to him with affected pique. He shook his head and chided, "No need to carp so, Heath. I was waxing metaphorical . . . naturally."

Heath allowed a small smile and then muttered wryly, "I have to tell you, I envisaged appreciating much more than the countryside in its natural state." He drew his feet restlessly close and tapped them against the wooden coach floor. He straightened in the seat and then sat forward, his elbows resting lightly on his knees. He clasped his hands and looked at Clifford, noting the self-mockery in the lean, shadowy face.

"Where are we going, Cliff?" he asked with gentle tolerance and a sympathetic smile. "Have you forgotten the way to St. Albans?" He indicated the coach driver with an abrupt jerk of his head. "Has David forgotten the way? We have been out for more than an hour now and stopped nowhere. And I am gasping for a drink."

Clifford smiled easily. "We shall be at Hatfield soon. There are a couple of good taverns —"

Heath interrupted with soft insinuation, "I was more looking forward to a cup of tea. I know this little place . . . comforting . . . welcoming . . . superb tea. We passed the turnoff miles back, where it was signposted 'St. Albans.' "

"And when did you ever drink tea after six in the afternoon?" Clifford parried with a derisive smile.

"Every chance I get, which of late, I have to own, has not been that often," Heath muttered with heavy innuendo and a dry laugh. Some of the humor faded as he studied Clifford penetratingly. "And by your look and manner, I should say you could do with a potful."

Clifford said nothing, but the sardonic twist further distorted his mouth. After a silent moment he said abruptly, "David can turn at the next suitable place. We can go back to St. Albans and I shall drop you off in town."

Heath sat back in his seat. He settled into the comfortable squabs, regarding his friend shrewdly. "And what are you intending to do? Tour the Hertfordshire countryside for the rest of the night?"

"Why not? I could sample the ale at every tavern I come across. It is a while since I did that. I believe I might quite enjoy it." Clifford leaned suddenly, his cane raised to rap at the driver's box as he noted the clearing ahead with space to turn the coach-and-four.

Heath caught at his outstretched arm, preventing him. "What the hell?" he muttered easily. "I was running out of excuses anyway. If I turn up once more without you . . ."

Clifford shrugged equably, indicating it was Heath's choice what he did. He inquired with mild interest, "What excuses have you used? I hope you have been imaginative." He recognized the gleam of arrogant amusement in Heath's brown eyes and qualified the statement with studied apology. "The excuses, I mean. I realize on other accounts your imagination never lacks."

Heath inclined his head in acceptance of the wry compliment. He looked exaggeratedly thoughtful before listing out slowly, "That neighbors had turned up unexpectedly and you felt obliged to entertain them; that a groom left the stables unlocked and all the horses escaped over the fields; that there was a riot amongst the kitchen staff over who had the last baked onion. . . ." He barely paused before continuing in the same monotonous drone. "That there is a lovely young lady in residence that you are in love with, and notwithstanding the fact that she locks herself in her room and only ventures out when she is sure you are away from home, she keeps you bound to her irrevocably and irrefutably."

Clifford's eyes slid back to his friend's for a moment before he turned away to the coach window again. "No need to have stretched your ingenuity quite so far, Heath," he dismissed quietly, "They sound implausible—every one."

Heath repeated softly, "Quite implausible. Especially the last, despite the fact that it happens to be true."

Clifford's eyes remained with the gloaming. Heath stared at the side of his face for a long moment, then remarked lightly, "This new tactic—feigning disinterest—it will never work. She can do it much better than you."

Clifford raised his eyes to the silvery moon that could just be glimpsed between the skeletal, lightly breezing tree tops. He gave a small, harsh laugh. "Ah, but she has an unfair advantage—she never needs to pretend."

"I am not so sure. She wanted you with her tonight—and not merely to talk." Heath added softly, "You should have stayed. What point have you made? She will merely distrust you more for indulging in what she imagines is rampant lechery." He laughed. "For what I too imagined was rampant lechery, for that matter."

The pearly moon escaped the trees, frosting the side of Clifford's face as his jaw set.

"I suppose it has not occurred to you to tell her you love her," Heath ventured calmly. He watched the averted face jerk away from him further, presumably to examine passing shrubbery. "Well, how about apologizing for abducting her?" he suggested smoothly.

Clifford swung to face him. "She was not abducted," he grated with perilous quiet, "I have her parents' consent."

"Yes, but not hers," Heath argued gently. He shook his head slowly. "We have been together a long time now, you and I; too long, I think. I worry about you. I thought I knew your moods—every one; yet since she has been at the Hall, you are completely different." He sat back further into the comfortable seat. One foot moved to rest on the other knee as he chided in a soft drawl, "You shore ain't no fun any mawh, Cliffuhd."

Clifford stared at Heath for a moment and then a small, acknowledging smile escaped him. "The Black Bull," he announced evenly, with a brief glance through the window.

"What have they got on offer?" Heath asked with a total lack of enthusiasm.

"Shall we see?"

Heath smiled, shrugging resignedly. "Why not."

Clifford called out suddenly to the driver and the coach pulled into the narrow, empty courtyard.

The two men had alighted before the footmen had time to dismount and help them. Clifford clapped his hands together to warm then, shouting to the driver and footmen that they should get themselves refreshment before he and Heath made for the door of the inn.

Total silence greeted their arrival in the small tap room, where it housed a rough wooden bar and equally rough and wooden locals who goggled, pipe-mouthed, at the new patrons.

A sparse-haired, boggle-eyed landlord crept tentatively from behind the bar, wiping his hands ceaselessly on a greasy-looking apron secured with string about his middle. He moved forward more hastily and obsequiously as he realized the two elegant men were not some wispy figment of his imagination.

"My lord . . . you do my humble drinking house immeasurable honor by stopping here this night," he groveled heartily. "What can I procure for you? Ale? A hot toddy? A dinner? I can get my wife to rustle up some pie—"

"Have you another room? Somewhere private?" Clifford interrupted laconically. "I prefer a quiet atmosphere, and I would not wish to curb these gentlemen in their revelry."

The granite-faced, silent men regarded him still, their expressions as inert as their limbs.

Heath let out a light, snorting laugh, disguising it immediately by shuffling his feet loudly against the rough-hewn floor as though to warm them. He stood slightly behind Clifford, as was his custom when in company. The landlord's eyes shifted to him uncertainly, noting the black, alien features and the expensive attire which seemed to contradict each other.

"I shall show your . . ." he stuttered and rumbled beneath his breath, then resorted to, ". . . man, into a room while you sup, my lord." He shuffled away, cringing forward subserviently.

Heath moved as though to follow the stooping man, but Clifford caught at his arm. "My friend drinks with me," he stated quietly.

Heath's eyes slid to his, rapidly cautioning, but Clifford merely smiled implacably.

The landlord dithered on the spot for a moment. Bowing low with the lank strands of hair flapping about his forehead, he agreed humbly, "Of course, your lordship."

" 'Sir' will do." The information was quiet and lightly amused.

The man bowed again and then held out a hand, indicating that they should walk through.

A low wooden door opened onto a moderately sized, whitewashed chamber. As they entered, a young woman looked up from where she sat fondling a kitten by the fire. She stared dumbly and slack-mouthed at the sight of the two refined, handsome men, her eyes lingering awestruck on Heath.

A furious, silent wagging of the old landlord's head was obviously a sign of her to remove herself. She did so, heaving her buxom form up and clutching the kitten to her bosom. She backed her way round the walls to the door, nodding deferentially the while.

Clifford walked into the room and close to the fire. He inspected a strange-looking armchair quite near the hearth. Having dusted it a little with his gloves and deemed it fit to sit in, he did so with a sigh. Heath did likewise, in a similar chair opposite, but dispensing with the initial housewifery.

Clifford looked up at the man who still gawped at them doubtfully, uncertain they were not some sort of mocking apparition. Clifford smiled encouragingly and received a wavering, broken-toothed one in return.

"Have you any brandy?" he inquired mildly.

"Yes, my lord."

Clifford smiled at his continual aggrandizement, but said nothing further. His eyes narrowed. "I mean the proper stuff—French and good," he informed with soft steel.

The landlord shuffled, then prevaricated, "Well, as you must know, my lord, it is never easy to get French goods during time of war." He haggled with a wringing of gnarled hands, "But I may be able to procure some, it depends. . . ."

Clifford withdrew a banknote from his pocket. Leaning forward, he placed it on the table in front of him. He smiled cynically up at the landlord. "Perhaps that may aid you in your search. Now move, man, else we shall die of thirst."

The man blinked rapidly and greedily at the twenty-pound note, then grinned blackly again. He bowed deeply, collecting the cash adroitly as he did so. "For that, my lord, I shall allow my own dear daughter to serve it to you, too," he muttered with a sly wink. When this seemed to elicit no great lascivious response, he advised hastily, "Oh, she is not . . . I mean she is used to gentlemen . . . a widow. Never fear, she is not as shy as she seems."

Clifford's eyes hardened a little at this unsubtle pimping. He glanced casually across at Heath. The black man made an almost imperceptible, neutral-looking grimace that was nevertheless well understood. "Get the girl to fetch it, then, but speedily," Clifford ordered curtly.

Clifford's feet raised to rest on the low, battered table. He leaned forward and sideways, collecting his glass of brandy from the floor, and then settled back into the surprisingly comfortable old armchair. He raised the glass to his mouth and drank, his face screwing up as the raw liquid scalded his throat. He mused idly whether to get the landlord back, but he knew it would be useless. If he'd had any better, he'd have brought it. He had seemed quite genuinely proud of his find when he placed it before him. No doubt he honestly thought it was the best the French could be expected to produce.

His head leaned back into the cushions, the glass by his face. A muted giggling reached his ears and his hand dropped and the glass was held low, by the chair arm. He watched for a moment as the plump blonde girl pulled the dark head close, burying it between heavy, uncovered breasts. She laughed again, wriggling and thrusting herself upwards into the appreciative dark features.

Aware she was being observed, she turned slightly and smiled tentatively, yet with clear invitation, at the hard, cynical face. Her purposeful clasp slackened and she squirmed on Heath's lap again but more this time as though to remove herself.

Clifford raised the brandy to his mouth once more and looked away dismissively. He settled his head into a more comfortable position. "Did you check to make sure that

David and the two lads have been attended to?"

Heath raised his face just slightly from its pleasurable resting place as he grunted assent.

Clifford removed his watch from his pocket and looked at it: twelve o'clock. He allowed the watch to oscillate on its chain for a moment, his eyes following its mesmeric swaying but his mind miles away.

He swung the chain, arcing the watch into his hand again before replacing it in his coat.

He closed his eyes and immediately a pale face surrounded by thick, dark-chestnut hair filled his mind. As the girl's eyelids raised, the striking violet eyes pierced him accusingly. He smiled to himself, wryly but content, holding tight to the dream. He breathed out to Heath on a weary sigh, "Wake me at eight o'clock."

Emily strolled to the library window and gazed out across the quiet lawns, where only sway-headed daffodils moved in the light breeze. Her fingers drummed idly against the window sill for a moment before she returned to the chair where Richard sat.

The boy was perusing a brightly colored picture book with much frowning interest, his absorption today unusually complete. Emily watched him as a thin index finger traced outlines with painstaking care.

Aware he was being observed, he glanced up. "Who are you looking for in the gardens? You have stared out there so many times," he remarked solemnly.

Emily smiled faintly, and a hand moved to part and straighten his fine hair. "Oh, I just have to speak to your uncle about something, that is all," she answered him lightly. "Have you seen him yet today, Richard?" she asked casually.

The boy shook his head idly, turning the pages of his book again. "Mama came home last night from her friends'. She will be ready to come out of her room soon, I expect. Shall we go and see her?"

Emily smiled and shook her head. "I have to see your uncle first, Richard. I think I might go and see if he is yet home."

As though to silently refute this courageous idea, she wandered aimlessly to the bookshelves. She removed volumes fitfully, replacing them with barely a glance at their titles, let alone their pages. She slid a book forcefully onto a shelf with a restless sigh and looked at Richard, but his interest was elsewhere. A slight tactful cough made her head turn in the direction of the door too.

Heath was standing within the room.

Emily glanced away from the attractive dark features with supercilious brevity. She moved closer to where Richard sat ignoring Heath completely.

As though sensing her abrupt detachment in attitude and sympathy and the reasons for it, he bowed and backstepped a little. "Miss Shaw, Sir Clifford bade me inform you that should you still wish to speak to him, he will receive you now," he advised in a tone more formal than he would customarily use.

Emily's gaze sought the man then, her assumption of his nocturnal activities as plain in her violet eyes as her disgust. His manner remained unflinching; he merely added in the same impassive tone, "Should you wish to speak to him he will be in his study for the next hour."

A curt nod of acceptance and dismissal was delivered before Emily turned her back on him. After a few moments she heard the door close quietly.

Emily touched the boy's soft blond hair again with unsteady fingers. She said on a tremulous sigh, "I shall be but a short while, Richard. Wait here for me and I will come back to get you before we go to find your mama." Richard nodded amenably without looking away from his book.

Emily walked to the door glancing at the clock as she went. It was a quarter to twelve—almost midday. She felt something within her tighten yet again in futile frustration and rage as she dwelt on the length and purpose of his absence. She tried to dismiss the smarting pain and affront, but it churned as remorselessly now as it had last night, keeping her tormented and sleepless. She had eventually risen abruptly at midnight and walked the cool dark corridors to find Margaret and some laudanum to banish the taunting images and numb her into sleep for a few hours. She clenched her hands as she stood by the study door, horrified by her awareness that she wanted fervently to lash out at him. She tried desperately to calm herself and regain some of the composure and impartiality she had managed yesterday evening. She knocked at the study door and entered at once when she heard the command.

He was standing with his back to the window, dressed in the same clothes as when he had left the house yesterday evening. Her eyes were drawn to them, noting that now they looked as though he had slept in them. The notion almost made her laugh aloud. No doubt the state they were in was more due to the haste and carelessness with which they had been discarded. She fleetingly remembered the wine velvet jacket that had spent time on her bedroom floor.

He was watching her blatant inspection of his appearance and she met his eyes briefly before looking away, antipathy patent in the averted face.

"Why are you looking at me like that, Emily? Have you perhaps been considering how night-long fornication must have stigmatized me? Left me cloven-hooved, perhaps, or sprouting horns . . . ?"

Storm-purple eyes slid to his as she returned falsely, yet with exemplary contempt, "You are quite mistaken if you believe I have thought of you at all."

The irony in his face strengthened. His head inclined, acknowledging the rebuffal. "Thank you, Emily, for those few kind words," he muttered with stinging sarcasm. "I wish dearly that I could return the sentiment."

She allowed her eyes to glide past him in a deliberate show of disdain. She knew that their estrangement was yawning ever wider and could only help her cause. He was obviously going to be as surely glad to be rid of her as she was to leave and marry Jonathon.

The air of calm belligerence made the words focus sharply and immediately in her brain. She was just about to speak when the drawer on his desk slammed sharply and she heard him mutter some incoherent phrase littered with almost inaudible expletives.

She glanced at him quickly, searching for some sign of the indifference that had been so evident last night. His eyes rose from the desk top and clashed with hers, locking inextricably for a moment.

Emily broke the trance with a long blink. "Are you my legal guardian since you coerced me into residence here?" she asked swiftly and in a reasonably civil tone.

A muscle hardened and jerked by his mouth but he sat down casually in the chair behind the desk. He indicated with an indolent movement of his hand that she sit also, in a chair close by. She ignored him, merely waiting tensely and silently for his reply.

He looked up at her standing before him and the chair he sat in swiveled sideways. "Yes . . . you are my ward during your father's ill health and while you are a minor," he answered calmly.

Emily nodded a brief, emotionless acceptance of this. "In that case, as I am not yet twenty-one, I believe I need your permission for my marriage to Jonathon. He has proposed to me and I intend to accept."

The chair ceased its idle swaying and his eyes already held by hers for the duration of this concise speech, became unwavering and black as the crumpled coat he wore.

He stared at her with such intensity that Emily picked unconsciously and quite impertinently at a few papers that were scattered on the desk top, shuffling them about. She repeated stiltedly, "I should like your permission, for I wish to inform Jonathan of my acceptance at once and make plans with him for our wedding."

He turned the chair slowly so that it faced forward again. "Would you, indeed?" he muttered slowly, in a strange, vehement tone.

"Yes. I would be grateful if you could let me have your decision today. I wish to see Jonathon later and advise him of it."

Clifford stood up so abruptly and forcefully that despite being on the opposite side of the desk, Emily sidestepped and knocked into the armchair she had declined to sit in. She steadied herself and as her eyes sought his again she tensed. He was gazing at her with a peculiar furious blaze in his eyes. As Emily stared into the satanic black eyes, she realized that the diabolical reference he had made was certainly apt. The consequences of his debauchery seemed indeed suitable and in evidence.

Clifford looked down abruptly at the desk top. He picked up papers in much the same way Emily had moments before her, long, lean fingers shaking the sheaf of notes he held for no more than a few seconds before they all fluttered back to the desk.

He turned from her abruptly and walked straight into the swivel chair just behind. He kicked it savagely away from him as he moved to the window and stared out.

"Is this what you wished to tell me yesterday?"

"Yes."

A coarse laugh erupted. "My apologies for deferring . . . I had no idea it was quite this vital," he rasped.

"I believe I made it very clear that the matter was

urgent," she retorted stridently. "But it was obvious that for you there was nothing quite as important as your. . . ." The crudity stuck in her throat and she merely added after a long, calming inhalation, "Your trip to town."

He turned back toward her, his hands thrusting deep into his pockets. He stared at her intently for a moment before his eyes sought the ceiling, and a sound of frustrated despair escaped him that nevertheless sounded quite like amusement.

His face lowered slowly and he gazed at her. "What do you think I did last night?" he demanded softly.

Emily's cheeks reddened furiously. "How dare you ask me such a thing!" she choked, outraged. "I am not one of your vulgar harlots waiting to be told the details of your disgusting behavior. Neither am I Amanda standing by meekly and silently while you abuse me in such a way."

He walked round the desk slowly, and in her rage and mortification she barely noticed him approaching her.

He stood before her but without touching her. "I apologize; I phrased it badly," he excused himself quietly. "Where do you think I have been?"

She backed away a pace, the ire still shaking her. Her hands clenched spontaneously as his nearness threatened, and she felt quite violently disposed to hit him. She swallowed repeatedly to try and calm herself. "I care not where you have been or with whom," she managed to force out.

"Well, perhaps I shall tell you anyway."

She backed away further, her hands moving up as though to prevent her ears hearing. He caught at her raised wrists and jerked her closer, holding her in front of him. "The extent of my vice the night long was to visit a country inn and down a bottle of very poor French brandy. Sin indeed, when I think what I paid for it, and that it was little consolation; but there was certainly no wanton rampage."

She twisted herself free of him and walked away, her arms crossing over her body and her hands rubbing at her arms as though to clear herself of taint.

He watched her for a moment, then stated quietly, "You don't believe me, do you? And it matters little what I say, or do . . ." he laughed bitterly, "or don't do. Have I wasted a night drinking and sleeping in some rural tavern, uncomfortable and miserable, for this?"

She jerked her head away from him farther as though every word was a lie that she cared little to hear.

"Emily . . ." he pleaded hopelessly before coaxing, "Shall I ask Heath to come and verify it?"

She swung back toward him, sneering, "Him? He is as depraved as you by all accounts. Why would I believe anything he says?"

Clifford smiled sardonically. "Ah . . . I see my wretched, downtrodden black has now lost all your soft sympathy. When was this, Emily? When you discovered he was also a man—one of those lecherous barbarians?" he taunted roughly.

He watched the flush rise in her face but she said nothing, merely gazed through the window close to her and out into the garden.

The silence continued for a few minutes more, yet it seemed to drag like hours. "And where is this ardent, inoffensive swain?" he asked with absolute control. "Has he no intention of coming himself to plead his suit? I thought that was the more familiar and gentlemanly course to take."

Emily turned then from examining the garden to look at him. "I felt I should ask, under the circumstances," she informed coolly.

"Which circumstances are they, Emily? Those that ensure you always get your own way with me, is that it?"

She remained silent and he added, "You won't this

time, though. And whatever happened to the demure, shrinking maiden who had no wish to be bound to any man . . . no wish to marry at all?"

"You destroyed her, as I remember." The statement was calm and very nearly untinged with blame.

He half-smiled, glad that at last she had openly alluded to it. He stressed gently, "I made love to you, Emily . . . against your will, I grant . . . but had I wished to destroy you, I could have done so and God knows you would have known the difference."

He gazed at her steadily, but she was now completely fascinated by a brass-based lamp on his desk. Her fingers explored it unsteadily, tracing outlines upon the yellowish metal.

Clifford's fingers moved to disturb the papers on his desk again as he murmured, "What passed between us that night, Emily . . . do you believe that was the worst I could think of? That I knew nothing more hurtful or humiliating to do to you just that once?"

Emily's fingernails grated jarringly against the glass lampshade and she returned them hastily to examine the dull metal of the stem.

Clifford looked up at her then from the papers on his desk. "I could have abused you, Emily, had I wanted to," he reasoned softly. "I could have done so nightly and for months past — until you no longer cared whether I touched you or not . . . or how. You would have been grateful for a smile — the slightest kindness and you would have willingly done anything for me. And you certainly never have stood before me now and raised your eyes, let alone your voice. It was exactly what your father dreaded and expected . . . and you too; for you are not nearly so unknowing or unfeeling as you would like to keep me thinking, are you."

He watched her as the hand at the lamp shook uncontrollably and knocked against the glass canopy. She withdrew the trembling fingers at once and put them behind her back, but her eyes remained with it. Her bottom lip trembled as violently as the hidden hands, and she bit it deeply, her head jerking as she quickly and quietly swallowed the sob that was threatening.

His hand rose to his face slowly, the fingers rubbing against his eyes. "I am sorry," he sighed softly. "I never meant to say that. It is true I have felt like doing so at times when you have provoked me . . . but I never meant to say it to you. And most certainly I could never have done it."

He looked at the still bowed head, and as though fearing part of the threat might have somehow come about merely by talking of it, he ordered harshly, "Look at me, Emily."

Her head sprung back and as their eyes met, his closed. "Why is it like this?" he demanded with quiet hopelessness. "It doesn't have to be this way between us, Emily."

"Of course it does," she returned quietly.

His mouth set. "Shall I take you home tomorrow?" he asked in a toneless voice.

She blinked rapidly, then stared, silent, for a full minute. Remembering then her reason for being here with him now, she stuttered, "But, I . . . I have . . . I want to be married. And you have not told me of your decision." She felt the tears heat her eyes in rage and futility. After all these months of waiting and hoping and pleading to be allowed home, he should relent now when it was too late. She glanced back at him sharply, wondering if he had indeed guessed she was pregnant and was taunting her with the choice of disgracing her family too.

He walked closer to her, and as though to endorse her fears, interrogated quietly, "Why this rush to be married? You will be twenty-one soon and then can marry without my permission."

She looked up into the shrewd, narrowed gray eyes.

"I will not go home now," she vowed softly, the truth of it wounding deeply. "I have no wish to go home any longer. I wish to marry Jonathon . . . and straightaway so that we can both move well away from here."

After a further silent moment, he probed quietly, "Do I take it your trip to London with Amanda is now canceled?"

She turned away from him to shield the guilty flush and her agitation, certain now that he knew.

A slight, unamused noise broke in his throat. "Perhaps I ought to see Cross. I believe there is something here to attend to, and the sooner the matter is concluded, the better."

"Will you give me leave then to marry?" she requested politely.

"Oh, yes, Emily . . . I give you leave to marry," he uttered vehemently, but in a way that allayed her anxiety not at all.

"I shall go and tell Jonathon that you will see him then. Would you see him today? Is that convenient?" she inquired nervously.

"I will send word to Cross and you are confined to the house till this matter is dealt with."

She swung round to face him then, as though to remonstrate. But there was something rigid and utterly forbidding in his countenance that made her simply murmur distantly, "Very well."

She hesitated on her way to the door. "But I would like you to see him today."

"Oh, it will be today, Emily, never fear."

She glanced at him with increased nervousness and uncertainty, then she opened the door and went back to the library and Richard.

Jonathon moved abruptly from the library window and

returned to his seat. He sat down and glanced at the clock on the mantel and then at Emily. "Does he think I have nothing better to do than wait for him to grant me his infernal presence?" he muttered testily. "If he is not here soon, Emily, I will have to go. It stated four o'clock in his note. It is now five and I have much to attend to."

Half-listening to these oft-heard, peevish complaints, Emily reassured him quietly, "I expect he will be here soon, Jonathon. He is no doubt delayed." As a niggling doubt recurred, she posed tentatively, "Will Lucy be living with us, Jonathon, after our marriage, wherever we set up home?"

Jonathon gazed across at her, confirming with astonishment, "Well, of course, Emily. Where else would she live?"

Emily gave a small, apologetic smile and gestured weakly. She looked at the clock herself then: the hands were just gaining ten past five. She was sure in her own mind that the delay was deliberate and guessed by Jonathon's irritation that he did too. No doubt Clifford was merely in another part of the house, laughing with his black comrade over this flagrant insult to her risible young suitor.

Suddenly the door opened noisily. Clifford strode in, dressed in dusty riding clothes and carrying his riding crop. He made no greeting to either Jonathon or Emily, but launched immediately into: "Sorry for detaining you so long. My horse threw a shoe near Hertford and I have been the while since three o'clock trying to get back here."

The riding crop he still held was dropped abruptly onto the desk top with a clatter. He brushed his clothes down in a cursory fashion, the dirt lifting visibly. He swung about then and regarded them both properly.

Jonathon had sprung from his chair on Clifford's entrance and now stood regarding him nervously.

Clifford smiled slightly at the young man standing

awkwardly in the center of his magnificent library. "Do sit down, Cross," he urged mockingly, "you make the place look untidy."

Jonathon's ruddy cheeks purpled further in embarrassment. Emily glanced sharply at Clifford, then patted the seat close by her and directed a meaningful look Jonathon's way. He moved toward her jerkily and perched himself clumsily on the very edge of the sofa.

Clifford approached them with a decanter and two glasses. He held out the brandy indicatively, asking Jonathon, "Do you want a drink?"

Jonathon looked uncertain, then, judging it would be the manly thing to do on such an occasion, he nodded. "Thank you," he accepted.

Clifford poured the drinks and Emily's eyes stayed with the one or more inches of brandy he handed to Jonathon. She cautioned in a whisper, "Remember you have work to do on the farm, Jonathon. . . ." Aware of Clifford's eyes watching her, she glanced at him, noting at once the hard amusement in them over her nagging concern. She returned his gaze defiantly until she could feel the color rising in her face, and he acknowledged her discomfort with a more pronounced smile.

Clifford seated himself opposite them, then drank lengthily from his glass. Jonathon copied his host and tipped his own drink for an equal amount of time. There was a splutter and sniff from one side of her as the fiery alcohol caught in Jonathon's throat, making Emily glance balefully at Clifford once more. He met her eyes steadily, one hand holding his glass and the other resting idly against his face.

After an amused, silent moment, he began genially, "So, Jonathon have you given further consideration to my offer for the freehold, Cross? It is a very good price, you know that. You will get no such elsewhere."

Slightly disturbed by the reference to business rather

than his impending marriage, Jonathon faltered, "Yes . . . yes. I . . . that is . . . we have. Emily and I have considered your proposal and have decided we would like to sell up to you now and move away from here."

Clifford sat back in his chair, one foot coming up slowly to rest casually on the opposite knee. "Just one point, Cross," he remarked mildly, "You talk as though my offer of five thousand pounds for the land included taking Emily with you also."

Jonathon stared at him, aghast and outraged. Emily glared too and, beating Jonathon to any such rebuke, she informed icily, "Jonathon has proposed and I have accepted. It has nothing to do with the offer for the land and I—"

"And *I* . . ." Clifford cut into the words quietly yet impacably, "have no intention of allowing any such marriage to take place."

Emily gazed unwaveringly into steel-gray eyes for a moment before glancing swiftly at Jonathon.

He sat rigidly, mortification once more apparent in his rubicund complexion. "May I know your reasons, sir, for that decision?" he inquired with formality.

"Indeed you may, Cross. Emily is already spoken for. She seems to have forgotten and omitted to tell you that. But I have not. I believe her parents will bear me out on the matter when I say she is destined to marry another. You could check with them should you so wish."

Jonathon looked searchingly and judiciously at Emily, as though trying to assess her culpability.

Noting the skeptical nature of Jonathon's regard, she flustered hastily and said, quite affronted, "You cannot believe him, Jonathon. He lies most terribly. He is just trying to spoil our happiness, I know he is. He is vicious and spiteful and. . . ." She would have berated her guardian further but Jonathon laid a heavy hand on hers, his face wary. As far as he could tell, Sir Clifford Moore had done very little today to merit such violent vituperation.

Jonathon's green-gold eyes slid repeatedly to Clifford as he rebuked softly, "Emily, you should not talk so. It is most unseemly for a young lady to be so . . . outspoken."

Clifford's mouth tilted very slightly in amusement before he provoked solemnly, "Yes, please calm yourself, Emily. Behave more rationally, else I shall have to send you to your room."

Emily jumped up abruptly. "Admit you are lying . . . admit it!" she demanded shakily. "There is no one I am promised to. I never have been and well you know it." She swung back to Jonathon and he glanced at her, amazed at the effrontery and disrespect she openly showed to this man who, it was well known throughout the county, was almost omnipotent in his influence and wealth.

Jonathon's eyes narrowed appraisingly as he looked from Emily, glaring fiercely, to Clifford Moore, regarding her equally steadily, if amused. He picked up his glass of brandy and drank deeply, his lips smacking together loudly this time as he savored and clung to the inspiriting liquor.

Clifford smiled, noting that the young man relished his drink. Ignoring Emily now, he resumed, "Now: about this transaction. I have the documents ready. I need no more than a signature before you have the cash and I will expect vacant possession within one calendar month. . . . Sit down, Emily." He tacked the light command at the end of the statement of affairs, making it sound as though she were some vexing, wayward child.

Emily sensed her self-control lost abruptly as he made such a display of his patronizing condescension—and in front of Jonathon, too. She approached Clifford and as she did so, he stood up leisurely. She trembled lightly as she glowered up into his silver eyes. "Don't you dare dismiss my life and future so," she breathed fiercely. "It is not some trifling matter to be tossed aside at whim as if valueless." Her eyes clouded and she sniffed loudly as she felt threatening tears sting at her eyes and nose. "I wish to be married now and—"

"And so you shall, Emily . . . so you shall," Clifford interrupted soothingly.

"I wish to be married to Jonathon," she declared through gritting teeth.

"Go to your room, Emily." The command was quiet yet imperious.

"I will not."

"I believe you will, Emily," Clifford contradicted softly. "You know my patience endures only so long, and once expended. . . ." He made no attempt to conclude the threat.

Emily's eyes lowered beneath his. She felt the compulsion to hurt him pervade her inexorably and she lashed out abruptly with a clenched fist.

He had easily anticipated it. She felt her flailing hands imprisoned before she was swung round immediately in his arms so that her back was held fast against him.

She was half aware of Jonathon crying out her name in restraint but even more in shock.

"You will have to excuse her, Cross," Clifford apologized with an even, unperturbed smile. "She has these bouts of tantrum. Did she not tell you? I fear we may have to discuss the matter of the farm at some other time."

Jonathon made no move to rise, and Clifford asked pointedly, with a meaningful tilt of his head toward the door, "Would you mind? Sorry. I shall send for you again, or perhaps drop by so that we can finalize things."

Jonathon stood then, wordlessly. His eyes moved to Emily's tear-streaked face before following the length of the dark-clad arm that ran with such familiarity and possessiveness across her squirming body. His eyes shifted to Clifford's, clashing competitively. "This man Emily is to marry . . . who is it?" he asked shrewdly.

Clifford smiled affably. "I believe I am not yet at liberty to say."

Jonathon stared at him assessingly. "I see," he uttered slowly and very clearly.

Clifford's equable smile deepened. "Good, I am glad that is settled," he murmured.

Jonathon glanced back at Emily, who rested quietly now within the proprietary embrace. He made a very slight bow to her before he nodded curtly at Clifford and made for the door.

"Jonathon," Emily called plaintively as a freckled hand touched the door handle. He hesitated only briefly before opening the door and quitting the room without a backward glance.

Emily moved a hand to smear away the trail of tears. Then she tried to prise away Clifford's hands.

He was unrelenting. His hand flattened purposefully against her stomach, following the soft, swollen roundness. His fingers skimmed up her side, just brushing the round, hardened breasts that now tautened the material of her bodice. Lulled by the gentle caress, it was a moment before she realized its purpose.

He held her close as she renewed her struggle to break free, back-stepping to the chair he had previously sat in. He sat abruptly, pulling her down onto his lap. She fought to stand up but he restrained her, his eyes slowly scanning the front of her figure, where soft scarlet wool was clinging and straining at hitherto less pronounced places. Emily sensed her face burning, sure it must match the gown she was wearing, so candid was his leisurely examination.

One of his hands went to her face and remained there, preventing her turning away as he murmured, "You appear to be putting on weight, Emily."

"I eat too much — all the time. What else is there to do

in this godforsaken place?" she parried hastily and acidly.

"Are you pregnant, Emily?" he asked directly.

She looked down quickly at her straining bodice, agonizing whether to trust him. She glanced up searchingly, as though she could glean the extent of his deceit from his face. Her eyes were drawn instinctively to the scar on his cheek and she forced out hastily, "'Of course not. How could I be?" She blushed further, knowing she had just made herself sound ingenuous in the extreme.

"Would you know if you were?' he asked gently. "Do you know how to tell?"

She attempted to shake him off roughly then, muttering, 'Of course . . . I know very well. My mother told me and that is how I am certain that I am not, for since you. . . ." She halted, her face stinging with embarrassment, hating him for making her feel so uneasy.

She turned her head away from him completely. "I have told you, I merely eat too much. In fact, I am quite ravenous now," she lied, the thought of food making the nausea incurred during her previous agitation increase. Nevertheless, she added for good measure, "I shall go and have tea now and dinner later this evening."

"I want the doctor to see you, Emily, tomorrow. I shall arrange it."

Alarm made her head spin back towards him at once. There is no need," she protested forcefully. "I have told you, I am very well . . . just hungry."

"Well, I would like him to tell me that, Emily," he countered.

"I shall not see him. You will waste your time bringing him here." She tacked on the end quickly, to distract him, "And why did you bother asking Jonathon here at all? You had no intention of considering his proposal. It was very. . . ." She paused and swallowed the insult and merely said distantly, "Very discourteous." She made to push away at that point, but his hand tightened spontaneously although he leaned his head back against the chair as if weary.

She knew he was still watching her shrewdly and thoughtfully, his eyes lingering on her body, but seeing him so relaxed made her want to be likewise. As though aware of her imminent capitulation, he drew her closer until she leaned back against him. As her head rested against his shoulder, he lightly touched his mouth to her hair.

"Did you mean it when you said earlier that I may go home?" she asked abruptly. She felt the hand stroking her hair lose rhythm. His nails scratched softly at her head as he corrected mildly, "That is not what I said. I asked if you wanted still to go." His arm tightened about her, anticipating her rejection, but she remained quiet and relaxed.

His fingers drew her hair away from her face. They rubbed gently against her cheek, insisting upon an answer as he demanded softly, "Tell me why you don't want to go home, now Emily."

"I have told you . . . I want to be married."

"Good . . . this hankering after the marital state . . . is it lingering still?"

Emily sighed bitterly. "What does it matter? I have little hope that Jonathon will ask me again now. After your lies, he now believes me a liar too."

The arm holding her gave a light, admonishing shake. "I think you know very well, Emily, that marrying him was not what I meant."

He sat up abruptly with her and the sudden motion made her cling to him for safety. As her arms went up about his neck for support, he shifted away from her as though to stand and she fell into the seat. He resettled himself on the edge of the chair in front of her and his hands went to her face, clearing the tumbling locks of hair away.

312

She watched his face lower but made no move to avoid it. His mouth brushed lightly against hers, the contrived caress parting her lips. His hands slid behind her, moving her close against him, and her arms tightened about his neck, clinging at once. Distrust and fears as to his motives and morals were abruptly forgotten, dispelled by a soft stroking along the hot, sensitive curve of her inner lip. She sighed deeply into his mouth, arcing towards him at the very moment he lifted his head and turned away from her.

Emily opened her eyes slowly, feeling dazed and weakened, unaware for a few moments that Amanda was even in the room with them, let alone that she had spoken.

Emily sat further upright in the chair, hastily straightening her dress.

Clifford got up slowly and as Emily's eyes rose tentatively to his face, she recognized the cold rage at once.

"Good Lord, this room is little better than a public lending library. It has seen more people this afternoon than it does in a week." The sarcasm was muttered slowly and in fury and frustration rather than uneasiness at how he had been chanced upon.

His head indicated the door before he pointed explicitly. "Go, Amanda," he gritted, his jaw rigid. "I have something of great importance to discuss with Emily."

Amanda sneered and agreed insinuatingly, "Oh, yes . . . I can see that. What was her answer? Yea or nay? Of course, it makes little difference whatever she decides, does it not? You'll have her."

Emily pushed herself further upright in the seat, her face crimsoning. Amanda's eyes pounced on hers, the fiery contempt in the blue depths lashing her, and Emily cowered back into the chair a little.

Clifford advanced toward Amanda, the lightness in his movement belied by a perilous menace in his face. "Go, Amanda, now," he commanded with ominous softness.

313

Amanda backed away slightly but ventured closer once more after making a detour of some of the furniture. "Oh, I am here for a purpose," she informed, viciously amused. "I come to deliver you some very interesting news. It should console you greatly, I think, for I do believe by the look of Emily now that her answer will most definitely be no." She barely paused before jeering further, "Well, it matters little anyway, for guess who has come to visit? And just dying to please you, by the breathless look of her." She hesitated and assessed him reflectively through slitted blue eyes. "Or perhaps you already know . . . perhaps it was arranged in one of your more abandoned moments."

"What the hell are you about, Amanda?" Clifford demanded with harsh exasperation. "What treachery and lies are these now?"

Amanda smiled waveringly. "None, I assure you." She watched intently as he turned then to look at Emily, who had risen, eyes downcast, from her chair. She redrew his attention immediately to herself with the repeated news,

"You have a visitor, Clifford. That is what I came here to tell you. It is a teashop waitress," she informed, smiling maliciously.

He looked completely bemused and dangerously impatient.

"It is a . . . lady . . . with a slight Canadian accent," she smirked, "and would you believe . . . she has brought with her a black maid—quite a lovely young thing, I'll warrant no more than seventeen or so. Do you think Heath might like an introduction?"

He stared dumbstruck and disbelieving for a moment, and then his eyes shifted to the door as though he might see through it. "If you lie, Amanda. . . ." he menaced huskily.

"Oh, I do not, I assure you. I asked Margaret to show them into the small salon. I hope I did right. I was not sure whether there or your bedchamber would be best. Such a pity that I overlooked to think of the library," she mused with malevolent ruefulness. "I am sure they would have been quite amazed by the display, but perhaps the Canadian trollop would not have been much amused. What do you think?" She walked away then as though to leave the room, but Clifford halted her with a crude oath coupled with her name and she swung back toward him at once.

As though remembering Emily was still standing silently behind, he swung round at once. He gazed at her as she stood there, her face as pale and striken as his. Their eyes met but briefly before she started to walk slowly toward the door.

He moved nearer to her. She evaded him at once, but he copied the path of her circumvention steadfastly, closing with her slowly until they met at last face-to-face by a bookcase.

She put out a small white hand at once to keep him away. He removed it from his arm and held it, and bending closer to her, murmured with plea and despair, "I did not know, Emily, I swear it. I had nothing to do with it. . . ." Realizing this disclaimer sounded quite absurd, his eyes closed and he raised the tightly-gripped hand to his face, pressing it against his cheek. Her free hand slapped at his face immediately and savagely, the other twisting violently free before she walked hastily away.

As she drew level with piercing, needle-bright eyes, she glanced involuntarily at Amanda. The withering derision was blatant. "You stupid fool," she hissed in an undertone, "you should heed what I say more carefully. Learn by this, Emily."

Emily looked away quickly as the blood suffused her face. She quit the room on legs that felt too unsteady to support her weight.

She walked hurriedly back to the hall. On crossing the

massive expanse to the stairway, she noted Heath standing with his back to her near the small salon doorway and her pace faltered. As he espied her, he straightened from his lounging position with one hand leaning lightly against the door. He moved away and Emily saw the small black girl positioned between him and the wall.

Heath walked the corridor a few paces aimlessly, his hands clasped lightly behind his back. The girl made a nervous show of straightening the pink bonnet she wore, her eyes on her feet.

Emily regarded them for barely a moment longer and then she mounted the stairs, slowly and outwardly quite calm. But acknowledging her credulousness and gullibility made her stomach heave with shame and rage, for today she had come very close to trusting him, believing that perhaps she was special to him: different from Amanda or this woman he claimed not to have seen last night, yet who was confident enough of her influence to visit him, uninvited, at home. She was sure his astonishment was genuine, which made the woman's power quite awesome. She had been conscious of the sound of swift, heavy footsteps across the polished wood floor of the hallway and knew that it was neither Heath nor the girl. They halted now at the foot of the stairs, and as she reached the top, they withdrew once more. She walked toward her room at the end of the corridor and halfway along heard the door of the small salon crash loudly shut.

Clifford walked into the salon quickly, ignoring the blonde woman who rose at once at his appearance. Heath and the black girl followed him closely into the room, and the girl stood silently and respectfully close by the wall near the door.

The decanter chimed sonorously and Clifford poured himself a large measure of brandy, which he downed in one gulp. He refilled it and then turned to glare explicitly at Heath, the woman still overlooked.

The servant's face was tense, and as he noted the wrathful accusation leveled at him, he shook his head slowly, shrugging and grimacing his innocence.

As though sensing from this silent exchange that she had misjudged the appropriateness of her audacious intrusion of his residence, the blonde woman approached Clifford slowly. An expensively gloved hand moved to rest on his arm and a pale cheek rubbed his shoulder affectionately, "Please don't be too angry with me, Cliff," she implored throatily. "I know I have been very foolish in coming here, but I had to see you."

He shook her off savagely and with a quite audible sneering oath.

He stared at Heath for a moment, then ordered quietly but imperiously, "Take Selina to the kitchen. Get her some refreshment and then show her back to the carriage. She will have but a short wait before her mistress joins her."

Heath returned the stare and then acceded with cutting servility, "Of course, master Clifford . . . at once, sir."

Clifford's jaw set at the bitter sarcasm and antagonism that built slowly between them. The servant turned away abruptly and taking the girl's arm, propelled her toward the door.

As the door closed, Clifford glanced at the blonde woman and then smiled tautly. "My apologies for being so inhospitable . . . you came upon me at rather a bad time."

He held out the decanter, silently offering her a drink. She smiled acceptance, but some mild, pouting reprimand was present too. He poured a small amount of brandy into a glass and handed it to her. He pointed to a chair and she moved to seat herself. He then sat opposite her but made no attempt at conversation.

Rouged lips sipped appreciatively at the brandy, and after a brief quiet, he leaned forward a little and gesturing with his glass asked with exageroated inquiry, "Well?"

She smiled uncertainly and a gloved hand pressed against brandy moistened lips. "Well what?" she repeated coyly.

"Come," he prompted too gently, "there must be some pressing reason why my mistress would visit and bother me at home. What is it? Some matter of life and death . . . or commerce? Are you run out of tea? No money to brew with next week?"

She gazed at him, tears glazing her cornflower-blue eyes at this scathing attack. His eyes rested briefly on the almost depleted glass in her hand. "Run out of brandy perhaps," he snapped. His voice savaged harshly, "Come, tell me what it is. I cannot believe you have merely come here to gawp at me. Or perhaps you thought we could all indulge in some bacchanalian extravaganza here at Malvern Hall for a change instead of using your place as we usually do. Is that why you brought Selina along? To keep Heath entertained? How very thoughtful."

The woman curled a long fair ringlet about an unsteady finger. "I always travel with my maid; you know that," she defended herself. "It is not safe for a woman to travel alone; the highways are full of marauding robbers."

"Well, let them know your price in advance—that should have them scattering for the hills," he muttered with a sarcastic smile.

He stood up abruptly and walked away from her. She withdrew a lacy square from her reticule and sobbed into it, bright blue eyes attaching to his every movement. He downed the remainder of his brandy, then sighed, "I am sorry, truly. I meant not to upset you so; but you should never have come. I thought I made that most clear when first I had this arrangement with you."

The blonde head bowed further into the scrap of lace as she wept daintily. She raised undamaged eyes to his, excusing herself plaintively, "It is just . . . I have not seen you for so long. It has been so long. I send notes with Heath, but you never reply; and you have never ever written to me explaining your absences. I have penned notes thanking your generosity when you send money with Heath, but you never acknowledge me."

He looked at the pretty young woman then, taking in the fair long ringlets that framed her smooth face, guessing now what he had never bothered to surmise before, that she was probably not more than twenty-five, younger than Amanda. Noting his perusal, the woman straightened herself slightly in the chair. Her shoulders unhunched from their humbled posture, then moved back so that her breasts strained enticingly forward against the thin stuff of her gown.

Encouraged by this length, candid appreciation, she got up slowly and more contentedly and swayed herself towards him. Her hands clasped at his arm and large blue eyes widened limpidly at his face. "I miss you so when you stay away. Have you. . . ." She hesitated and a sob choked her as she croaked, "Have you been visiting elsewhere?"

"No."

"Then why?"

He removed her from him, but more gently. "I am sorry, but it is finished now, and I wish you had not come here and learned of it this way. I would have told you and more kindly if you had allowed me to do so in my own time and in an infinitely better state of mind."

She looked at him blankly, as though she understood none of what he said. He neared the door, instructing, "Come, I will see you to your carriage." She made no move to leave but merely gazed at him still and then the wistful sadness cheered a little. "I suppose it is that bitch of a sister-in-law," she said. "She has ensnared you once more with those oh-so-obviously flaunted charms. And you have the nerve to insinuate that I am some sort of mercenary harlot. I thought she was the reason for your lengthy absence . . . I thought so."

Clifford shut the door again quietly and then leant against it. As the total farce of the situation hit him abruptly, he started to laugh. He laughed so infectiously that after a stunned moment the woman approached him laughing herself, thinking that perhaps the whole episode was just an eccentric joke that he and Heath had concocted to vex her.

She leaned against him heavily, simpering up into the laughing face. He removed himself and walked away, still rocked with mirth. He shook his head a little as though to impose some sort of control. One hand moved to his face and splayed the width of it, pressing against his eyes for a long moment. "Come, I will show you to your carriage," he said.

As they walked through the hallway, she looked up into his face. "Will you come later to visit? You know you are always well rewarded when you do." The throaty enticement drew no more than a cursory glance. "It is you who are well rewarded," he muttered quite impersonally.

Amanda stepped out of the shadows at that moment, and so abruptly that it was obvious she had been waiting quite some time to do so. The two women approached each other, gazing disdainfully at each other. Amanda gave the woman a brazen head-to-toe inspection and then emitted a sharp hoot of derision. "God, what a mess!" she muttered witheringly.

The blonde woman turned to look after her. She started forward, presumably to make some physical remonstration, but Clifford caught spitefully at her arm. He pushed her slightly in front of him as he strode without losing pace to the great doors.

He stopped halfway down the stone steps. She turned, tempting with a meaningful pout replete with promise, "Until later then . . . tonight? Please. . . ?"

He said nothing but merely smiled neutrally and waved a dismissing hand. She swung away with a half-hearted flounce, descending the remaining steps to the carriage. She passed Heath with barely a glance as he climbed the steps to stand with Clifford.

They watched her alight; then Clifford turned and glared stonily at the man by his side. Heath shrugged and shook his head in denial. "Nothing whatsoever to do with me . . . I swear," he muttered emphatically.

Clifford nodded once. "Well, you can go into town later. Give her some money—a final settlement." He glanced down laconically at the carriage as it moved off. "She could have at least used the back door like the rest of the pedlers," he muttered drily. He had turned and was remounting the steps before the coach had moved two yards.

Heath gave a hard smile at his back and shook his head slowly. "God, you can be a callous bastard at times. And I thought it was my job to be the unfeeling savage around here."

Clifford smiled, unaffected. "Just goes to show," he remarked carelessly as he pushed open the oaken doors.

Chapter Ten

"Do you believe me now, Emily?"

The query was witheringly scornful, but Emily continued dressing for dinner. After a moment she answered quite dispassionately, "I have said already, Amanda, I believe you now, and I did believe you before. It is just. . . ." Her eyes lowered to the buttons she was fastening. "He can be so duplicitous—quite ridiculously charming at times."

"Oh, yes, we all know that, Emily: how charming and persuasive Clifford can be," Amanda sneered. "Ask the trollop downstairs. No doubt she could relate much of his delightful allure."

Emily allowed her mind to dwell then on the faceless mistress. "How does she look?" she asked quietly.

Amanda glanced at her briefly. "Completely smitten—as lust-lorn as he," she scoffed with a curl to her rouged lips.

"No . . . I meant her appearance," Emily hastily corrected. "Is she fair? As you are?"

Amanda glanced astutely at the dark-haired girl as she stood fiddling with the buttons on her dress. "Yes," she answered slyly, "I have to admit that he chooses blondes for his longer relationships—the more serious of them—if you can ever call it that, of course. I have to admit also, though she is fat and her hair colorless, she resembles me a little." Amanda moved one of her hands to touch her own whitish hair. "I do believe he chooses mistresses that resemble myself on purpose." She sighed, "Such a fool . . . I feel now quite certain that he shuns me merely out of guilt and tries to ease his pain by hurting me also. I am convinced he is tormented by what Stephen would think of us together. No doubt he feels it is something incestuous for us to be lovers, for him to love the wife of his dead brother."

Amanda moved to Emily's dressing table mirror. She swayed her head from side to side, inspecting and wallowing in her reflection.

Emily looked at her intently, trying to imagine a plumper body and paler hair. One of her hands went to touch her own loose hair. She drew a dark, sheeny strand forward and gazed at it before she let it drop. Her eyes lowered to critically scrutinize her own, still relatively slender body. A hand traveled the curve of lightly rounded abdomen as his had done barely an hour before.

"I cannot come to London at the end of the week, Amanda." Emily halted and swallowed. "I just cannot do it," she averred steadily. "I cannot, and besides, there is now an alternative. I have had a proposal of marriage from Jonathon, and I want to accept it. I just hope I can persuade him to reoffer it to me after what he heard this afternoon."

Amanda straightened away from the mirror at once and stared, bewildered. She stepped quickly closer. "What is this? It makes no sense. Jonathon proposed but must do so again? Explain everything."

Emily did so, calmly and quite objectively, describing all that she had not been able to tell Amanda yesterday: Jonathon's proposal and his visit to the Hall that afternoon, and the outcome.

Amanda sat next to her on the lilac-draped bed as she talked, and her eyes were estimating and shrewd throughout.

Emily sighed hopelessly as she finished recounting the tale. Amanda regarded her thoughtfully. "Do you think he will propose again?" she probed.

"I know not." Emily shook her head slowly. "It depends on whether I can make him believe that I have not lied to him. Of course, should he wish to verify the facts with my mother, all is lost. I know she will allow nothing in my favor before she has first checked with . . ." she hestitated, then merely finished, "him."

"Well, suggest to Jonathon that he speak to your father if it is likely he will be more amenable."

Emily shook her head sadly. "He is gone into hiding somewhere, a quiet convalescence in the countryside. He does not want to be disturbed, I know that. He has written me a letter with the address of the boarding house, but I know he wants his whereabouts kept secret; so does my mother." She gave a melancholic smile. "Poor papa. He is such an embarrassment now that the earl has proposed. Papa's health is so very poor, and I gleaned from mama's last letter that he is not always . . ." she hesitated and then murmured, "rational. I believe his mind is . . . disturbed . . . . Poor papa is going mad."

"Write him a note."

Emily looked up from her mournful reverie at Amanda. She studied the calculating face, but it displayed a total disregard for anything she had just recounted. Emily clasped her hands in her lap. "I have just said . . . I know he wants to be left in peace now. He cannot be bothered with such matters. But besides all that, his reason is not to be trusted, and Jonathon would discover that quite easily."

"No . . . no. Write Jonathon a note pleading your case," Amanda huffed impatiently. "Say you are still ready to wed him. Hint at an elopement; that should fire his ardor and enthusiasm, knowing that you are ready and willing to risk all for him." She gave a knowing laugh, muttering, "Men can be such vain creatures."

Emily said nothing; she bit at her lip and examined the red wool threads in her skirt, plucking at them with nervous fingers. Amanda gazed at her shrewdly, guessing correctly that what troubled Emily now was her conscience.

"For God's sake, Emily, be sensible!" Amanda encouraged heartily. "You need to marry now, and very soon. You cannot wait until you are of age. Babies may be a month or so early, but not several—and you would then never be able to pass the child off as Jonathon's. If you do not act, and at once, all the security and respectability he offers is lost. Oh, he will suspect nothing," she reassured, quite blasé. "He will probably be quite delighted when you tell him in the first month of your marriage that he is to be a father. No doubt his ribs and back will be quite black and blue from all the nudging and back-slapping of his chums. So virile so soon, and all that rot. You know what men are like. . . ."

Amanda glanced at the ingenuous face and gave a small dry laugh at the absurdity of her utterance. "Well, never mind," she muttered to herself.

Emily sighed, "I know I should, Amanda . . . but it is just that I am not sure I can dupe Jonathon so. He would surely hate me if ever he should find out."

"He cannot feel disgust for what he does not know," Amanda soothed. "He looks as though he has little experience of women. Trust me, he will discover nothing. You have to be as selfish now, Emily, as those around you . . . as Clifford is . . . and as your family has been, to allow you to be sacrificed to his malevolence. Forget all of them now. Think only of yourself and of your unborn child."

Emily nodded, knowing the wisdom of it. Amanda watched her carefully, noting the logic being dissected and finally accepted.

"Write a note, Emily, and I will deliver it for you," she urged at once. "Clifford will never be suspicious of me leaving the house, even at this time in the evening. I will be back by dinner time, never fear. You will not have to sit with him alone. We will eat together tonight, you and I, and we will completely ignore him henceforth."

Amanda's face became yet more animated. "An elopement . . . how exciting," she exclaimed, genuinely enthralled.

"I doubt very much that Jonathon will agree to it, Amanda," Emily despaired. "Even if he agrees to marry me still, he will not elope, and certainly not immediately. He would never leave either his sister or his farm so abruptly."

Amanda stared silently for a moment, disheartened by this overlooked point. "Well, write to him anyway, Emily," she encouraged, but with less zeal. "Let us see what he has to say. I will stress that we need a swift reply and wait for one."

Emily pointed out slowly, "Well, it might be best to adopt a little casualness, lest he becomes suspicious of our motives."

Amanda smiled slyly. "It is up to you, Emily, to persuade him that any haste is merely due to your uncontrollable desire to be his true wife." She glanced at the paper and pen Emily had drawn close. "Write the note, Emily," she instructed firmly.

Amanda peered over Emily's shoulder as she broke the seal on the letter and unfolded the paper. Emily read the sloping script through twice and then handed it to Amanda.

Amanda read it quite unemotionally, then her face blossomed in sheer glee. "He agrees and suggests tomorrow night . . . so soon," she squeaked ebulliently. "Oh, I am so pleased for you, Emily. How thrilling!" She barely hesitated before prodding, "Now, come write a reply and I will make sure he has it this very night."

"You cannot go out again tonight, Amanda," Emily deterred hastily. "It will most definitely look suspicious."

Amanda gave a crafty smile and a sly wink. "Oh, I have no intention of doing so. I have a good friend who works in the stables, and he would do just anything for me, Emily, and die before he breathed a word of it to anyone."

Emily chewed at her tender bottom lip yet again that evening. She tried to think clearly, knowing that events were sweeping her along much too fast. "What of Clifford, Amanda? I can hardly just walk out of the house tomorrow with a bag in my hand. He will never let me. If he is about tomorrow evening, I might never get away."

Amanda waved an airy, dismissive hand. "By the look of him and that strumpet today, I should say they have about a week's worth of business to tarry over," she sneered coarsely. "He will be well occupied for evening aplenty yet." Amanda curled her lip further. "How very obvious that slut is! No sense of good taste. That dress . . . with that hat. I feel now, the more I dwell on it, that she resembles me not at all." She finished savouring her contempt and looked back quickly at Emily. She smiled conspiratorially. "We shall dupe Sir Clifford Moore. . . ." She drawled the name disparagingly. "We shall retaliate for all our slights by wounding him where he is most sensitive: that gross pride. We can outwit him, and that will rankle so very much. And how I shall love the doing of it!"

She glanced at Emily's wan, tense face. "Well, you cannot deny that he has hurt me," she goaded harshly, "or you, for that matter." She watched as Emily bit nervously at the side of a finger. "Never fear that Clifford will retaliate once you are married. He still wants that land and for such as he business will always be dearest to his heart." She gave a small, ironic laugh. "Pardon me, I ought to say 'of utmost importance,' for of course he has no heart. He will care little about the marriage once the thing is accomplished and probably console himself with building a new wing to this palace he has here. Or by gloating over the deeds to Jonathon's acreage. Or by treating himself and Heath to a week-long orgy in town with those whores that were here today."

Amanda's vitriol faded away as she noted Emily finish writing.

The folded paper was proffered as Emily said faintly, "Thank you, Amanda."

"I have checked, Emily. He and Heath are safely installed in his room, and by the raucous sound of things, with a case or more of brandy in attendance. There is much rollicking amusement issuing forth — perhaps they have dragged in a couple of kitchen girls too." She shrugged that the notion bothered her little. "I know not how they avoid waking the household when they have these sessions," she threw in casually.

"Do they often, then?" Emily asked, trying to calm her trepidation and nausea with bland conversation. She added through chattering teeth, "I have never heard any noise." She pulled on long, warm gloves carefully, straightening and stretching the fingers.

"Well, they used to, but not so much since you have been here, I have to admit," Amanda said casually.

"No doubt the black will be up and about as po-faced as ever in the morning, as though the only diversion he ever indulged in in his master's room was an amount of servile boot-licking. Clifford treats him just like an equal and a friend when alone, I know it: I have at times seen it. It is quite disgusting to be so familiar with such—" She broke off abruptly as though realizing that she was time-wasting, and at such a time.

She stared at Emily as she examined her unbending fingers in the stiff gloves. "Come now, Emily," Amanda chided softly, "make haste, just in case for some reason they thwart our plans and go downstairs to finish this drunken spree."

Emily nodded and collected her small carpetbag from the bed. She straightened her hat methodically and nervously and then looked around the room as one does when seeing a place for the last time.

She moved to the sitting room door and gazed in, then turned abruptly and walked close to her bed to pick up her bag. Her eyes were arrested then by the book of translated verse she had been given. She walked to the table near the bed and picked it up. Her fingers smoothed the soft leather cover, tracing the gold lettering with a fingernail. She flicked the pages quite casually knowing, as she glimpsed odd words, that she would like to read it once more. She moved away holding it gently and then as she passed the newly-made blazing fire, she threw it in quite abruptly, without looking at it again.

She walked to the door. Amanda opened it cautiously and peered the length of the corridor before Emily stepped out. They made silent, quick progress toward the stairhead.

As they neared it they both gazed into the gloomy corridor of the east wing that housed Clifford's rooms.

Emily allowed herself a brief thought of him then and her heart palpitated as she realized she might never see him again.

They had met last night at dinner but not spoken, apart from a brief exchange of words at the end of the meal. She and Amanda had sat close during dinner and had had time and attention only for each other as they spoke of Richard and other harmless topics in low, exclusive tones. They could have been alone for all the notice they had taken of him, and he had made no attempt to intrude his presence on them or on their conversation. He had eaten abstemiously and risen early with the light but unmistakable command that he wished to see Emily in his study as soon as she had finished her meal.

She had agreed tonelessly and without looking away from the coffee cup she held but had returned immediately to her room with Amanda to discuss plans for this escapade. There had been no further summons to insist she meet him.

He had not dined with her and Amanda that evening. Amanda had merely lifted cynical eyebrows and sneered that she believed he must be taking tea instead of dinner tonight.

Obviously he had returned, though, for Amanda had seen them and by all accounts heard them too.

As though reading her thoughts, Amanda put out a restrictive hand and Emily halted at once, alarm making her catch her breath. But Amanda merely looked silently ahead, her face up a little as though listening.

Silence filled the colossal hallway for a moment, and then Emily heard a loud male laugh issuing forth, muted by distance but quite distinct nevertheless.

Amanda nodded her satisfaction as she glanced at Emily; then they began to descend the stairs.

The hallway was empty and quiet. They crossed it noiselessly and approached the corridor that led to the kitchens and a door which opened onto the back courtyard.

They halted on reaching it, both breathless despite their lack of any real exertion.

Amanda leaned forward suddenly and clasping Emily's face, she kissed both cheeks lightly. She rocked the pale face in her white hands, almost fondly but certainly with gentle vehemence. "Good luck," she mouthed soundlessly.

Emily nodded slowly. She felt tears start to her eyes at this unexpected show of affection. "Say goodbye to Richard for me," she whispered hoarsely.

Amanda nodded quickly and then gave Emily's arm a light push as she opened the well-oiled door.

The fresh night air assailed their nostrils and Emily breathed unsteadily, yet deeply, of the aromatic humidity.

"Jonathon is waiting behind the stables, but you will have to walk to the carriage I hired for you for fear of making a noise. It is barely a quarter of a mile away and the night is not that cold," Amanda informed softly.

She looked up at the cloud-scudding sky. "There is hardly a moon," she murmured contentedly.

Emily nodded and then, as a sob broke in her throat, a culmination of her lingering uncertainty and fear, she turned and walked away quickly, out into the dark night and Jonathon's care.

Amanda shut the door at once and locked it.

She leaned back against the hard wood and closed her eyes before she allowed a wide smile of pure, malicious satisfaction.

Her mind traveled up the dark staircase and along the corridor to a certain door, one that she would enter quite willingly even now and not emerge from till morning.

She thought of the blond man within and the malevolence increased as she acknowledged that even pleading with him to bed her would raise no more than disgust or a lust to go into town.

A white hand went to her throat and she caressed it soothingly and dwelt on her own revenge. For that was indeed what it was, and exceedingly sweet. Losing Emily to a peasant might dent his pride, but it was his heart, which she now knew, incredibly, he did have, that was going to shatter beneath the damage of this night's work.

She dwelt on Emily and smiled, but with less spite this

time. She quite liked the girl in a vague, peculiar way. But then, despising her was easy too; for any woman so completely blind to such utter devotion and reverence when it was quite obviously what she most yearned for was indeed unworthy of it.

Heath let the curtain drop back into place and raised his glass to his lips. He drank deeply, savoring the warmth. He raised his eyes to look gravely across at the man slumped low in an armchair with his boots resting on an expensive mahogany table.

He watched him push his fair hair away from his eyes, then a clumsy foot kicked the table away suddenly. It crashed over but he took no heed, sitting upright over-quickly and spilling some of his brandy down the front of his shirt. He brushed it away carelessly before turning his head toward Heath, beckoning with hand and head. "Bring the cards," he slurred.

Heath nodded slowly and smiled. "In a minute," he replied easily before he drank again from his glass.

Clifford shrugged and sank down once more into the yielding armchair, the fair head thrown back heavily into the cushions as though he had forgotten about the cards and was ready to sleep instead.

The edge of the curtain lifted casually once more and Heath turned back slightly to the window and looked out. He cursed quietly as he realized that his restlessness had prompted him to move from his own comfortable spot by the fire. Desire to perhaps see Selina later had made him hanker, stupidly, after peering toward the pinprick lights of the distant town. He gazed now at the firefly glow afar in St. Albans before his eyes were redrawn to a spot quite close by. He closed his eyes, wishing desperately he had remained unaware.

Clifford watched his comfort swirl higher in his glass.

He smiled to himself and said quite lucidly, "Go on, if you want to see her — go."

Heath moved away from the window and sat in the chair he had recently vacated opposite Clifford. He leaned forward, righting the upturned mahogany table, and Clifford's boots rose at once to rest against the polished red wood.

Heath relaxed back in his chair and closed his eyes immediately, shielding guilt and indecision.

Silence ensued and after a few moments, Heath opened his eyes to regard Clifford. He had fallen into a similar sort of half-slumbering repose. As he watched him, the hand holding his glass slackened further on the armchair edge until golden liquid tilted perilously close to the goblet rim. Heath reached forward, gently removing the glass from the relaxing fingers and placed it on the table.

Clifford's eyes opened slowly and he smiled. "Am I quite drunk, Heath?" he mocked himself.

"Not quite . . . but almost. Slow down for a while. It is early yet. What are we going too do for the rest of the night if you are to drunk to drink even or play at cards?"

Clifford smiled wryly. "Sleep, Heath, that is what," he murmured. "Sink into sweet, gentle slumber. . . ." He allowed his glazed gray eyes to close once more.

Heath listened to the wistful aspiration with a sad smile, knowing that the object of those yearning dreams was even now moving further out of reach. He watched broodingly, studying him carefully, as one does when regarding something dear. His eyes scanned the still lightly tanned face and sun-bleached tips of hair, now contrasting quite clearly with darker, new growth closer to his scalp; his thin mouth still cynically aslant, even in rest.

Heath stared unwaveringly at the man who had given him everything in life that he cherished. In fact, life itself; because he was wise now and knew well enough that the

Jamaican cane fields would have very likely claimed him, and very early too. At thirteen and on the auction block, the only work he had experienced in that murderous land was filling in ledgers and fetching and carrying within doors. But he was young and strong, and such blacks were destined for other things in the West Indies. Had the sugar cane spared him and he had adjusted to that work, then some sadistic-minded planter with a liking to set savage examples of uppity blacks would have broken his spirit and probably his body and relished the doing of it.

In those early days and when barely older than himself, Clifford had been everything to him: employer, brother; all the family he had ever known or needed. He had been tutor too and taught him not only facts but the worth and satisfaction of learning. He taught him of self-esteem and dignity: that he was no less a mortal being than the white slavemasters merely because they told him that was so, or because he recognized in himself that he looked different than they did.

But now the finely-honed intelligence was menacing him, confusing him in his loyalties and making him selfish.

He was sensitive to that magical emotion, and so acutely that he oddly envied Clifford experiencing its potency. For something so subtle, yet capable of humbling and ruining what no Jamaican hardship had touched, was indeed worthy of respect. Yet he hated it too, passionately, for he knew well enough that he was losing him . . . his closest kin.

Emily . . . he thought of the name and the girl with a wry smile, for despite her punishing power, she had always had the ability to charm him. And within that innate sweetness of dignity and compassion lay the essence of why a man would keep himself in some brandy-soaked celibacy when he could go into town now and allow himself to be tempted to indulge in all manner of distraction.

During the years in Jamaica, Heath had never realized Emily's significance; it was merely the name of the eldest daughter of a squire Clifford hated, and with whom he had old and implacable scores to settle.

It was also the name he had painted diligently across the prow of the first merchantman Clifford had owned. The first attempt had left the vessel graced with "Emma Lee." Clifford had been amused, but, Heath had thought at the time, quite unreasonably adamant about using the correct spelling. With the name then printed on a piece of paper and a fresh pot of paint at hand, Heath had set, mutteringly, once more to work to amend his artistry.

He reflected on that ship with some fondness. It was hardly the best Clifford had owned, but of those bought at that time it was the only one he now still retained. And unnecessarily; for he currently owned a fleet of traders sailing out of Liverpool that could rival that of the greatest shipping merchant in the country. The "Emily" was there too, crumbling in some dock but no doubt never to be sold off.

Heath's eyes focused on Clifford as he shuddered slightly on drawing a long, deep breath, as a child might after crying too lengthily and violently, exhaling air lingeringly through softly pouting lips. The fair head dropped abruptly to one side and then righted itself with a jerk although his doze was unbroken.

Heath gazed at him with platonic adoration, knowing that if his own life were to end tomorrow or in fifty years' time he would never love another person as he loved this man. Gratitude barely touched it any more. He knew equally well that Clifford was bound just as inextricably in his love and that the girl who held sway over him was even now leaving him for another man.

If he told him, he would bring her back, keep her tantalizingly close again because the torment of letting her go was worse. And if she hurt him because of it, he would die a little more. And if he harmed her again in weakness and retaliation, it would inevitably fuse them further though self-disgust tore him apart.

Heath closed his eyes to the tragic irony that the man who had bestowed on him the ability to acknowledge and nurture his own self-respect was now in peril of losing grasp on his own.

Dark brown eyes closed wearily; he smiled ruefully and waited indecisively for no more than a few minutes. For he knew in his own eternal reverence and affection that he could not presume to deny him what he would choose to know.

His boots raised to rest beside Clifford's on the table, then made hard, rough contact with those close by. Clifford jerked upright in the chair. He stared across sightlessly at Heath, startled and unaware for a moment. As his brow creased and his lips drew back slightly from his teeth, Heath realized he was about to be regaled with some oath-ridden remonstration.

Heath held up a restraining hand and gave a wry smile as he removed his feet from the table.

Clifford shook his head to clear it, one hand moving to push the hair from his face before his forehead dropped to rest in gently massaging hands.

Heath leaned forward then and a black hand caught at one of Clifford's, pulling it away from his gaunt face. Clifford looked inquiringly at Heath and the black man smiled, asking evenly, "How long does it take you to sober up? I think you might want to go out tonight after all."

"It was very good of Amanda to procure this coach for us, do you not think?"

Emily glanced across at Jonathon, her fingers tightening spontaneously on the carpetbag in her lap as she

336

regarded his indistinct face. "Yes, indeed." She smiled at him, unobserved, in the dusky coach interior before turning and gazing sightlessly once more out into the dark night.

"We shall have to stop soon to refresh ourselves and the horses—at a tavern or such."

"Yes, indeed we shall," Emily agreed in the same polite tone, but she did not turn from the window.

A low laugh met this uncertain certitude. "You sound unsure, Emily. Do you suspect I may attempt to seduce you prior to our wedding?" he asked bluntly.

The hard lump in Emily's throat was swallowed quickly. "Of course not. Why are you talking like that, Jonathon?" she demanded in an anxious whisper. "You seem so different tonight." She stared across at him intently, wishing that she could see his face clearly through the gloom.

"You sound and seem different also, Emily," he insinuated softly.

Emily glimpsed the brief whiteness in the sombre coach interior and realized that he was smiling.

"Perhaps I alarm you tonight now that we are alone and in such a compromising situation," he suggested. He paused before remarking carelessly, "Your reputation is quite ruined now, whether we marry or not."

Emily felt the skin of her face chill and tauten. "What are you trying to say, Jonathon?" she demanded shrilly. "If you are regretting this, if it was a rash decision on your part, then we can turn about right now."

He leaned forward suddenly, one of his work-roughened hands groping in the darkness for one of hers. As he sought and found, Emily recoiled a little.

"Don't be silly, Emily," he soothed. "You know I wish to marry you as much as ever I did. It is just that I have to admit to being a trifle surprised that you suggested we elope." The reassurance was uttered mildly but Emily was sure it required explanations from her.

Jonathon smiled into wide, glossy eyes that regarded him doubtfully, but Emily looked away from the fixed gaze and out through the carriage window.

"I have to admit also, Emily, to being quite shaken by what Moore had to say the other afternoon," Jonathon commented much too casually. "What he told me of your being promised to another. Your reaction to it and to him was most . . . unusual."

He gazed at her and murmured relentlessly, "You were most familiar, Emily, and he looked as though holding you as he did, with such little respect and decency, came quite naturally—perhaps quite often too."

Emily blinked rapidly at the dark, shadowy trees. Her hand withdrew easingly from his clammy clasp as she excused in a whisper, "It was no more than his arrogance that makes you think so. I believed you realized just how highly he regards himself."

Emily turned then, away from the murky night and to look at Jonathon directly. She stared, wishing she could see the green-gold of his eyes and the freckling on his face and all the familiar, pleasant things she liked about him. But the dusk dissembled well, making his features merge into a bland, insipid moon.

Sensing her uneasiness mount, Emily insisted with sincerity, "I swear to you, Jonathon, I have never been betrothed or promised to any man at any time. I can only imagine he said it to be spiteful. And I know I behaved badly, recklessly, toward him; it is just that he infuriated me so. He is double-edged, all the time appearing one thing one moment and another the next. I would never have humiliated myself or you by arranging the meeting had I realized how he would react." She halted, then added quietly and forcefully, "I believe that I hate him now."

She sat back completely in the seat, her head moving to

rest against the squabs. Jonathon straightened from his slightly stooping posture and did likewise. "I wonder, though, Emily," he reflected quietly, "Does he hate you too? Or is his passion perhaps otherwise motivated?"

Emily gave a short, bitter laugh, aware of the probing and the innuendo. "Oh, yes. I believe he dislikes all the Shaw family very much. My father he certainly hates and he has done so since he left his employ when he was seventeen."

She glanced at Jonathon, sensing his keen interest. "Yes, he used to work for my father after his own family was bankrupted and his father died," she explained quietly. "He and his mother worked on our estate when we lived in Hertfordshire but they left under . . . acrimonious circumstances. It matters little now," she concluded abruptly.

"But I would like to know more about it, Emily," came the immediate disagreement.

She remained silent and Jonathon persisted, but quite mildly, "Well, are you going to tell me, Emily?"

"Perhaps one day . . . but not now." She uttered the words in a tone that begged indulgence but as she looked at him with a small smile there was no answering whiteness in the gloom.

Emily looked away from him hastily, her disquiet increasing treacherously.

From the moment they had settled into the carriage together, she had sensed something indefinably different about Jonathon. The shy awkwardness that usually embarrassed him and endeared her had disappeared completely. He seemed confident and eager to be on the road, yet oddly supercilious to her.

As they rattled along the sombre roads in a strange uncompanionable quiet, Emily had more than once wanted to beg him to turn the coach round and take her back home . . . until she realized there was no home.

At one time, the opportunity to travel in a carriage away from Malvern Hall would have prompted her to beg her savior to take her to London and her parents. But she knew now that no comfort lay in the small Clapham house for her any more, not even of the meager variety she had once belittled but had, since being deprived of it, grown to cherish and yearn for.

Besides, her father was now gone from there. Emily allowed a small, sad smile. She knew well enough that her mother and sister wanted no upset to hazard the forth-coming nuptials. No doubt she was a greater liability than her poor, drink-decrepit papa. Should she saddle them with her presence it would not be for long. Once her condition was discovered, she would soon be banished to join him in exile.

But they deserved to be humiliated too. Why should they not? Her mother especially—for using her and aban-doning her while still so vulnerable. The likely outcome of seduction was well known, yet she had not warned or advised Emily on how to deal with it.

But her mother would simply say it was her own fault. She would say she should have married him when she had the chance. Yes . . . she should have done so. She realized that now. For she could never have had the kind of marriage she had imagined—if such a thing even existed. It would have been best to have ceded at once, before she left home at all, and arrived at Malvern Hall as a married woman.

Men were to be encouraged in their infidelities, her mother had said so, and it was wise. For to be married to a man who was easily distracted away to town must have advantages. He bore little malice towards her—she knew that was true—and she would have become tedious quite quickly. He would have left her alone; they probably would have lived separate lives as most married couples of her acquaintance did. Yet even as the meandering reason linked together and flowed through her mind, she knew it was useless. She could never be indifferent, never share what she wanted for herself alone, and having nothing was better than having a heart-breaking portion.

Emily glanced at Jonathon. But how much better had she made her lot? She closed her eyes, knowing that things were hideously wrong. She was marrying a man she knew now she felt very little for, yet would be obliged to tolerate knowing intimately. She would bear a child whose father was not her husband. It was quite ludicrous in its ghastliness. And at the back of her consciousness niggled constantly the realization that ultimately she knew where she would rather lie at night and with whom.

But her child would now have a name. Her hands gripped at the seat on either side of her. She prayed that it would have life too and her with it. As long as Jonathon did not change his mind, they seemed saved for the moment from poverty and others' disgust and exploitation.

Emily glimpsed the lights of the tavern just as the driver informed them of their arrival at the hostelry.

Jonathon leaned through the window as the coach pulled into the courtyard. He cursed below his breath, then looked back at Emily. "He is stopping already," he muttered irritably. "I shall see why. I had wanted to be more than two and a half hours on the road."

He swung the door wide and jumped to the ground. Emily pushed at the door as it swung closed and she descended the rough wooden steps to the ground. Her legs wobbled a little in the cool, damp night air as her trepidation took hold with a vengeance.

The coach driver strode away to the tap room and after glaring at his retreating figure for an instant, Jonathon swung back toward Emily. "He wants to tend to the horses. And to himself as well, I'll wager, with a jug or two," he ground out irascibly. "He is a surly enough fellow and spoiling for a fight, I am sure of it. Come, we will have a drink and something to eat before setting on the road again."

He caught hold of Emily's elbow and propelled her toward the welcoming, orange-glowing windows.

Emily went gratefully, glad to be away from the musky, dark coach. She glanced at Jonathon, hoping that perhaps in the light and warmth he might display some of his usual charm and consideration. The alternative was too distressing to contempate. As she walked shakily by his side in the deserted courtyard, she clasped at him instinctively as he guided her, desperate to endear him.

He smiled down at her and Emily relaxed a little, certain that she had indeed recognized the tenderness she so desired to see.

Jonathon pulled a chair close to the fire and held out a hand, indicating that Emily should sit. She did so and he proffered her hot drink. Emily smiled thanks before sipping gratefully at the warming brew, sensing the alcohol in the mixture roughen her throat.

She glanced about, examining the pub interior. The landlord, a small, round man of ample girth and practically completely bald plate, gave her a familiar leer as their eyes met.

Emily replaced her glass on the wooden table in front of her just as an equally obese aproned woman bore down on them carrying a tray containing steaming soup plates and chunks of bread.

Jonathon moved from his position gazing silently into the golden-glowing coals and seated himself opposite Emily. The food was placed on the table in front of them.

Emily looked into the gray, scummy broth in which indistinct matter was floating. She glanced doubtfully at Jonathon as he dipped his bread immediately and started to chew. She regarded her own dish once more, realizing she had no appetite for it at all.

"Eat it, Emily." The command was quiet yet firm, and as Emily raised her eyes from the unappetizing mess to meet his, he repeated remorselessly, "Eat it. There will be nothing else for a long while, and I hardly want you fainting away from hunger."

Emily peered sideways at the disgusting brew, murmuring plaintively, "But it looks so —"

Jonathon laughed coarsely into the words, "This is not Malvern Hall, Emily. Nor is my farm. You can forget now about silver cutlery and finely prepared fare. I have eaten worse than this, and in my own home. It is quite amazing how long a potato broth can be made to last when you are starving. I remember once, Lucy and I had one on the boil for a week or more."

He paused and watched with an ironic twist to his mouth as Emily picked up the spoon quickly and touched the top of the greasy soup with it, sinking the metal slowly beneath the surface before lifting it reluctantly to her mouth.

Jonathon watched her, unpleasantly amused. Emily tried to join him in his humor by wrinkling her nose and smiling at him before sipping delicately at the broth. The stench of it as it neared her face made her stomach lurch, but she finished the spoonful and then chewed hurriedly at the solid hunk of bread to try and rid her mouth of the foul taste.

Jonathon was now reapplying himself enthusiastically to his own food, and Emily looked away from him and once more inspected the cozy, low-beamed bar room. There were no other occupants; it was hardly surprisingly, considering the lateness of the hour. Only the landlord and his wife were in the room with them, sitting and supping by the bar. Emily knew the coachman and groom were about the building somewhere too, no doubt insulating themselves more pleasantly against the chill spring night with hot toddies or jugs of warm ale.

She looked back at the revolting soup, aware that she would attempt it now before it cooled, for then it really would be noxious. She dipped the chunk of inflexible bread and looked towards the fire and was trying to engage Jonathon in a little conversation when the tavern door opened.

Feeling weighted by melancholy, Emily did not look up. Neither did Jonathon, engrossed as he was with his food and his silent mockery in watching Emily trying to force down her soup.

His gaze roamed leisurely across the side of her fair face and dark, curling hair that trailed against the cowl of her cloak. His ruminations now had little to do with the food he ate; he mused that the sacrifice of leaving his sister and his farm in the hands of Jacob Matthewson and his wife would be well rewarded—and this very night. And not simply by the havoc he knew would erupt when her absence was discovered.

He thought of Clifford Moore and his eyes narrowed with his mouth in hard satisfaction. Aware of someone standing quite close now, he turned casually, and as the object of his malice smiled at him, he even managed to return a small one before he froze.

His soup spoon clattered against the dish, falling from nerveless fingers and splashing fat globules onto the rough wooden table top. Green eyes remained slanting upwards, held easily by the steel ones gazing down. Clifford's eyes shifted then and settled on the side of the averted dark head. Emily sat composed and quiet now, momentarily contemplating wistful dreams in the shifting, glowing mass of coals and leaping flames in the hearth.

Jonathon glanced hastily toward the door, noticing the black servant leaning back against it. His eyes darted to Emily, but she was watching the fiery dance still. But, perhaps aware of his attention, she inquired softly, "Who will deal with your business for you, Jonathon, while you are away?"

There was no reply. Sensing that this awful friendliness in him might turn into discourteousness as well, she lowered her eyes to her soup plate. She picked up the spoon again and let it sink into the muddy broth.

"Are you going to eat that swill, Emily?"

As though the ironic comment made her once more regard the food in exactly the same light, she grimaced and let the spoon drift into the soup, the handle sliding away beneath the grease-glossed surface. The familiar, welcome voice registered then, lifting her eyes and her spirits as she spun in her chair, startled, toward him.

Her hands went to the table as though to push herself up and rush to him but his gray eyes were stone-cold despite the enlivening rage. Emily gripped at the table edge until her knuckles whitened. She looked away from the frightening, hostile gaze and back at Jonathon.

He was inspecting his hands in his lap, turning them palm upwards and examining them as though for callouses before they fell with a slap against his thighs. He looked up at the man by his side and gave a thin-lipped smile. "How did you know? Did you see her leave?" he asked. "What matter? It was worth a try." His eyes sought Emily and lingered broodingly. "How much, I wonder, would my farm have been worth had I managed to spend the night with her? How much to rid yourself of me then, and buy her back?"

Clifford smiled slowly and enquiringly, as though quite amused but puzzled too by the suggestion. Long fingers came out leisurely as though to rest casually upon Jonathon's shoulder but they jerked him upright in an abrupt instant.

Clifford spun him about before knocking his head sideways with the back of a lean, savage hand. Jonathon tottered back on his heels a few paces before crashing into the brick fireplace.

Emily was on her feet in an instant, whispering Jonathon's name, astonished by what she had witnessed.

Jonathon rolled himself hastily away from the burning grate and leaned his head and shoulders against the rough, crumbly red brickwork. A shaking hand went to his split mouth. He inspected his sticky crimson fingers.

Clifford seated himself in the chair from which he had just ejected Jonathon, shoving away in disgust the almost empty soup bowl.

Emily shook herself from her daze and moved then to go to Jonathon's aid. As she neared the other chair, her wrist was gripped painfully. Clifford moved her in front of him again and without looking at her bit out, "Sit" as he pushed her backward toward her seat.

She swiped violently at the arm that restricted her as the full force of his brutality and arrogance permeated her shock. "How dare you treat Jonathon so!" she choked out. "He gave you no cause to hurt him like that, you . . . you barbarian!"

The fingers at her wrist increased pressure. "Sit, Emily," he ordered menacingly, "for if I have to stand again to make you do so, I believe I might be tempted to. . . ." The threat went unfinished, but as his metallic eyes lifted, making contact with hers, his contained wrath somehow unleashed her own. She lashed out recklessly, giving him a hefty slap about the side of the face.

Clifford ducked, managing to evade the worst of the blow as he dodged sideways.

He pushed himself upright again wearily, but his hand flashed up, making Emily flinch and cower instinctively. His fist rested against the side of her face for no more than a few seconds before his hand opened, spanning her jaw and jerking her round to face him.

Fearful yet defiant violet eyes gazed up, noticing then panic as well as fury darkening the steel of his eyes. They closed for a second as he rasped, "No more, Emily, or I

346

swear. . . ." His hand dropped away from her just as abruptly as it had taken hold.

Clifford addressed Heath without naming him or turning toward him. "Get him out of here. I shall be back in the morning."

Heath pushed himself away from the door and paced toward Jonathon. As he neared, Jonathon scrambled up, wiping a smear of blood across his cheek.

"Suppose I don't want to go," he hissed with a sneer. "You have no right to dictate to me where I go or when. Keep that for your nigger slaves."

Clifford glanced back at him and his mouth tilted, but nothing in the smile suggested amusement. "Suppose I want to make an issue of the fact that you have abducted my ward," he parried softly. "Suppose I have you imprisoned and suppose your sister finds she is left to cope alone . . . with a farm which just dropped quite considerably in value, to a sum that more reflects its true worth. Think carefully on it; for if you intend remaining close you will regret it." He laughed with soft poison, "But if you intend crossing me again, for any reason, I promise you now, you will regret the day your mother gave you life."

Jonathon smirked. "Threaten me all you like. Coerce . . . intimidate. I have witnesses, you know." He glanced meaningfully at the rotund, gawp-mouthed couple at the bar who sat, statue-like with tankards raised in perpetual salute. "Perhaps I might prosecute you," Jonathon mused happily.

Clifford's eyes followed Jonathon's gaze. He smiled easily at the landlord and the man's fat lips tugged at the sides in acknowledgment. Apart from that his fleshy face remained petrified.

"Did you hear that, my good man?" Clifford inquired.

The man stirred at last, replacing his drink upon the bar. He stared assessingly at the expensively dressed yet haggard blond man, who despite the equable words and outward calm was wound tight as a spring, about as innocuous as a powder keg in a fire. He shifted small, squinty eyes to the roughly clad, smaller man on the floor, pressing at his bleeding mouth with agitated fingers. Piggy eyes then settled on the beautiful white-faced girl who glanced at him at that moment with terror in her wide violet eyes.

He looked back finally at Clifford. "What was that you said, sir?" he asked slowly and deliberately. "You shall have to speak up a bit. Me and the wife here, we been afflicted this past year or so. Martha here — she be deaf as a post at times, you know."

His wife's pouched cheeks bagged further in affront at this easily interpreted slight to her good health. But she sat uncomplaining, staring at Clifford warily and with the same intensity as her husband.

Clifford's mouth thrust in a cynical smile. He removed a five-pound note from his pocket and let it drift to the table close to Jonathon's soup dish. He glanced at the mortified man, breathing heavily as he rested against the fireplace still.

"Well, let me at least pay for your meal, Cross, before you leave," Clifford murmured patrionizingly as he re-seated himself in the chair he had occupied before.

Heath beckoned to Jonathon, indicating they leave now. Jonathan pushed himself up slowly, dusting his clothes in a cursory way, saying nothing else although his eyes were deadly. He approached where Emily stood and hesitated. He seemed about to speak or go to her, but instead merely bit his lip, looking sheepish, then gave a hopeless shrug as he walked on.

Emily took two steps, as though about to go to him instead; but there was nothing after all that she wanted to say or do.

Heath passed Emily with his customary nod and a

small smile, and Emily followed him uncertainly. As he neared the exit, she speeded up considerably and caught at the dark-clad arm.

The servant turned toward her and she gazed imploringly up into his dark features.

"Please . . . don't leave me with him," she begged softly. "May I come with you . . . please?" The entreaty was as low as she could make it as she was unaware of whether Clifford was looking or listening, positioned as he was somewhere behind her now.

Dark brown eyes smiled before Heath's full mouth lifted, twisting wryly. "It is all right . . . trust him," he murmured.

Emily shook her head immediately, denying the reassurance vehemently. Her fingers tightened desperately on his sleeve. Her head swayed from side to side slowly as she beseeched, "Please . . . I am frightened. He frightens me more than anything tonight."

A dark hand raised, just skimming one of Emily's ashen cheeks. "That is because you frightened him more than anything tonight," Heath soothed gently. He gazed across the top of her dark-chestnut head to Clifford, sitting with one hand resting by his mouth, as he watched this unusual discourse, narrow-eyed.

"But I know not how to pacify him . . . what to do or say," Emily choked in despair. "He will beat me, I know he will."

Heath shook his head, but whether in denial or hopeless disbelief, it was hard to tell. But he looked back at Emily, suggesting wryly, "I think a smile might do the trick." He removed the grasping hand from his sleeve and held it for a second before lifting it briefly to touch his lips.

He returned the small shaking hand gently to her side and then walked away, nearing Jonathon. He opened the door for Jonathon with customary civility and a deferential nod. Jonathon left without another glance Emily's way and the black man followed him closely.

Emily watched them go, realizing then quite detachedly that Heath's docile servility was a facade behind which mockery dissembled.

She approached the exit and stood looking at the door for a moment, undecided whether to leave with them anyway. She swung about, aware that Clifford was watching her, but her eyes were with the innkeeper and his wife, searching for some glimmer of compassion or aid there.

The man glanced away hastily and busied himself clearing away jugs and pots with one hand while the other grasped at a grayish cloth. He commenced wiping the same spot on the bar with great thoroughness, in wide sweeping circles. His spouse now seemed equally conscientious. She eased her bulk away from her stool with surprising agility and, gathering an armful of the dirty tankards with an encompassing grab, she shambled away into a back room, clinking loudly, without her eyes once meeting Emily's.

Brightening violet eyes traced reluctantly back to the man who did look at her, and most steadily. Clifford stood up slowly and walked toward her leisurely. She backed away from him spontaneously and her heels crashed against the wooden door behind.

"Can we go now?" Emily asked in a breathless rush, without looking at him once.

He smiled as he closed with her. "Go where?" he inquired with suspect calm.

"Back to Malvern Hall? I came on horseback. Heath will have taken the coach and I have no intention of setting upon the road again tonight. It is past one-thirty and I am ready for bed."

Emily started, setting the wooden door at her back shuddering. She gave an emphatic shake of the head, the door's shuddering renewing. "They might not have taken

350

it. I heard no coach leave."

Clifford smiled very slightly, his eyes narrowing as he dashed the hope quietly, "Oh, they took the coach, Emily. I told Heath to."

He halted just in front of her, now so close that she could recognize the gauntness and exhaustion that sallowed his skin.

Emily made to slip sideways and past him, murmuring distractingly, "I should like a drink—"

A hand leaned against the door abruptly, halting her movement. Her shoulder knocked into it and she retreated hastily from him and flattened herself against the door again.

His eyes were intent, traveling her face slowly before lowering to the heavy draped cloak fastened at the neck. He remained leaning heavily against the door, but his free hand moved to the buttons and undid them. He pushed the cloak open and gazed at the lines of her figure closely encased in the clinging red woollen dress. His eyes slid to her feet and then back again with leisurely purpose, raising to her face. Silver eyes regarded her steadily, heavily-lidded with desire and threat, and a mockery that could have been directed at either of them.

"Have you a room? A bedchamber?" he asked evenly of the now busily observant landlord behind him. He had not turned while making the inquiry and Emily's eyes darted to his, widening, her mouth parting as though to speak but no words formed. He was unmoved, his stare unwavering, watching every nuance of reaction.

"Yes, sir," came the landlord's affable reply.

"Clean?"

"Yes, sir," came the slightly affronted affirmation.

Clifford smiled in sardonic appreciation of this pleasing news, then pushed himself away from the door and nodded, murmuring, "Good," as he walked back to his chair and sat down.

Emily followed him hesitantly. She halted in the center of the room, her heart thudding so slowly and heavily that she sensed at any moment it must soon cease functioning completely.

"I only . . . I told you I wanted to be married now. I did tell you . . ." she tried to explain in her defense.

He gazed up at her quite mildly for a minute before his fist smashed into the wooden table in front of him. The crockery jumped and Emily's forgotten, cold, thick soup escaped the dish and landed heavily on the floor.

The landlord crept from behind the bar, easing his turgid body carefully between it and the wall. His eyes attached to his best crockery, and his inaudible curses were for his wife, as he realized she had omitted to make use of the chipped set on this occasion. He was prepared to waive the loss of the dish's contents, although it could have rejoined the pot; but his china was definitely worth the saving.

Clifford's stone eyes ground against apprehensive violet ones. He gritted slowly through teeth that seemed to have difficulty moving at all, "I asked you to marry me. And more times than I should have." He gazed at her, his face utterly set. "But no more," he concluded softly.

He noticed then the stealthily sneaking landlord and he rose away from the table, allowing the man access to clear the mess.

Pudgy fingers scraped together the crockery and the soup-splattered five-pound note that was waved deftly to be cleaned before it disappeared like greased lightning about his person. He bowed obsequiously to Clifford, who demanded tersely, "Where is the room?"

"Top of the stairs and first right, sir."

Clifford nodded curtly. "You and your good wife should retire now, I think. It is exceedingly late." He produced another note from his pocket as he spoke and proffered it. It was slipped away from his fingers with expertise and deposited with its mate in a cavernous pocket about the man's waist.

The bald pate dipped low in thanks as he agreed in a humble tone, "Exceedingly late sir. I was thinking the same thing myself this very moment." He gave a loud, open-mouthed yawn to emphasize the extent of his fatigue before he sloped off. He closed the door quietly as he left the room.

Clifford's gaze returned to Emily as she stood twisting her hands in mute desolation in the center of the room still. She was sure she was chilled so she shivered ceaselessly, and as though to warm herself, her body swung from side to side, making it appear she might at any one moment walk either one way or the other, but she remained rooted to the spot. Her agitation was controlled abruptly. She approached him tentatively, gazing up into gravel eyes. On impulse, her arms lifted and went about his neck, her forehead resting lightly against his abrasive, unshaven chin. "I am sorry . . . truly. I am sorry for running away. Please don't be so angry with me," she begged.

She felt him tense but his arms remained at his sides. After a moment she drew back and looked up anxiously into his face and with the closeness she could suddenly smell the alcohol about him.

His mouth lowered to hers abruptly, kissing her coarsely and selfishly, insulting in its violence and disregard. His head raised and he watched as a trembling hand withdrew from him to press against her bruised mouth. Her wide, large-pupiled eyes glossed with tears as she whispered huskily, "Are you drunk?"

He laughed shortly and a sweet, alcoholic breath assailed her nostrils more pungently. "Yes, Emily," he slurred carelessly, "although I surprised myself tonight by the speed with which I can sober up when need be. I am sober enough . . . never fear. I have no intention of passing out — not for a good while yet."

She gazed into ruthless silver eyes and as his mouth descended, she turned away quickly, unable to bear that he should kiss her so again. Her other hand slid away from his shoulder hastily, but his arms coiled about her then, keeping her relentlessly against him. One unyielding hand restricted her evasive face, his mouth violating hers with punishing force before sliding to savage hotly and lingeringly at her neck.

His hands moved to her cloak, opening it and sliding in to assault her with immediate unrestrained sensuality. They stroked up leisurely from the curve of hip and waist to longer at her breasts, heavy thumbs tormenting with calculated skill before long fingers moved to unfasten the small buttons at the front of her bodice.

Humiliated beyond further endurance, Emily slapped up viciously in the direction of his face. She pushed herself violently back from him and stared up frozen-eyed. She back-stepped again, separating them with a distance of a few feet.

"Do you think you might possibly wait? Just until we are upstairs. I would rather undress myself, and do it somewhere a bit more private," she lashed glacially.

His mouth set in a hard smile, no sign of remorse apparent. He shrugged an immediate, indifferent acceptance of terms, the lust in his eyes intemperate and quite deliberately so. He held out a hand, indicating wordlessly that they were to go now.

Emily hesitated, wondering if pleading and crying would work, for she could sense both were imminent. She dismissed the craven notion, but only because she remembered that neither helped anyway, the self-abasement involved was disregarded.

Ignoring his outstretched hand, she moved past him and to the stairway that was set at the back of the room. She mounted the narrow, steep stairs as quickly as her trembling misery would allow. She faltered on the low-ceilinged landing and looked forlornly at the four or more closed doors that led off. She tried to remember the landlord's directions of which room was theirs, but her mind was dead, and her memory beyond resuscitation.

She approached one, then hesitated, with her fingers outstretched for the handle. The sound of her name from behind made her swing about. She walked back slowly toward the door he held open with one hand while the other clasped a bottle and glass. As she passed him she wondered absently where he had got them.

She entered the room reluctantly and glanced at once at the bed. The whole room had an unexpected, fresh air of cleanliness; the sheets were pristine and frostily white, already turned back neatly for the bed to be used.

A small, dainty oil lamp glowed by one side of the double bed on a light-colored wooden table. The curtains were open and the metal lattice windows seemed to beckon. Emily neared them and gazed out into the pitch night, then down into the somber courtyard. "The coach is there still, I can see it," she remarked softly.

Clifford moved closer, looking over her shoulder. "So it is," he agreed drily, "they must have returned on horse-back."

A light touch on her shoulders made her flinch and move away at once to close the heavy, dark-blue velvet curtains against the moonless night. Tremulous fingers brushed against the soft fabric for an anguished second before she turned away and into the room again.

He appeared to have taken the side of the bed where the lamp was and had placed his bottle and glass down by it. Emily moved to the other side and stood by a small armchair, her fingers raising at once to the small buttons at her bodice. She began to unfasten them, easily at first and quite rapidly. But as her hand neared her waist and shook clumsily, and she was aware, despite her lowered eyes, that he was standing quite still watching her, she asked on a light sigh that tore at her throat, "May I undress alone at least? I will be quick."

There was no reply and he remained motionless for so long that she was sure he had simply ignored the request. But he walked past her wordlessly and removed the key from the lock as he left the room.

Emily finished undressing hurriedly. She tidied her clothes on the small chair as neatly as a few seconds would allow before shielding her nudity inside the bed with the cold white sheets held tightly to her chin. She lay on her back with her eyes closed.

He was gone for so long that she was even beginning to feel relaxed, sleep leadening her eyelids, when she eventually heard the door open and close quietly.

The key grated in the lock and her lashes raised slowly, sleepy violet eyes gazing up at him as he stood over her. He sat down on the bed close by and she instinctively turned from him and tried to shift away. His hand leaned on the other side of her, prevening her moving far, before it slid along the bed to her face, turning her back to look at him.

She gazed up at him unblinkingly. She inquired softly and quite steadily, "Where will I go when we leave here?"

"Where do you want to go?"

She stared past him, wide-eyed and thoughtful. "I should like to see my father," she decided quietly. "He is dying. He told me so quite honestly in his last letter. The doctor has warned him that he has but a few months. He is away from home now while my mother and sister prepare for the wedding. I should so like to see him again before he . . . I wonder if George knows?"

"Knows what?"

The query was mild but lightly probing. Emily focused again on the man casually leaning over her. "Well, knows of the marriage, and that Papa is dying," she explained in a small voice.

"Does he know where you have been staying?"

Violet eyes skimmed past narrowed gray ones. "I believe my mother wrote to him that I was staying with friends a while ago now," she replied with no irony.

Her eyes retraced to his, momentarily surveying the drunken dissipation quite evident in his face, and as it monopolized her consciousness, dread overwhelmed her once more. A hot stinging behind her eyes forced her lids suddenly closed. She turned hurriedly sideways so that her face was half-hidden by the pillow. "Where will I go tomorrow?" she asked in a muffled mumble.

Clifford slid a gentle hand to her face, stroking the strands of clinging hair away from the deathly pale cheek presented to him. After a moment, the caress ceased abruptly and he stood up.

He walked away and started to undress as he said coolly, "Amanda has no need of a companion at the Hall now. She is moving out at the end of the week. I realize she was prime instigator in this little plot — but no matter. She is going to London and will not be back. So . . . there is no ostensible reason for you to be there either. I hardly think I can take you back as companion to myself. . . ." A low laugh was followed by, "Much as I would like to. No — I think what I shall do with you is what I should have six months ago. What I most need is a mistress. I seem to remember putting mine off for some reason. I can't imagine why . . . for she was most obliging and accomplished." He looked at Emily as he shrugged out of his shirt. She was lying with one hand at her face now, although she was utterly silent and still.

He stared at her for a lengthy moment, but the pain and fright of nearly losing her lingered, spurring his need to wound her in retaliation. He looked away from her deliberately, tormenting softly, "But in time, no doubt, you will learn just how to be nice to me."

A faint voice asked on a quick gasp, "Where will I stay?"

"In town," he answered tersely. "What would you prefer? A milliner's? Haberdasher's?" He laughed. "I realize a dressmaker's would hardly be a possibility. With your skills it would be a ludicrous undertaking." He paused before taunting slowly, " A bookshop . . . how would that suit? Too well, I imagine. No doubt you could arrange business to keep you occupied the night through. What do you think, Emily?"

The silence throbbed, Emily holding her grief so rigidly that it was hard to tell whether she breathed.

He tormented her further, but in the same reasonable tone, "No, I think just a house would be best with plenty of servants and no books. No distraction . . . nothing at all for you to do the day through except think of me, and my visits, and how best to please me."

The quiet sob she let out was stifled as her face turned suddenly into the pillow and rubbed against the cotton, drying and easing the ache in her eyes.

He remained motionless, watching her as she shuddered but tried to conceal her anguish from him. His eyes closed in utter despair and his mouth tightened in self-disgust at how he had quite purposely brought her to such misery. Ridiculously too, for he had hurt himself equally in achieving it. He threw his clothes abruptly toward an empty chair before moving round to sit on his side of the bed.

Emily recognized the sound of decanter touching glass, and she turned slowly toward him and watched as he raised the glass to his mouth. He held it there for a moment before downing the topaz liquor in one swallow.

She turned toward him fully, oblivious to his naked torso—tanned, broad shoulders and narrow waist and hips—as she gazed at the comfort in the bottle. She sat up, clutching the cover to her, her hair tangled thickly about her face and shoulders.

"May I have some?" Her voice was thin and quavering, yet the plea was woundingly clear. "I would like some. I wanted a drink . . . may I?"

She stared longingly at the rum or brandy or whatever it was, caring little for its flavor but craving its power to warm and calm and obliterate.

He replaced the empty glass on the table without answering. After a further silent moment, Emily sank back into the bed, quite deadened already by her conviction that his cruelty tonight was boundless and quite unrelenting.

He got into bed slowly, relaxing beside her with a long, deep exhalation.

"Would you turn the lamp out?" Emily asked huskily after a few minutes of unbearable tense quiet.

His hand reached out toward the oil lamp. He lifted it and went onto one elbow as he adjusted the glow but left it burning. He replaced it carefully on the table and then turned her, one hand cupping one side of his face as he regarded her steadily and silently.

The sob gathering momentum within erupted violently, rocking her against the bed. A small, white hand sped to cover her face as she pleaded gaspingly, "Don't be so callous . . . so tormenting. I would rather you. . . ." She trailed into silence, unable to voice the lunacy that she would rather he begin the violation than torture her with its imminence.

He moved a hand toward her spontaneously, wanting to soothe and comfort, reassure and attempt to initiate apology, but as she caught sight of it, she instinctively cringed and choked simultaneously.

Clifford jerked her close abruptly, his arms enfolding her and holding her tightly. His face bowed forward, resting against soft, dark hair, his hands caressing ceaselessly. He kept her hard against him, stifling the jolting sobs against his body, until they quietened to an intermittent racking hiccup that faded slowly away into nothing; her breathing steadied, and the night lengthened, and she slept in his arms with her hair matted wetly about her face.

Chapter Eleven

Emily woke at dawn. Her eyes felt hot and uncomfortable and they parted slowly and painfully. Her aching head moved back tentatively and a hand went to clear straggling hair away from her face. She gazed at the bare, dark shoulder she had been resting against. Her head straightened then and she stared at Clifford's face as he slept. She blinked, trying to clear her vision of distorting film as she regarded him for a few minutes with unbroken attention. One of her fingers stretched out slowly, tracing with feather lightness the scar that marked his cheek.

He was laying on his back, one arm about her still and the other resting open against the side of the table by the bed.

Emily focused on the glass with a small amount of alcohol still in it, barely inches from his hand, placed as though he had relinquished it, then slept immediately. The bottle had been full the previous night, she knew that; yet now there was barely more than a glassful of color at the bottom.

She studied him again, carefully noting the light sheen of sweat against the sallow skin of his face and strands of fair hair caught damply at his forehead.

She lowered her face to his. The cloying scent of the alcohol made her recoil and she realized he was quite drunk.

One of her hands slid below the sheet to instinctively touch her thigh. She moved a little, wondering, but there was no soreness or discomfort. Her hand skimmed up, traveling her stomach and breasts slowly, but she sensed she was the same.

She murmured his name softly, testing, but not too courageously. There was no response at all, so she eased away slowly. His hand fell from her to the sheet with a thud and Emily tensed rigid, petrified for a moment that he might wake. But he frowned and stirred, moving the hand by the glass to his forehead. His tongue touched his lips, moistening them, and then he had once more relaxed into deep, intoxicated slumber.

Emily backed away from the bed stealthily and stood shaking, watching him unwaveringly for any further sign of wakefulness.

She dressed hurriedly in silence, her eyes ever vigilant, then tried to untangle and neaten her hair. She approached the window on swift, quiet feet and lifted the curtain edge. She gazed down at the carriage, her eyes closing in heartfelt thanks as she saw it was still there. She felt automatically in her cloak pocket in a vain attempt to locate some money, even though she knew she had none.

Her eyes were drawn then, involuntarily, to Clifford's clothes, heaped together on the chair as though thrown there. She glanced away quickly, knowing she would never be able to take money from him.

362

Emily's fingers twisted the small pearl ring nervously and then she looked down at it more purposefully. She spun it round completely on her finger before removing it. She walked quickly to the door and turned the key, her mouth pursed tight lest it grate, but it turned quite smoothly. She pulled the door open abruptly and then hesitated. She turned and gazed toward the bed, her eyes anguished. A hopeless sigh escaped and her head inclined to lean against the barely open door edge as fear of the unknown and uncertainty at leaving him warred within. She dwelt on St. Albans—a town she hardly knew, and a large lonely house where she could expect random visits for an unknown time, until he tired of her, or her pregnancy rendered her of no further use; and then . . . . she opened the door hastily and made her way softly downstairs.

The embrace tightened, rocking her ceaselessly, and moist, hot breath steamed against her neck.

Emily smiled into the rough woollen coal of the man who held her, feeling more surely happy than she had in a long while. She disentangled one arm with difficulty from within his grasp and her hand ruffled thick, wiry hair before she eased herself gently away.

She gazed lovingly into his ravaged face, pinkish, almost sightless, eyes blinking rapidly to focus on her in eagerness.

"It is so good to see you, Papa . . . so good."

He merely nodded, tears tracking his cheeks once more, merging with the wet already there. He snorted and reached for her again, swaying her continually in grasping, greedy arms. "I had not thought to see my Emily again in this life," he mumbled out on a long sniff. "I

363

prayed to see you . . . just once more before I died. I prayed it nightly the weeks and months I have been here, and now you are come to me like an angel." He pushed back to look at her again. "So beautiful . . . so beautiful still," he murmured, shaking his head slowly.

A rough square hand went to smear tears and mucous across his face and he rubbed his cuff into the mess to clear it.

Charles snuffled loudly and then coughed to cover some of his embarrassment at this display of uncontrollable emotion. He straightened himself in the chair and knocked at the front of his jacket to neaten it. "How are you, Emily, my dear," he asked quietly and calmly. "How have you been these months I have not seen you?"

"Well, Papa. I wrote to you that I was well, did I not?" she replied gently. She smiled and nodded reassurance at him, but he shook his head savagely and a hand went again to clear his eyes of yet more tears.

"I could believe none of that, my love. How could I believe it unless I saw you and heard you say so? Did he read your letters? Those you sent me? Did he tear up the first that accused of vileness and make you redo them?" His voice became guttural as oft-imagined torments bedeviled him. Thick fingers scrabbled at his blinded eyes, pressing to deny the tears further access.

Emily swallowed the throbbing lump in her throat. "It is true, Papa. I was well then and I am well now." She paused before avowing softly, "He never asked to see my letters."

The iron-gray head lifted and pale pools of eyes sought and found her anxious violet ones. Charles stared silently, too distraught to show any further sign of his anguish.

"Did he hurt you, Emily?" he asked in a hoarse murmur. "Tell me true how he hurt you; for I have to know to beg forgiveness before I can rest," he explained with quiet, controlled reason.

Emily put out a soothing, stroking hand, moving a thick lock of coarse hair away from his damaged eyes. She reassured softly, believing the words as she uttered them, "He never hurt me, Papa. I would not lie. I swear, He did not hurt me."

She rose then from the small couch they sat upon and walked to the open french windows that looked out over the small, spring-flowered gardens. She breathed deeply of the mildly redolent air. Her eyes encountered distant meadows and she murmured quite happily, "This is such a lovely place, Papa. Who would have believed it . . .? She laughed softly, "You have been so close to me. Barely fifteen miles from Malvern Hall and the Grange and within the same county."

He smiled and nodded forcefully, informing gleefully, like a boy in a prank, "On days when I have felt well in the past, I have asked Jeremiah—oh, he is oddjob man here—I have asked him to drive me there. I have sat in the coach, out of sight, close to those excluding, high gates of his, and gazed through at what these old eyes could see of that palace he owns. I would look and stare and look . . . sometimes for two hours or more . . . until I was sure I could see you laughing at a window and waving to me. Then I would come back here and rest a while, quite peacefully."

Emily smiled sadly through the tears misting her eyes. She swung about suddenly to look around the small, comfortably-furnished room. "Who is your landlady here, Papa? Is it she that showed me to you? She seemed most pleasant when I arrived, most obliging and not at all put out by my unexpected visit." She walked back slowly to the couch and sank down, feeling exhausted by the day-long traveling and her rising at dawn that morning.

Charles reached out a short, thick arm and drew her close, and Emily rested her head gratefully against his sturdy shoulder. She relaxed against him and sighed softly and deeply, and for a moment they both sat, mute and still, with eyes that were sightless and minds that were distant, wandering through history and the Hertfordshire dirt tracks.

Emily stretched out a leisurely hand to touch the wooden table to one side of the couch. "There seem to be quite a few guests at this lodging, Papa. I noticed about five young ladies sitting in the garden when I arrived, taking their afternoon tea."

Charles withdrew his arm from his daughter slowly. He asked in a low, weary voice, "How have you come here today, Emily? Does he know where you are? Have you run away or been discarded now?" He repeated softly with barely a pause, "How have you come here today, my dear?"

Emily straightened, sitting unsupported now. She picked at the cloth of her cloak. "I have run away," she admitted quietly, "and he has no idea where I am. But I think it will worry him little now, Papa". She blinked at her cloak before adding, "No one, not a soul, knows where I am. I have told no one that I know of this address, for you did write and tell me not to. Once I had memorized the location, I burnt the letter, just in case at some time he should find it and want to terrrorize you further."

Charles lifted a hand to his daughter's cheek and rubbed softly. He smiled before muttering conspiratorially, "So no one knows where either of us be. For I have told nobody either. Your mama and Jane, and George too, believe me still to be in Surrey. I have been honest though—I did stay there for a while, with an old friend." He gave a self-pitying grunt of laughter, adding, "And about the only one I do have left, I freely admit." He sighed lengthily. "Of course, I write to your mama from time to time, just to let them all know I survive still, but I doubt they take that as any comfort. I doubt too that they would worry should they discover I am no longer in Surrey, for that address they did have, but I heard nothing from either Jane or your mama the few months I resided there."

He halted and stared through the open french doors before informing slowly, "I had a nice letter from your brother, though, while in Surrey. He asked most kindly after you, Emily. He believes you to be well and with friends and was looking forward to receiving a letter from you. . . ." Charles trailed into silence, his ashen complexion brightening with mortification. "I just never had the courage to tell him the truth," he admitted gruffly. "I could not *tell* him how I had disgraced and failed you all, but especially not how I had brought my Emily to such jeopardy. I just could not tell him," he whimpered, his weak eyes pinkening again.

Emily soothed him spontaneously, a small, pale hand stroking against the coarse skin of his face. Charles sniffed and shook his head a little to compose himself. "And George is coming home in July," he informed with an attempt at brightness, "to give your sister away when she marries her earl. For even had I wanted to undertake the duty—which a year or so ago I should have loved, I freely admit—I fear I can no longer travel far at all. The very thought of journeying to London makes me feel weak."

Charles gazed into space. His face softened as his eyes roamed Emily's face adoringly. "But of course, you will be there, my Emily. And when the grand occasion is over with, you must sneak away one week. Come to your old papa and tell me how fine you all looked and how happy your sister is now that she is wed."

Emily glanced at him briefly before her eyes sought her hands, unsteady now in her lap. "I . . . I wanted to stay here with you, Papa," she murmured. "I have no money, though, to pay for my keep. All I had was Grandmama's ring, and that I exchanged with the coach driver for my passage here. I know that I overpaid him badly, for I believe it might have fetched fifty pounds or more if pawned; but I had nought else to use. Now he is gone. He told me on the journey that he is away up to Liverpool to work on the docks."

"You cannot stay here, Emily," Charles said firmly, but with sadness, "It is not a place for young ladies to stay, not at all. But especially not for one as pure as you: for I know that whether you tell me he touched you or not, in your heart you will ever be pure . . . it is the way you are."

Emily turned away from him. "I want to stay here with you, Papa," she insisted quickly. "I cannot go home to London, not now."

"You can, Emily, and you must," he countered with equal resolution. "Never fear that he will persecute you longer. Jane is to be married soon, and he will not trifle with an earl and his wife or her family. He has had his rapine and it will need to suffice. It is me he hates, in any case, and should he wish to come here and torment the life out of me, I would thank him for it. It would be sweet relief, for some days the pain—"

His anguish was assuaged abruptly by two slender arms closing about his neck. Emily held him close for a moment, her dark head rubbing easingly against his rough, bristled face.

"I have to stay here, Papa, I have to," Emily mumbled against his clothes. "If need be, I will work for the landlady—do jobs of some sort to pay for my board."

Charles pushed her head up gently and looked at her. He gave a short, acrid laugh. "You will never work here, Emily. Over my dead body would you work here. I would cheat death a year or more to see that through." He looked about the room then as though searching for words to explain further. At that moment a light rap sounded at the door. The woman who had shown Emily to her father on arrival poked her dant curly head about the door.

"Would you like tea, Charles?" she inquired pleasantly. "Would your daughter like some? The girls are having theirs now and I should like to offer your daughter some refreshment before she journeys on."

Charles nodded a mute acceptance and the woman looked at him curiously, sensing his distress.

Emily rose and walked slowly closer to the door, smiling tentatively. "I hoped I might be able to stay a while— here at this boarding house. I have nowhere else to go."

The woman opened the door wider and walked in, shutting it softly behind her. She turned to scrutinize Emily carefully and with very great interest.

Aware of this thorough examination and misconstruing its reason, Emily admitted slowly, "I am afraid I have no money to pay for my keep. I believe my father is also embarrassed for funds, but. . . ."

Emily halted as the woman's attention shifted from her to her father as he rose sharply. "I have told her she must not stay," he ground out, "and now you must tell her the same for I will not tolerate that she remain at this place."

The woman smiled wryly at Charles before looking at

his daughter. "I believe it is for you to tell her why she cannot stay, Charles," she declared succinctly and with a quite pronounced London accent. She looked Emily over from head to toe before announcing, "For my part, I would indeed welcome her enrollment; she is one of the most beautiful creatures I have ever seen."

"No."

Both Emily and the woman stared at Charles as he stood, fists clenched and his whole body rigid.

Emily neared him uncertainly, wanting to comfort or ask what ailed him so, but he relaxed and avoided her. He turned back toward her abruptly and began, "Emily, I should like to introduce you properly to this fine lady who has given me shelter in her house. And she is fine . . . and a lady . . . no matter what you may hear to the contrary at any time. She has ever been fair and honest with me and more open-hearted and generous than some I could mention." He coughed awkwardly and glanced at Emily as she undid the top fastening of her cloak.

"My dear, this is Hannah Watson, an acquaintance I made in London, a friend of some years' standing who has kindly allowed me to board here and at a most reasonable rate."

Emily smiled automatically at the woman, musing that the name sounded familiar and that her father must have at some time introduced her into conversation. She approached the woman then to shake hands, and on closing with her, noticed just how handsome she was. She was quite tall and very rounded, although not plump, and despite the curvaceousness, quite graceful. Her neck was long and slender and her bare shoulders creamy pale and well sculpted. Her dark hair was cut modishly short with a mass of tiny curls adorning a pale, unlined forehead. As Emily looked into sharp, brown eyes that returned her gaze squarely, she realized that Hannah Watson was probably no more than thirty or so years old although, on first brief encounter, she had imagined her to be nearer forty.

There was a slight air of debility about her that Emily found difficult to pinpoint. For examining her closely, feature by attractive feature, the general overall appearance was one of salubriousness. Nevertheless, a slight shading beneath her expressive, dark eyes and a certain lining about her mouth hinted that something was not quite right.

Emily proffered one of her hands and Hannah clasped it and held it rather than shaking it. "So this is your daughter Emily, Charles," she said to him, although her eyes never left the fair face close by. "The daughter you have not seen for so many months. She is, indeed, quite beautiful." Hannah regarded Charles's ravaged countenance. "I find it difficult to believe that such a lovely child is yours, Charles," she mocked gently.

He harrumphed a short laugh. "As you can tell, Emily, she is not without her faults. She teases your old papa something dreadful. I know not why I stay with her."

"Who else would put up with you and your constant bewailing of fate and life in general," Hannah rejoined at once. She gave Emily's hand a last pat and then let it fall. Without looking at her, she said quietly, "Your papa is quite right, Emily. You cannot stay here."

Emily looked from one to the other of them, trying to recollect where it was before she had heard of Hannah Watson.

The memory seemed to link to the army, and she thought of George but knew Hannah was no friend of his. Then she thought of regiments and of Wellington and the piece fitted the puzzle. She stared across immediately at the woman who had once been mistress to the man she had left drunk in bed that morning.

Hannah met her steady violet gaze and smiled slightly in acknowledgment of the recognition.

Emily walked slowly to the open windows and gazed out at the girls still grouped about a table. It was shaded by a large, sprawling apple tree that was just coming into blossom.

A light shriek of laughter drifted on the balmy air and Emily turned slowly back into the room. "Is this place a brothel?" she asked quite normally.

Charles choked on an uneasy cough and sank back to sit on the sofa with his face held in his hands. Hannah's bright brown eyes met Emily's unflinchingly. "Yes," she assented evenly, "although, I have to own, we usually term it something slightly more—"

Emily cut into the mitigation with a derisive laugh, "Well, no matter how it is dressed up, the trade is the same." She looked at her feet abruptly and swallowed, immediately ashamed of her arrogance, the more uneasy for knowing she had no right to be so self-righteous. She added quite humbly, "I would like to stay . . . if I may and am prepared to work hard to earn my keep, although not as—" She faltered bluntly and flushed, finishing hastily, "But not as the other girls do. But if you need kitchen staff, or help with cleaning, I would undertake—"

Charles gritted forcefully into Emily's words, "You go to your mother and I will hear no more such rubbish of cleaning or cooking." He dribbled foamily at the mouth with the vehemence of his speech, flecks of spittle daubing his chin.

"I cannot, Papa," Emily breathed, barely pausing before informing quietly, "I am pregnant and I cannot go to London and ruin Jane's wedding preparations."

His pale, watery eyes lifted slowly to her face, staring, as did Hannah's piercing brown ones, which cut Emily like glass shards, so keenly did they observe.

Charles shuffled nearer to his daughter, shaking his head as though he had perhaps not quite heard her correctly. Emily drew a deep, shuddering breath, then repeated tremulously, "I am to have a baby, Papa. I should imagine about September, but I am not too sure; I know so little of these things."

She saw the anguish in her father's colorless eyes as he made obvious connections. Emily dissembled quickly and quite truthfully, "I did not tell you, papa, but yesterday evening I tried to elope with a young man. He lives quite close to where we used to in Hertfordshire. He has a small farm of his own there." She hesitated, then added quietly, "He told me that he loved me and wanted to marry me and I believed him. But it was not the truth. He . . . it does not matter now anyway, for Clifford was against the marriage and forbade us to wed. We decided then to elope, but he found out and stopped us. He would have brought me back with him but I cannot . . . I cannot go with him anymore. I cannot go anywhere and would as lief stay here with you, no matter what the place is we lodge in," she concluded on a soft sigh. As the ensuing silence lengthened and her father looked just as stunned, she glanced down quickly at her intertwining fingers. She twisted them painfully together, saying quietly, "I am sorry, Papa, if I have shamed you."

He stumbled the few steps that separated them and fell upon her at once, clutching her to him and rocking her in his arms. "It is I who shall apologize," he cried wretchedly, "for even if I say the words every minute of every day until I rest at last, it will never be enough times to atone for what you have suffered on my account."

Hannah approached them, and clasping Emily's arm, she gave her a light shake. "Come, Emily, I will find you a room. I believe I have a small one; near the attic I am afraid, and rather dusty, but then if you are to work for your keep, you might as well start with cleaning out your own lodging." She scanned Emily's face slowly and then sighed a light laugh. "I cannot say that I am at all gratified by the arrangement, for you are indeed fair of face and figure. The child is not to be born for some while yet, I can see that from the look of you, and I would prefer you used your natural assets for your own and my good. We could both be rich women . . . but never mind." She waved a dismissive hand. "I am prepared to allow you to stay on your terms for the moment — for the amity I share with your father. After the baby is born I would need to review the situation, for in truth I have no need of kitchen staff that look as you do but great need of something so beautiful to lure the customers."

Emily met the honest brown eyes and smiled very slightly, tacitly accepting the terms.

Hannah lead the way to the door and Emily followed slowly, turning about just before she quit the room to look back at her father. He still stood quiet and slack-armed as though in shock. Emily managed a small smile as she promised, "I shall come back down and see you later, Papa."

Hannah waved a hand in front of her face as disturbed dust flew up. She pushed the ill-fitting door wider, wrinkling her nose and forehead as the dispersing hand worked frantically. She allowed the dirt time to resettle and then walked in, Emily following close behind.

Emily maneuvered carefully past dusty trunks and packing cases, glancing about her constantly as she moved to the window. She looked out over the garden; the girls were still sitting out in the bright afternoon, their faces sunny as they talked and laughed. Her eyes raised, gazing out over distant hills dense with spring greenness.

She turned about to meet observant brown eyes. Emily smiled slowly and said, "Thank you. I like it very much; I believe it will suit me very well." She glanced down at the iron bedstead, bare of mattress or covers, and then regarded the rickety-looking wardrobe. She moved to it with a childish thrill of excitement, keen to explore.

Hannah walked further into the small room too, kicking some of the cases to the side walls, coughing as the dust drifted up again. This is going to do my ailing lungs the world of good," she remarked drily.

Emily watched motes of dust eddy in a solitary strip of yellow sunlight, spinning and milling like so much gold dust, gilding the otherwise somber room.

"Thank you," Emily said again. "I really am very grateful. I will work hard—anything—I don't mind what I do."

"Have you thought of ending your pregnancy?" Hannah asked baldly.

Emily glanced at her astonished, about to prevaricate or object to this presumption. She merely looked at her fingers, answering honestly, "Yes, I did think of it at one time; at first, when I initially found out. But I believed I was to be married and now . . . now I have felt it move. Just this week I have felt him wriggle inside me . . . and I cannot," she said softly.

"Is the child Clifford's?" Hannah asked candidly.

Emily's head jerked up at once.

Hannah smiled and said, "Oh, I know you have been

375

staying with him. Your papa told me that. He hates him, does he not? And most violently. I could not understand why at first, for he has told me little of it; but things fall slowly into place. He did tell me though, and most smugly, that you spurned marrying him." Well-shaped, dark eyebrows rose, begging a reason for such odd behavior.

"I told you and my father," Emily blurted quickly. "I told you both that Jonathon and I wanted to elope to be married."

"But you have not answered me, Emily," Hannah chided gently, "Were I with child and unwed, I also should probably look about for a nice young man willing to protect me. But no matter . . . it is your own concern. Remember though, in six months or so when the baby arrives, it will not be easy. Babies need much provision: clothes and food, as they grow they need more and more. You have a right to some aid and the father has an obligation."

Emily swung away abruptly and gazed through the window again. "I believe you were correct when you said it was my concern," she uttered stiffly.

Hannah looked at the rigidly turned back. She rose away from the bed, offering cheerfully, "I shall ask the girls to come and help you. They can bring you up some bedding and a mattress. Let them move some of these trunks and stack them away against the wall. Don't you attempt it," she cautioned, wagging a raised finger. "Perhaps one or two of them might even offer to give you a hand sweeping it out. They never start work themselves much before seven." She explained lightly, "We have a small gambling hall here, downstairs in the large front room. We open that at seven, but Tuesday is a quiet night, in any case."

She approached the door and then swung back. "It might be as well, Emily, for you to keep out of sight at night. The landing below and left of the stairs leads to the rooms the girls use. Keep away from there at night, for if a client were to spot you and offer me exorbitant sums, well, I might find it hard to refuse. I am first and foremost a business woman. Providing gentlemen with pleasure as a livelihood has ever been my forte." She gave a small laugh before continuing, "Even if this vexing ill health I suffer lately will not allow me to take such a personal interest in them as I used to."

Emily stared at her honest, open countenance. "I am very grateful that you are so . . . frank and sincere. I prefer that you be truthful with me. I will indeed remain in my room from seven onwards, never fear."

Hannah nodded and smiled but did not leave. "Once the baby is born and once your papa is no longer with us, things will have to be different. As I have said, you are wasted in my kitchens. I feel it is sacrilege to employ you to skivvy". She paused and then added softly, "I do so hope that Charles sees the baby but I fear six months for him might be a very long time."

The stiff, warped window pushed open at last and Emily allowed cool, clean air to freshen her face. She breathed deeply of the exhilarating draught, trying to clear her nose and lungs of clogging, irritating dust. She turned back into the room and leaned the broom she clutched against a bare plaster wall.

A light tapping made her head spin towards the door just as a dark-blonde head poked around it tentatively.

Emily stared at the girl for a moment and then smiled nervously. "Do . . . do come in, please," she invited in a strange, high-pitched voice she barely recognized as her own.

A small, plump body followed the round face that now smiled sweetly at her. As she emerged completely, Emily noticed she was carrying a bundle of blankets.

A taller, dark-haired girl followed after a few seconds, and breathlessly, as though she had just arrived up the stairs. She knocked the door wider as she entered with a rolled mattress beneath her arm and Emily's carpetbag in the other.

"Blimey . . . wotta mess," the newcomer judged jauntily as she gazed about the room. She scrutinized estimatingly as she approached the bed. Unrolling the mattress, she let it drop and then placed the bag upon it, ignoring or not hearing Emily's quick thanks for bringing it.

The girl bounced back into the bed and her legs drew up as she rested back on her elbows. Emily glanced at the thin muslin shift she was wearing, noticing that it was almost transparent and had fallen back from the girl's raised knees to collect about her thighs. The girl scanned the room slowly again with large, blue-black eyes. " 'Course, it's gotta lotta room for improvement. You could move that over 'ere. . . ." she suggested helpfully, pointing at the wardrobe and then at a patch of bare wall by the bed.

Emily gazed at them both still, entranced by the newness of their faces and voices and at knowing how they earned their living. Realizing then that the sloe-eyes were upon her, and that the girl was awaiting a comment from her regarding furniture arranging, Emily mumbled quickly, "Oh, yes, of course. I had not thought of it."

The dark-haired girl bounded from the bed, her thin cotton dress falling about her bare legs. "Want me to do it for you? Don't mind—honest."

Emily merely nodded and smiled and then the plump, blonde girl approached her. Blue eyes gazed up into

Emily's face. "You are pretty," the girl said softly. "It is just as well you are not joining us on the landing — we might all be out of work."

Emily managed a smile but could not prevent a light choke as her throat tightened in embarrassment. She was prevented the necessity of seeking for some reply to the expectant-faced girl as her friend called to her raucously.

"Do come on, fatso . . . give us a lift 'ere with this thing, else I'll put out me back and no use to any cove at all tonight."

Emily followed the blonde girl, going to help herself with shifting the furniture.

"Not you," the dark-haired girl bossed. "You might strain yourself — damage the baby."

Emily retreated, sensing the stinging in her cheeks as her face colored. She watched as the two young women, neither of whom she guessed to be more than twenty-one or -two, scraped and pushed and dragged the heavy wardrobe across the floor.

"I'm Sylvia and that's —" a thumb jerked towards the blonde girl, "Fiona," came the abrupt information.

Emily nodded a greeting and introduced herself politely. "I am Emily and my father has been staying here for a while."

"Oh, yes, Charlie. We all like him. Not too good though, is 'e, poor old soul," Sylvia remarked sympathetically. "Somedays, I wonder 'ow 'e drags 'isself outta bed."

The wardrobe crashed into position against the wall. Sylvia turned about then, clapping her hands to dust them. "Sorry to hear about your husband. Wotta shame; you look so young to be a widder." She glanced at Fiona and demanded, "Don't she?"

Fiona nodded with a spontaneous, heartfelt smile.

Emily moistened her lips and asked faintly, "What did

379

Hannah tell you of . . . him?"

"Killed in the war, weren't 'e? Fighting with Wellington?" Sylvia shook her head slowly and muttered something disparaging about the French that Emily could not seem to comprehend.

Black hair was tidied back from Sylvia's pale face with filthy hands, leaving dust trails on her clear complexion. "Be nice to have a baby about the place," she announced. "My sister has a baby . . . four months old. Bit of a snot-faced brat . . . but then so's she. Suppose it follers." She gazed estimatingly at Emily, concluding after a thoughtful moment, "You look nice though. If the little baby is like you, we shall all be petting him. Spoil him rotten, no doubt." She swept the cotton skirt from about her legs and advanced towards the broom. She started pushing dirt about in various directions. The broom crashed back against the wall again and she shook her head.

"Stop gawping and give us 'and with these cases," she directed Fiona.

Fiona tripped towards her obligingly, banging her shin hard against the iron bed as she went. Sylvia guffawed loudly as the blonde girl's face screwed in pain and she massaged her bruise.

Sylvia advised Emily drily, "Clumsy cow, she is—crashed about everywhere. Falls on her back so often, 'er mother sent 'er 'ere. Said she might as well get paid for it."

Emily managed a constrained laugh and turned hastily to the window. She pushed it wider, glad of the mild air that cooled her hot face. She looked down into the garden but it was empty now. With one last look over green meadows she turned back into the room, watching for a moment as the two young women toiled quite voluntarily and happily on her behalf. She smiled at them both as

380

they simultaneously looked at her.

"Thank you for helping," Emily murmured sincerely before she moved to the bed and started unfolding the blankets.

A black hand sprang to the bottle, moving it and shoving it so forcefully away that it skidded against the glossed table a foot or more.

Clifford looked up and smiled sardonically and then rose from his chair a little. He leaned forward, reaching for the brandy again.

Heath's hand approached it too, nearing the bottle simultaneously with Clifford's. The paler hand slapped viciously, knocking Heath's outstretched fingers away from his and a snarl took thin, colorless lips back from his teeth.

Clifford picked up the brandy and placed it close to him again. He refilled his empty glass with great deliberation until it was almost half-full.

He leaned back in the delicate yew dining chair and raised the glass to his mouth. He drank lengthily before his eyes slid to meet Heath's. He smiled at him, exaggeratedly, and raised the glass slightly in mocking salute. He pushed himself back further from the dining table and dirty hessian boots rose, scraping against the mellow, golden wood of the dining table as they settled noisily and comfortably.

Heath stared at him for a moment impassively, then he ordered quietly, "Get your feet off the table."

Clifford merely smiled infuriatingly at him and returned the glass to his mouth.

Heath stood up from the table where moments before they had dined together. He walked around the table to where the child sat. He pulled the chair back for Richard in case he wanted to get down, then moved to stand by the hearth.

Richard frowned at his uncle a trifle anxiously, but Clifford smiled at him and the boy seemed reassured. He jumped down from his chair and walked closer.

"Is that nice?"

"What nice?" Clifford muttered.

"That stuff you drink . . . is it nice?"

Clifford's narrow mouth twisted. He regarded the amber liquid, rocking it in the glass a little as he murmured, "Very nice."

"May I have some? Would I like some?"

Silver eyes darted to the bright, innocent face, staring for a moment at glossy blue eyes and pale skin. He looked away abruptly. "No, it is not for children," he muttered huskily.

Richard pouted sulkily but walked away without another word. He selected an apple from the heaped fruit bowl, then approached Heath. He gave it to him silently to peel. The servant smiled indulgently at the small boy and, taking a penknife from his coat pocket, he started to strip the apple skin slowly. His eyes remained with Clifford, relaxing back into the chair, the glass constantly at his lips.

Heath cut the apple into quarters for the boy and gave it to him. He discarded the peel abruptly into the fire before he walked close to the table again.

"Are you coming into town later?"

Clifford looked up and grunted a laugh. "I think not," he slurred sarcastically. "Should I manage to mount a horse I doubt I would stay in the saddle long. And as for any other physical activity . . . well. . . ." He smiled up meaningfully at Heath before downing what remained in the glass. The tumbler found the table again heavily.

"Well, take the carriage — play cards, billiards — do something for God's sake," Heath urged forcefully. As he passed behind Clifford's chair, he savagely swiped the dirty boots away from the priceless table as he went.

Clifford said nothing but made to replace them immediately. Heath swung about and gritted out sneeringly, "You think she would come back to you anyway? A drunken slob? You would have to drag her here again."

Clifford reached for the bottle once more, his face tense and expressionless, no more than a tightening at the side of his mouth indicating he had heard as he replenished his glass.

He raised the alcohol to his mouth and drank, watching as Richard finished his apple. The boy walked off to gaze through the half-open doors that led to the gardens and the warm, late-summer evening air.

"It is your bedtime soon, Richard."

The boy spun around at his uncle's words, looking as though about to dissent. He merely nodded dutifully before asking with a wrinkling of his nose, "Do I have to go to London again? I would rather stay here with you. I hate it in London. There is nothing to do."

"It is up to your mother," Clifford informed gently. "I have said you may stay but you must ask her first if she will allow you to come back again."

Richard pursed his mouth peevishly and a foot stamped loudly. "But I don't want to go and I shan't," he whined gratingly.

Clifford's eyes raised from his glass. "Richard . . ." he cautioned very quietly.

The boy looked at him at once, his mouth still pinched, but his eyes were wary. Small lips tightened further, helping to contain any further disobedience. He swung back to look out into the summer-flower bedecked garden. He strolled out onto the stone-flagged terrace and started to descend the steps to the gardens.

Heath looked at Clifford steadily. "You are starting to frighten the boy," he stated quietly. "You should set some example. He treats you like a father — why can't you try to act like one? He is your brother's child; how do you think he would feel, leaving his only son in the care of a self-pitying sot who treats his father's house like some Jamaican shack?"

Clifford closed his eyes and smiled. "It is mine. He lost it and I got it back. And what is it anyway but an ostentatious palace . . . a monument to my avarice and arrogance?" He glanced up at Heath with a querying lift of his eyebrows and a sarcastic smile distorting his mouth.

Heath returned the irony, provoking deliberately, "Well, if you terrified her before, I wonder how she would feel now?"

Dirty boots scraped back, dropping away from the table abruptly. Clifford straightened in the chair, his hand moving to his glass as he rasped gutturally, "Shut up." He put a hand to his face and shook his head a little to clear it. His fingers pressed at his eyes as he demanded in a coarse, liquor-thickened voice, "What time is it?"

"Eight-thirty."

Clifford nodded slowly and stood up. He walked quite steadily to the open doors to look out over his garden.

Heath followed him and stood some way behind. "What did he say?" he asked abruptly.

"What did who say?"

Heath smiled to himself and turned his head a little but he repeated gently, "What did Shaw's friend in Surrey have to say this time? Anything new? Any hint at all?"

"Nothing," came the terse reply. "He knows nothing other than what he told me before. He has not the vaguest idea where he is. He left without saying where he was going . . . but he thought he might be returning to Herfordshire."

Clifford's gaunt face tilted back a little and he laughed at the ceiling. "Hertfordshire," he mocked. "Perhaps he moved in here and I missed him."

Heath nodded slowly, "In the state you have been in, it is a possibility."

"So everyone has disappeared," Clifford murmured harshly, "Fathers . . . daughters . . . coachman bound for Liverpool docks . . . all disappear. Perhaps it is a conspiracy. . . ."

Heath interrupted abruptly, "What of her mother? Did you stop there on the way to Surrey?"

Clifford nodded. "There and back. She has heard nothing at all from either of them and she seems to care little." He laughed bitterly, then ground out, "Bitch . . . her own daughter and she is more distracted by this damned wedding at the weekend. But perhaps I will go, just in case." He sighed hopelessly, "It will be a waste of time, I know it." His mouth tautened and he bit at his lower lip for a moment before swinging back into the room. He headed for the table and the brandy, half-filling his glass again and lifting it immediately to his mouth. Before he drank he inquired mockingly, "Well, had you not better be off? Time is getting on."

Heath stared at him, then commanded softly, "Stop that. You are killing yourself with the stuff. It has been three months—how long do you think you can keep up drinking at such a rate? You look terrible; soon you will not even be fit enough to look for her, and what then?"

He gazed at Clifford unwaveringly but he merely raised

his glass again, lost in reflections of his own.

"Well, you have to forget then," Heath urged desperately on thoughtless impulse.

The glass splintered into the fireplace, brandy inspiriting the blaze and making it roar into the chimney.

Heath stared tensely at the averted fair head. Clifford turned, savage-eyed to glower at him. "Do you think I don't want to?" he choked out with a bitter laugh. "Do you think I haven't tried to? Every day for three months . . . no — every day for eleven years I have told myself that such obsession is madness." An unsteady hand went to his mouth, wiping slowly. "I have to know where she is. How she is." He inhaled shudderingly, but said with more composure, "I have to know that she is alive and . . . whether there is a child." The mention of a baby made a hand spring to his eyes and press there for a moment.

He turned abruptly from the table and walked toward the garden again, passing Heath wordlessly. He delivered a dismissive farewell to the black man as he moved out onto the terrace.

Clifford threw his head back, surveying the lucid blue sky and puffs of pure white cloud before he scanned the garden for Richard. He noticed him sitting on the grass, head bent, and he descended the stone steps.

He strolled springy emerald turf towards his nephew. He called his name and as the child looked up from his absorbing task, he beckoned briefly.

Richard swung the daisy chain he had been crafting between thumb and forefinger, then stood up carrying it with him. He approached on dragging feet, whining sulkily, "Is it bedtime then?"

Clifford nodded, signalling for him to come before he turned away and started back to the house.

Richard ran to catch up with him. He clutched at one

of his hands and raised the daisy chain to display it.

"Emily showed me."

Clifford glanced down and quickly away. "Mmm . . . nice."

"Is she coming back home yet?" Richard clasped more tightly at the hand he held as it spontaneously tried to remove itself. He gazed up curiously at the tall man at his side who turned suddenly from him.

"Is she?" he persisted.

"No. I don't know."

Richard dropped the daisy chain suddenly to the grass, purposely crashing it underfoot as he walked. "She has gone away for good," he moaned. "I know she doesn't like me any more. I know she was cross because I used to be naughty. She said I was naughty sometimes and now she has gone."

"She does like you, Richard," a hoarse voice corrected kindly, "it is not that."

"Why then? She didn't even say goodbye to me. She went away without telling me or saying—"

Clifford's hand tightened sharply on the small one within it, halting the boy's complaints. "Be quiet, Richard, there's a good lad," he pleaded on a small, awkward laugh.

"Where is she then?" Richard demanded, undeterred.

Clifford sighed and murmured, "With her papa, I expect."

"She has seen him for a long while. Now she can come back home," Richard decided. They began to ascend the stone steps to the house as Richard insisted, "Well, can't she?"

"She likes to stay with him, I expect."

"Well, he could come too and live here, then she would come back," Richard declared confidently.

"Heaven forbid," Clifford muttered drily.

Richard looked sideways up at him. "Well, when is she. . . ?"

"For God's sake, Richard!" Clifford choked out on a spontaneous, harsh bellow.

The boy jumped, startled, and Clifford gripped at his small hand quickly to prevent him tumbling back a step or two. He looked down at wide, frightened eyes and a large, shaking hand went to soothe and smooth the boy's fair head. "I am sorry, I did not mean to shout."

He started to reclimb the steps and Richard went with him, clutching feverishly at the reluctant hand in his small grasp, gripping at it with tiny nails as Clifford tried to slip free.

"Will you read me a story before I go to bed?"

"Ask your nanny; I expect she will."

"Emily used to. She read to me a lot. Can we go to the library . . . just for half an hour?"

"No."

"Well, ten minutes then?" Richard wheedled plaintively. "Heath reads me stories," he informed accusingly with narrowed eyes and petulant mouth.

"Heath likes books."

"Don't you?"

They had reached the top step and walked into the house through the dining room doors.

"Will you then?" the boy cajoled in a tinny, high voice.

"Just ten minutes and no more."

They entered the library and Clifford glanced reluctantly toward the book shelves, trying to close his mind to the slight, dark-haired wraith that roamed them in graceful silence.

"Which book?" he asked abruptly as he turned to the fireplace.

"The one with small people in it," came the immediate response.

Clifford frowned and looked thoughtful. "Gulliver's Travels," he murmured. His eyes returned slowly to the shelves. "But where is it?" he asked with a slight smile, raising inquiring eyebrows at Richard.

The boy approached a spot close to the long window at the farthest end of the room. He confidently removed a brown, leather-bound volume and returned quickly with it.

Clifford sat in the chair by the fire and the boy moved towards him and sat by his side.

Clifford opened the book and looked at the print and then at the top of the fair head. "Ten minutes only," he reminded firmly.

Richard nodded silently and then settled back but stared forward as he listened.

Half an hour later, the elderly woman stood, nervously clasping her hands, just inside the library door. She coughed, barely audibly, to gain attention and then a hand flew to her mouth as though to apologize for the interruption.

Clifford looked up and faltered in his reading before he shut the book in his lap with a snap.

Richard's nanny began to make some humble excuse for disturbing him but he beckoned her in. She approached a few paces and bobbed low. "It is past his bedtime, sir," she advised in a whisper.

Clifford nodded and gave the small, fair head a couple of light, dismissing taps.

Richard turned to grimace disappointment at his uncle, his face screwing up and begging indulgence.

"Go on . . . it was more than ten minutes after all," Clifford said lightly. He stood abruptly to show he was not to be disobeyed. His hand went to steady himself against the chair as he felt himself sway and the inside of his head rotate.

Richard pushed himself upright and made his polite goodnights to his silent uncle before moving to the door and leaving the room with his nanny.

Clifford returned the book to its allocated space in the densely filled shelves. His eyes rose, roaming the volumes, and as he tilted his head back suddenly, the sick vertigo took hold again. He lowered his face carefully and shook his head to clear it, then neared the table where the decanter and glass were located.

He unstopped the bottle and poured, carrying the glass back to the chair by the fire.

His head rested back against the cushion and his hand against the chair arm. He allowed the tumbler to oscillate a little between thumb and forefinger as he gazed unblinkingly into the fire and the images flickering amid the shifting embers.

He turned his head abruptly and closed his eyes, but the vision was the same, indelibly printed on his eyelids. They opened abruptly and he stared at the comfort in his glass instead. Violet sparks floated dreamily in the tawny pool and he gazed mesmerized for a moment before the sob racked him, slopping brandy wetly about his fingers.

He replaced the glass carefully on the chair arm and stood up, slowly and tentatively this time.

He walked toward the library door and quit the room and was halfway toward the stairs when he noticed Heath descending them.

The man was immaculately attired, his clothes of fine, dark material and extremely well-cut.

Clifford watched, a sardonic twist distorting his mouth, as Heath neared the bottom with an agile grace.

Heath noticed him then and as his feet hit the hall he slowed and gave a slight mocking bow before walking toward him.

Clifford looked him over slowly from head to toe. "You look as though you own the place," he remarked softly.

Heath grinned whitely and nodded in acceptance. "At one time, you looked as though you did," he countered with intentional provocation.

Heath regarded the sallow, drawn face and crumpled clothes. He took out his watch. "Nine-thirty," he murmured blandly. "I shall be off soon . . . coming?"

Clifford shook his head, turning away.

"Come on," Heath coaxed, "The carriage is out. It is still light — a lovely evening."

Clifford's hand raised automatically toward his mouth, as though he believed he still held a glass. He glanced at his empty fingers and let them drop before looking at Heath.

The black man returned the gaze steadily, his empathy tangible.

Clifford walked past him and toward the stairs, saying as he walked, "Wait for me then . . . I shall be but a little while.

Chapter Twelve

"Thank you so much for the beautiful present: David and I are most thrilled with it."

A slight inclination of the head acknowledged the gratitude. Silver eyes lingered on the upturned face, taking in the rose-entwined coronet set atop fawn-colored hair. "You look very beautiful today," Clifford murmured with a smile.

Jane raised her eyes to his, some of the coyness gone as she gazed into the lean face that seemed to her more attractive for its gauntness.

Clifford smiled at her again, as her gaze lingered on him, and the blood flooded her face.

She glanced away hastily, sure he had read her wistful reverie of what might have been had he settled for her, and second best, all those months ago.

"Have you heard anything of Emily?" he asked quietly.

Jane glanced back at him, the intensity in his stare making her blush renew, although she knew quite well that in his mind he saw nothing other than a girl with dark hair and eyes the color of violets. She glanced at her satin slippers before lifting her eyes to his face again, hoping perhaps to tempt him at least to tell her once more that she was beautiful.

His eyes were no longer with her but scanning the wedding party bunched about the flower-decorated drawing room.

"I am sure she is with Papa," Jane reassured him timidly. "I expect they are holidaying somewhere. By the sea perhaps, or taking the spa water at Bath. It would benefit papa's health."

"They are not there," Clifford advised curtly. "I have been there myself, and detectives after me, several times. They are not there." Realizing then how brusquely he had spoken, he glanced at the diffident girl and smiled.

He looked across the top of Jane's head, about to start another fruitless visual search of the room when he espied her mother approaching swiftly and purposefully.

Isabelle Shaw halted with a bright smile for her daughter and an even warmer one for Clifford. "Ah, Sir Clifford, I am so pleased you came after all. Such a beautiful Dresden service you have given the lucky couple—"

"Have you heard from your husband?" Clifford interrupted in a hard, pointed tone.

Isabelle looked a trifle peeved by this blunt curtailment of her appreciation. She smiled at Jane as she withdrew a few paces and took a whispered leave of them both. Isabelle glanced sideways at Clifford, then informed quietly, "No, I have still heard nothing from either of them; which of course indicates that they are together. I know Emily had the address at which he lodged—she wrote and told me so. I just wish now I had had the foresight to inquire where it was."

Clifford stared at her relentlessly and she glanced about her, a trifle flustered. He smiled slightly to himself on noticing her agitation. "It seems to bother you little that your daughter is missing—has run away. I quite expected you might demand some explanation from me as to why she has so abruptly absconded."

Isabelle was well aware of the hard irony and his tacit condemnation. She looked up, meeting his narrowed eyes squarely. "I need no explanation. I know why she has gone: because you have not yet managed to convince her that, despite everything pointing to the contrary, your intentions are honorable and you care for her." She gave a sympathetic smile. "I own it must be no simple task. She is . . . difficult to understand and control, I know that well enough; for I never, in all the time she was with me, managed to achieve it." She looked at Clifford and said quietly, "she is your responsibility now, not mine, and it is right that you should have her. I know you care; I always have, or truly I would never have allowed her to go with you. It is just a pity that you seem unable to convince her of how you feel, for it is all she wants really — to be loved and protected, as we all do."

Isabelle stared into the lean, handsome face assessingly, noting a more pronounced cynical twist to his mouth and dark hollows beneath the sleep-deprived eyes.

She raised a hand and gripped at his sleeve, shaking it a little in reassurance. "Never fear . . . they will turn up. I know Charles will . . . like the proverbial bad penny. And who knows, perhaps a little real hardship might not harm Emily that much. It could mature her and she might return to you a woman; for despite all her intelligence, that girl seems to me to be an eternal child."

A vague noise issued involuntarily from Clifford as he wryly acknowledged the acuity of that observation.

Isabelle started to say something else to him, but he was barely listening to her lauding her new son-in-law. His eyes were with a mirror-bright tray which was approaching, balanced upon a footmen's steady palm. As it came within his reach he removed a ruby-filled goblet deftly, placing it to his mouth immediately.

Isabelle halted in mid-sentence and stared, then opined quietly, "You look ill."

Clifford withdrew from her a few paces. He gave a cool smile and murmured, "I am fine." He bowed with polite formality, then turned away.

He started to make for the door, draining his glass as he walked. Just as he looked about for somewhere to deposit it, he felt his arm caught in a cutting grip.

He turned slowly towards the dark-haired young man, resplendent in his hussar's uniform.

Fierce deep-blue eyes raked him hatefully. Clifford stared, stunned for a moment by the aching similarity in features and coloring. He raised a hand automatically, removing rigid fingers from his arm.

"I want to talk to you," George gritted.

Clifford nodded and deposited his empty glass on a window ledge. "I was just leaving; come outside."

"Yes . . . outside," George repeated in a low mutter.

They walked the remaining length of the drawing room in mutual silence; but both murmuring occasional greetings to acquaintances as they passed on toward the door.

They crossed the polished wood floor of the hallway of the Earl of Creighton's country house. Then they were out in the hot summer air, descending the few steps to the gravel driveway.

A carriage started to move forward, and as Clifford noticed it approaching, he raised an idle hand, gesturing that the driver wait a while.

He strolled away from the front of the house and round to the side of the building so that he and George were out of sight of the main entrance.

After walking for about two minutes he swung about abruptly, his hands thrusting deeply into his pockets. He regarded, silently, the tense-faced young man, poised expectantly on the balls of his feet.

"Where is Emily?" George gritted out through white, even teeth.

"I don't know. I wish to God that I did."

"My father?" George interrogated with the same hard vehemence.

Clifford shook his head, indicating the same was true.

George looked sideways down at the gravel at his feet for a moment before intense blue eyes gazed back at the taller, fair man.

"What the hell has been going on while I have been away?" George choked passionately. "It has been barely eight months since last I was home and I come back to this—my father and sister missing and no one knows where. They cannot even be found to attend my sister's wedding." He gazed silently at Clifford and then demanded abruptly, "Why did she go to stay with you? In letters I was told she stayed with friends. I return and she is not at friends but missing while in the care of an old enemy and no-one seems to give a damn."

Clifford ground out on a despairing laugh, "You think I don't care? I have had detectives scouring the country. I have searched myself. I have even sent people abroad—in case they travel to Europe—"

"But why has she gone?" George cut in with lethal quiet. "What made her leave your house? My mother tells me she visited her there and she was living comfortably. Why would she shun that shelter? It was security of sorts, and I know Emily well enough. She would not take desperate steps unless forced to. She was ever a home-loving child, never went anywhere. It was not in her nature to be adventurous."

Clifford nodded and admitted softly, "I know that . . . I know."

"Why did she go then, and without giving word of it to anyone?" George demanded in a harsh, anguished tone.

"She tried to elope with a neighboring farmer. I stopped them and would have brought her back but—"

"Is she gone with him again then?" George suggested in a lighter tone. "Has she run away to marry?"

"No. He lives nearby still, but soon he is moving away from the area. He has heard nothing from her at all. His was the first place I looked."

"Did you have to spoil it for her?" George accused. "If she loved him, could you not—"

"It was not like that," Clifford rasped hoarsely. "She went with him for the same reason she has gone this time—simply to be free of me." There was a brief pause before he stated tonelessly. "I made love to her and she believed I would do so again."

George stared at him. His fist swung out automatically, his face contorting as a string of oaths and foul remonstrations came tumbling out through barely parted teeth.

Clifford made no move to avoid the blows or retaliate, and the beating knocked him back into the cream-gray stone of the house.

He shook his head to clear the film from his eyes, his hand moving briefly to ease his face. George advanced purposfully again and Clifford dodged sideways, knocking away the vicious fists flailing savagely near his face again.

He backstepped cautiously, ever alert to a renewed attack, his weight shifting from foot to foot expediently.

"I am going now. There is no point in this. It will not find her quicker. I deserve your hatred and disgust, I know that. But never torment yourself with your absence abroad. Had you been here those months ago when I first took her with me, it would have made no difference. I wanted her then as I do now and in the same way; as a wife. I love her more than anything but I desire her too, and she will not yet accept that."

George advanced slowly once more, his misery apparent as he sneered abrasively, "Why harm her then? Why hurt her so? My mother tells me the same," he spat out jeeringly,—that you love her. It sounds like sheer sophistry to me—fallacious rubbish to shield your depravity and real character as lecher and despoiler of young innocents." He paused, wiping the spittle away from his mouth with the back of a shaking hand. "Were there not enough whores in London to satisfy your foul purpose?" he screamed, respattering his chin with saliva.

George paced steadily closer, fists clenching and relaxing spasmodically as he neared Clifford.

Clifford avoided him again as he vowed vehemently, "I love her, George—more than life. I admit I was wrong to take her with me as I did—unwed. I should have insisted we marry first instead of letting her have her way. I was sure I could control the situation until she accepted me as a husband, but it was not so. It was madness to try and endure the temptation of having her so close." He gave a spontaneous choke of hopeless laughter. "Your sister can be the most annoying, provocative. . . ." The fond, despairing words halted abruptly and Clifford looked appealingly at George. "She needs and wants me too . . . I know it. If I was not absolutely certain of that, I would have allowed her home months ago and unharmed. But she wants to keep me as a friend, as we were years ago, and I will no more allow myself to be just a friend to her than she will allow herself to be my mistress."

George wiped a rough hand across his face and eyes. "She might be dead. She might be lying even now, ravished again, in a stinking ditch somewhere, covered in blood—"

He was jerked forward by the shoulders abruptly, almost off his feet. Clifford snarled out, "Shut up . . . shut your mouth. Never say so. She is not. She is with your father and safe. We have to believe that . . . I have to, or I would end my own life now. I have thought of doing so, longed to do so; for the grief of losing her is killing me anyway." Wet gray eyes closed abruptly and he inhaled raggedly before wiping a hand savagely across his face.

He stepped back from George slowly and carefully. "I am going now. My apologies to your mother and sister. Perhaps you would convey. . . ."

George was not listening. He interrupted harshly. "My father is ill, I take it. My mother tells me little but I gather he is dying. I guess too his health is ruined by you taking Emily away. He must have tortured himself hourly, brooding on how you tormented and defiled her." When Clifford made no plea in his defense, George demanded hoarsely, "Is he dying? Do you know?"

"I believe so."

"And what will become of Emily when he is dead? Who will protect her then? Perhaps he is dead already."

George sprang forward suddenly, teeth bared and lips tautened thinly.

Clifford ducked sideways to evade the first blows. "George—" he said, but George was past hearing or heeding.

A single punch rocked George on his heels for a moment before his legs collapsed and he crashed to the shingle.

Clifford sighed heavily in regret and his eyes raised heavenward. He looked down at the young hussar and said with slow vehemence, "I am sorry . . . truly, George. But this gets us nowhere. Let me find them; after that you are welcome to kick the hell out of me; but let me find them first."

Clifford approached the panting, mortified young man and held out a hand to aid him to his feet.

George stared at the long, lean fingers stretched towards him. He jerked head and shoulders forward and hawked fully at them.

Clifford remained motionless a moment longer, his hand still proffered in reconciliation.

He turned and walked away abruptly, shaking his fingers casually to free them of clinging spittle.

George pushed himself upright painfully and slowly, dusting his down uniform. Blue eyes watched brightly as Clifford withdrew, then tears of utter futility split and streamed uncontrollably down his cheeks.

"It's no use, Emily, I shall never get this right." Sylvia's stub of charcoal fell clattering to the table.

Emily pushed back onto her knees slowly, away from the grate. She dropped the brush she held and knocked her hands together, rubbing soot absently onto the grubby pinafore she wore. She smoothed the apron down, across her swollen abdomen. A sudden, sharp twinge from within her gasp and Sylvia looked up from her writing at once.

"Wot is it?" she demanded quickly.

"Nothing," Emily dismissed with a cautious smile, "he is just a bit lively today."

Sylvia smiled sympathetically and then glanced back at her alphabet with a plaintive sigh.

Emily moved across on her knees the few feet to the sofa where Sylvia and Fiona were sitting. Her head tilted and she studied Sylvia's wavering, heavily-scripted letters. She swiveled the paper on the table and examined the writing more carefully.

"That is very good. The letters are well formed."

"Are you just saying that? To make me feel good?" Sylvia accused with narrowed, suspicious eyes.

Emily shook her head. "It really is very good," she said again, "especially as you have been learning only a few weeks—" She halted in mid sentence and looked up as the door opened and two girls entered the parlor.

The taller girl, with light-brown hair and hazel eyes, squinted at Emily. She turned to her companion with a curled-lip sneer. I see Miss 'Igh 'n Mighty 'as got the school out again today," she advised her friend, who seemed totally indifferent. That girl merely continued filing her nails assiduously as she approached an armchair and sank into it.

The malicious girl followed slowly, feline eyes still directed toward the three young women grouped about the low wooden table with work spread out.

Sylvia looked up slowly and counseled in a reasonable tone, "Shut your mouth, Pauline." Her tongue tip removed from the corner of her parted mouth and she held her paper in front of her as she examined her letters.

"P'raps Miss Virtuous might 'elp me learn to read and write," Pauline antagonized further. "Then perhaps I could get work like she 'as — sweepin' out the cinders, 'stead of indulging in all sorts of lewd goings on with the gents upstairs."

Sylvia stood up casually, still inspecting her writing with an assessing grimace. She walked close to the armchair where Pauline sat perched on a soft, rounded arm by the side of her friend. Sylvia carried her work with her as she approached, as though she might show the two newcomers her efforts, but as she came within reach a hand snaked out abruptly and grabbed a fistful of Pauline's long, brown hair. She twisted it viciously, wrenching the girl's head to one side at a hazardous angle. "I told you to shut your mouth, slut," she reminded in the same even tone. She released the girl after giving a final spiteful wring to the thick tresses.

Pauline sprang up at once, fingers crabbed into claws and raised, ready to retaliate. Sylvia casually stood her ground. She shoved the irate girl heavily in the chest with an open palm, saying contemptuously, "Sit down, stupid." And the girl bounced back against the chair she had previously perched upon.

"You got very matey with 'er, ain't you?" Pauline hissed jeeringly. "She laughs at you, you know. Turns 'er nose up, don't she. Too good for this lark, ain't she? She 'ud rather skivvy honest like than make a few bob the easy way. And she could've months ago, 'fore that belly swole up. 'Er with 'er blasted airs 'n graces and 'er full belly. But no ring on 'er fingers, 'as she?" She finished with a sneer and an emphatic nod.

Emily returned to her bucket and brushes and hastily pushed herself to her feet. She averted her hot face from the malevolent girl who glared at her with unwavering spite.

Sylvia returned to her seat next to Fiona and relaxed into the cushions. "Stupid bitch," she scoffed, amused. "She is a widder. So wot if she don't have a ring. Pawn shop's full of weddin' rings and country's full of women who 'ud rather eat than wear a lump of metal."

Emily dropped her cleaning tools to the floor and crouched, pressing a hand to her stomach as a pain creased her.

Emily's head spun towards her at once. "Wot is it?" she demanded urgently.

Emily shook her head a little and tried to smile. "Nothing . . . I am sure it is nothing. He is just kicking, that is all."

Fiona approached Emily quickly and slid one of her hands gently across Emily's distended stomach. The swelling distorted and heaved, and Fiona's small blue eyes widened in awe.

"Better tell, Hannah," Sylvia decided. "I'll do it."

She made for the door but Emily straightened carefully. "No, it is all right. I am sure it is nothing. There are weeks to go yet."

Emily collected her bucket and brush from the floor and left the room. She walked along the corridor in the direction of the kitchens.

Hannah was already there; she was made rudely aware of that as she neared the door. Raucous chastisement could be quite easily heard coming from within.

Hannah stood by the scrubbed wooden table, berating a young kitchen maid who was blubbering and holding a solitary bloodied finger up in the air. Enough could be gleaned from the commotion for Emily to realize that the young girl had almost sliced off the top of her finger and left the onion completely intact.

Hannah shook her head in disbelief muttering disparagingly about the intellectual worth of her menials. She gave the girl a last cuff round the ear, making the wailing increase, but Emily could tell the blow was delivered more in relief that the damage was not worse than in any sense of real malice.

Hannah turned to Emily as the girl deposited her bucket and brush by the door.

"I have been looking for you, Emily," Hannah declared, and without another word she quit the kitchen and was walking toward the morning room.

Hannah picked up the newspaper from the hide-covered sofa. She proffered it but Emily made no move to take it. Hannah drew the paper close again and looked at it, then read steadily: "Charles and Emily Shaw: should anyone know the whereabouts of either of—"

"Yes, I know. You have told me before and I have read it myself," Emily interrupted a trifle tartly.

"Do you think it is your mother?"

Emily shrugged and shook her head. "I know not and care less," she muttered fiercely.

She paused with her face turned away, then sighed and admitted softly, "No, that is not true. I do care, and I think Papa worries too that they know not where we are. But I just cannot get in touch—not yet. Not till after the baby is born. What could I truthfully say? I would have to lie about how I am and where, for I could not stand it if they came looking for me and saw me like this." She glanced down at her bloated abdomen, her dirty, white apron stretched taut across it. One of her hands went to rest on the mound as she said softly, "I thought it might be George. I know he came home for the wedding. He might still be in England. I am sure he must be wondering what has become of us. I would so like to see him." She bit at her bottom lip before saying faintly, "Should anything happen to me . . . when the baby is born—"

Hannah interrupted her, murmuring something soothing, but Emily shook her head, persisting bravely, "I know it can. Childbirth can be dangerous, I know that. I have written some letters to my family and I would like you to make sure they have them." She glanced up at Hannah, her eyes anxious and pleading.

Hannah smiled and said quietly, "Of course." She paused and raised the paper in her hand again. "This is not your mother or George though, Emily."

Emily glanced up swiftly as Hannah added mildly, "It is Clifford. It is the work of a detective agency in London. Their client resides in Herfordshire—at Malvern Hall, would you believe," she said wryly.

Emily looked away from her, feeling the pain in her throat and around her heart ache more than the knotting contractions that held her baby.

"Why do you think he looks for you still?" Hannah asked gently in the ensuing silence. "He must have more than a dozen willing *belles amies* all eager to help him forget you, don't you think?"

The intentional provocation did its work. Emily swung back about to retaliate, but folded forward instead as a contraction doubled her.

Hannah was with her in an instant. "What is it?" she interrogated brusquely. "Surely not . . . not yet. Not for three weeks or more. We worked the date out."

Emily managed to move her head, indicating that she was just as confused. She straightened a little, fearful violet eyes seeking Hannah's. "I don't know, but it hurts so much." She stared at Hannah, her eyes purpling with trepidation, "I hope it will be all right . . . I don't want to die . . . I don't want to," she gasped.

"Hush . . . women have babies all the time. It is most

404

natural. None of us would have a mother alive, or brother or sisters, else." Hannah smiled reassuringly and stroked Emily's dark hair soothingly as she helped her to seat herself on the sofa.

She smoothed strands of hair away, from Emily's sweat-beading forehead, then caught sight of her sooty hands. She grabbed at them at once and turned them palm upwards. "What have you been about?" she demanded. "I told you weeks ago to leave those hearths and let Maria do them. Your papa will flay me alive if he knows you have been sweeping out the grates."

"Where is he?" Emily panted.

"In the garden, taking some sun. Do you want him?"

Emily shook her head quickly. She gave a small, soft smile and murmured, "Perhaps he will see his grandchild after all."

Hannah gave a low laugh. She nodded, consenting wryly, "Yes, Emily, I believe he will. How, I shall never fathom, for he is the illest man that still lives that ever I have known. He cheats death daily and will keep doing so until he sees you settled. He cheats me too," she acknowledged drily, "for he knows that I have given my word and will not break it. While he lives your place here is secure and as you want it. He protects you now, Emily. Belatedly perhaps, but he will not allow himself to rest, though he wants to so much. He will never leave you until you are safe. He is surviving on will power alone, and how he achieves it I honestly do not know."

Emily nodded sadly, feeling the tears blur her vision. They increased, but with physical pain this time, and she pressed a hand quickly to her stomach.

Hannah approached the door swiftly, saying as she walked, "I shall send Jeremiah for the doctor or the midwife, then get your room ready.

Emily jerked her head back quickly. As the terrifying imminence thrust upon her, she called quickly after Hannah, "No, it is not. It cannot be. It is too early, too early. He is just kicking. . . ."

Hannah walked back toward her and placed comforting arms about her. "Don't be frightened. Babies will just not wait. When they are done, out they must come. A bit like cakes, really, and you would not want to spoil, would you?"

Sylvia poked her head about the door and peered into the room. She tiptoed in and Emily turned her head on the pillow, her dark hair spreading against the snowy cotton. She smiled at the sloe-eyed girl as she advanced lightly toward the bed.

" 'Ow are you?" Sylvia asked gaily, although the blue-black eyes were betrayingly wide and brimming with concern.

Emily simply nodded in reply and managed another small smile.

"Brought you these." A bunch of roses was whipped out from behind Sylvia's back, and she laid them carefully on the bed.

Emily glanced down at them and moved a hand to touch a soft pink petal.

"Charlie's in a state," Sylvia advised thoughtlessly, "blubbering 'n all sorts." She noticed Hannah's stony-brown glare and added quickly, in an apologetic tone, "Shall I tell 'im he can come up and see you?"

"No," Hannah interjected firmly from her chair by the window. "It will not be long to wait." Her eyes sought Emily, and she smiled and added softly, "It will be quite soon." She raised her eyes sharply to Sylvia and quizzed abruptly, "Is Jeremiah back yet?"

Dark curls moved about Sylvia's face as the girl shook her head. Her eyes were anxious, held by Hannah's for a long moment. Hannah looked away deliberately and said brightly, "Well, find a vase for those blooms, Sylvia, before they wither away. A pink rose is my favorite," she murmured conversationally, her eyes with the posy. Sylvia moved to the window ledge obligingly and removed a plain pottery vase. She began stripping away some of the leaves and thorns as she arranged them with undue attention.

Hannah rose from her chair and moved to the bed. Taking a cloth from a bowl on Emily's bedside table, she wiped it across her chalky brow, pushing damp, dark curls away.

Pain-darkened violet eyes stared up widely at Hannah, terror and uncertainty apparent, although Emily uttered not a word.

Hannah smiled gently at her. "My friend Julia has six children," she informed lightly. "She has only to look at her good friend the colonel and there she is, in a delicate condition yet again. I am quite sure that woman will end up with a brood of ten . . . if not more."

Emily frowned up at Hannah. "Good friend? Is she not married to him?"

"Heavens no," Hannah remarked with a laugh. "He has a wife. Julia has been his mistress for the past. . . ." She attempted some calculation but gave up with a laugh. "Well, more years than I care to remember."

A low moan escaped Emily's tightly compressed lips and her legs drew up instinctively in the bed.

Hannah turned to Sylvia just as the girl spun away from the window and her flower arranging.

"See if Jeremiah is back with the doctor or Mrs. Meaker," Hannah ordered quietly and calmly.

Dark hair streamed out behind Sylvia as the girl made a hasty dash for the door, completely negating Hannah's attempt to maintain an air of serene control.

"I am scared, Hannah," Emily sobbed out, her eyes squeezing tightly shut.

"I know." The damp cloth cooled and gently relaxed her fair, furrowed brow.

Hannah perched herself on the edge of the bed and instructed firmly, "You must tell Clifford that the child is born, Emily. He is looking for you still and you must tell him. Did he know you were pregnant?"

Emily moved her head restlessly against the pillow. "I am not sure. I think he guessed. I know not how, for I never said," she replied, unconsciously acknowledging him now as the father.

"You have to marry him now, Emily. Do you want the child to be a bastard its life through? It would not be fair."

A small, bitter laugh escaped Emily and she turned her head away on the pillow. "He has no wish to marry me now, he said so."

"But why do you think he looks for you still, Emily?" Hannah posed reasonably.

"I know not," Emily gasped on a sob of pain and misery. "Perhaps because he said he would have me as a mistress. He said he would take me to St. Albans and put me in a house there for him to visit. I know not why he should still bother with me. He had a mistress there already and if she was no longer willing, I know there would be others who were. I think he might have some obsession for me. We were childhood friends . . . we liked each other once, when young. But then . . . then he left. He and his mother were sent away by my father to the workhouse. Katherine Moore died there; very sadly, and Clifford hates us for it. Mostly my father, I know. He took me away to Malvern Hall with him primarily to torment my papa; for he can hurt him so much more by harming me." She closed her eyes and breathed, "And he has done his work well, has he not? My father is now dying . . . and so slowly. He has been torturing himself to death for months past and in a way more agonizing than any physical barbarity Clifford could have devised."

One of Hannah's hands located clutching fingers that

gripped the covering sheet. She smoothed white knuckles, then loosened inflexible fingers from the cotton and held Emily's hand.

"While we wait for the doctor, I shall tell you a little of my life and the people I knew in London. Some of it is quite amusing and it will while away the time and perhaps entertain you." She stroked thin, stiff fingers as she related causally, "There was one little incident, with Wellington; he was once a good friend of mine."

Emily wriggled her fingers from Hannah's cool grasp. "Yes, I heard of it," she said in a brittle voice. "Amusing, was it not?"

Hannah recovered the small hand, clasping it within both of hers to keep it still. "Not nearly so risible as the truth, Emily," she remarked wryly. "I can say that now, for the incident was a year or more ago, and the other gentleman in question tugs not so deeply at my heart anymore. Some details that circulated were true: Wellington did indeed stand beneath my window in the rain like a drowned rat. But the gentleman above—"

"I care not to hear it, Hannah, really," Emily forced out quickly, grimacing as a contraction racked her.

"I think you should. It was not Clifford, Emily. It was a man I loved dearly. He was married . . . is, I should say. He had every respect and affection for his wife and did not want her to discover our relationship. He was always determined, in his own hypocritical way, that she should never be humiliated or betrayed." She gave out a small laugh. "At the time, I own, I used to love him the more for his consideration. Of course, once this tale was broadcast about, it would no doubt sooner or later have come to her ears. I agreed to say that it was another I spent time with that evening. Clifford was a good friend and I knew he would care little. But then Clifford always cared little when amorously involved . . . or so I believed at first. Great passion seemed ever to escape him. He was always so controlled, calculating in all he did. He was never my lover, although a great friend in the years I knew him. Of course, that is not to say he had no mistresses. He did, and when in England he would visit one or other of them and that would suffice. He never had any intention of letting any woman distract him or get too close. He was waiting for someone else, merely biding time with all of us." She paused and looked at the side of Emily's averted face.

"I have known Clifford some four years or more now, Emily." Emily's head turned slowly to look at Hannah then. "How could you? He is back in England but eighteen months or so."

Hannah smiled and wiped the damp cloth across the already moist forehead. "Oh, he has been back in England for a short while, these past four years. He would come back every summer for a month or two. I liked to think it was to see me, for although I was never his mistress, that is not to say that at one time I would not have like the opportunity to become so." She gave a small, self-mocking laugh. "I still like to believe he resisted because he was too fond of me: never wanted to use and discard me as he did the others. But the reason for those annual visits to England had nothing to do with me . . . or any other woman. He came back to see a girl. She was sixteen the first year he returned. She must be about twenty or so now, I suppose. I remember the year she was eighteen and had her come-out. Not that he spoke of her much, but once he let slip that during her launch into society that summer, she had several proposals of marriage. He was like a man possessed, on edge and quite unusually so for him. Although he never discussed her, I could tell he believed she might accept one of her suitors. He could have prevented it, or course. For even two years ago he had money enough. But he wanted more, wanted circumstances to be ideal, so that no one could ever deny him anything. He went back to Jamaica that autumn, much relieved by the news that apparently this young lady had little inclination to marry at all. I can remember the day he left, teasing him with why he wanted a child when he could so easily have a woman."

Emily stared at Hannah still as she finished speaking, violet eyes large and wondering. Then her face screwed abruptly and her head threw back into the pillow with her face toward the ceiling. She was half-aware through the knotting, throbbing agony, of the sound of her father's muffled voice.

Hannah got up quickly, trying to prevent him from entering the room, but he jerked himself clumsily free and rushed to sink to his knees by the bed.

Emily relaxed slowly and tentatively, allowing her back to retouch the mattress. Her head fell to one side as she regarded her gray-faced papa.

He clutched at a limp white hand and she squeezed his hand weakly and managed a hesitant smile. Dull violet eyes roved his exhausted face, the stubble on his cheeks and chin snowy against the muddy complexion.

He attempted to return her smile but found it impossible and instead patted heavily at her hand in a gesture of encouragement.

His head dropped forward suddenly to rest against their clasped fingers and Emily felt the wetness slide warmly against her skin.

She raised her free hand, touching his gray hair lightly. "Don't fret so, Papa," she soothed him softly. "I shall be all right — Hannah says so. Hannah knows of these things; you ask her. She has a friend with six children, and unwed too."

Charles mumbled hotly against their entwined fingers, "When you are feeling well again and the darling child is with us, there are things I must say to you. Things I have to tell you of myself and . . . and the Moores. Of myself and Katherine. For indeed he — Clifford Moore — although I hate him as much as any man can hate, I have to own that he has as much right to detest me in return. And I must tell you, for indeed you deserve to know — "

"I do know, Papa."

Charles nodded vigorously against their hands, scraping both their fingers with his abrasive face. "He told you so . . . all about it. I thought he would, and enjoy describing my vileness to you. For indeed I was vile and not a day since has passed that I have not regretted my disgusting weakness and what I did to my Katherine, for in truth I loved her."

"Papa . . ." Emily pleaded, wounded by him sharing his private truths and anguish. "You do not have to say anything to me, Papa," she said gently. "I do know, but it was not he . . . but no matter now. You must not upset yourself more by it."

She ruffled his thick, pewter hair until he raised bloodshot eyes to search blearily for her face.

He raised her hand, holding it tightly against the scratching bristle on his cheek.

Sylvia entered the room breathlessly and behind her followed a giant of a woman. She was tall and large-boned and completely enveloped in a voluminous black cloak. A coiled snake of hair wound into a bun at the nape of her neck, as black in color as was the cloak she wore, yet threads of silver circled it.

The woman clapped her massive hands together briskly and then flapped them indicatively toward the door in an explicit way. Sylvia crept back to the exit, worried eyes with Emily until her head disappeared from view.

Hannah helped Charles to his feet. He attempted to leave the room with his hand still clasped tenaciously to his daughter's. Hannah eased his fingers away gently and led him to the door.

The large, black-cloaked woman turned to gaze at

Emily before swinging her cloak from her shoulders.

She gazed with professional intensity at the small, slender frame and gross bulge that distorted the bedclothes. She smiled at Emily then with understanding and sympathy before she walked to the jug and bowl and washed her hands thoroughly.

"Clean linen and plenty of it," she instructed Hannah authoritatively. "Hot water and the hotter the better."

"It is done already and waiting this past hour," Hannah advised quietly.

The woman turned to look at her, then smiled and nodded.

"Emily, this is Mrs. Meaker, the midwife from the village," Hannah introduced quietly, with a reassuring, encouraging smile.

The midwife drew Emily's covering sheet carefully away and Emily flinched instinctively, trying to force herself, panic-stricken, into the bed.

Large hands approached and touched and Emily winced and jerked. But they probed and examined with smooth, gentle strokes and a confident skill and purpose that relaxed cramped muscles the longer they worked.

Emily opened bright, dark eyes to look into the black ones that lifted from her pelvis to gaze at her. Mrs. Meaker smiled and nodded and remarked in a voice that soothed like warm honey, "A good job I came . . . for you are nearly there, my love. So very nearly there."

Hannah placed an index finger to her mouth explicitly, cautioning and silencing as the girls trooped solemnly into the room. They stood grouped at the bed end, staring with fixed, wondering eyes at the sheet-shrouded forms.

Sylvia gazed at Emily's pallid complexion and wisps of damp, dark hair stuck to her forehead and cheeks. Blue eyes slid to the wrapped bundle at Emily's side, a small, slack hand resting possessively upon it.

"I feel as though I am in church," Sylvia sighed with

awed reverence, "all sort of tingly and timid. I don't know why, for I have seen babies as new before and mothers as young. But now, today, it seems like close to God and 'ere of all places."

Pauline turned to her and giggled shrilly and nervously, as though embarrassed by words that had been her own thoughts.

Emily stirred and five pairs of eyes glared at Pauline for having disturbed her. Pauline twisted her mouth and shrugged a mute apology.

Emily's eyes opened with several long blinks. As her vision cleared she smiled at the young women grouped about the bed. "I feel so tired," she whispered. "I cannot keep awake a minute."

"We will be but a moment," Hannah said softly. "They so wanted to see . . . but just for a short while, then you must sleep again."

Emily turned her head on the pillow to gaze at the swathed infant. She slid the hand resting there to ease the cover away from a tiny face. She stared in adoration at the sleeping child, marveling that it really was still there and hers.

The silent girls shifted closer, bending and contorting as one, to look at the fair face, the translucent skin and mauve-threaded eyelids that brushed satin cheeks with long, fawn eyelashes.

"I still feel like I'm in church," Sylvia choked on a gurgle. "I think I might blubber."

"No you don't," Hannah threatened fiercely, "else you'll start us all off."

Sylvia gulped quickly and asked on a controlling sniff, " 'Ave you chosen a name?"

Emily smiled at her sleeping daughter. "Katherine Emily," she advised proudly.

Sylvia repeated the name with a slow, approving nod. "Yes . . . that is nice."

All eyes were with the child for a long, silent moment, then Sylvia queried brightly, "Is Katherine your mama's name?"

Emily's eyes lingered on the wispy, fine fair hair that peeped from beneath the baby's blanket. "No," she informed quietly, "It is . . . was her other grandmama's name, but she is dead."

Emily's eyes rose then and met Hannah's. The woman smiled and said softly, "I am sure the girl will be as gracious as her mother . . . and she resembles her father so exactly."

Mrs. Meaker finished tidying away her things just as a light rapping was heard at the door.

Before Hannah could move to open it, Charles had entered and shuffled into the room. The girls moved back from the bed, allowing him passage through to see his granddaughter. He remained motionless, his eyes blinking rapidly and ceaselessly in the direction of the indistinct white forms on the bed.

"Come now, all you girls back downstairs," Hannah ordered firmly. "Emily needs to sleep and time is getting on. We are opening in just over an hour. Business . . . business. . . ." she reminded them mockingly.

The filed out quietly with last smiling glances at the bed.

Mrs. Meaker swung her black cloak around her shoulder and buttoned the throat. She smiled at Emily and looked at the child, nodding in silent satisfaction.

As though aware of this acknowledgement, a minute fist thrust free from its restricting cover and waved in the air. A squeaking mewing spun Emily's startled face immediately in the direction of her daughter and her hand sprang away from the newly heaving bundle. She gazed up immediately at the midwife with imploring, questioning eyes, acknowledging at once her ignorance, and allowing it to fluster her.

Mrs. Meaker walked to the side of the bed, close to the child. She dropped to her knees, her cloak billowing about her as she settled. Large, sinuous fingers deftly unwrapped the straining child, freeing her arms and turning face. The midwife quickly and wordlessly unbuttoned the front fastening of Emily's nightgown before she shifted her gently up in the bed, plumping the pillow for support. "Your daughter is hungry already," she informed with an amount of contentment. "But that is because she is very healthy. She will feed well even if she is a few weeks early. She is strong and robust for all that she looks a mite small."

Capable, strong hands placed the child against a breast she bared abruptly. Without any further aid, the baby's face spun against firm, warm flesh for an instant before locating and attaching to the nipple.

Emily gazed down in wonder at the steadily suckling baby. Mrs. Meaker smoothed clinging strands of hair back from Emily's cheeks, taking it behind her shoulder and away from the feeding child. "Not so difficult, was it? One of the easiest and quickest births I have known. You are very lucky, my dear, for I own, when I first saw those narrow hips. . . . But no matter now. You are a natural mother—quick and easy, and it will always be so. For other times too."

Emily's rigidly held back relaxed slowly into the supporting pillows as she sensed a drenching warmth saturate her with serenity. She gazed down lovingly as soft eyelashes stroked against her breast, Katherine lifting tiny lids so deep blue eyes could regard whence sweet contentment came. One of Emily's hands moved instinctively, cradling the back of the velvet head, caressing slowly as she explored every precious inch of skin and bone and learned every color and mark.

She remembered then her father, standing by the door still. As Mrs. Meaker rose away from the bed, Emily called his name and beckoned him closer.

He approached slowly and knelt beside the bed, as Mrs. Meaker had just done.

Emily smiled at him, absently aware that she felt no embarrassment at all at him watching her thus and not only because she was aware his failing sight allowed him to see so little. She knew too that his tears were blurring what poor vision he did have.

Broad, blunt fingers moved out shakily to tentatively search for and touch a minute, curled fist close by. A tremulous thumb skimmed silken baby skin lingeringly. "How will she be called?" he whispered hoarsely.

"Katherine Emily."

He nodded slowly, the tears dripping from his nose now, but his grief was quite quiet. His eyes never left the perfect infant as he murmured thickly, "It is fitting; for she is most certainly a Moore. I know that even though I see so very little of her beautiful face."

Emily's eyes rose from her daughter to her father and then slid briefly to the door as Mrs. Meaker left quietly.

Chapter Thirteen

The letter completed, Hannah gazed at the few lines of script for a moment before her eyes settled on the tissue-wrapped pearl ring. She picked up the tiny parcel and placed it on the letter, then folded the paper with the ring enclosed inside. She sealed it quickly and rang the small, brass bell on the desk top.

Her maid appeared practically at once and bobbed to her mistress.

"Is Emily up yet, Maria?"

"Indeed she is, madam," Maria advised roundly. "Her first day out of bed and she has taken that lovely baby into the garden for a little sun. Can you not hear the girls cooing and aahing from here?" She smiled widely and then shook her head and looked wistful. "I remember when my Robin was a tot, he was the most —"

"Yes, yes," Hannah interrupted but with an indulgent smile. "Fetch Jeremiah, would you please, Maria. I have an urgent letter to be delivered."

Maria stood unheeding, lost in nostalgic reverie, doting on babes in arms.

"Hurry if you please, Maria," Hannah urged sharply, "lest I change my mind and unseal this betrayal once more — for I know not if I do right."

Maria focused on her mistress then and stared, bemused by this enigmatic declaration. She stood motionless, as though perhaps awaiting some explanation to the riddle.

Hannah flapped her hands expressively and raised her eyes heavenwards with equal exasperation.

Maria bobbed quickly, confusion still in her face as she turned and scuttled to the door, apron tails flying out in her haste to be dutiful now.

"Who brought it?"

"A young man about twenty two or so, on horseback." Heath paused before adding slowly, "He was most insistent that he hand it to you personally, but you were not back from Liverpool."

Clifford nodded and stared at the open letter lying on his desk. A dry laugh preceded, "All this time . . . six months . . . and within the space of twenty-four hours I twice find out where she is."

Heath neared him at once. "Twice? Did you find him then?" he interrogated keenly. Clifford nodded. "Yes, Heath, I found him," he muttered tonelessly, "and he told me where she asked to go." He looked up at Heath, deliberately disregarding where Emily lodged for a moment, as he informed casually, "He was in Liverpool, but not as a stevedore. He was miles from the Mersey — working as a wheelwright's apprentice." His eyes were redrawn to the black ink on the paper in front of him. "He took her to Hannah's, six months ago now," he said almost impersonally.

"She paid him with the pearl ring and he left it with Hannah — payment for services rendered."

"Is the letter from Hananh?" Heath probed quietly and tentatively, knowing how tenuous was Clifford's self-control despite this apparent cool composure.

Clifford grunted a hard laugh. "Oh, yes. It is just a brief cryptic clue. She feels I might find something of interest at White Lodge, Sawbridgeworth." He picked up the small pearl ring and gazed at it as he gritted savagely, "Perhaps she is reduced to touting for business by post . . . what do you think?"

"I think you are being ridiculous," Heath rejoined gently. "She is there simply because her father is. I'll wager a thousand pounds he is there with her." He smiled and then laughed, "No wonder the old dog kept his whereabouts secret from everybody. But especially his family—hardly the sort of lodging you would tell your wife of, is it? Certainly the last place we would have thought to look."

Clifford stood up abruptly, kicking the leather swivel chair back from him. He started to pace the circumference of the room, head bent, and then went to stand by the window and look out over the garden.

Heath regarded the line of emaciated cheek presented to him. He watched as Clifford's back teeth met then ground, jerking his jaw temporarily out of alignment.

"You know as well as I do," Heath persuaded forcefully, "she would as soon have drowned herself in the nearest cesspit as taken a client upstairs at Hannah's. If it had ever come to that, she would have returned here of her own volition." He halted and closed his eyes, knowing that for all his caution, he had just blundered badly. He raised a dark hand to massage his forehead and said on an uneasy laugh, "I really didn't mean that the way it sounded."

Clifford swung back toward him, a sardonic smile just touching the scar near his mouth. "Don't apologize . . . you are right. I think she always believed that that was how I regarded her. And serving me alone would have appeared preferable to entertaining some unknown quantity. Better the devil you know . . . she was ever logical."

He approached his desk again and picked up the pearl ring and dropped it into his pocket without looking at it. "Get David to bring the carriage round for me, will you?"

"Let me come with you," Heath coaxed.

"No, I want to go alone." The rebuff was quiet and adamant.

Heath nodded acceptingly, then turned and walked to the door.

"Would you mind, Emily?"

Emily grimaced and sighed. "Well, truthfully, Hannah, I would rather not. I realize it is harmless, but I have no idea how to deal cards and I would feel . . . uneasy. Quite out of place. I am sure my awkwardness would show. It might put the clients off," she emphasized, hoping to deter Hannah from asking again. She tucked in the bedding about her daughter as she spoke. She gazed down with maternal attentiveness, judging that the pink cheeks were rounding and the small fist lying lightly clenched on the coverlet was indeed quite fat. She smiled, contented: her daughter was blossoming.

Hannah was not dissuaded. She coaxed with a smile, "You know I would not ask, Emily, but I am so short-handed tonight. Both Rose and May are ill. They tell me they have the stomach cramps again," she shook her head and sighed exasperatedly. "I know the pair of fat gluttons have been in the orchard again—at the apples before they are properly ripe. It serves them both right . . . but helps me not at all." She paused, then cajoled, "There is nothing difficult about it. You just throw a card in front of each of the gents till they tell you to stop. It really is simple enough." Hannah noticed apprehensiveness in Emily's face as she chewed worryingly at her bottom lip. "I shall be close at all times, Emily," Hannah reassured. "If any one of them dares to even think of taking liberties with you. . . ." She raised a clenched first and shook it indicatively.

Emily allowed a small, uncertain laugh, relenting very slowly, "Very well. But only for an hour. Katherine's feed is at eight o'clock."

Hannah smiled her thanks, then approached the crib and the sleeping baby. "The only thing in the world I would have loved—even unwed—but never managed to get for myself." She coughed an ironic laugh. "Now you would think in my profession. . . ." She sighed into silence without finishing the sentence.

"Had you any desire to marry, Hannah?" Emily asked interestedly.

Hannah smiled wryly. "A few times. Men have professed to desire marrying me but I believe that talk was all it ever was. Most of my lovers were of the gentry and they rarely marry courtesans—they do not need or want to. They marry girls of good breeding—for breeding." She shrugged easily. "After all, it is quite likely I may not only have amused one man but a number of his cronies in the course of my professional life and no man, however infatuated, wants his wife's charms tattled over by all and sundry in Brook's Club."

"I understand how girls can be set on the road to ruin," Emily said quietly. "Even those who should be secure because of birth and position. It need be nothing to do with what they want or their characters. It takes no more than financial hardship and a callous opportunist. Blackmailed into seduction, henceforth they are trapped by shameful circumstances. There is no way out, nowhere to go but back to more of the same if they choose to survive with life. And why not? For self-respect and dignity would already be dead." She halted abruptly, aware that she alluded to her own coercion and dishonor.

Hannah started to say something comforting, but Emily laughed with unusual shrillness. "You should catalog some of your youthful exploits, Hannah. I am sure it would make interesting reading, a book I should love to read. I am certain others must too. Most enlightening and amusing, learning of the gentility of some of this country's finest gentlemen."

Hannah smiled and nodded reflectively. "I have to own, Emily, there have been many times over the years when much the same thought has occurred to me. So much so that I have been prudent enough to keep notes of interesting events and all the sweet *billets-doux* that have come my way. Passionate yearnings and professions of undying love that gentlemen commit to paper in moments of weakness can be of inestimable value to a courtesan once she meets financial difficulty or her twilight years."

Emily stared at Hannah, aware that she was instructing how blackmail could be a double-sided tool. "I should keep them safe, Hannah," she counseled softly. "I am sure you have at some time merited every penny they might bring you."

"So young to be so cynical, Emily," Hannah chided gently but with a short laugh.

Emily said nothing further on the matter. She grasped a handful of the gray serge work dress she wore. "But I have no decent dress to wear downstairs tonight, Hannah,"

Hannah removed the objection before it rooted. "I have already thought of that. Rosemary is about your size. She has a rather fine lavender gown she rarely wears, for it reveals not much." She ran her eyes over Emily's figure judiciously. "It will suit you—the coloring is right—and fit too, I judge. You are still a little rounded from the baby."

The mention of her increased curvaceousness made

Emily skim the bodice of her gown unconsciously and grimace to herself, once more dwelling on the fearsome gentlemen who would later that day be downstairs.

Noting the dissension once more in the brewing, Hannah walked swiftly to the door, saying just before she left the room, "I shall send Rosemary with the dress as soon as I can find her."

Hannah leaned forward and kissed both hollowed cheeks. She raised large brown eyes with innate coquettishness, regarding the attractive male face close to hers. Her rouged lips lightly re-touched a lean cheek before a slow fingernail trailed the scar from cheekbone to chin.

"No more ardent greeting for your old friend Hannah after all this while?" she pouted provocatively. "I thought you might at least pretend slightly more pleasure at seeing me, Clifford."

She made a small bud of her mouth and glanced up coyly from beneath dark lashes.

He removed both of her arms from his shoulders, gripping them by the wrists as he held her firmly back from him. He gazed at her for a long moment and then smiled before his eyes raised, scanning the empty parlor slowly and thoroughly as though he might locate Emily within the room somewhere.

"Where is she?" he asked with admirable control.

Hannah removed herself from his grip and walked to the table that held decanters and glasses. She poured two measures of brandy and then returned, proffering his glass.

He took it immediately and downed it before hers had raised to her lips to be sipped at. The hand that still held his empty glass pressed to his mouth for a moment; then the glass was lowered abruptly to a table.

Hannah watched him shrewdly, then smiled and

nodded with a hint of contentment. "As bad as that, Clifford?" she murmured ruefully.

She looked him over slowly: he was dressed well, in dark, expensive clothes. But her eyes were redrawn to his cynical face, mouth set permanently aslant and silver eyes never seeming fully open. He was smooth shaven and extremely clean, his hair thick and shining but far too long—well past his collar. He smiled sardonically at this blatant inspection and raised idle eyebrows, tacitly inviting her opinion.

Hannah smiled, acknowledging the mocking query. "You look quite terrifyingly dissolute, Clifford. I am not sure I should allow you to see her. You might frighten her the more."

"Fetch her now." The command was soft and he smiled still, but Hannah was well aware that he was utterly devoid of amusement.

She replaced her glass on the table and said quietly, "She has no idea you are here, or Charles. Both made me promise never to divulge their whereabouts. I agreed and I have adhered strictly to that, for I actually never did. I would like Emily to know that: that I never literally betrayed her." She paused and added softly, "She is most beautiful, Clifford; also in a way that has nothing to do with how she looks. That is why I wrote to you. I cannot see her stay here . . . she is not made for this life. Yet if she went elsewhere, I know that she could be coerced into something much worse. Charles is with us still but—"

Clifford interrupted hoarsely, "Is he dying?"

"Oh, yes . . . these past six months or so I would never have given him more than two weeks longer. But he hangs on . . . to protect her. He is quite literally safeguarding her with his life, for I told them both that once he is no longer with us, she must work here as the other girls do."

The immediate dangerous flare in his eyes made her smile. "I did it for you, Clifford," she placated, "to try and make her see sense. Which girl in her right mind would choose this place and my clients above Malvern Hall and you?"

The increased twist to his mouth answered her.

"Come," Hannah said abruptly and walked to the door.

Hannah opened the door to the long gaming hall that ran the entire width of the front of the building. She and Clifford entered the room. A few clients were already assembled and also four girls, dealing cards at green baize tables.

Silence ensued on their entrance, all eyes staring at the tall, imposing man, elegantly dressed, yet with his long, fair hair contradicting the sartorial sophistication.

Sylvia and Fiona exchanged glances, covert smiles and widening eyes expressing immediate professional interest in this new and attractive stranger, who despite looking haggard to the point of exhaustion, nevertheless possessed that heady aura that lingers about those with power and money.

Having scanned the room's occupants within a few moments, Clifford turned as though to leave the room, frustrated impatience darkening his eyes.

Hannah caught at his arm and urged him further into the room, toward a blackjack table.

She invited him to be seated but he ignored her. A portly, bewhiskered gentlemen seated in the next chair smiled up at Clifford and made some polite greeting as soon as he was sure he did not recognize him from the magistrates' bench.

Clifford nodded curtly and then swung away again to leave the room.

Hannah blocked his way and he halted and drew a deep, calming breath. He glowered over her head at nothing in particular. "I came here not to play games, Hannah, or do business," he bit out. "Where is she?"

"I remembered you liked to play cards, Clifford," Hannah stalled, hoping that Emily would hurry up and put in an appearance before he wrecked the place.

Hazardous silver eyes glared at her and she drew him slightly to one side. "That pearl ring, Clifford; it is in fact mine. I was left it by —"

"Yes, I know the story," he interrupted curtly. "How much?"

Hannah looked thoughtful and pursed her mouth. "Well, I am a business woman, and as it seems you intend spending none of your cash on either my tables or my girls, I think a hundred pounds for my trouble?"

He nodded abruptly, gray eyes flicking over the room's occupants again in fruitless search.

As his eyes slid past Sylvia, she moved forward and Hannah gave her a subtle, sanctioning nod as she approached.

"Sylvia will keep you company while I go and see what I have got within this establishment to interest you."

Sylvia slid a lace-encased hand along his dark-suited arm as Hannah neared the door leisurely.

It opened at that moment, just as Hannah was within two paces of it. Emily entered, clad in the borrowed lavender dress. Her mahogany hair was very loosely curled, dropping way past her shoulders in soft ringlets.

Silence enveloped the room once more that evening. The seated gentlemen gawped, their gambling utterly forgotten, as they ogled Hannah's latest and most welcome new recruit. They might have deemed her slightly overdressed; with the pale mauve dress buttoned through to the throat, but her beauty was startling and they stared, utterly enchanted, with many a lusty mind toying with forgoing cards and retiring unusually early.

Emily stood nervously, her eyes immediately with Hannah's close, comforting presence. She was oblivious to all others in the room and she bit her lip anxiously and frowned at Hannah, wanting to flee this new and daunting territory at once.

Hannah smiled at her and Emily relinquished her grip on the door handle and it swung shut.

Clifford was as mesmerized as the other gentlemen for a brief instant, then he thrust Sylvia, still clinging to his arm, ungently aside. The abrupt movement made violet eyes slide past Hannah and cling with equal intensity to the gray ones that regarded her.

Clifford turned slowly from the wall he rested back against to face her completely, his eyes never once relinquishing hers. He once more disengaged Sylvia's perservering clutch from his arm and pushed her more firmly away this time.

Emily looked then at Sylvia, reaching for him again already. She turned and groped for the door handle and quit the room at speed.

She hoisted the lavender skirt from about her feet and fled to the stairs, ascending them frantically. She pushed blindly through two girls who were descending leisurely and chattering. They protested in a lively, good-natured way about this cavalier treatment, but Emily heard nothing. She gained the landing and raced along the narrow flight that led to the attic rooms.

She entered her small sanctuary, gasping for breath, and leant back heavily against the door. Her head rested firmly into it and her eyes closed as her lungs and heart fought to pump fast enough.

She opened her eyes and grimaced in despair at the ceiling. She breathed deeply, then pushed away from the door and walked unsteadily into the room. She neared the crib by the side of her bed and stared down at her sleeping daughter. This time she barely saw her, her mind in turmoil as she tried to reason why he was below, whether he had come for her or merely for the entertainment that all gentlemen came for. She recalled Sylvia attached to him and realized that it was most likely that his presence was just an awful, ironic coincidence, for he lived, after all, not very far away. Perhaps he came regularly and Hannah simply never mentioned it to her.

Sensing her mother's presence and her feed imminent, Katherine clenched fists and stretched tiny arms, baring pink gums in readiness to squeal.

Emily stooped and picked up the child, wrapping her shawl tightly about curled legs as she settled her in her arms. She cradled the baby against her rapidly pounding heart, embracing her tightly, then more tightly still as she tried to ease the trembling that still rocked her.

Katherine's small, puckering face turned against her shoulder; the pouncing mouth searching ceaselessly for food.

Emily approached the window and swayed herself and the child in comfort as she stared sightlessly out into the mellow Indian Summer evening. The trees were abundantly leaved still and the grass vividly green and lush.

One unsteady hand moved to cup the back of Katherine's soft, downy head, and Emily lowered her mouth instinctively to touch the throbbing pulse beneath the indented skull.

The infant whimpered, seeking her milk still. Emily inserted a knuckle between the gaping lips and Katherine enclosed it immediately, sucking vigorously and only occasionally squeaking her discontent with this unyielding consolation.

Emily's head raised slowly away from the child, sensing his presence far before she heard or saw him.

He moved to the right of her, leaning back against the wall by the window so that her faced her. At the first, brief glimpse of him, Emily turned sideways so that the child was protected from view. Her head bowed too, dark curls falling forward; shielding part of her face and the small bundle she clutched so closely.

She could feel the relentless, scorching regard traveling

over her from head to foot, but he seemed in no hurry to speak. Unable to bear the tension longer she asked with peculiar calm, "What do you want?"

"What else would I want in a whore's bedroom?" came the deceptively soft reply.

Emily felt her face redden, but she kept her eyes and voice lowered. "You have lost your way," she replied coolly. "The girls' room are below — on the landing to the left of the stairs."

"Hannah tells me much the same. So what do you do here, Emily?" he demanded exceedingly quietly.

She decided at once to ignore the question, then just as abruptly informed, "I work here as a general domestic — if it is any business of yours — and will continue to do so until my father dies." She had barely finished speaking when Katherine abruptly relinquished her fruitless comfort and wailed thinly and so suddenly and unexpectedly that Emily practically dropped the baby from her arms.

A firm grip on her arm spun her to face him. As she glanced up tentatively and watched awe-filled gray eyes lower to her precious burden, she realized that she had managed to conceal the child very well. His eyes lingered on the restless, squawking baby before raising to her mother.

Emily looked down at once at the top of the silky-fair head, he face moving closer to it, avoiding the immediate question and wonder in his eyes.

"How old is he?" he asked in a choked rush.

Emily sensed a hysterical urge to laugh, sure that any other man would simply have demanded to know whether it was his. "It is a girl," she prevaricated with an amount of pique.

"How old?"

"Two weeks."

Silver eyes resought his daughter as he muttered, "She was early . . . nearly three weeks."

Emily looked at him immediately. "How did you know that?" she asked, astonished.

He stared at her, gray eyes glazing with emotion as he choked, "Thirty-eight weeks from time of conception until the birth. It is not that for five days more."

Emily gazed at him with equal intensity as he watched her. Reading her bewilderment at his knowledge, he smiled. "There were many babies born on my plantation in Jamaica. I came to know a´little of childbirth. The duration is thirty eight weeks or thereabouts." A hoarse, despairing laugh escaped him as wet eyes raised upwards. "Not yet thirty-eight weeks, and it seems like half a lifetime."

One of his hands moved toward her very slowly, touching her face tentatively and extremely gently before it lowered to tenderly enclose the fragile head of his daughter. He stroked and felt her face with ceaseless soft touches before his hand moved to a small clenched fist. He uncurled fingers with clumsy gentleness regarding the tiny fingers and nails.

"The most beautiful sight there is," he murmured thickly, "a perfectly formed infant." His eyes raised to Emily, roving her face with such intensity that additional words were unnecessary.

"How was it when you had her?" he asked abruptly. "How was it when she was born?"

He allowed her no time to reply but gritted almost immediately, "Why did you not stay with me? I could have provided you with everything. The best care; the best doctor; everything that money could buy to keep you both safe." He inhaled deeply. "Emily. . . ."

He held onto his daughter with one hand while the other wiped roughly across his face. He gazed out through the window into the sunlit evening, remaining silent and composed for a few minutes.

"Why could you not tell me? I had a right to know."

Emily swallowed, knowing his distress moved her deeply, but uneasily aware too that she was quite unkindly gratified by it. "Tell you what?" she inquired coolly. "Tell you that you had fathered a bastard? It can hardly be the first time you have been apprised of the fact. What did you do for the others? Nothing, I imagine."

He turned from the window to look at her. "I have no other children. I am most careful in making sure I leave no child of mine where I know not how it will be cared for. I have none, I swear it. It is possible to take precautions. . . ." He faltered, noting the perplexity in her face that required an immediate explanation. He glanced out through the window again with a small, wry smile, realizing that it was hardly the time for an impromptu lesson on crude birth control methods.

"I shall tell you another time. Get your things now; we are leaving."

Emily shook her head. "No. You have to leave me alone now. It is not fair." She sensed tears sting and wondered remotely why knowing that he loved her wounded. In the same instant she realized that it was because she still needed to hurt him, that he had not yet suffered enough.

"You have had your revenge . . . all that you will get," she told him quietly. "My sister is married now. She and my mother are protected by the Earl of Creighton. My father is all but dead, and you cannot hurt him more. You have certainly done your work well there. George can look after himself. You have nothing left to blackmail me with. It is finished."

His hands cupped her face gently as he murmured persuasively, "There was no revenge, Emily. You know that very well. It was never why I wanted to keep you with me."

She jerked herself away from him and his hands fell to his sides for a moment.

He removed Katherine from her abruptly and moved back into the room with her. He supported the baby on his palms and studied her lingeringly from wispily covered head to toes. He held her carefully as he unwrapped the shawl and examined quivering arms and legs that jerked and twitched ceaselessly as she gazed quietly up into her father's face. They stared at each other lengthily, then Clifford stated proudly, almost arrogantly, "She looks like me."

"Yes, she does," Emily admitted softly.

"How is she called?"

Emily remained silent and looked away from tiny features, asking simply, "Is she named yet?"

"Yes."

He regarded her expectantly and she answered suddenly, "Katherine . . . Katherine Emily."

He looked back at his daughter for a long emotion-filled moment. "Thank you," he muttered thickly, then coughed clearing his throat. "Who told you how she died? Your father?" he asked quietly.

Emily shook her head very slightly, murmuring "No."

Clifford looked at her again, searchingly, and as she glanced at the floor, he breathed hoarsely, "That bitch, Amanda." He stared at her, his mind working furiously. He said slowly, "She told you before you left, didn't she? She must have; you have not seen her since. You never surely believed that I wanted. . . ." He halted abruptly, feeling what he was about to say was too ludicrous actually to be voiced.

The astonishment and disbelief in his face as he mused on the unspoken lunacy was scornfully intense, and Emily felt her face flood with betraying color.

"Emily?" Her name, uttered softly and questioningly, displayed the depths of his heartbreak.

"It was your fault," she accused quickly. "You made it seem that you would have me suffer as your mother did—"

"Is that why you went away?" he interrupted. "Because you believed I might turn you out? Might want you and my own child to die?"

"No . . . yes . . . partly, I don't know any more. Once I knew the truth, of how your mother died, I understood. I could imagine feeling exactly the same way—wanting to be just as vindictive." A sob brought the faltering excuse to a close.

He placed Katherine in her crib and walked back slowly toward Emily.

He stood close, but without touching her. "How could you believe that I did not care? Did not love you? When every day I lived for you, just to smile at me—sit with me—laugh and talk to me for an hour or so. It was enough at first that we should get to know each other again, although I always wanted you so. But I would have waited until you were ready, I swear. From the first night you stayed with me, I knew I never wanted to hurt you. It was just . . . I needed you too much, and you gave me too many opportunities to lose control. But it was never meant, never planned that way." He paused, his eyes roving her tear-streaked face. "I wanted it to be different, Emily, truly. I am so sorry . . . so sorry for everything. Do you believe me?"

Gentle hands tilted her wet face up to look at him, cupping then sliding across her damp cheeks. "Tell me you believe me now," he exacted huskily. "I never intended hurting you, Emily. I love you too much and I have ever loved you . . . for far too long. It was difficult waiting so many years. Since you were a child I have wanted you, and in a way that at seventeen made me feel ashamed and uneasy. There was not one day in Jamaica I did not think of home . . . and you. I thought of you, Emily, every day for ten years, and now you have to come home with me."

She shook her head without looking at him, quite

startled by her own action, for she was sure she had been about to indicate the reverse.

His hands tightened on her face. "Please, Emily," he begged, "You have to come with me and bring my daughter. I love you both so much."

"You have killed my papa," she accused fiercely.

"He was killing himself anyway, Emily, you cannot truthfully deny that. But I am sorry . . . believe me I am sorry, and I will tell him so. I will apologize to him today for taking you away as I did, for I admit, exacting redress from him was always what I intended."

"I will not come," Emily stated stubbornly. "But if you want to take your daughter you may. It is not that I do not want her, or love her. I do. But I must leave this place soon or work as the other girls do. Either way, I would prefer she was safe elsewhere. I know you will provide well for her."

He stared at her, misery brightening his eyes, but he encouraged coarsely, "Well, stay here, Emily. I am sure I could easily make some arrangement with Hannah. She would keep you exclusively available for me." He turned his head savagely and rasped in fury and frustration, "This is quite ridiculous. Get your things . . . no, forget them. You need nothing. Come — we will leave now."

He caught firmly at her arm but she pulled away, knowing as she did so that she was indeed behaving quite idiotically. But the perversity seemed quite uncontrollable.

He gazed at her as she backed away a few paces, then up at the sun-dappled ceiling. "You may come back on any terms," he offered quietly. "We marry, but if you wish, in name only for as long as you want it so."

He looked at her for her answer, but she remained silent and fierce-eyed.

He made a small, hopeless noise but closed his eyes and half-smiled. "What do you want me to say then, Emily?" he asked softly. "Tell me and I will say it . . . anything."

She said quietly, with words chosen for their power to wound rather than their honesty, "I cannot forgive you; nor have I any wish to. You have destroyed the family life I knew. All I ever wanted was to be with them, but it is all gone now. My mother will never speak to me once she knows I have a. . . ." She trailed into silence, unable to brand her beloved daughter so.

"Do you think I like it, Emily?" he demanded on a despairing laugh. "That my daughter is born out of wedlock and in a whorehouse? There was no need for it to be so. We could . . . should have been married a full year ago now."

The logic rang in her ears, making her bridle further. "Please go away now," she dismissed coldly, swinging away from him. "I have said you may take Katherine, for much as I hate to lose her, I know it is best and you will care for her."

"Emily. . . ." Her name was protracted beseechingly, controlled misery almost strangling him.

She shook her head without turning. Two minutes of silence passed, no more than Katherine's gurgling and fist sucking breaking the quiet.

Finally, footsteps moved closer to her, halting just behind. "Very well," he said quickly. "I will go and not bother you again, but only if you promise me now faithfully that you will adhere to the provision I make for you."

Emily turned to look at him, alarmed by the fact that he seemed now so composed and willing to comply with her lunatic game.

"The Grange is ready," he informed quietly. "I have had it renovated." He smiled humorlessly at the wall, amending drily, "Well, the glass is back in the windows and all major repairs are finished, but apart from that . . . I left the rest. I thought that when I found you, you might like to choose yourself how to finish it."

He glanced at her upturned, wide-eyed face. "It is comfortable. I have been living there myself on and off for the past three months or so."

"You have?" she queried wonderingly.

He smiled vaguely. "Yes. I moved in, intending only for a night or two, while I supervised the builders. I just seemed to stay on."

He walked away from her and to the crib and stared down at Katherine, curled fingers jerking at her mouth. "There was nothing of you at Malvern Hall. Nothing at all, despite the wardrobe full of clothes and the books and Richard pining for you constantly. And yet I have only to walk through the stable yard of that accursed white building and you are all about. I can see you there . . . hear you . . . smell and taste you almost. Ridiculous, I know, for you have not set foot on the grounds for more than eleven years. I suppose it is because I know it is where you would choose to be. So I stayed to be close to you."

A hand moved spontaneously to his eyes. "So, you must promise to stay there with Katherine. Money will be provided for all your needs — anything you want." He gave a brief, mirthless laugh. "Despite six months of insanity while I have searched for you or drunk myself insensible, Heath has managed to keep my business affairs in order. No doubt if he had not, I would now have nothing of worth to offer you anyway."

"Where will you be?" Emily asked in a small, frightened voice, "At Malvern Hall?"

"No. I shall put it in trust for Richard. I have no need or liking for it longer. It was always my father's house, never mine."

Emily stared soulfully at him, the need to capitulate now and act rationally tearing into her. She knew that if he would but ask her once more to go with him she would agree at once and most gratefully. She tried to force words from her mouth, but pride had lodged them tightly in her throat.

"Heath and I will go abroad," he informed her abruptly. "I had decided to do so anyway if I could not find you. I gave myself two years to search before I went away. There is nothing else for me here."

"Whereabouts abroad?" came the faint, apprehensive query.

He shrugged. "Anywhere. Perhaps the East Indies—there is money to be made there."

"But you just said you have money enough still," she reasoned desperately.

"Yes, I do, but what else is there for me but work. It is a satisfaction of sorts. It is what I know . . . what I am good at." He snorted a sharp, self-mocking laugh. "Working and acting the fool are what I am good at, Emily. Perhaps I shall be able to fire myself with vindictiveness. I did once and it provided me with everything: a new life in Jamaica and a fortune from nothing other than cunning and backbreaking, interminable work. It kept me warm and fed when I was cold and hungry and alive when I wanted to die. So I clung to it, sure it suited me and would serve me well. But I was deceived, for I know now it has destroyed what I wanted above all else. Now I have wealth and privilege and no use for either. Playing the country gentleman for no reason seems pointless. It is tiresome, Emily; I think I may go back and find the reprobate I once was."

He changed the subject abruptly. "I should like to visit you. Perhaps once a year—in the summer. Would you mind?"

She moved her head a little in acceptance, unable to speak now that remorse had closed her throat.

"Heath will settle you at the Grange," he said without looking at her. He picked Katherine up suddenly and touched his mouth to forehead and both cheeks before replacing her gently in her cot. Without a further glance Emily's way, he had turned and left the room in an instant.

Emily heard the clatter on the stairs as he descended swiftly. A sob rocked her, tears streaming down her face and into her mouth. She walked to the crib and took out the baby and placed her mouth to her forehead as Clifford had just done.

Emily ran to the door, carrying her daughter with her. She descended the rickey stairs as speedily as safety would allow, one arm fast about Katherine and the other gripping tightly to the handrail. She ran the length of the landing and descended the stairway to the main entrance hall with even greater haste.

He might want to see Katherine once more before he left.

Muted laughter and noise of gaming emitted from the front of the house, and Emily hesitated, wondering if he had gone back to that room. But she knew he had not; he had left. She walked intuitively toward the back of the house and the kitchen.

Hannah was standing by the kitchen window gazing out. With her was Maria, contorting her neck as she tried to peer past her mistress and out into the meadow.

Hannah turned as she heard Emily approach, and they stared at each other wordlessly for a moment.

"So you have sent him away," Hannah stated evenly.

Emily made no reply as she approached the window and gazed out. Her eyes located at once what Hannah had been watching and what the maid still gaped at. Emily noticed the dark shape of the carriage, stopped in the road at the bottom of the meadow he was crossing, and she wondered remotely why he had not brought it closer to the house and saved himself the walk.

Her eyes darted back to his fair head, staring fixedly for a moment, before violet eyes closed and she willed him, yearningly, to falter and come back to her.

Interpreting the wistful silence exactly, Hannah declared provocatively, "He won't be back and begging again. He has pride too, and plenty of it."

Emily heard the goading but could not retaliate. She moved to the kitchen door that lead out to the gardens. She opened it and gazed out. Hannah followed her to the doorway, advising in the same cheerful tone, "Never mind. He is sure to find solace somewhere. He will allow himself to be comforted now that he knows it is hopeless." She gave lascivious-eyed Maria a cursory glance as she added drily, "And I do not mean of the sort likely to be offered in an establishment such as this. No . . . he is ready to settle and put down roots. And there will be plenty—and from good families too—more than willing to encourage him to it. Sweet smiles and silken arms tempting him to love them."

Emily turned then, terror and uncertainty mingling with reproach in her eyes for how Hannah was tormenting her.

"You cannot bind him to you with nothing for ever, Emily," Hannah counseled with fierce caution. "There are too many girls extremely adept at snipping through invisible cords, and he will let them do it now that he accepts you as lost."

Emily's dark head spun anxiously in the direction of the meadow. She noted the dark figure far in the distance now. She rushed out into the garden, instinctively allowing Katherine a finger to suck as she whimpered.

The crude wooden gate that lead into the meadow was swung open, creaking back on rusty hinges. She walked through and into the meadow, trailing slowly through the long grass. Her eyes were intent, fixed on the man so far off now—quite close to his transport home and away from her forever.

Her pace speeded suddenly and then she began to run,

jerking the child heavily against her as she did so. Katherine bawled immediate objection to this rough handling and Emily halted quickly. She bent swiftly and uncovering the baby, laid her shawl on the grass and placed Katherine upon it. With one last, long glance at her daughter, she ran on, her skirt clutched tightly and up high, about her knees, as she sped through the tall, swaying reeds.

She wanted to scream for him to come back, but it seemed her breath was all taken up; too badly needed to keep her moving forward, and not a sound was expelled. She saw him withdraw his hands from his pockets as he reached the opposite gate that led to the road. One hand went to his head, pushing long, fair hair away from his eyes before it lowered to open the gate.

"Oh, don't go, Clifford . . . please don't go," she gasped out at last. Her anguish tore into her throat as painfully as the breathless exertion, but he faltered then and swung about. He remained still, without moving forward to meet her.

He stood motionless, watching her, as she ran the last yards towards him. Then she was within reach at last and his arms jerked out, snatching at her and lifting her off the ground and bringing her hard against him. His arms coiled around her, enfolding her so close that she was bent back at the waist at a seemingly impossible angle. But her arms grabbed, clinging to him violently and pulling him down so their necks entwined, entangling them completely.

They shook together, straining and gripping ceaselessly for an interminable, intense moment of aching rapture. Clifford lifted his head slowly, away from the hair he had wet at her neck, finally allowing her to slide down his body and her feet to retouch the springy turf.

Emily kept her arms locked about his neck, her face burying in his coat as she accused brokenly, "I thought

441

you meant to leave me . . . really go away this time."

He smoothed her untidy, dark hair with shaking fingers. "I was coming back for you tomorrow, Emily, I promise . . . and not taking no for an answer," he reassured thickly with a light hint of laughter.

Emily looked up at him through glass-bright violet eyes, and she laughed and raised her face to kiss a lean, sallow cheek. She drew back then and stared at him assessingly, for the first time that day, becoming aware of his gauntness. She raised a finger to trace the scar before it moved to the deeper crease near his mouth.

"You look . . . you seem different, as though unwell."

He turned his face into her hand, his cheek rubbing against the finger that caressed him. He kissed it before muttering, "I am all right. I just drink too much lately — since you went away, that is all." The mention of alcohol made the craving stir, and an unsteady hand wiped across his mouth as he admitted with husky self-mockery, "Actually, I could do with a bottle right now."

Emily pressed her hand against a thin cheek as she cautioned with alarm and fear, "But you must not, else you will end up like my papa."

"It will be better now you are with me," he promised, smiling tenderly. "It will pass in time."

She raised her face again, kissing him gently on the mouth to emphasize just how certainly she was with him. He returned the kiss softly for a moment before his arms tightened. He clung to her, his mouth parting hers urgently, needing her for a lot more than the mild comfort she had intended.

Emily laughed into his mouth and pushed at him lightly, but his hold strengthened, one hand sliding up to the back of her head so the pressure on her mouth increased. His head raised at last and he looked at her uncertainly, but she half-lifted languid eyelids and her moist, parted mouth slid away across his cheek.

"You see how easy it is for me to forget about the compulsion to drink," he murmured against her hair.

Her arms tightened about his neck, twining into soft, long hair. "Well, next time the longing bedevils you . . . every time . . . you must tell me and we shall think of something else you like to do—to distract you until it troubles you no more."

She felt him jerk as he laughed but he said quite solemnly, "I am quite certain to be afflicted for the next thirty years, Emily . . . possibly longer."

She pushed back and gazed up steadily into silver-black eyes. They caressed her face before dropping to linger at her body, desire blackening his eyes completely and tautening sensually stroking hands at her waist.

Emily nodded and murmured, "Good." She remembered then their daughter, lying in the grass, and turned to look at her.

She clasped Clifford's hand wordlessly and they started to walk back through the meadow.

Katherine Moore was placidly consoling herself with a tiny thumb; no more than occasional mewing noises displaying her dissatisfaction as did her free, waving fist that punched up angrily at fluffy, white clouds.

Charles Shaw sat by the parlor window, leaning forward in his armchair and squinting out into the green meadow. His eyes fixed on the indistinct forms—one small and pale in colour and the other tall and dark. They dropped to the ground then; a small white bundle positioned between them on the emerald grass.

Hannah removed the empty goblet from his fingers and placed it on a table. Aware of her again, Charles looked up sharply and demanded on a long, sniffing sigh, "How did you know, Hannah? How did you know that he would come? You must have told him that she was here.

It was a false wager . . . I know it was. You have cheated me, you witch, I am certain of it."

Hannah laughed lightly. "I swear, Charles, on the life of that darling baby girl, that I never told him that either you or Emily were here."

Charles nodded slowly in acceptance of the vow and a fumbling hand went to his pocket. It delved and searched by touch and he withdrew a half-sovereign. Dying eyes reluctantly relinquished the blurred family grouped on the grass. He looked instead at the gold coin in his palm, then settled it carefully on the tips of thumb and forefinger before flicking it into the air. Hannah caught it adroitly with one hand and pocketed it in her dress with a smiling mutter of thanks.

Colorless eyes resought the figures on the grass, Charles gazing unwaveringly. "I do believe, Hannah, that is the last wager I shall ever lose."

She nodded agreement at the top of the iron-gray head, murmuring inaudible assent.

"And I would lose it a million times, and most gladly," he choked emotionally, "for she is happy now, is she not, Hannah?"

"Oh, yes, Charles . . . much more than happy. They both are, for despite everything, he loves her more than life itself, and at last she believes him."

Charles nodded slow, gasping satisfaction, watering eyes spilling as the light and dark figure merged together on the grass. He sobbed out a bubbling breath, "They put me in mind of two children I knew once . . . it seems such a long time ago." He sank back from the window to lean comfortably into the chair, but his eyes remained constant.

Hannah tidied the glasses away onto the tray, then walked close to the window. She watched as fair hair separated from long, chestnut tresses. Clifford stood up, cradling his daughter in one arm while with the other he jerked Emily to her feet and immediately pulled her close. They turned together and started to approach the house.

"How happy are you, Charles?" Hannah asked softly, "for I believe they come now to see you."

The silence stretched and Hannah felt tears spiteful against her eyes and stinging her nose, but she made herself turn to look at him. She gazed down at eyes wide and sightless but bright, and a mouth still and slightly parted but serenely curved; and she smiled, then laughed wryly, knowing Charles kept his joy for eternity.

CHILLING GOTHICS
From Zebra Books

HEATH HALLOWS (1901, $2.95)
by Michele Y. Thomas

Caroline knew it was wrong to go in her cousin's place to Heath Hallows Abbey; but the wealthy Hawkesworths would never know the difference. But tragedies of the past cast a dark and deadly shadow over Heath Hallows, leaving Caroline to fear the evil lurking in the shadows.

SAPPHIRE LEGACY (1979, $2.95)
by Beverly C. Warren

Forced into a loveless marriage with the aging Lord Charles Cambourne, Catherine was grateful for his undemanding kindness and the heirloom sapphires he draped around her neck. But Charles could not live forever, and someone wanted to make sure the young bride would never escape the deadly *Sapphire Legacy*.

SHADOWTIDE (1695, $2.95)
by Dianne Price

Jenna had no choice but to accept Brennan Savage's mysterious marriage proposal. And as flickering candlelight lured her up the spiral staircase of Savage Lighthouse, Jenna could only pray her fate did not lie upon the jagged rocks and thundering ocean far below.

THE HOUSE AT STONEHAVEN (1239, $2.50)
by Ellouise Rife

Though she'd heard rumors about how her employer's first wife had died, Jo couldn't resist the magnetism of Elliot Stone. But soon she had to wonder if she was destined to become the next victim.

ROMANCE — WITH A TWIST
From Zebra Books

TIMELESS PASSION (1837, $3.95)
By Constance O'Day-Flannery

When Brianne Quinlan woke up after the accident, her car, and even the highway, had vanished. Instead, her eyes met the magnetic blue gaze of a remarkably handsome man. Ryan Barrington was on a routine tour of his own plantation; he never expected to find such a beautiful woman, in such strange clothing. Ready to send her on her way, he kissed her ripe lips instead — and vowed to find out her true identity and make her his own with TIMELESS PASSION.

TIMESWEPT LOVERS (2057, $3.95)
By Constance O'Day-Flannery

Corporate executive Jenna Weldon was taking a cross-country train as part of a promotional gimmick. All too quickly, she realized the joke was on her — somewhere along the line she had fallen backward in time, and into the arms of the original Marlboro man! Morgan Trahern had never seen such astonishing beauty in his life, and he was determined to capture her heart and unite their souls as TIMESWEPT LOVERS.

CRYSTAL PARADISE (1894, $3.95)
By Johanna Hailey

Aurora thought she had finally found happiness with Frayne, but her joy was short-lived when he had to leave her on his quest for a perfect crystal rose. Once separated from him, Aurora knew that she would never again be whole until their flesh touched in a raging embrace . . . and they joined together again as one in passion's burning fury.

BELOVED PARADISE (2014, $3.95)
By Johanna Hailey

Lost and lonely in an enchanted land, beautiful Aurora searched for the secret of her true identity. And just as she thought all hope was gone she saw the handsome warrior appear out of the rainbow mist. His passion-filled kiss aroused her desire, his heated touch against her ivory flesh caused her blood to stir. He promised to help her in her desperate quest — but only if she'd pledge her love in return.

Available wherever paperbacks are sold, or order direct from the Publisher. Send cover price plus 50¢ per copy for mailing and handling to Zebra Books, Dept. 2192, 475 Park Avenue South, New York, N.Y. 10016. Residents of New York, New Jersey and Pennsylvania must include sales tax. DO NOT SEND CASH.